THE
LION AND
THE ROSE

THE LION AND THE ROSE

RICCARDO BRUNI

Translated by Aaron Maines

amazon crossing

Previously published as *Il leone e la rosa* by Kindle Direct Publishing in 2014 in Italy. Translated from Italian by Aaron Maines. First published in English by AmazonCrossing in 2015.

Published by AmazonCrossing, Seattle

www.apub.com

Amazon, the Amazon logo, and AmazonCrossing are trademarks of Amazon.com, Inc., or its affiliates.

ISBN-13: 9781503948327
ISBN-10: 1503948323

Cover design by Edward Bettison

Printed in the United States of America

CHAPTER 1

Venice

The last days of January 1502

Golden rays of dawn filtered faintly through a thick fog sliding across the frigid waters of the Canal Grande. Darkness receded from alleys and quays along the Rialto, where the first fish-market stalls were opening up.

Fishermen tied up their boats and unloaded their merchandise. Fishmongers cleaned the larger fish, dumping guts on the ground and fighting off the cold sinking into their bones. Puddles of blood pooled alongside the stalls, and slimy offal turned the stone slick. Voices rose up along the bridge and continued through the market, all the way to Piazza San Marco. Soon the crowd would thicken. Merchants unfurled brightly colored fabrics and Oriental rugs. The scent of spices and roast eel intermingled with the smells of wine, urine, chickens, and the acrid blood of butchered beasts.

The old man bit down on one of his hands, which had gone wooden. He felt pain. That was a good sign. He dropped the day's earnings into his pocket, then walked down the stone steps and picked up the rope tied to his little boat.

That's when he saw it.

There was something in the dark water. Something floating, near the sturdy wood bridge that joined the Rialto with San Marco. The old man set the rope back down and looked closer, trying to figure out what it was. He called to another fisherman who hadn't yet come ashore. That man followed the arc of the old man's arm to the exact spot he was pointing to. The fisherman maneuvered his boat toward what seemed like the carcass of some strange animal.

But once he was closer, he understood.

He looked around, feeling lost.

A few moments later, other fishermen joined him, driving their small boats across the water as the fog seemed to melt away, drawing back the curtains on the horror. They surrounded him, their eyes betraying the fear consuming them and clutching at their stomachs.

"It's the work of Satan," said the old man with the wooden hands, by the water's edge. "The Lord has forsaken us."

Everyone was watching, glancing around at one another. One man made the sign of the cross.

"We have to take it out of the water and call the guards," said one of the younger fishermen.

"A priest. That's who we have to call! Someone who can bless this water. It seems infected with hellish intent," said another. He looked around, searching for confirmation in the other men's eyes. "This is the second one we've found. It can't be by chance. You know. You understand what I'm saying. These waters are cursed, inhabited by devils!"

"These waters feed us every day, and they deserve your respect," said the fisherman who discovered the body. "The fish we eat is as good as it ever was. The boy is right—we need to call the guards again."

The wooden hull of his boat almost touched the object in the water now. He knelt down and leaned his face over to get a closer look. The others watched his every move, transfixed, even as they hung back a bit.

The floating object had once been a man, before he'd been chewed up and spat out by the Devil. The face was almost devoid of flesh. The gaping mouth hung open in an expression of terror, crystallized by the cold and by the salt in the lagoon. Blood was clotted around empty eye sockets, from which the eyeballs had been ripped away, and the flesh inside the wide-open mouth was butchered meat. The ears had been cut off, leaving behind pus-filled shreds of something white that welled up from beneath the swollen skin still stuck to the skull.

The torso stuck out of the water, nailed to a broad plank of wood. The arms were stretched wide as if in crucifixion, and the hands were hammered into the wood with two large rusty nails. Both arms appeared to have been burned.

A long gash had slashed open the throat.

Suddenly, a horrible stench enveloped the fisherman—a cloud of rotten blood, of beaten and burned flesh. The smell of death. He spun around to the other side of his little boat, to keep from inflicting yet another insult on the tortured body, and emptied his stomach into the canal. Afterward, he cupped a handful of salty water to clean his mouth.

"You can call the guards now," he said.

The other men looked away. Their heavy breathing became vapor that blended in with the last tendrils of fog. Fear snaked among them, scratching its way up their spines. It was a terrible feeling. It slithered its way amid the men's motionless, silent stares and glided over the water, all the way to the nearby landings where a crowd was gathering. People craned their necks, staring out at the little group of fishermen in an attempt to figure out what was going on. Fear worked its way among the people of Venice, convincing them they were condemned, that God had turned his gaze elsewhere. It wended through the words of priests who'd been accusing La Serenissima, this "most serene" republic, of arrogance even before the first body had been discovered. That, too, had been the Devil's handiwork.

Rumors swirled through the markets and the passageways known as *calli*. Whispers and exhortations. They said that Venetians had been called upon to offer up a tribute to their lagoon, the echo of ancient sacrificial rites that old people spoke of softly. They said that this place had earned the title of "Sodom on the water"—and the Lord's wrath—because of the habits of its denizens. Because of its whores, orgies, and banquets. Because of sexual acts practiced between men. For the vulgar rhymes of its poets and bards. For its obscene books.

"We need to bring this back to shore," insisted the fisherman who had gone to give the body a closer look.

A woman screamed. The sound came from near the bridge, on the side that descended near the fish market. Like a wave that erupts in a boat's wake, everyone began running in that direction. The group of fishermen turned to look, filled with foreboding. A fisherman who had remained in the market ran over the bridge to where the boats were gathered and, his voice cracking, confirmed the worst.

There was another body.

The third.

CHAPTER 2

The University of Padua

The next day

Mathias closed the little book he was holding in his hands. He was sitting in a secluded portico next to a courtyard. The morning was sunny and bright, and frost in the garden reflected the sunlight all around. The monk had a sturdy athletic build and was ruggedly handsome, even though he was fifty.

He was looking for answers. He was trying to understand. And every time he found himself in this state of mind, he would sit down somewhere, his back against a column, just as he had when he was a student. While he thought, his gaze moved around restlessly, from the garden to a stone arch, to the book he held in his hands—a gift from one of his Venetian friends, Giacomo Foscarini. Correspondence to Mathias from Germany was still getting sent to Venice, even though he'd been teaching in Padua for more than a year. So every time something arrived in Venice for him from the university in Leipzig, where his old study partner and fellow monk Gheorg was working, or from the little village of Stolberg in the Harz mountain range, where his family lived, Foscarini made sure it was forwarded. That morning, along with a letter from Gheorg, Foscarini had sent a personal gift: Petrarch's *Canzoniere*, published by Manuzio in a new small format, which, prior to a brilliant departure by the talented printer, had been reserved for prayer books alone. It was a simple idea, but one with enormous implications. It cost far less to produce such a small book than it did to commission a group of inscribers to make a copy. Lots of people were investing large sums of money in printing. The result, as Foscarini had described in his letter, was an extraordinary circulation for *Canzoniere*, a work written a century and a half earlier that everyone was talking about now.

Mathias had leafed through the precious pages and then closed it, tucking the tiny volume into the pocket of his wool frock. He knew what the book contained; it was the way the information could be carried around now that made it such a prodigious invention. His superiors wouldn't appreciate his passion. They seemed less and less tolerant of Mathias and his controversial ideas, believing them inappropriate for the rigor that a monk, a follower of Saint Augustine, must honor.

He was guilty of arrogance, and he knew it, but Mathias couldn't find it in himself to feel guilty for his sins. The Church had a strong presence here, and despite the fact that the University of Padua proudly asserted its autonomy, considerations like that should have driven him to behave more humbly. But now it was too late. Gheorg's letter had taken him by surprise, but it came at a good time.

After leaving Leipzig, Gheorg had traveled as far as Frankfurt an der Oder, where he remained for a year. Then he'd gone back to Thuringia, stopping at Erfurt, where he made contact with Johann von Staupitz, the vicar general of the Augustinian order.

Frederick III, elector of Saxony, was about to open a new university in Wittenberg and was looking for new teachers. The vicar general was charged with selecting people he believed would be up to the task.

Staupitz was struck by how well prepared Gheorg was and offered him a position. Before accepting, Gheorg traveled to Wittenberg in order to get a better grasp of the situation. Then he wrote his old friend, Mathias, asking him to join him and explaining that conditions there were more than adequate to allow them to continue on the path they'd chosen, to continue studies that they couldn't pursue elsewhere.

Mathias had been suspended from teaching for a month now at the University of Padua, the same place where he'd been enthusiastically summoned from Venice eighteen months earlier. Some of his students had told the rectors about a few mentions he'd made of the studies of John Wycliffe, and *Tractatus de civili dominio* in particular. More than a century earlier, that work had driven Pope Gregory XI to call for the English theologian's head. The accusation was that his writings offended the Church by questioning its authority. His opinions were considered heretical, but Mathias and his study companions believed those texts expressed a very real and urgent need for change. And according to Gheorg, their thinking would find fertile and welcoming terrain in Wittenberg. The vicar general hadn't fully comprehended the passions driving Gheorg, but at least until a new vicar general was nominated, Johann von Staupitz's somnolence would guarantee that they'd both avoid the risk of being expelled for their ideas, which involved seeking out a new path for the Word of God, a long route but one that everyone could join in equally.

Mathias thought back on those nights. The dim candlelight and true faith. The Word read in the people's tongue, and therefore comprehensible to every farmer and peasant. Excitement and fear. Truth and heresy. *Might such small, unimportant men actually change the world?* he wondered. Or was their passion merely vanity? A passage from Ecclesiastes popped into his head.

The words of the Preacher, the son of David, king in Jerusalem. Vanity of vanities, says the Preacher, vanity of vanities! All is vanity.

His vanity, buried in Venice.

Could an imperfect servant of God still comprehend the right path for his Word? A man who had experienced the abyss of sin. A man who still felt no remorse. Could he be redeemed, and did he need to be?

There was a woman . . . Angelica. Her face haunted his thoughts, restoring the endless arrogance of a sinner who couldn't manage to reconcile his own sin.

How can I know God?

He had convinced himself that Padua was a grand opportunity, and that leaving La Serenissima behind was a necessary step along his path to fully understanding who he was. But deep within himself, Mathias could sense the hypocrisy of that move. His adventure at this university kept him at a distance, putting him in a position where he could avoid coming fully to terms with something he should have faced a long time ago. Wittenberg seemed like a perfect destination, but he had to be sure his heart would follow his mind, because once he traveled north of Munich, he would never come back again.

As he sat thinking, Mathias fingered the book Foscarini had sent him. It was a precious gift. But then the Venetian had always looked after his needs while he was in Venice, and over the course of the years they had spent in that city, he had become like a brother to him.

Foscarini was a nobleman, a member of one of the most influential patrician families in La Serenissima. In the letters he'd written over the past few months, he'd told Mathias about the difficult period his faction was experiencing following the death of Agostino Barbarigo, the doge who had led the republic into a ruinous war with the Turks that had brought Venice to its knees. When Barbarigo died, the various noble families had engaged in an unprecedented series of vendettas, settling old disputes and ultimately producing a new doge. For a few months now, the situation remained calm, but these were hard times in Venice.

Mathias got up and walked along the cobblestones, then sat down again in the portico gallery. The sound of footsteps drew him back from his meditations. The sun was high, revealing how much time he'd spent lost in his own thoughts.

Ubertino was walking through the entryway to the internal courtyard. At that time of day, he should have been busy cleaning the refectory. He walked quickly over to Mathias. Ubertino looked worried—the way he always did when something unexpected came up.

"Two men are here for you, Brother. They've come from Venice."

Mathias got up and rubbed a hand across his chin, smoothing his blond beard, which was starting to turn gray. His expression mirrored Ubertino's worried visage. Two men from Venice, for him? He'd only just received the letters the day before. Why would they travel all the way to Padua to see him?

He nodded to Ubertino, but the two men who'd come looking for him were already heading his way. Although the daggers they carried were supposed to be hidden, Mathias noticed their outlines beneath the long dark cloaks of the men. As they drew closer, he could see that they kept themselves clean-shaven and groomed, despite the dust and other signs of travel. They both wore gloves made with fine fabric and boots of high-quality leather. They didn't seem like mere guardsmen from La Serenissima, more like private emissaries from some nobleman.

"Are you Mathias Munster?" asked the leader of the two.

"Yes, I am."

"My name is Marigo. We've been sent to escort you to Venice, where someone wishes to meet with you. This should be explanation enough," said the man, handing him a letter.

Excusing himself, Mathias took the letter and walked out into the garden where the light was better and he could read it more easily. It contained a very brief explanation. In reality, it explained little other than the identity of the man who was calling him back to Venice, a man Mathias had never met in person, a man he only knew by name. His friend Foscarini had mentioned the man more than once, especially in the most recent letters he'd written following Barbarigo's death.

The monk's eyes read the name over and over. He was stunned. The man inviting him to return to La Serenissima as quickly as possible was none other than Leonardo Loredan, the seventy-fifth doge of the Republic of Venice.

CHAPTER 3

Venice

"Our elders can't recall worse times. We must do something. It's our duty." Young Corner spoke with animation, but everyone knew full well he was merely saying something others had commanded him to share.

Inside the small room within Palazzo Ducale, where the Council of Ten gathered, the faces of the members assembled could be easily confused with the painted portraits that adorned the room's walls. That afternoon's meeting was rife with a strong sense of impending danger. The most controversial executive branch of the Republic sat upon wooden chairs, and the silent tension in the room was only interrupted by the creaking of the old wood.

The Council was made up of ten consiglieri, elected for a term of one year each; six members of the Signoria of Venice, the Doge's personal advisors; and Doge Loredan himself, who sat in as chairman for every meeting. The Council was expected to handle primarily issues of safety and security, but since it was the most exclusive and secretive element of Venice's government, it was often accused of taking on issues that should have been the province of other, larger institutions that were therefore slower to make decisions. Now, conflicts between different Venetian noble families were about to come to a head again.

"Nobody doubts we need to do something, but we're still not in agreement about what we should do," said Marcello Foscarini, the young nephew of Giacomo Foscarini. "The solution you've been insisting upon for some time now hasn't garnered the support you hoped for, and the fact that you continue to bring it up here is insulting."

"We'll never tire of attempting to save the Republic from catastrophe," countered Corner. "Even your uncle knows full well that Venice won't survive much longer caught between two fires. The war at sea with the Turks and continued conflicts with the Pope here at home will crush us. Nothing will be left of our power but a fistful of ashes."

Venier, a member of the Signoria, responded to this. "You know full well what we intend to do, Corner. Stop trying our Doge's patience in this manner."

"If you're referring to making peace with the Turks, the latest military affairs should be enough of an answer for you," said Morosini, an old man who sat alongside young Corner. "If that's the path you're proposing we follow in order to put this situation behind us—a situation that is exhausting our economy, disrupting commercial routes, destroying our businesses, and leaving our ships loaded with merchandise at the mercy of predators paid by the Sultan . . . If the only solution you can see for this mess is an armistice with that blasphemous criminal, you should at least be able to demonstrate that he's willing to sit down and talk. In reality, you know full well that the conditions the Sultan would impose are too onerous for our city to bear. I find it insulting that you'd rather form an alliance with that scoundrel than with Rome."

At this, the Doge spoke. "Your arguments are nothing new."

Everyone remained silent while Loredan laboriously adjusted his position on the bench. His illness was gaining the upper hand, making it hard for him to shoulder the destiny of the Republic in such dark times as these. Some believed that the loss of his wife, who died just the year before he was elected, had left an indelible mark on him, pushing him away from life and closer to death. This opinion left him even more greatly exposed to criticism.

Loredan tried to find color in the sky outside the window, which was even now turning red with the end of the day. Then he nodded for young Foscarini to light more candles, which would brighten the entire room. The discussion continued.

"We're back on the same old issues, my dear Morosini," the Doge said. "You all know what I think, which is what most of our nobility thinks. Going against the Turks will cost us a few possessions, but going against the Borgias would cost us much more. Still, these kinds of issues are the province of the Great Council of Venice and the Pregadi, and they have already had their say on the matter."

"Rejecting both proposals, my signore," responded Morosini. "Demonstrating yet again their habitual inability to make quick decisions. We all know that in truth, we need nothing more than the willingness of a few key people in order to safeguard the future of Venice."

"In order to hand Venice over to the Pope, you mean," said Marcello Foscarini.

"In order to obtain his support against our real enemy and wipe him off the face of the earth once and for all."

"Fattening the coffers at your shipyards with money from the Republic, I imagine."

Morosini's temper flared, and he turned to the Doge. "Perhaps your young friend should learn a little more respect for his elders!"

"And you for the law," responded Loredan. "It's unheard of for you to come here and talk to me about the willingness of just a few people when you know quite well that these kinds of issues should be addressed elsewhere."

"But while these issues are being debated, Venice lives in terror." The voice came from the only corner still in shadow. It was Trevisan, the oldest member of the Council.

Loredan knew that his adversaries had been aiming to get to this point all along. Trevisan shifted in his seat, allowing the candlelight to illuminate his face. "The things taking place right now are something this assembly should deal with. And Venetians believe that the recent events are connected with the arrogance their city has displayed when dealing with those who are here to represent God on earth."

Young Foscarini hammered a fist into his thigh. "If you intend to use these events to leverage fear and superstition to convince a few houses to join your side, then you're more wretched than I'd imagined."

Morosini raised his voice. "Are you calling our oldest advisor 'wretched'? Your uncle should teach you how to behave at this assembly when he's putting the words he wants you to say right into your mouth only to be spit out here."

Young Foscarini leapt to his feet. "How dare you!"

"That's enough," interrupted the Doge. "Trevisan, what do you want to say?"

"These"—the elderly man placed a handful of letters and notes on the small table next to him—"are complaints people have left in the *bocche*. The magistrates handed them over to us."

The *bocche di leone*, or lions' mouths, were stone sculptures set into the walls at various points around the city, which contained small letter boxes. The magistrates used them to collect anonymous complaints—often about issues like adultery or contraband.

"As you can see," said Trevisan, "the sheer number of these complaints has turned this case into something more than just an issue for ordinary administration and justice." He spread the letters out to underline just how many there were. "Look at how many Venetians have felt it necessary to turn to the law to denounce pagan rites, occult congregations, demon worship, and sodomy. Some have even written of black priests who evoke the Devil in order to drive Venice to terror. You have to do something, signore. Three deaths in such a short time, the bodies ruined and disfigured until they no longer look human. How long must we wait before asking the Pope to send us an inquisitor?"

"We already have an inquisitor in Venice," answered the Doge in an icy voice. "He knows how to do his job. I won't let fear force the Republic to step aside in order to grant free rein to Borgia's emissaries. I am the law here in Venice, not the Pope. If that's not to your liking, then go join your family in Rome, where you'll feel safer. I do not intend to sit here any longer and listen to such insinuations."

"Insinuations, my signore?" said Morosini, intervening on behalf of the elderly Trevisan. "The people are afraid. They're unsettled by these events. The faithful view these events as divine punishment for your refusal to rely on the Church. You spurn a sacred alliance that would sweep away the Turks in the name of the Lord. Instead, you try to make peace with those barbarians, offending God and remaining helpless as our people pay the price for your arrogance!"

"You! You of all people speak to me of arrogance?" Despite his illness, Loredan knew how to be imposing when he needed to be. "You come here to offend me and then accuse me of arrogance?" His voice grew thick with rage. "Is there anyone here willing to claim seriously that a demon is wandering around the calli of our city, exacting revenge for presumed insults I've paid the Pope?" Pushing down on the table, Loredan stood up, assuming an unnatural but majestic pose. "Do you believe God can punish me for having failed to respect Rodrigo Borgia?"

"He's the Pope, my signore," said Trevisan.

"The Pope?" shouted the Doge. "If God seriously wished to punish Venice by sending a demon, then Rome would be overcome by all the hordes of Hell!" His voice echoed around the small room. Young Corner was rendered speechless, staring at the floor. Morosini looked shocked.

"My faith forces me to abandon this meeting," said the elderly Trevisan, slowly pulling himself upright. "You have offended God, my signore. I pray this will not bring disaster down on our blessed city."

Loredan sat down again. His voice still shaking with rage, he barely managed to call the meeting to a close and send everyone away. "If there's nothing else," he said, "then we can stop here."

The others stood up and headed for the door through which Trevisan was already leaving. The old man was smiling. He was well aware that more and more Venetians would be convinced that the Doge's attitude toward the Church was driving Venice into ruin.

Loredan returned to his chambers and stayed there, staring out at the dark, starless sky, which now seemed to hang over the city like a threat. He'd barely won a difficult election, achieving victory only with the help of his friendships. Now his enemies were growing stronger than ever, attracting more and more support from Rome. Asking the Pope to intervene in the war against the Turks, putting their faith in a Christian alliance in order to defeat Bayezid II, would mean submitting the Republic to the Pope. It would mean renouncing autonomy. Pope Alexander VI would pay back his faithful supporters, Venetian families that in some cases could vaunt a cardinal or two in their lineage who had in turn supported Borgia's election. Thanks to them, the Pope would be able to overturn the majority and remove anyone from Venice who didn't submit to his authority altogether.

And those corpses popping up in the Canal Grande risked dealing a deathblow to the precarious equilibrium that kept Loredan in power. Fear was running rampant among Venetians, and there was no shortage of people willing to use that fear, to feed it until fear had the citizens in its grip and they could be convinced to attack the Doge and insist the Pope intervene. Inquisitors sent from Rome would be Borgia's Trojan horse—the key to getting his hands on La Serenissima.

Loredan had told the Council that Venice already had its own inquisitor, but he knew he couldn't let that man investigate, since that might mean the inquisitor's superior would come from Rome. Loredan had only been in office for a few months, and he had to surround himself with guards in order to feel safe. He needed an outsider, someone who wasn't involved in any of these complicated political stratagems. Someone who couldn't be bought, and who wasn't afraid to investigate the mystery surrounding those terrifying mutilated corpses.

The sound of footsteps tore the Doge away from his thoughts, and he turned his gaze from that black, wondrous night sky. He heard the swish and sweep of his guards' clothing as they stepped aside to let Loredan's most trusted servant through.

The Doge turned around to see Marigo walk through the small wooden door and into his lord's chambers.

"Welcome back, Captain," he said.

"Good news, my signore."

"It will be the first I've heard in a long time."

"Mathias Munster is on his way to Venice."

CHAPTER 4

The gondola floated along in darkness, on its way to the pier in San Marco. Mathias was seated on board, motionless in the cold. A reflection of the city rippled on the water. The monk adjusted his velvet cap and then buried his hands deep in his wool frock, underneath his cloak. He was about to see everything he thought he'd left behind, yet he knew nothing would be the same. Even though he'd been gone just a year and a half, he felt different, older, more resigned.

The gondolier maneuvered the long oar he'd set in the forked lock. As the boat drew closer to the pier, the silhouette of Palazzo Ducale gradually emerged from the dark night. Mathias didn't know why he'd been summoned here, and none of the private guards who had come for him had provided further information. Perhaps they didn't know either.

The boat docked. Only then did a man wrapped in a thick cloak step out where he could be seen. Mathias recognized him as Marigo, the man who had come to find him in Padua. Marigo stepped close to the boat and offered a hand to help Mathias up onto the pier.

"Welcome back to Venice, *magister*."

"Did the Doge tell you to call me that?

Marigo didn't answer, instead motioning for him to follow.

When they were closer to Palazzo Ducale, Mathias could see the piazza that opened up in front of the basilica. It was extraordinary. Work had continued in his absence, and the piazza had changed a great deal since the last time he'd had a chance to admire it. Only now did he feel like he'd truly returned.

Marigo slipped into a narrow calle. Mathias hesitated, then summoned his courage: if they had wanted to harm him, they would have done so already, somewhere far more convenient than this. During the long trip back to Venice, for example.

He followed Marigo into the alleyway, which opened up onto a *rio*, or small internal canal, just a few yards later. A covered gondola with a *felze*, or private cabin, which protected the passenger not only from rain and foul weather but from unwelcome eyes as well, was tied up near a footbridge. It was an elegant vessel, undoubtedly the property of some nobleman, but he could see no insignia on it anywhere. A dark-skinned man, perhaps an African, stood in the stern, grasping the oar with both hands. He was waiting for the order to depart.

Marigo opened the door of the felze and invited Mathias to step in. He closed the door behind his guest and went to sit in the bow, out in the open, alongside another man. Both of them pulled their hoods up over their heads, protecting themselves from the cold and keeping their identities hidden from any curious onlooker they might pass.

Mathias sat on the little bench inside the cabin. Almost immediately, he realized he wasn't alone in that small space, and after he saw who there, he was so surprised he sat in stunned silence. He knew the Doge was waiting for him, but he was sure he would be received by one of Loredan's emissaries, not the man himself.

"Please excuse my methods, but as I'm sure you know, the Doge can't meet anyone without the presence of his advisors," said Loredan, smiling. "Every time he requires a private conversation, he's forced to rely on this sort of stratagem."

"M'lord need excuse nothing," the monk managed to say, still stunned to find himself face-to-face with the highest authority of the Republic of Venice.

"We don't have much time. You'll forgive me if I'm abrupt, but Venice has been shaken by terrible events, and I need someone who can help me shed light on what's happened."

"And m'lord believes I can do so?"

"The Republic stands divided." Loredan knocked on the roof of the cabin to signal that the boat should leave. The gondola glided down a narrow passage between two looming palazzi. Then the Doge began to speak again. "On one side stand the noblemen, convinced that La Serenissima should remain autonomous and independent, and for the time being they are the majority, though by a very slim count. On the other stand our adversaries, who, in their own efforts to gain a majority and thus seize power, have accepted the help of their family members who live in Rome and wear cardinals' cassocks." Mathias listened, but the whole conversation seemed unreal. "These adversaries of ours know full well that if Rome were to take control of La Serenissima, they would be able to pocket most of the money guaranteed by the Borgia family, which currently owns the papacy. Land, contracts for merchant ships, power . . . Do you follow?"

Mathias nodded. He had no idea what was going on, but he tried to concentrate on the Doge's words.

"My enemies have found an opportunity to close ranks in this cursed war against the Turks, a war that my foolish predecessor did little or nothing to avoid. The Republic has lost important territories. Some key strongholds for our ships en route to the Orient have fallen to the Sultan. You can imagine the damage this has done to our merchants. And I'm sure you're equally aware that here in Venice, noblemen and merchants are one and the same." Loredan seemed exhausted. Illness had left its mark on his face. "If Venice were to ask the Pope for help, for his partnership in a holy alliance, Borgia would be more than happy to honor the request, drive the Turks away from the sea routes, and put Venice beneath his fist.

"You are a smart man, magister, and particularly insightful. I'm sure you can see how the argument to protect that which the nobles hold most dear—in other words, their wallets—is more than enough to convince where mere faith could not. Right now, any and every Venetian can be convinced, threatened, extorted, bought, and sold. Or worse still, made the victim of violence. This is why I felt compelled to turn to you, someone who is both a foreigner and a man who knows our Republic intimately, since you lived here for so many years."

Mathias had listened carefully to the Doge. After his initial shock subsided, it seemed to him that Loredan was both tired and in danger, but not in the least bit resigned to his fate. Therefore, he decided to speak to the Doge as frankly as possible.

"Pardon me, m'lord, but I still can't see how I can be of help to you in all of this." Mathias was already aware of most of what the Doge had said and the situation Venice now found itself in. But he couldn't understand what role Loredan had in mind for him. "I'm a monk, a scholar. Certainly not a politician, m'lord."

"I know you're someone I can trust. You know Venice, and you can help me gather information."

"Information?"

"Yes, concerning three crimes."

"Crimes?"

"Three people, only one of whom we've been able to identify by name, have been found brutally murdered. Their bodies were found floating in the Canal Grande. Their faces were horribly mutilated. It was quite terrible, I can assure you. Terrible enough to spread rumors around Venice that these atrocities are the work of some demon or, even worse, that they are manifestations of a divine punishment. You can imagine how useful all this is for my adversaries, who have wasted no time turning these terrible events to their advantage."

"Issues of commerce do not excite the people's interest," said Mathias. "But I can imagine that fear of a demon is a far more effective lever for convincing them to support someone invoking the Holy Father's name to save Venice."

"As I said, you are a smart man, and particularly insightful."

"So your adversaries are making these events, these three crimes, their own in order to win the people over to their side?"

"Yes. And now they're calling for inquisitors from Rome, who represent the Pope's power. By searching for a demon, the Pope would seize the right to rule over our people. An inquisition would be a Trojan horse."

Mathias nodded, concentrating on pulling all the individual pieces of information into one coherent whole.

The sound of the oar creaking filled the short silence, then the Doge spoke up again. "People are leaving crazy letters in the lions' mouths. They fear the gates of Hell have opened up beneath the foundation of our city. There is a very good chance I'll be forced to submit. That would mean the end of the Republic."

"M'lord, you're speaking to me of important events, but I'm simply a humble scholar, *mio signore*."

"I have to trust someone, and it can't be anyone who holds a public office, who can be traced back to me directly. It has to be someone who doesn't have any interests at stake, and therefore cannot be blackmailed. Most importantly, it has to be someone who possesses the qualities necessary to reconstruct what's happened and figure out what killed those three poor souls. You possess all of these characteristics."

An investigation, conducted for the Doge.

Loredan waited in silence while his guest reorganized his thoughts.

"I hope you will pardon my frankness," said Mathias, "but don't you realize you're asking a humble servant of God for help in keeping the Pope out of your affairs?"

Loredan's eyes bored into Mathias. A small smile spread across the Doge's lips.

"Unless I'm mistaken," said the Doge, "you were suspended from teaching because of your rather unorthodox ideas."

"M'lord is well-informed, but I'm still a monk."

"You are a free man, and that's worthy of respect. If I've judged you correctly, you'll help me save everything Venice represents—especially for men like you—from falling into the hands of Alexander the Sixth."

"Who gave you my name?"

"You have many admirers. Many men who have learned to appreciate your qualities as an inquisitor. Or as a defender, if you prefer."

"I helped catch a few petty thieves who were pilfering a sacristy and a couple of bars, that's all."

"You saved a woman from certain execution."

"I don't know . . ."

"Angelica Zanon. Don't worry, you merely helped the truth emerge from a deep pile of slander and lies."

"So m'lord knows about that, too."

"As I said before, you have many admirers."

"My role was far more marginal than m'lord believes."

"I'm asking you to be my eyes and ears, to serve a cause you believe in as deeply as I do. It's a service for which you will be well paid in any case, believe me."

"You're asking me to find those responsible for these three deaths?"

"I'm asking you to find out information that will help me understand. And to do so without breathing a word of our agreement to anyone, an agreement I wouldn't have the authority to make in any case."

Outside the tiny window, Mathias caught glimpses of the palazzi lining the Canal Grande. Weak light from bars that were still open, even though they were supposed to be closed at this hour, reflected on the still, icy waters dividing the city in half.

"Where are we going?"

"I've taken the liberty of providing you with a house in the Rialto," said Loredan. "I hope that you will find it adequate to your needs."

"And I hope I can satisfy at least half of your expectations."

"You've spoken sincerely, and I appreciate that."

"Sincerity, mio signore . . ." Mathias searched for the right words. "Alexander the Sixth is not exactly the best thing that I could wish on Christianity, but I am nevertheless a servant of the same God. I will try to be useful to you, but only within the limits of what I am allowed to do."

The Doge thanked him again for his frankness and told Mathias what he would pay the monk for carrying out this task. It was a considerable sum of money, more than enough to support him while he rebuilt his life after he returned to Germany. Mathias was surprised to find he no longer considered Gheorg's invitation as merely a possibility to consider sometime in the future.

The monk got out at the Rialto pier. He took with him the large bag he'd filled with his luggage and, after saying good-bye to the Doge, headed toward the house where he'd been told to go. Everything was still confusing. The meeting with the Doge, corpses found floating in the canal, schemes and conspiracies, not to mention the fact that he, Mathias, had been called upon to resolve the situation. His thoughts drifted to the affair that took place when he was last in Venice, the one that had made him so famous. He would have to face that part of his past as well.

He'd been convinced that Venice would help him see what God wanted from him, and why he continued to test Mathias's faith so relentlessly. That Venice would help him understand if he still had faith enough to tolerate what was happening all around him. The events in Florence, for example, and the stake upon which Girolamo Savonarola—the Dominican priest who had led the city into a blind religious fervor—was incinerated. The widespread corruption defiling the house of Peter, where all sorts of assassinations were carried out.

The dirty blood-spattered money fattening priests and cardinals, who in their generosity with pardons were confusing punishment with guilt and canceling out both. All in the name of a God who was farther and farther away, a God Mathias hadn't known how to turn to for some time now. Maybe if he shared Gheorg's conviction, that everything was wrong and should be done away with out of a pure love of God, then he might have fewer weaknesses to reproach himself for. But in the flesh that had betrayed him, Mathias still hadn't managed to find something resembling sin.

In Venice, he would encounter his guilt once again. Or he would rid himself of it forever.

***

As soon as the monk disappeared into the calli of the Rialto, a hooded man entered the cabin and moved to sit across from the Doge. He had remained by Marigo's side for the entire voyage. Now he uncovered his face, and spoke.

"He seems like the right man, if he manages to survive his own turmoil."

"He's a quiet man. He doesn't display much of this torment you've spoken of," said the Doge.

"He'll do anything he can to help you. His anxious desire to make sense of things won't give him a moment's rest. He's condemned to feed his own demons, no matter what happens. But you have to be careful how you manage him. There's always a risk that a man like that will escape your grasp."

The Doge knocked on the ceiling. The gondola slid away into the night.

CHAPTER 5

Weighed down beneath the large bag he was carrying over one shoulder, Mathias was accompanied during his walk through the Rialto by nothing more than the sound of his own footsteps on the stone. Everything was stilled, suspended in the cold night air. In his mind, the monk went back over his conversation with the Doge.

He knew the situation inside the Republic was truly serious. The Pope and the Doge had been clashing with one another for a long time, the result of long-standing animosity. As a result, their respective supporters had been battling one another for at least as long, pushing back a final, decisive, and devastating act, thanks to their political skills and the art of compromise. Until now, no one had been arrogant enough to believe he could resolve the conflict: every nobleman had focused on taking advantage of it instead, leaving the clashing powers fundamentally in equilibrium.

Most of what the Doge had shared with Mathias was known to everyone. But not everything. What shocked the monk the most was the issue of the three murders.

Mathias remembered that once when he was a boy, he'd gone up to a pile of red apples that lay in a cart, in the market near Stolberg where his father often took him. He'd always loved apples, and he couldn't resist the temptation of grabbing one out of the pile. He chose the closest, a splendid red piece of fruit that he would never forget because of his overwhelming desire to take it and hide it in the folds of his clothing. A moment after Mathias reached out and snatched it, the pile slid and apples tumbled down all around him. The farmer, who knew his father, would have been satisfied with an apology. But his father, a successful craftsmen who was well-known and respected in the town, had insisted on purchasing an entire basketful of apples, because of the trouble Mathias had caused. Mathias got the worst scolding his father had ever given him. Not because of the money, but for that small act of petty thievery, which an upright man like his father would never tolerate. He shouldered his punishment, and in the end was only allowed to eat a single apple from the basket. He spent that night thinking about the pile. He had to remove only one and the whole thing had come down. He wondered if the same thing might happen with any tower, no matter how majestic and imposing it might seem, were someone to remove the right stone from its base.

That thought would stay with him throughout his life. Venice now seemed a lot like that pile of apples. If three murders truly represented an irresistible opportunity, then which nobleman would have seized it, knowing that such a thing would cause La Serenissima and everything it represented to come crashing down?

Whose hand was concealed behind the crimes? And why didn't Mathias, a man who had dedicated his life to faith, believe for even one moment that the murders were truly the work of a demon? He felt a strong desire to see his old friend Brother Serafino once again. Serafino would have chastised him for this unwavering focus on rationality, which often made Mathias incapable of accepting the incomprehensible as a necessary act of faith. Serafino had been his teacher and confessor, and he'd always felt great respect for the man, but Mathias had always been drawn down the path of reason, even as his old friend constantly reminded him of the supremacy of faith. Perhaps it was precisely this love of reason that deprived him of certainties that should have been guiding tenets for a man of God, and should have helped him to feel a little less lost in this world.

Mathias sifted through the confusing ideas in his head, leapfrogging from the Doge to the murders, Venice's destiny, the Pope, his own personal faith, and a woman. Her silhouette seemed to emerge from every corner in the city. He could almost smell her perfume hanging in the cold, dense air. But when, turning a corner, he found himself facing San Giacometo Church, something completely different attracted his attention, drowning out memories that he didn't even bother to suppress anymore.

A funeral vigil was being held inside the church. At least twenty people crowded around the entrance and appeared to be pushing to get in. Several night guards, the Venetian officers who kept the peace after the sun went down, were trying to keep people calm.

Mathias decided to go see what was happening for himself.

"Let the Devil take him, that goddamned sodomite! Nobody here is going to cry for him," yelled one young man angrily. "The faithful know. Satan has left Hell and come to our city because of people like that one in there!"

Alongside the young man stood a Dominican friar. His order was the most important in Venice, emphasized by the order's marvelous San Zanipolo Church. Gheorg called the Dominicans "*Domini canes*," God's dogs. They were the fiercest fighters in the Church's absurd war on heresy.

"The Church must change, Brother," Gheorg had said one day long ago, back when they were still theology students at the University of Leipzig. "Christian faith cannot be the tool of a monarch who sells God's pardon in exchange for money and power. Our Lord speaks to *all* men, Mathias. The Church must be a place where all men can meet and pray, not a place where they must submit to the power of other men. God's word must reach everyone equally."

That thinking had cost a lot of people their lives. Priests were excommunicated by mad visionaries who claimed they spoke directly with God, assuming a power that the Church gave its priests. Often the Dominicans were assigned to interrogate those accused of heresy. According to Gheorg, the Dominican order had gained greater prestige thanks to those trials and interrogations. If he had been there, standing alongside Mathias, he would undoubtedly have contested the speech the Dominican was now making there amid the crowd.

The eyes of those people were so utterly blinded by ferocious hatred that it seemed impossible for anybody to suppress them. *Hatred such as this,* thought Mathias, *can only be born of great fear.* He moved around the group, trying to reach the church entrance so that he could see what was going on inside. One of the night guards came over to him.

"Stand aside, together with the others," he said.

"I'm sorry. I've only just returned to Venice, and I was trying to figure out what kind of problems my fellow citizens are dealing with," responded Mathias, smiling.

"It's nothing that should concern you."

"Let Our Lord be the judge of that," replied the monk, making the sign of the cross and showing the guard that he was a man of the faith. After that, the guard took him aside and accompanied him to the church entrance.

"The man they're holding the vigil for is Mariolino Scarpa. He was a printer, a bookseller. His body was found in the Canal Grande. These people here are convinced that the prints he sold in his shop offended God or some saint."

"What convinced them?"

"You didn't choose a very good time to return to Venice," the guard said. He seemed to want to confide in someone. "Three dead bodies have been found floating in the Canal Grande, bodies that seemed spit out from Hell. People are afraid and looking for someone to blame. These people are convinced that if they burn the printer's body and throw the ashes into the Canal, their problems will be over."

"Is the Dominican friar standing with them convinced that's the right solution?"

"He's spent the entire afternoon out here stirring people up. He said that unless Venice earns God's forgiveness, every day more people will die the same horrible way."

"What happened to the other victims?"

"Nobody knows who they were. Maestro Scarpa was the only one who could be recognized."

While he was talking to the guard, Mathias noticed that another guard stopped an old man from entering the church. The old man was saying something, but his voice was drowned out by the noise of the crowd. When the guard let him pass, the old man slipped between the columns and into the church. Mathias was now close enough to see inside. A small group of people were kneeling in prayer to the left of the nave. On the opposite side, a young man, seated alone, turned his gaze to the old man who had just come in.

"If you're not going to pray for the deceased, I advise you to go back home," the guard said to Mathias.

Mathias was still exhausted from his travels, but he needed to think more clearly about his encounter with the Doge. There was something in all of this, in everything that was happening, that still escaped him. It had developed too quickly, Mathias told himself, for him to get a clear sense of what was going on. He needed to rest. Then he could try to fit the pieces together, to get a clearer picture of what was happening.

There were people he needed to see, among them the woman whose face that had begun to reappear in his thoughts. Her lips, her eyes.

He took one last look inside the church, then turned on his heels. The old man who had talked his way past the guard was seated alongside the young man who had been holding vigil alone.

One of the three victims had been a bookseller. Who were the other two?

CHAPTER 6

Lorenzo Scarpa was seated just a few yards from his uncle Mariolino inside San Giacometo Church.

He'd decided to have his uncle's disfigured face covered with a veil.

Lorenzo had started to worry as soon as news of the discovery of another body reached him. His uncle hadn't returned home that night. He didn't know where the man was. When he reached the pier in the Rialto where they'd put the two bodies found by the fishermen, he immediately recognized his uncle by a scar the man had on one side of his torso, a long wound that Mariolino had gotten late one night outside the Due Mori bar, arguing with another man.

Lorenzo was the illegitimate son of a priest who lived near Bologna but who wasn't an important enough man to keep the son he'd fathered with a prostitute nearby. When twelve-year-old Lorenzo's mother died from an illness that didn't even have a name, he had been sent to live with the priest's brother, Mariolino, who hadn't heard from the priest in a long time. That's how Lorenzo had first come to Venice, six years earlier.

His uncle had taken Lorenzo in and showered him with all the affection the boy had never had from his own father. Lorenzo quickly understood the secret harbored by his uncle, a man who venerated books and had never taken a wife. Mariolino had never spoken to him of it, but he had helped Lorenzo understand on his own, before other people could tell him. The man had wanted Lorenzo to be prepared if something should happen to him someday, because love between two men was forbidden in Venice. Some people had been condemned to death for sodomy.

Mariolino had been an extraordinary man, and Lorenzo venerated him. He had been an attentive tutor to the boy—teaching him to read, teaching him about books—and took care of his every need. For Lorenzo, his uncle's small shop in the Rialto was the center of the universe. He often spent hours there, looking through the books that were offered for sale. He had learned to recognize which volumes were better to buy from a printer, and which from the merchants that traveled to La Serenissima from the East, from Germany, and from Paris.

The business had become intense over the past year, because Mariolino was working on a project that he said would change things for them forever and solve all their problems. He had explained to Lorenzo that he was going to buy a press from an old printer who was retiring. Mariolino was planning to ask for a loan to start printing a very important book. The movable-type system was widespread by now, making it possible to print more quickly and economically; print plates that were useless after they'd printed a page could now be taken apart and used again. Often, when Lorenzo and his uncle were talking about that project, the two discussed what book they should give the honor of printing first. Lorenzo got the impression that his uncle kept returning to the subject in order to get an idea of what Lorenzo was thinking, how he was growing up, and what kind of man he was becoming. He thought that in reality, Mariolino had long ago decided which book he would print first with his new press, the incredible tool that his uncle believed would change the course of history as much as the very invention of writing had so many centuries ago.

In his last days, his uncle's behavior had changed. One moment he seemed consumed by worry, the next unable to contain his enthusiasm for what they were about to do.

Now it was all lost. Stolen away. Torn away by a pitiless monster. His uncle's body lay there in front of him, covered by a cloth and with only a single hand showing.

Lorenzo had cleaned off the blood. He had sewed up the deepest wounds with a needle and thread the way Mariolino had taught him to fix the binding on a book. He'd spent hours looking at that same hand he'd spent most of his life watching at work. The long, slim fingers caressing paper, flipping through a book to let his nephew hear the incredible sound so many pages made.

The little flame on the candle Lorenzo lit seemed to dance in the faint whisper of wind that came in from outside the church. He was alone. Recognition of this was transformed into a sense of relief when he saw Niccolò Zaugo, a fellow bookseller and friend of his uncle's, who had been printing on his own for over a year now. Niccolò had crossed through the piazza, and Lorenzo could hear the people yelling all the terrible insults from there. He wished he could go outside and tear apart the first person he met, but he couldn't do so because of respect for the man who had taught him only to pity those who suffered from the terrible illness known as ignorance. Mariolino had always asked him to never resort to violence, not even when faced with the insults people flung in his face for his uncle's secret—which, precisely because it was a secret, everyone in Venice was aware of. Lorenzo knew that if his uncle could see him from wherever he'd gone after leaving that mutilated body, he would have been happy to find him seated inside, far from the crowd and its chaos.

Before Niccolò came, the only people who joined him to pray for Mariolino's soul were eight young monks, who did the same for any poor soul who wound up inside San Giacometo. They were kneeling on the prayer benches, and had been there for hours. Lorenzo had watched them for a long time before he saw Niccolò in the doorway.

"You must be tired, Lorenzo. You should go home and sleep," he said as soon as he reached the young man. Niccolò patted Lorenzo's brown hair and laid a hand on his shoulder, squeezing it to give him courage.

Out of the corner of his eye, Lorenzo noted a faint shimmer on Niccolò's hand. He turned his head a little and saw a small ring, a gold band, on the man's finger. Lorenzo knew the ring. His uncle had one just like it. In someone else's eyes, this wouldn't have seemed like much, but the boy had seen his uncle's ring up close and knew that there was a symbol carved into the gold. But a symbol for what? His mind drifted back to a day several months earlier.

He was waiting for his uncle so that they could have dinner together. He'd already laid out two bowls filled with minestrone downstairs. Their home had three rooms right above his uncle's shop. That night Mariolino was late coming down for dinner, which never happened. So Lorenzo went up to his uncle's room, where Mariolino usually went to change, and he found his uncle sitting at the little table near the window. He called out to him, and his uncle, drawn back as if from deep, distant thoughts, told Lorenzo he'd be down in a minute. But just as he was heading back downstairs, Lorenzo noticed a gesture Mariolino made. His uncle removed the small gold ring he was wearing and put it in a small drawer underneath the table. At that moment, Lorenzo realized that his uncle had always worn that ring and he'd never asked the man what importance it held for him. He'd always assumed it was a gift from a lover, a topic they never discussed. Long ago Lorenzo had decided he'd respect his uncle's freedom and let Mariolino be the one to address the forbidden subject first.

But the boy wanted, even needed, to know more. He felt as if a woodworm had burrowed its way into his mind. He decided that even if his uncle chose never to talk to him about it, he, as nephew, should know the secret. If nothing else, so that he could protect Mariolino. A few months earlier, his uncle had almost been killed by a man who had waited for him in the dark, hiding in the shadows of the calle outside the Due Mori. If his uncle wouldn't tell him anything, he could never be sure that a better-timed blow wouldn't take his uncle away from him forever. Mariolino was the only person Lorenzo had, and he wasn't about to take that chance.

So over the following nights, Lorenzo spied on his uncle as he removed the ring and put it away in the table, closing the drawer with a key that Mariolino then hid behind one of the bedposts.

A few weeks later, when he had a particularly successful business deal to celebrate, Mariolino broke out some fine wine and the two of them drank together. Lorenzo's uncle seemed like his old self again, making jokes and having a good time. Late that night, when he could hear his uncle snoring, Lorenzo took a candle and went into his room to take a closer look at that little ring. He went over to the bed, got the key, and opened the drawer. He took the ring and brought it close to the weak candle flame. That's when he noticed that in the space where a goldsmith could have inserted a gem, there was the faintest trace of a design, a decoration. It looked like a rose. Examining the tiny ring up close, he also discovered writing on the inside.

Lorenzo turned the candle to one side in order to bring as much light to the words as possible, but in doing so he forgot about the hot wax.

Just as he was about to read the writing, a few scalding drops fell on his bare foot. He managed to stifle a shout, but automatic reflexes made his leg jump and he kicked the leg of the table. Then he froze while his uncle stirred in his sleep. So Lorenzo put the ring back in the drawer and closed it with the key, then hid the key back in its place behind the bedpost.

He could never shake the feeling that his uncle had seen him snooping through his personal things that night.

Now that Niccolò was sitting beside him, holding vigil over Mariolino's body, Lorenzo recognized the same outline of a rose on his ring. A secret symbol?

Was there something important that Mariolino had never told him? Maybe his uncle meant to, someday. Maybe he wanted to share everything with Lorenzo. But that absurd and terrifying death had shut Mariolino's mouth forever.

He decided to ask Niccolò about it. He turned back toward his uncle, searching for the words that he'd need to broach a subject his uncle had never been able or willing to address. His eyes came to rest on the hand sticking out from beneath the cloth. Only then did Lorenzo realize that Mariolino's ring was no longer there.

Had the assassin taken it? Was the demon everyone was talking about drawn to the rose? Lorenzo realized he knew far too little about many things. And he was sitting with the only person he knew who might be able to answer his questions. But when he turned back to Niccolò Zaugo, Lorenzo caught sight of someone else entering San Giacometo Church.

It was Simone Luzzatto, the Jew.

His face bore an expression of triumph and joy.

CHAPTER 7

Mathias entered the house the Doge had made available to him. He tucked the large iron key into the inside pocket of his frock and went to the fireplace. The wood was crackling pleasantly, indicating that someone had prepared for his arrival. Evidently, the Doge had been sure he would accept. Mathias wondered if he'd only had the illusion of a choice.

He had been planning to return to Venice to resolve issues that couldn't wait any longer, to understand who he'd become over the past few years. He'd felt shadows grow all around him, and especially within his own heart. Instead, he had returned because he'd been drawn into an intrigue, the shape and extent of which he had yet to fully comprehend.

Mathias held his hands out to the fire to warm himself, dropping the bag of personal belongings he'd brought from Padua on the floor. The cold seemed to have worked its way into his bones, but the heat from the fire provided a measure of relief. He stood there a while, staring into the flames.

He'd never felt farther from the faith that had made him a strong, courageous man.

Can a lost man confuse light with shadow?

Reason with faith?

The Doge had called him back to Venice. Was it merely fortuitous that this task had led him to a place to which he had not yet found the courage to return and face his past?

Venice.

Angelica.

Three corpses.

Three mutilated faces, only one of which had a name. He knew where he'd find the others: they could be only in one place, where a doctor whom Mathias knew would now be preparing them. He would pay the man a visit.

CHAPTER 8

"Get out of here, Jew. Can't you see I'm mourning my uncle?"

Lorenzo's voice was laced with rancor. He could see Simone Luzzatto's satisfaction at the trials that had befallen his family.

"You should have paid your debts, Scarpa. Now, because of those debts, my father is going to seize your worldly goods, calculated to include interest."

"Your father wouldn't dare! . . . Would he?" Uncertainty and fear replaced rancor in Lorenzo's voice. His uncle's worldly goods meant the shop, the books, the press and paper, those three rooms they'd lived in together, and everything else Lorenzo had left. "I'll pay my debts, but I can't do so if I can't work."

"You can always go fish for sardines, Christian."

Lorenzo leapt to his feet. Niccolò managed to stop him before he attacked the other young man.

"The guards are right outside," said Simone. "You wouldn't want to wind up in the wells, would you?"

Lorenzo stared into Simone's eyes. Their look spoke of hatred and vendettas. Simone took a step backward. Lorenzo shook Niccolò's hands off his shoulders, giving the older man a curt nod to show he had control of his temper again. "The wells" was slang for the subterranean holding cells of the Venetian prison: rarely did those who were locked up there see the light of day again.

"Heed your friend, Scarpa. If you know what's best for you," said Luzzatto. Then he turned on his heel and left the church. Lorenzo collapsed on the wooden bench, trying to let go of the rage coursing through his heart. He felt lost, alone. His dark eyes filled with tears as he looked at the body of his uncle, laid out beneath that cloth.

Presently, Lorenzo looked up and around the church, searching for something, anything that would warm his soul from the cold anger filling his body. His eyes came to rest on the profile of a young woman. She was dressed in black, indicating that she would soon become a nun.

Luzzatto would be his ruin. He'd been expecting this for some time now. Their history had begun one morning in the middle of summer, near the Rialto market stalls. It all played out there, near that large wooden bridge, which was equipped with an ingenious, almost magical mechanism that lifted it up every time an important vessel had to pass underneath.

***

The heat around the Canal Grande had been oppressive. Lorenzo had taken refuge in the shade of a pear tree, in a garden someone had set up behind a small wood shed. His uncle had sent him out on a series of errands, and he'd completed them as quickly as possible so that he could relax and do nothing but doze. He liked working in the shop, but that little strip of earth in the sweet-scented shade of the pear tree was a delight that no one would have been able to resist.

After a while he remembered that his uncle had invited guests for dinner and had asked him to buy some meat, perhaps a chicken, and some wine. Lorenzo shook off his slumber and headed back into the market. A group of boys were playing alongside the dock, gripping wooden staves as if they were swords, play-fighting one another in an imaginary battle between Turks and Venetians, getting knocked into the water and clambering back out again. Lorenzo walked around them, then past a spice stall that reeked of the powerful aromas of pepper imported from the Orient and mixed into different varieties. Farther along, he could smell roast eel that a merchant was slicing into succulent strips and skewering on thin wooden spears.

He turned a corner and ducked beneath the portico that opened up below a warehouse containing merchandise that had been brought to Venice by boat and levered out of the vessels using long wooden "arms," with which the workers were able to lift extraordinarily heavy loads.

Lorenzo had just passed alongside one of these large shipping boats, laden with woven rugs and fabrics from the East, and stepped down the last step along the passage that led beneath the warehouse when he first saw the girl with the blue eyes the color of a summer sea. He'd barely had time to draw a sharp breath, and then the girl turned back to the swathe of cloth in her hands.

Unbeknownst to Lorenzo Scarpa, Simone Luzzatto already knew that girl. Her name was Caterina Marin, and she was a merchant's daughter. Simone was so in love with her that he felt as if he could sacrifice anything for her. He'd been watching her for some time, following her and waiting for the right moment to talk to her. He had learned her schedule by heart and had decided to give her that cloth as a gift, because he'd noted that she often stopped at the fabric stall in the Rialto, there beneath the warehouse, to pore over the latest merchandise arriving from the Orient.

That morning Simone had watched as Caterina examined a roll of scarlet velvet, asking the merchant how much it cost. He hoped he had enough money tucked into the little pouch he kept close to his body, clutching it with one hand for fear a thief might steal it away. His father,

Moses, didn't know anything about Simone's intentions for that little bag of money, but that was a problem he would have to deal with later. He caressed the little stone dolphin he wore on a cord around his neck for courage. It was a gift from his mother, something that helped him feel as if her protective presence were still nearby.

Walking over to the stall, he picked up the other end of the roll of scarlet velvet.

"It's really beautiful, isn't it?" he said to Caterina.

She turned to him, and Simone smiled, trying to keep his emotions in check.

"Unfortunately, I only have that one roll," said the cloth merchant.

That was perfect. Simone was ready to ask how much it cost and purchase it so that he could give it to Caterina, but a voice behind him interrupted his plans. A harsh sound upsetting what he'd hoped to turn into a perfect tableau.

"Your hair is already quite close in color, Luzzatto. I'm sure this splendid fabric would look much better on that young lady."

Scarpa, the bookseller's son. He'd showed up at precisely the wrong moment. Simone never got a chance to say his piece, and his face reddened to match his curly head of deep-auburn hair.

"I hope your friend agrees," said Caterina to the intruder. "I absolutely love this color."

"Butt out, Scarpa. This one's mine."

"What exactly would you have be yours, Jew?"

"The fabric, I'm sure," said Caterina. "It's not worth getting upset over. Please, take the whole roll if you'd like."

"The roll?" stammered Simone. "I didn't mean to . . ."

"Sure, you keep it," said Scarpa before turning to Caterina. "It won't be hard to find another that looks just as good on you. And I know a stall that has cloth far more beautiful than this one."

"The fabric at this stall is among the best in Venice," replied Caterina.

Simone had already taken a step back. He felt excluded. He'd been thrown out of his own narrative, erased from the perfect scenario he'd drawn in his head. The rest of what Caterina and Scarpa said to one another was lost in the sounds of the surrounding market. Caterina left the roll of fabric Simone had meant to buy for her lying on the stall. Scarpa was motioning for her to follow him, perhaps to go look at another stall somewhere. Caterina called a woman over to her. A servant followed, lugging her bundle of purchases.

While Simone was left stewing, Lorenzo had no idea where he was going to lead the girl, much less how he could possibly buy fabric worthy of her with the few coins he had in his pocket for chicken and wine. But he knew that they would walk a while together, and that all that mattered was being able to talk to her.

No sooner had they left the stall, however, when Lorenzo felt a hard grip on his shoulder. He turned around to find Simone, his face twisted in anger, standing behind him. The smaller man moved suddenly, and Lorenzo stepped back, easily dodging a clumsy punch. Then he sidestepped another, even clumsier than the first. Lorenzo twisted his torso a little, and Simone's third attempt at landing a blow threw him off balance, sending the red-haired fellow tumbling into the canal.

All the people walking through that crowded stretch of market turned to watch the scene.

"Did you see that?" said Lorenzo to Caterina, who looked upset. "He brought this all on himself. At least in this heat, he'll dry out as soon as he gets back on land."

Simone dragged himself to the edge of the canal, accompanied by a chorus of laughter rippling up and down the marketplace. He'd never learned how to swim very well, so he'd flapped and flopped about in the water. Then he realized he'd lost the little pouch full of gold ducats.

"My money, my money!" he shouted just as a group of boys happily leapt into the canal to collect it. They were much better swimmers, and more laughter erupted. Someone helped him climb onto land.

"My money!" he cried again, looking around at the faces staring down at him. Fortunately, Caterina's wasn't among them. He felt ridiculous and defeated.

"That'll teach you!" said the man who had helped him up out of the water. "At least you'll learn how to swim."

***

Now, so long after that afternoon, Lorenzo still remembered every moment, every word of the encounter. He could still see clearly the sunlight reflected in Caterina's eyes. He could still feel the way her smile made his heart race. They'd stayed together for hours, and when he finally made his way home, bringing back neither chicken nor wine, he'd told his uncle about the entire affair, confiding in him the way one might with an older brother.

Now, drying his tears and returning from his reveries into the cold air of the dimly lit San Giacometo Church, Lorenzo reached out to clasp his uncle's hand where it stuck out from beneath the cloth. But there was no comfort in a dead man's hand, and clutching it made him feel more lost than before.

Niccolò accompanied Luzzatto out of the church, asking him to please respect Lorenzo's suffering and let him grieve for the loss of his uncle in peace. The group of monks had finished and was preparing to leave.

Lorenzo raised his eyes again to find the young woman dressed in black huddled down in prayer. At the same moment, she turned and her eyes met his: clear blue, light as a summer sea, but full of sadness.

Caterina.

Under the circumstances, neither of them could do anything else, and both knew it. He answered her stare with a sad smile, then watched as she walked slowly out of the church.

Once again, he was alone.

CHAPTER 9

"Venice has changed. These are terrible times. You'd have done better to stay in Padua." Majid was a doctor, and an Arab. His family had come to La Serenissima when he was little more than a baby. Now he gave lessons at the city's school of medicine. Mathias had decided Majid was the first person he should meet for his investigation. In the frigid morning, they walked together beneath a pale sun that barely warmed their shoulders at all. Descending into the subterranean rooms of the building where he taught, Majid told Mathias, "After a life spent here, certain looks I get while walking through the city streets are enough to make me still feel like a foreigner."

"The war is over." Mathias was following the doctor down a damp, narrow corridor lit only by a few oil lamps.

"And another one will start as soon as possible. Wars are necessary. Ship owners fatten their coffers, and a foreign enemy focuses people's attention and keeps the city united."

"Venice has always had plenty of enemies."

"Of course. And you know which ones are its worst?"

"The Genoese?"

"The nobility. They're the ones who've reduced the entire Republic to poverty in order to embellish their palazzi. They surround themselves with prostitutes, eat five full meals a day, and fill the streets and canals with their shit, and all while they're busy convincing people that their real problem is the Turks. And now I can't even walk down the street without getting glared at, and I'm an Arab, not a Turk! If only they knew how much Arabs hate Turks . . ."

"You're getting old Majid. You're starting to complain about the same old things as before."

"Everybody's feeling insecure and frightened. Jews, Dalmatians, the Spanish, the Portuguese, and even the Germans, my friend. And those speaking in your God's name aren't helping any, either. Here, life has become one constant call for everyone to make war on the infidels." Majid glanced over his shoulder and smiled as he led Mathias deeper into the belly of the building. "I'm sorry," he said. "I tend to talk too much when I meet an old friend I haven't seen in a while."

"And I'm sorry I don't possess a German disposition, so that I might keep my mouth carefully shut and not say a word about the reason why, after more than a year has passed, I should suddenly show up back in Venice, searching for a couple of cadavers!"

Majid came to a stop and turned around, piercing Mathias with his dark eyes.

"I'm looking for someone," said Mathias. "A stranger I was supposed to meet here in the city. He never showed up. I want to know if he's one of the two dead men you're keeping down here."

"How did you know *I* was keeping them?"

"Two nameless cadavers, two poor souls no one has claimed? That's high-quality merchandise for someone who studies human anatomy, Majid. I was quite sure you wouldn't let them get away. As sure as death itself."

"High-quality merchandise, my foot. You should see how they massacred those two poor souls." Majid kept walking, then stopped and turned around again. "And don't think for a minute that I believe your nonsense about a meeting, either. I may have a gift for gab, but I'm not an idiot."

Mathias nodded but didn't say anything else. The stench of rotting flesh grew stronger with every step they took toward the holding room. Mathias felt his stomach twist and turn. The walls were dripping with humidity. The surrounding lagoon seemed to want to repossesses these walls, to take back this underground space that had been stolen away from the water and walled up. Finally, the two men came to a short wooden footbridge.

"Hold this under your nose and try not to faint," said Majid, handing the monk a small bouquet of strong-smelling aromatic herbs. "I've already started working on the smaller one, the one that showed up the first day. Otherwise, the worms would have ruined him for me," said Majid as he opened the door.

Blood. Red, dark, coagulated. Something that looked like a gigantic rope web. Hell on earth. Majid moved around, as at ease in that chamber of horrors as a barman behind the counter of a local tavern.

"This one, you see? I discovered that he wouldn't have lived much longer anyway. You see here? His intestines were rotting."

The cadaver was spread out on a wooden table with high legs, split open from just below his neck all the way to his genitals. The flesh had been hooked with a series of thin cords attached to small iron fishhooks, while the cords were kept taut by the webbing that surrounded the table. This allowed the doctor to keep the body open so that he could better study its internal organs. Another cadaver lay on the next table, still intact. Mathias could see what he recognized as an Arabic copy of Avicenna's *The Canon of Medicine* sitting on the heavy lectern between the two tables.

"The external parts of the corpses were almost entirely unusable due to the wounds and burns. It's hard for me to believe that another human being could have done this," said Majid, pointing to the first man's disfigured, almost entirely fleshless face.

"Are you afraid a demon has escaped Hell in order to descend upon the Venetians?"

"I think there are a few who'd deserve it, but I'm also a man of science, and I believe that we all carry our own private infernos inside ourselves."

"What can you tell me about that one?" asked the monk, going over to the second, larger corpse. The flesh was greenish white and emanated a ghastly, fetid stench. The doctor seemed to be used to it, but Mathias had to press the little herb bouquet into his nose to keep from being overwhelmed by a wave of bile rising from his stomach.

"A tall man, muscular. I believe he had very long black hair. And there's one other thing, something particularly interesting." Majid picked up a small iron implement that he used to make incisions and pointed at the corpses.

"As you can see, the first thing the demon did was entertain himself by making a series of cuts all over his victims' bodies. Even on the arms. Then he covered them with oil and lit a bonfire. But the cuts were made before he burned them, and in fact, in a certain sense, the fire cauterized the wounds. I believe that the demon then put out the fire and continued to torture them."

"Torture?"

"What else could it have been?" said Majid. He put the little iron instrument down on the table. "What motive could he possibly have for having used a method that could prolong his victim's suffering this way? He wanted something from them. Otherwise, why go to such great lengths? I believe whoever did this reasoned in much the same way as your inquisitors."

"I've got nothing to do with those people, Majid, and you know full well I don't."

"Perhaps," said the doctor, picking the iron tool back up. "Our assassin paid special attention to the face. First, he removed the flesh from one part, cutting away some of the skin. It's hard to even imagine the pain he inflicted on these poor souls. He worked with a knife that had a very thick blade. A butcher's knife. Here, look at this." The doctor waved Mathias over, pointing his tool into one of the empty sockets from which the assassin had ripped out an eyeball. "He stuck his knife in right here. I can guarantee that kind of suffering would drive somebody crazy. Then he used the bone as a lever, and the eyeball must have just popped right out. And he did the same thing with the other eyeball. But there's another thing I can't figure out.

"The blood that's all over the face. Look at this. It's very difficult to make out, probably because these two bodies were floating in the canal and the water undoubtedly washed something away. But I have the impression that in this case, unlike with that smaller fellow over there, the eyes were ripped out of the head in anger. The work is rougher, cruder. Maybe his intent wasn't so much to cause pain as it was to express anger, to punish." Majid pointed out the differences around the eye sockets of the two cadavers to Mathias.

"Could there have been two different assassins?"

"I'd rule that out. The rest of the work is identical. There are only two things I don't understand. This thing with the eyes is the first."

"The second?"

"This," said the doctor, pointing to a wound on the left leg of the larger cadaver, the one that was discovered the same day as the bookseller's. "Cut this artery and you'll be dead before you can say one of your Ave Maria prayers from start to finish."

"What don't you understand about it?"

"Why torture somebody, and then decide to kill him in just a few seconds?"

"Maybe because you're satisfied. You got what you wanted."

"There's no mercy in a man who's capable of ruining another human being like this."

"I imagine you have an alternative explanation?"

"The wrists on this cadaver are much more lacerated than those wrists over there, especially the left wrist. And the bones of the left hand are broken, here," said Majid, pointing to the thumb. "I believe this poor fellow broke it himself, struggling to free his hand from a cord that bound him by the wrists, and then took his own life."

"He broke his own hand, then took his own life?"

"A deep cut into this artery, inflicted by someone who knew what he was doing. A quick death, like the one they used to give a defeated gladiator. Back then they would cut the vein on the neck. Effective, but a little slow. Cutting the artery here on the leg is faster. This makes me think he was a military man. Perhaps a guard or a mercenary. Somebody who knew certain things."

"But why would he take his own life?"

"He knew it was over. His legs were broken. He couldn't escape. And he'd suffered horrible wounds. He gave his soul up to God."

Mathias tried to keep his gaze on the disfigured face of the man Majid believed had been some sort of soldier. "And you've deduced all this from the wounds you found on the cadaver, or have you found a way to talk to the dead?"

"A corpse is like a scroll of parchment. As long as you know how to read it, the body can't hide many secrets from you."

"I'm shocked, I have to admit."

"While you Christians are busy sticking bloodsucking leeches on each other to purify your moods, we're busy studying medicine."

Mathias stared at the lifeless body in silence. "We can't be sure," he said at last. "He might have decided to kill the man and dump the body once he'd gotten what he wanted."

"As I said before, I don't believe in an act of clemency from the man who did all this. And in any case, this body was found on the same day as the bookseller's body. If the torturer really got what he wanted, then we won't find any more corpses."

Struck by those last words, Mathias looked around the room, trying to organize his thoughts in this truly terrifying place. The instruments Majid used to open up bodies and study them were stacked on tables all over the chamber. A book lay open on a small table.

"Impressive," said the monk, going over to the book. "A valuable copy."

"It's a copy of Galen's *Therapeutics*," said Majid. "Published by a Greek printer, Zaccaria Calliergi."

"Isn't he the same man who printed the *Mega Etymologikon*?"

"He's partnered with a certain Vlastò, a man from Crete who's the trusted servant of Anna Notarà, the daughter of the latest Byzantine prime minister to arrive in Venice with a bag full of money to spend. And apparently he's spending a great deal just to make books."

"Some prefer to decorate their palazzi. Others prefer to print books."

"Of course," said Majid. "That's the way it is everywhere, in Venice just as in Rome, don't you think?"

Mathias lifted his gaze from the book and directed it at the doctor.

"Since when do the sons of Allah interest themselves in the goings-on of Rome?"

"And since when does a man of the Church take an interest in printers?"

"I admire their work," said the monk, picking up Galen's volume to examine it again.

"I'd have thought you'd prefer the palazzi, like your Holy Father."

"The first book printed with this new technique was a copy of the Bible," said Mathias.

"If you want to catch him, try to understand his mind, the way he thinks."

Mathias spun around to stare at the doctor.

"What? I'm not—"

"Don't worry. You didn't say anything to me. I have no idea why you're hunting this demon, but whatever we've said here will remain between the two of us."

After taking his leave of Majid, Mathias walked as quickly as he could out into the fresh, open air. He drew great, deep breaths into his lungs. The sun had already disappeared behind thick clouds, which threatened snow by nightfall. The cold air cleansed the smell of death from him.

Mathias felt the need to sit down, and sat with his back against a low stone wall that surrounded someone's tiny garden. Little by little, the hubbub of passersby helped push the horror back. Those men had been the victims of atrocious torture. The demon had driven them into an abyss of fear and pain.

Why?

That was the first question to ask.

What did he want to get from them?

A soldier, a military man, more accustomed than most to the trials of physical pain. A man who could bear it. He held important information. The killer knew it. He wanted that information. The soldier had seen the brink of the abyss, the horizon of his own mortal existence. A man of war, someone who knew how to control his fear, he knew he was approaching death. He broke his own left hand and freed himself from the binds that held him, that kept him at the mercy of his torturer. Mathias imagined him falling to the ground, dragging himself away. His legs broken, blades of pain carving up what was left of his body, he dragged himself toward the knife.

Majid's voice came back to him. *A deep cut into this artery, inflicted by someone who knew what he was doing.*

Something wasn't right. Mathias imagined a silhouette emerging out of the darkness, and he imagined talking to the demon.

Where were you while that man was taking his life?

Majid's voice again. *Maybe his intent wasn't so much to cause pain as it was to express anger, to punish.*

A demon's fury. By taking his own life, the soldier had also taken the power the demon exercised over him.

He played with you.

He gave you the wrong information.

And when he escaped to take his own life, you weren't there.

They were pieces of a mosaic. Torture. A demon who left the soldier alone. A soldier who had enough time to free himself, take his own life, and escape into the afterlife with his secrets. The demon who returned, furious, and ripped out the soldier's eyes in a fit of rage.

He gave you the wrong place, the wrong location.

There it was. The truth.

You're looking for something, and he told you where it was. But he gave you the wrong location. He sent you away so that he could free himself from you in the meantime.

Something was hidden in Venice. Hidden in a place that the soldier knew but hadn't revealed. He fooled the demon. The hiding place was safe. But why crucify the cadavers? Why dump them in the Canal Grande? Why the spectacle?

You want people to know what you're doing.

Those corpses are a message, a message you're leaving for someone.

The monk leapt to his feet without even realizing it.

"You're still looking for it," he exclaimed.

Only then did Mathias realize that two boys were standing there, staring at him. Both were carrying large bags of flour over their shoulders. Their eyes were wide with surprise.

"Are you feeling all right, old man?" one of them asked.

"Everything's fine. Thanks all the same, boys," he said, spreading out his hands and smiling. "No problems."

The two glanced at each other. One made a face and jerked his head for them to leave. They walked away.

Mathias realized suddenly that he was shaking with cold. He started walking and kept walking for nearly an hour, wandering along calli, becoming completely lost in Venice. Pieces of the mosaic. Three men tortured and killed. The first was still completely unknown. The second was a bookseller. The third knew the place where something the killer was looking for was hidden.

The monk looked up and realized he was near the canal where the bodies had been found. He headed in that direction, looking around while he walked. He crossed a narrow bridge, offering to help a woman carrying a basket heaped with rags. He smiled at her, a broad grin fueled in part by his excitement at the new things he'd discovered. The woman looked down and ran off.

Mathias needed to keep walking, both to release the tension he felt in his body and to warm up. He looked up at the palazzi of the city's oldest families, painted in brilliant colors that favored shades of red. Once he reached the Canal Grande, he could see the Rialto on the other side. He continued walking, following the waterway that was the city's main street. It was flanked by the newest, most modern palazzi, their facades dressed with marble imported from Istria.

The bridge to the Rialto was being lowered. A rich vessel had just passed beneath the bridge and was navigating the canal alongside the market. Mathias had heard talk of an upcoming wedding between two prominent Venetian families. Evidently, the guests were arriving in the city.

He reached the bridge, an impressive wood walkway that connected the island of Rialto to Piazza San Marco, Venice's economic, political, and religious center. The decision to release the bodies here may have been deliberate, he thought, surprising himself by returning so quickly to the unpleasant issue. He decided not to cross the bridge, but to continue walking along the same side of the canal. In just a few minutes, he'd reach the basilica. Suddenly, he heard someone call his name.

"Mathias!"

The monk turned around.

"This way, my friend."

He saw a luxurious gondola pull up to the stone bank. A corpulent gentleman was waving his arms at him, drawing the attention of pass-ersby. He watched as the well-dressed man got out of the gondola, and people gathered around him, each one elbowing his or her companion and pointing to the heavyset man, who was one of the most illustrious personages in all of Venice's nobility.

"I was wondering when you might come by to pay your respects, magister," said Giacomo Foscarini, calling Mathias by the title he had always used with him.

CHAPTER 10

Lorenzo lit the last few candles he could afford. Niccolò had left already, and now he was alone, listening to the murmur of voices from the crowd gathered outside the church. They were calling for his uncle Mariolino to be burned on a pyre, a sacrifice to satisfy the thirst of an increasingly unmerciful God. Lorenzo was sitting on the stone floor now, his head leaning back to rest on the seat of a bench, his eyes fixed on the ceiling.

He felt detached from the present, leaving behind the difficult days he'd been experiencing to reminisce about happier days past. One October afternoon, there was a downpour, the rain marking the end of an exceptionally long summer. After that first day in the market, he'd sought out Caterina whenever he could. They had a special place where they could meet, the rooftop of a palazzo inhabited by two elderly sisters who left them in peace. They were planning to watch an afternoon parade held on the Canal Grande. Caterina loved celebrations, perhaps because her name linked her to Venice's most important one. She was always reminding Lorenzo that she had been named for Caterina Corner, or Caterina Cornaro, as others called her, who was the queen of Cyprus until just over a decade ago, and now the Lady of Asolo.

Her father, Alvise Marin, had admired the queen so much he'd named his daughter for her. She was an important noblewoman, explained Caterina. She sat next to the Doge on the *bucintoro*, the ship the Doge took out every year on Ascension Day to celebrate Venice's matrimony with the sea.

But that day it was raining, and since they couldn't very well sit on the rooftop in the rain to watch the flotilla parade, they stayed in the little room that led to the roof. It had just one tiny window through which the gray light of day filtered in. They sat on the floor, and Lorenzo's senses were aroused by the sound of the rain falling outside, the musky smell of his own body, and the fragrant scent of Caterina's hair. A single blonde strand wound down her slim neck.

They kissed, taking off their rain-washed summer clothes so that their bodies pressed, naked, against one another. Long, delicate lovemaking. Caresses, kisses, shivers, and sighs of delight.

Lorenzo would have gladly spent the rest of his life preserved in that single moment, as if in amber, abandoning reality to live in the memory of that one single day. But his neck hurt, and as he lifted it off the hard wood, he found himself staring straight at his dead uncle's hand. The ring finger still had a mark, even though the gold band was no longer there. There was something important connected to the symbol on the ring, to that rose. Or at least Lorenzo hoped so; he clung to the force of that assumption in order to keep sadness from overwhelming him.

He saw three religious men enter the church. They'd come to take his uncle's body away and perform funeral rites, taking advantage of the fact that the crowd of Venetians who had spent the entire night outside calling for the body to be burned had finally broken up and melted away. Lorenzo gathered his courage and followed the men as they carried the coffin to the cemetery where his uncle would be buried. He stayed silent throughout the morning, listening to the sounds of Venice waking up and coming to life all around him—a life that no longer felt like his own. No longer a life in which he and Caterina spoke of marriage and living together. No longer a life in which he and his uncle discussed printing books.

Lorenzo felt Niccolò's hand on his shoulder again. He turned around, drying the tears that left damp trails down his cheeks. Wet earth was thrown on his uncle's grave. He thanked Niccolò for keeping him company at this terrible moment. The man remained silent, standing at his side. But he seemed tense, hurried, and after the short prayers had been said he explained why.

"Luzzatto is on his way to your uncle's shop," said Niccolò. "He wants to seize all your possessions as payment for the debt."

CHAPTER 11

Aboard the gondola, Giacomo Foscarini sat facing Mathias. They were crossing the Canal Grande, then they would navigate around San Marco and return. Foscarini loved to travel around Venice this way. They stopped briefly at a mooring near the bridge to the Rialto, and Foscarini had a servant fetch green olives, fresh Piacenza cheese, a few sausages from Modena, and wine that had just been delivered from Crete. The nobleman often dined aboard his gondola, looking out over the city, watching his world. "Seen from this vantage point, Venice doesn't seem like it's in any of its terrible troubles at all, magister," said Foscarini.

"You appear to be doing well for yourself," said Mathias, pointing to the banquet the nobleman had set before them. Giacomo smiled, spitting the pit from a flavorful walnut-sized olive out into the water.

"I'm a man of privilege, as you know. But even among my fortunate friends, there are many who are extremely worried about the way things are going."

"I've heard that foreign guests like me are no longer blessed by your favor," said Mathias. Foscarini was privy to every issue concerning the

Republic, and unquestionably the best man to talk to if he wanted to gather information.

"The Orientals aren't particularly welcome, but that's normal," said Foscarini. "But with the war and everything else, all you need is sun-darkened skin to be taken for a damned Turk."

"Nobody likes the Turks."

"And if you've talked to a few Jews, especially those who escaped persecution in Spain, you already know that things are starting to get unbearable for them, too."

"Has Venice forgotten it stands at the center of the world?" asked Mathias.

"Venice stands on the edge of a precipice."

"And that's the Jews' fault?"

"You know what I mean. I don't have anything against the Jews."

"I've got a friend who is convinced that having a foreign enemy—any foreign enemy, regardless of whether it's the Jews or the Sultan—helps the Venetian nobility to direct attention away from all the wealth they've accumulated and squandered in the meantime."

"Merchants and artisans keep this city on its feet and put food in its belly. But plenty of them have taken out usurious loans that only the Jews can provide, because the pawnshops can't provide the sums they need. Venetians have gone into debt while the Jews have grown rich."

"So better people should blame them than blame those who borrowed money they couldn't hope to pay back, right?"

"We're at war," said Foscarini. "You seem to forget that we have to face down Bayezid the Second and deal with everything that means. We're losing territories, shipping routes, and ships in the meantime."

"Wars cost money because someone's making a profit."

"The Doge has cut the salaries of every single public official. Do you know what that means? It means that the aristocracy who fulfill those positions are ready to rebel. The Republic no longer has the money it needs to pay them, and the merchants no longer have the liquidity to cover their needs, so they have to go into debt."

"I imagine all this weakens Loredan and reinforces his adversaries, doesn't it?"

Foscarini was quiet for a little while before answering. "Do you take an interest in politics, magister?"

"I'm just afraid that tomorrow someone will decide the real problem is the Germans."

"This war with the Turks has been going on for too long. It chews up resources that would be better spent on exploring new trade routes, like the Portuguese are doing. That's exactly what Loredan would like to do, but he's too busy looking over his shoulder, keeping an eye on our neighbors."

"Rome?"

"The Borgias haven't given up. For them even a simple vineyard becomes an appetizing bite when it means stealing the morsel out of our mouths. They've been dreaming of getting their hands on Venice for generations. In the end, this might be their chance."

"If the Pope called on all Christians to wage war against the Turks," said Mathias, "you'd win back your interests across the Mediterranean."

"The price would be too high. And in any case, it's a matter for those who still enjoy these power games. The Pope's supporters simply want Loredan's position. The merchants just want to recover their trading routes. Those who oppose the Pope's intervention merely want to protect what they have now."

"You speak as if you were standing on the outside, looking in."

"I am, at least in part."

"Your nephew Marcello is a member of the Council of Ten. You yourself wrote to tell me so. Are you going to try and convince me that you're not interested in his affairs?"

"In part. Remember that: always *in part*. What I wanted to tell you was that these games and machinations bankrupting Venice have become the heritage of a merchant class that is completely out of touch with the times."

"Enlighten me."

"The future's no longer the Mediterranean. We certainly won't make history for the Republic by winning back a couple of ports from the Turks. The ocean. That's where everything will happen now. And while everyone else is headed in that direction, we're lazing about here for a handful of grapes, fattening the Pope by paying indulgences and buying discounts for purgatory. Our splendor is destined to fade." Enjoying the sound of his own voice, Foscarini settled back and bit into another plump olive. "Do you like these olives? The man who sold them to me has the best olives in Venice."

Mathias nodded. He picked up a piece of cheese and complimented that too. Then he poured some wine into two goblets and handed one to his friend.

"If our adversaries' plan," said Mathias, "is to convince the merchants that the Pope has to intervene in order to safeguard their trade routes, don't you think they'd need some less sophisticated approach in order to convince the common man? Most people don't care one whit about commerce, trade routes, and political intrigues."

"What are you trying to say?"

"Last night I spent some time outside San Giacometo."

"Ah. The dead bookseller. Scarpa was his name. He loved men. Did you know that?"

"Do you think that's why he was murdered?"

"I hope not, but it wouldn't surprise me. The Republic won't tolerate certain things. That's nothing new. In the past we've even supported prostitution as a way to keep young men from resorting to sodomy. Take a walk around the calli in the Rialto one evening. You'll see."

"The fact is that there were people outside the church calling for the body to be burned on a pyre. They claimed God has turned his face from Venice, and that a demon has been unleashed from Hell to castigate La Serenissima."

"Superstition. You know how these things go."

"Fear is easy to spread but can become difficult to manage."

Foscarini took a deep swallow of wine. He closed his eyes. He appeared to be thinking about what Mathias had said.

"You know what's strange, Mathias? You still haven't told me a word about what all this has to do with you."

"I did tell you. I'm simply worried about certain ideas I see spreading among the Venetians."

"If the demon is intelligent, it will be able to tell the difference between a German and a Venetian."

"So I'm safe."

"At worst, he'll offer you a mug of beer."

"Yes, of course," said Mathias, giving up. "A mug of beer would be a pleasure."

"Well then, let's not wait for the demon! I'll take you to a place where they have excellent beer." Foscarini signaled to his oarsman to turn around and head back to the market. "Maybe a mug or two will help loosen your tongue!"

"It doesn't seem like my tongue needs loosening."

"I think *you* do."

"Why do you say that?"

"Because you still haven't told me why you've returned to Venice with no advance word to me, nor why you're so interested in the war, nor why you're busy talking about demons climbing up out of Hell, nor why you're asking me strange questions about a dead bookseller!"

"It's not just the dead bookseller. You know what I'm talking about. Three corpses have been found in the Canal Grande, and someone is busy convincing people that they're part of a divine punishment. All this at a time when the only thing the Pope's men lack is the right opportunity to launch a definitive attack on Loredan, the Doge that you yourself support."

Mathias's eyes bore into his friend, trying to read his every reaction, no matter how small.

"You're not going to tell me anything, are you?" said Mathias at last.

"Not right away. Otherwise, we won't know what to talk about when we're finally enjoying a beer. But surely you'll agree that you have to answer a few questions yourself, no?"

"All right. What haven't I explained?"

"The reason you left."

"They offered me a job in Padua."

"That's an excuse, and I've heard it before."

"If you want a more direct answer, then ask a more direct question."

"Have you seen Angelica since you returned?"

There it was. That name. Her image was clearer than ever, as if burned into his memory. Foscarini was staring at him with a gaze that seemed to penetrate Mathias's every defense.

Angelica. The desire to see her again was stronger than his desire for God. Had he lost the light? Would he still be able to stare down darkness?

"Things haven't gone well for her," said Foscarini, "since you left the city."

His friend's voice seemed to reach him from a great distance, pulling Mathias back to the present.

"What are you saying?" demanded the monk.

"She refused anyone's help. She could have sold it all and moved on, but right from the day you left, she decided to keeping running the inn and the few clients her husband had left, before . . ."

Foscarini stopped there.

"Before he was killed," said Mathias. "Of course."

The pair had just disembarked and was walking toward the Rialto, looking for the tavern Foscarini claimed served the best beer in Venice.

Leaving the pier behind them, crowded with heavy vessels designed to load and unload cargo, they'd wandered into the narrow calli that criss-crossed the island, the economic center of La Serenissima.

The Rialto was full of banks, fish markets, chicken stalls, and spice sellers. It hosted the San Giovanni School of Philosophy, where Mathias had taught when he'd lived here. Food stalls opened onto the street, offering small chalices of fresh wine and pieces of salted fish. Here and there, prostitutes hung out of open windows, showing their breasts. At night they would come out into the streets, welcoming clients at the doorstep of houses of sin across the quarter.

The Rialto pulsed with life. Every person out on every street was looking for something. Mathias was, too. He was looking for his past.

Angelica had been the wife of an old man, Sebastiano Zanon, who owned an inn and a few small shops, and who had lost interest in Angelica not long after they'd married. She was far younger than her husband, but she had always respected the man because by marrying her, out of friendship with her father, he'd lifted Angelica up out of a life of certain hardship.

She and Mathias met by chance, at a time when they were each trying to understand their place in this world. She shared her story with him, and they talked together for hours during long walks through the city, slowly but surely growing closer. That was why they'd started seeing one another in private, secretly. Neither one wanted to arouse suspicion in those who saw them together every day. But the clandestine nature of their encounters had only driven them closer still.

Mathias believed himself to blame for Angelica's adultery. But somehow he couldn't regret it, and he knew this risked driving him away from God. And he didn't feel like a sinner, like someone who needed to be pardoned.

"You saved her life." Foscarini had intuited part of what Mathias was thinking about.

The nobleman had defended Angelica before the Venetian judiciary when she was accused of killing her husband. Mathias was the one who'd convinced him to accept the case, because he was sure of Angelica's innocence. He wanted to investigate the murder himself, uncover the necessary proof and identify Zanon's real killer. And that's what he did, allowing Foscarini to clear Angelica's name before the judges.

He'd also admitted to his friend the reason he'd risked facing down the inquisitor of the Republic. It wasn't simply out of his feelings for Angelica, but because the night Zanon was killed, Angelica was with Mathias. But in order to keep Mathias from being tried and condemned for adultery, she hid the relationship, relinquishing the one thing that could have saved her. Mathias had labored day and night, obsessed with the idea of finding a solution that could save Angelica's life. His efforts were rewarded, but Angelica's exoneration was a Pyrrhic victory, since it made him a number of enemies, and not just among Angelica's accusers. Everyone knew he had found the proof that set her free. Yet they'd challenged him—a man of the Church, a servant of God—saying that he was wrong, and that his conduct was unacceptable for a monk.

"We made quite a few enemies with that affair," said Mathias. "I am in your debt."

"We also won quite a few admirers, magister."

A doubt assailed Mathias. Marigo and later Loredan had also called him "magister," just as his friend did. The Doge even mentioned that Mathias had saved Angelica, in order to spur Mathias to aid his cause. What did Foscarini mean by "admirers?" It was the same word Loredan had used. What did Foscarini have to do with all of this? He was about to ask his friend precisely this question when someone bumped into him and interrupted his thoughts.

Two guards were running in the same direction the two friends were heading. He noticed a large group of people moving there as well.

CHAPTER 12

Lorenzo and Niccolò were walking quickly. Crossing the last bridge, they were nearly knocked into the icy water as they twisted to avoid a man carrying an enormous basket of apples on his shoulder. When Lorenzo turned onto the calle where his uncle's house was, he discovered a young man with red hair in the small plaza right in front of his uncle's shop. It was Simone Luzzatto.

"Scarpa didn't pay his debts. Therefore, his possessions, offered as collateral, now belong to my family." Simone was talking to a group of onlookers who had followed his father, a well-known moneylender, to the Scarpa house. Moses Luzzatto was watching his son with a severe eye, as if the young man were being put to test.

"Only a Jew could come here like this, the very day of Mariolino's funeral!"

The voice emerged from the crowd that had gathered around Simone, who had climbed up on a low stone wall in order to address them.

"If you honored your debts the way you honor your deceased, my father wouldn't have been driven to this. What would you have us do? Do we not have the right to demand what is due to us?"

Lorenzo pushed his way through the crowd, reaching Simone. He could feel Niccolò behind him, ready to stop him if he were to go too far. He concentrated all the hatred he could muster into his dark glare.

"Out of my way," he said to the red-haired young man.

A murmur went through the crowd as those present recognized him. Simone looked at his father, then turned back to Lorenzo, seething with anger. Lorenzo didn't budge.

"What's happening here?" demanded an official peacekeeper who had been drawn by all the commotion.

"My father and I have come here to collect on a debt, for which we have a contract," said Simone, pulling a creased and wrinkled letter from his pocket.

"That's my uncle's shop," said Lorenzo. "I'm responsible for his debts now."

"Based on what principle? This one here isn't even a Venetian," said Simone, pointing at Lorenzo, "while my family has been Venetian for generations." He raised his voice to reach the entire crowd. "This letter states quite clearly that if Mariolino Scarpa is unable to respect the terms, my family takes ownership of this property: a few rooms and a hole-in-the-wall shop that will barely be big enough to function as a warehouse."

"It's not a warehouse," said Lorenzo. "It's a bookshop. And if my uncle is unable to pay, then I'll pay in his stead. I'll assume responsibility for that contract, under the same terms and with the same obligations."

"You're nothing but a poor illegitimate bastard, and that's not a decision for you to make," hissed Simone.

Lorenzo leapt at Simone. He felt Niccolò's hand on his shoulder, grabbing at him and trying to hold him back, but his rage was so complete that his uncle's friend could never have stopped him, if it weren't for a voice booming out behind them.

"But then it's not your decision to make, either."

Lorenzo stopped and turned around to see who was talking. So did everyone else, including the guards.

A gasp of surprise raced through the crowd, and the throng split apart in immediate deference, as if the people were curtains opening on a stage, revealing the heavy man whose voice they'd all heard. Lorenzo recognized him immediately. They all did.

But the person who truly captured his attention was the man standing to one side of the speaker. A man with graying blond hair, deep-set blue eyes, and a profound gaze. He seemed able to stare straight into Lorenzo's soul.

***

Mathias and Giacomo had followed the guards to see why they were running. As soon as he realized what was going on, Giacomo explained the situation to his friend, even as it unfolded before them. When they reached the square, Mathias recognized the young man he'd seen sitting inside San Giacometo Church, crying over his uncle. The bookseller, one of the three victims. A man who sold books murdered by a demon who was searching for something.

"I need to ask you a favor," said Mathias to his friend.

"Aren't you already in my debt?"

"Protect that bookshop."

Giacomo turned and stared at him. No one had yet recognized the nobleman standing in their midst, because everyone was still concentrating on the young men who appeared intent on ripping one another apart.

"Out of all the things I might have expected you to ask," said Giacomo, "this is far and away the most—"

"There's no time, Giacomo. You need to intervene. Do it now," said the monk, aware that the situation was getting out of hand. "I'd love to explain everything to you, but I need to look around that bookshop first. Alone and undisturbed."

"There are many more bookshops in Venice, and with far better books. I've never even heard of this one . . ."

"I need *this* bookshop. Find a way to safeguard the shop and all its contents. You're a lawyer, remember?"

"This is a truly bizarre request, magister," replied Giacomo, glancing around. "But you're lucky. I think I can see a solution."

"What solution?" said Mathias.

"Calling for the judiciary to intervene. The guards will have to sequester the bookshop in order to give the Quarantia the time it needs to make a decision on the matter. That's the law. Once the young man's right to succeed his uncle has been recognized, even if he isn't afforded the same terms set out in the contract his uncle signed, he would still have the right to a two-month delay to pay his debt. That would give you all the time you need, no?"

"Do it."

You're nothing but a poor illegitimate bastard, and that's not a decision for you to make, Simone Luzzatto had just said.

"But then it's not your decision to make, either," said Giacomo, earning stares from everyone present.

Mathias took advantage of the moment to study the bookseller's nephew, the young man he'd seen seated on a bench in San Giacometo. The man standing at the nephew's side right now was the same one who'd entered the church after weaving his way through the crowd clamoring for the bookseller's body to be burned. Mathias met Lorenzo's eyes: the young man seemed to realize he was being studied. Did he know something? Did he know why his uncle had been reduced to mangled flesh? Would he be able to supply some explanation for why the demon had been after him? He hoped so.

But the more information the Lorenzo could give, the greater the danger he'd face.

***

"What's going on?" said Lorenzo Scarpa to Niccolò Zaugo.

"I have no idea."

Simone was thunderstruck. He felt as if misfortune had singled him out in order to crush him. Right when he finally had Scarpa squirming in his grip, one of the most famous men in Venice was intervening on his behalf. The God his father believed in so fervently was once again turning his back on the Luzzatto family.

"This is a complex dispute, and I believe the Quarantia should deal with it." Foscarini had everyone's attention. "Furthermore, in the event that there are problems with precise deadlines—for example, payment of the outstanding debt—then the officials would do best to provide a response quickly. I've bought a few books from this little bookshop, and I'm quite fond of it. Frankly speaking, I'd be more than a little upset to see it turned into a common warehouse, to be stuffed with baubles and junk, most of which was confiscated for unpaid debts." The crowd was silent, staring at Foscarini in shock. "Of course these are simply my own personal opinions, but please allow me to present this young bookseller's case before the Quarantia, because I believe he has every right to inherit his uncle's property, house and shop, debts, and profession."

The guards nodded, then one of them turned to the nobleman. "What would you have us do with the shop in the meantime?"

"Sequester it," responded Foscarini. "I believe I speak for the authorities when I say that it must be placed under the Doge's stewardship until such a time as the Quarantia rules on the matter."

These last words took the wind out of Lorenzo's sails. When Foscarini had arrived and started speaking, he'd become convinced that fortune had finally smiled upon him. But if the shop was seized, he wouldn't be able to do anything. He didn't understand what was going on. Who was that man staring at him with the piercing eyes? Why was such an important nobleman bothering with a simple dispute between citizens? Because, despite everything the nobleman had just said to justify his interest in the affair, Lorenzo was dead certain that Giacomo Foscarini had never set a single foot in his uncle's shop.

CHAPTER 13

When there was nothing left for Simone Luzzatto to do except walk home with his father, the young man hung his head and avoided people's gazes. He was furious.

"You should have interceded, Father. This decision may disturb our business. The last thing we need is some bankrupt person managing to get his way."

"Things went this way because of how you handled the situation," said Moses.

Simone turned on his father.

"What are you talking about? You didn't say a word! You let—"

"You must always conduct your business with a clear mind, free of personal issues. Until you learn this simple fact, you'll never get anything out of life."

Simone clenched his fists so hard that he drove his fingernails into his palms until they bled.

***

Outside the bookshop, the crowd was breaking up. The show was over. Lorenzo met Foscarini's eyes and bowed slightly to thank the nobleman. Foscarini responded with a small smile.

"You could have paid him a little more respect," said Niccolò, turning to Lorenzo. "Foscarini spoke on your behalf. You have no idea how important that can be for someone in your situation."

"I know what it means, Niccolò. What I can't figure out is why. But I want to find out."

"Be careful. That's not the kind of man you can question."

"I just want to try and understand. Who was that other man, the one standing with him?" Lorenzo gestured toward Mathias.

"I've never seen him before in my life."

Mathias was unaware he was the object of scrutiny. He looked up at his important friend, who waved regally to the assembled Venetians paying homage to the nobleman in their midst. "Now let's go have that beer and you can explain a few things to me, *friend*," said Foscarini.

"I'll explain," said Mathias, "but not right now."

"At least tell me why you had me speak out for that tiny bookshop."

"I've already wasted too much of your time. Besides, now I have to leave you."

"What? What are you saying? Where do you think you're going?"

"Somewhere I should have gone a long time ago."

"Will you *never* grow tired of speaking in riddles?"

"You know full well where I'm going."

Giacomo came to a stop and stared at his friend, who kept walking. "Mathias!" he called out.

The monk slowly turned around to face him. The heavyset nobleman was standing in the middle of the calle, his eyes on Mathias. "At least tell her she has nothing to be ashamed of."

Mathias smiled at Giacomo, then started walking again. Angelica's inn wasn't much farther.

***

"They've left, my lord," said one of the onlookers to a man who had remained apart from the crowd, half hidden in a passageway between two buildings that was so narrow it almost didn't exist.

"Did you get a good look at that man who was with Foscarini?" The man in the shadows had a deep, raspy voice.

"We can find out who he is, if this is what my lord wishes," said another onlooker standing just a few yards away from the first, out in the square. He had blended in perfectly with the rest of the crowd.

"Ask around," said the hidden man, half stepping out of the shadows in order to look around the square and observe the stragglers. He scratched his chin, covered with a perfumed gray beard. His thumb and fingers were decorated with gold rings and precious gemstones, including a splendid red ruby on his ring finger. "Try and figure out who he is. He may be a German, a certain Munster. If so, he left Venice well over a year ago. Find out why he has returned," he said to one of the two men. Then he turned to the other, handing him three folded letters. "As usual, make sure no one sees you."

The bearded man drew back again, disappearing down the passageway. He walked until he reached a rio, where a lordly gondola was waiting for him. He boarded and settled into a small felze, pulling the hem of marten fur on his large cape tight around his neck and face. The Rialto was a place where anything and everything could happen, but a man of his stature would be ill-advised to let himself be recognized out among the whore-filled calli, even in the light of day. Some people seemed like they didn't care about being seen—Foscarini, for example, who never missed a chance to express his disdain for the hypocrisy of noblemen "who live in the Rialto, yet disapprove of it."

Foscarini had always been his adversary. But he was weak now, and increasingly alone. Soon it would be time to act.

CHAPTER 14

Angelica's inn faced Rio San Silvestro, on the opposite side of the market. At night it was the least well-lit area of the Rialto, and the one with the least street traffic by day. A safe place, protected from uninvited eyes. The inn had been one of the main business activities of her husband, along with a few minor trade routes he ran on the mainland, for spices arriving in Venice from the Orient and then sent on to the north. These were small affairs to begin with, and even fewer of them were left when Sebastiano died. Too many ducats had been lost at the card table. In the end, Angelica had salvaged the inn and little else.

After Sebastiano Zanon's murder and the subsequent trial, Foscarini had offered to buy the inn, providing Angelica with an annuity. But she'd turned him down. Mathias was convinced she'd chosen to punish herself, oppressed by the weight of her own feelings of guilt.

The monk turned the last corner onto San Silvestro and walked until he came to the inn, Due Spade, meaning "two swords." He stepped inside. There was a small wood bar and a few little tables, the smell of roasted vegetables, and the murmurs of a few patrons heady with wine. The elderly barmaid, Mimosa, recognized him. She was holding a bottle of liquor in one hand, which she placed on the bar extremely slowly.

Mathias nodded to her, tightening his lips as if he were lifting up a great weight. She responded in kind, nodding, and then, with a furtive gesture, pointed up the stairs. After that, she picked up her rag and began wiping down the bar.

Mathias started up the stairs.

Memories assaulted him at each step.

"It's raining again. Sometimes it seems like it will keep raining forever . . ." When Angelica had said that, they were still in each other's arms, buried beneath a heavy wool cover. He would always remember the way Angelica looked that day—her lustrous brown hair mussed up, her red lips, her eyes gleaming in the light.

"I want to show you the land I come from, someday," he'd said, forgetting in that moment everything that lay outside that room. Sebastiano was dead. Angelica was a widow and, according to the laws governing La Serenissima, was required to observe a period of mourning. Mathias had turned his life over to God and, under the laws of his order, was bound to chastity. Yet letting himself slip down into that sweet chasm had been so incredibly simple . . .

"Someday, when it finally stops raining, you'll take me there."

Mathias stopped in front of the door to Angelica's room. He gathered his courage and raised his hand to knock.

"I saw you down below," said a voice from inside the room. "What are you waiting for? Come in."

The monk opened the door. Angelica stood beside the window. She had turned to face him. Weak light from the evening's first candles glimmered on her dark hair, pulled back against her head, and her simple dress.

"You look older," she said.

"I have grown older."

"So quickly?"

"To me, eighteen months seems like a lifetime."

Angelica smiled. She sat down at the foot of the bed. "Do you think you can step a little closer?" she asked.

He sat down next to her. They looked at one another in silence, staring into each other's eyes, as if searching for their lost intimacy.

"I didn't think you would come back," said Angelica.

"You were wrong. I was always going to return, no matter what."

"For one final good-bye?"

"Is that your desire?"

"I spent more than a year asking myself what I wanted. I'd hoped that if you ever came back, at least you'd come back with some answers."

Mathias took a deep breath. He had no answers. Angelica reached out and brushed a few stray hairs from his forehead.

"Don't look so concerned," she said. "Come here. If I didn't owe you my life, I'd have stabbed you in the heart by now."

They embraced. It took no more than a few moments for the gap between them to close. They sat together on the bed, watching the sun set over the rooftops. They never lacked for conversation: The university in Padua. His suspension from teaching. The inn and her business.

"Why have you returned?" It seemed like Angelica had kept from asking that question as long as she could but now could hold back no longer.

Mathias had been thinking about the answer from the moment he left Padua.

"I think I'm going back to Germany."

Angelica lowered her eyes, a fragile, bittersweet smile on her lips.

"So you've decided," she said.

"I think that in the end, it's inevitable."

"So I was right." Angelica looked up again, staring into his eyes. "You've come to say good-bye."

"Not exactly."

"I'm sure you've had plenty of time to prepare a speech. Why don't you summon your courage and tell me why you are here, in my room."

"It seems time hasn't changed you all that much," said the monk.

"I'll take that as a compliment."

"It wasn't."

"Mathias . . ."

"I came back because I have things I need to take care of, things I must resolve and put to rest. Does it truly seem so outlandish to you that I would come here as well?"

"It seems outlandish that you would come here yet can't explain why. If you have things to work out, you could just as well have worked them out in a library. I want you to tell me why you have come here, *to me*."

"You once said that the day it stopped raining you would come away with me, to Germany. Do you remember?"

"Yes. Of course I remember."

"Did you mean that?"

"What about the things you must resolve?"

"I'm working on them."

"I've been living suspended in time," said Angelica. For the first time since he walked into the room, she seemed tired. "I waited. I waited for you. But I can't wait for you forever. There's nothing left for me here. I could go with you tomorrow. But before I do, I have to be sure. Because leaving Venice would mean putting my life in your hands, and I don't want to do that until you have worked out your problems with your God. I don't want to live with your inner turmoil."

"It's not that simple. I'm a servant of God."

"The way you choose to serve your God is your decision. Yours and yours alone. But I ask you to come back to me only once that decision has been made."

Angelica stood up and walked back to the little window. She looked outside. The day was growing dark. A few lights moved around down in the street. A soldier had thrown a prostitute over his shoulder and was carrying her up the stairs into an inn. She heard laughter coming from far away.

Mathias searched for something to say, but once again he found nothing. Silently he stood up and walked to the door. He opened it and, without turning around, disappeared into the darkness of the stairwell.

He'd barely taken a dozen steps outside the inn when he was enveloped in frigid air. He would have liked to shut himself up inside, but he had other things to do. There weren't bars or inns in the little square outside Scarpa's shop. No nighttime attractions. Darkness would give him cover while he broke into the shop. He still wasn't sure what to look for, but he was convinced it would be the same thing the demon was after.

He took one last look up at Angelica's window. Now the curtains were drawn, and he could barely make out a glimmer of weak candlelight inside the room. Drawing his cloak tightly over his shoulders, he walked quickly down the calli that led to the shop.

When he got there, Mathias held back at first, checking to see if there was anyone else around. With his face hidden beneath his velvet cap and a scarf he'd wrapped around his neck to keep warm, he turned the handle, testing the door.

He walked over to a window. The shutters were locked from the inside. He wanted to try and force them open, but he couldn't risk someone in a neighboring house overhearing him.

Mathias examined the windows on the second floor. From what he'd understood of what people were saying while Scarpa and Luzzatto were arguing in the square, that section of the building belonged to the bookseller as well; he had lived in the rooms above the shop. Up there, the hinges of the shutters seemed old and half-rotted-away. He noticed a nearby wooden building, probably a warehouse, and decided he'd break in from there, taking advantage of a small spiral staircase that rose up near a few large bales of hay. Once he was inside the warehouse, he'd try to get in through the window. He headed for the staircase.

"What are you looking for?" said someone behind him. He'd been careless. Mathias stopped in his tracks, standing still, afraid a knife was pointed at his back.

"Don't do anything foolish. I don't have very much money," he said, raising his arms.

"Turn around."

Mathias did as he was told and found himself facing someone he recognized. At that moment, he realized that when all was said and done, it wasn't really such a surprise to find himself face-to-face with this young man.

Scarpa.

"I'm looking for something," said Mathias. "Maybe you can help me."

"Why should I?"

"Because today I helped you. I made sure you didn't lose everything you own." The young man wasn't carrying a weapon. Mathias lowered his arms. Scarpa was potentially an excellent resource. Perhaps he could help the monk find out what kind of trouble his uncle had been mixed up in. "And you should help me, because the thing I'm looking for may help us understand why your uncle was killed."

"What do you have to do with my uncle?"

"We'll have plenty of time to explain things to one another, but right now we need to move fast."

The boy looked unconvinced. The monk gave him a little more time to realize that helping him was the only thing he could do.

"You're looking in the wrong place," said Scarpa at last. "The shop is over there."

"I know where it is. I was trying to find a way in."

"Then I believe you'll find these keys useful," said the young man, pulling them out of a pocket in his heavy wool coat.

"We're making progress," said the monk.

But just then, they heard footsteps drawing close.

"Did you come alone?" asked Scarpa.

"Yes."

"Then someone else is on his way here . . . Hide!" whispered Lorenzo. The bookseller's nephew pushed the monk backward, into the spot where the bales of hay were stacked and stored. An animal stench emerged from the depths of the wooden structure, perhaps a pigsty, from somewhere beneath an arch of rotting wood. The pair remained immobile, watching as a dark shadow made its way closer and closer to the bookshop.

CHAPTER 15

His face hidden beneath the hood of his wool cloak, Righetto moved along the calli in the Rialto protected by shadow. Once again, he was faced with the same task. Leave the letters his lord had given him in a lion's mouth. Anonymous accusations, just like the others. His lord wasn't the only one who sent them, and he'd never understood what all the secrecy was about. He couldn't see the reasons why his signore and others like him refused to conduct their business in the light of day.

If it were up to him, he would have done things differently. He would have grabbed his dagger and carved his way forward, because it wouldn't have made a whit of difference if the blood to be spilled was that of a thief, or that of a nobleman. Blood is red, no matter what. It has the same taste.

He thought about the demon. The things people were murmuring around the city seemed much more likely when darkness fell. Righetto felt his spine tingle, and it wasn't because of the cold. He climbed the wood steps that led to the raised portico near the flour warehouse. One of the lions' mouths was located here. Ever since the mutilated bodies had been found in the Canal Grande, the contents of the lions' mouths were collected daily and brought to the authorities.

The symbol of La Serenissima sculpted onto a stone disc, the lion's mouth had a hole carved inside the creature's jaws. Righetto dropped his letters in, then looked furtively about again to see if any vagabonds happened to be hiding there.

There was no one around. The night shrouded that part of the city in silence. He had just one more thing to do, then he could go out and find a woman who would caress the cold away. Righetto traveled through the minor labyrinth of calli that crisscrossed the central part of the island. He had to check on a shop, to make sure no one was inside. He reached the square where the bookshop his lord had told him about was located. The door was closed, and he couldn't detect any movement within. Yet perhaps he should check a little more carefully, he thought. Maybe his lord would want him to wait and keep watch, making sure no one else showed up, not even in the wee hours of the night.

Righetto stood there for a while, mulling this over. He knew that his lord was sitting in front of a warm fireplace this very minute. And Righetto felt sure no one would brave the cold air just to break into that tiny shop filled with nothing more worthwhile than ink-stained paper. It certainly wasn't the kind of place that might contain something precious. He thought about the women who were waiting for him. He hadn't fondled a female body for far too many days. He'd been too busy working; there'd been no time for carnal pleasures. Righetto decided he wasn't going to spend another night doing someone else's busywork. He took one last look around, then disappeared into the dark night.

"He's gone," whispered Lorenzo to Mathias.

For some reason, Lorenzo wasn't surprised to find himself facing this man. He'd recognized him immediately: the monk who'd shown up in the square with Foscarini. The man who had stared at him with those ice-blue eyes. He had a strange way of speaking Italian, a foreign accent.

"You saw him," said Mathias. Do you know who he was?"

"No idea whatsoever."

"You'd better get one. He was checking on your shop."

"It's not my shop yet, as you should know. If I'm not mistaken, you were here today with Giacomo Foscarini." The other man nodded. "What do you want with me?"

"I will tell you my name, Mathias Munster, but for the moment, that will have to be enough. I need to look around in your uncle's shop, and for that reason I asked Foscarini to intervene on your behalf and make sure Luzzatto didn't empty it out and fill it up with his own things."

"Where are you from?"

"I'm from a lot of different places. I'm a monk. And a German."

There was no time to waste. Better to go straight to the heart of things, Lorenzo thought. "Were you a *friend* of my uncle's?"

"Would that help alleviate your suspicions?"

"It's just that I've never seen you before. Among his friends, I mean. It's okay by me. I don't have any problems with it."

"What are you talking about?"

"Whatever you prefer. It's just that you could have told me straightaway."

"Let's go into the shop," said Mathias. "It's time to get moving."

Motioning for him to follow, Lorenzo stuck his key into the heavy lock and opened the shop door.

The shop was small, but well supplied. For Mathias, walking into a bookshop was always like going home again. Several dozen books—perhaps a hundred in all—were stacked on the shelves. Some were of low quality; others were valuable incunabula built by very talented artisans. It was a relatively valuable patrimony, for the right person. He picked out a book and ran his finger down the stitched binding.

He noticed another door.

"What's through there?" he asked. The boy seemed distracted.

"The press," he said, walking over to the door.

Mathias reached out and pushed the door open. He glanced at the boy for permission, and Lorenzo nodded for him to go in.

The printing press was similar to the one vintners used to press grapes in the Rhine Valley. The printing plate meant to be filled with movable type, which was usually crafted by an engraver in a blend of lead and tin, was set up below the lever. A print that reproduced the alphabet hung on one wall, made up of all the typeset characters used in Venice, for a total of twenty-six different letters. There was a lowercase, uppercase, and large initial version of each. On the floor lay containers full of ink. A table covered with tools and thread for the binding stood nearby. Johannes Gutenberg's invention had transformed the book into an industrial object, and Venice had become the center of the publishing industry. The city boasted over a hundred printers, some of whom produced so many copies that they could send them to any market anywhere.

Mathias was fascinated by the extent of that change. Books had always been hostages to monasteries, kept in libraries that were accessible to only a privileged few. Monks had preserved ancient writings, copying them out by hand and thereby guaranteeing their survival. Now books could be picked up, perused, and bought at market stalls. Now the ideas of Seneca, Aristotle, and Plato, the poetry of Sappho, the doctrines of Christian philosophers, and writings from all over the world were available to anyone who knew how to read. If Giacomo Foscarini was convinced that the discovery of unexplored land on the other side of the ocean would transform markets and commerce, Mathias was convinced that printing would change the course of history forever. He knew it the moment he first read a few pages of the Bible translated into German. That evening, he realized that anyone and everyone would now have access to the Word of God, and could search it for his own meaning and understanding.

He couldn't help wondering what might have happened if someone like Wycliffe had had access to a printing press. The Church had not been supportive of his enthusiasm, which was hardly a surprise, but he'd found willing ears in Mathias's friends, like Gheorg, through whom Wycliffe's ideas began to circulate in universities. What would *they* be able to do, he wondered, when printing was available to everyone? A great change, a sea change, was in the offing. Mathias could feel that such a shift was possible, and he was increasingly certain that he knew whose side he would be on.

Lost in his contemplation, his gaze came to rest on a wooden chest.

"What's in there?" he asked Lorenzo.

"Paper."

The young man lifted up the top of the chest and showed the monk the paper that his uncle must have bought only recently. It was good quality, covered with rags, leather, and dry straw to protect it from humidity. Mathias riffled through it with one finger, enjoying the pleasurable sensation the touch of paper gave.

"What was your uncle going to print?"

"I don't know. I was hoping *you* could tell me that." The boy seemed disappointed. "Mariolino took out a large loan from Luzzatto in order to buy all this. It took him a long time. The press, the ink, the paper . . . And then the typeset, engraved by hand by a goldsmith in Florence. All my uncle would say about it was that this was his great opportunity. I don't know what he was referring to."

Mathias listened, his hand still on the paper.

"He wasn't a man who put great value on money," said Lorenzo, "but he loved all this, his work. I met him when I was still a little boy, and ever since then he's only talked about books. He's always loved books more than anything else." Lorenzo checked himself. "Of course, he loved people too. I didn't mean to say—"

"That's clear," said Mathias, attempting to console the young man. But he didn't understand what the boy was alluding to.

"But to really know him, you should have seen him when he was here, in the shop, talking about his books with the few people who came here to buy copies from him. He was convinced he would become a printer too. We talked all the time which book we should print first. But I always thought he had his own precise idea, as if he already knew which book he wanted to print and he wanted me to figure it out for myself."

"Why would he do that?"

"Because that's how he did everything. Even when it came to his . . . well . . . I mean, his tastes . . . his friends . . . He never told me clearly, and we never talked about it directly. He just did things in such a way that I understood."

Mathias remembered what the guard outside San Giacometo had told him about the printer's sexual preferences. Perhaps Lorenzo had misunderstood something, but this was neither the time nor the place to talk about the issue.

"So you have no idea what he intended to print?"

"No, but as I've said, I'm sure he had a specific plan. If you talked to him about Virgil, he would say that he was leaving that stuff for Manuzio. Do you see what I mean?"

"In part."

"I mean, if . . ." But there he stopped. Lorenzo started looking around, as if he'd only just then realized something he'd never thought of before. Mathias followed the young man's eyes as they darted left and right, from one corner of the shop to another.

"What's going on?" asked the monk.

"The books."

"What's wrong? Is something missing? Is a book missing?"

"Not exactly," said Lorenzo, going over to the door. He checked the lock. "I know where each and every book is supposed to be. Mariolino had his own ideal order, difficult for an outsider to understand. To someone who didn't know him, it would look like they were just put down here and there."

Mathias looked around, still not understanding what Lorenzo meant. The young man continued to fiddle with the lock until he pulled out a little shard of key tooth. "I knew it."

"What? Will you please tell me what you're doing?"

"Somebody forced the door, came in here, and searched the shop. Then he put the books back, but not in the same order." Lorenzo handed the iron shard to Mathias. "Whoever broke in here must have forced the lock with a very small iron tool."

"Do you have any idea who?"

"None." The young man scratched his chin, thinking. "It might have been the same man who was outside just a little while ago."

"I don't know," said Mathias, "but it seems like this shop has had a lot of visitors lately. It might be best to leave now before anyone else shows up."

"We could wait and see if someone else comes. Then we could ask him some questions."

"First, we need to figure out what's going on. And I don't think the man who killed your uncle is going to be interested in answering our questions."

"I'm staying," said Lorenzo.

"To do what?"

"I'm staying. This is my shop now."

"No. Right now, this shop belongs to the Doge, and if one of his guards finds you here you'll wind up in chains."

"Where else should I go?"

Mathias thought about that, a new and unwelcome complication.

"My uncle met with someone just a few days ago," said the young man, bringing the monk back to the present. Mathias stared at Lorenzo, waiting for him to go on. "If we work together, we might find the answers you need. Let me stay with you tonight, and I'll tell you about their meeting. Let's go. I'll die of cold if I sleep outside, and thanks to you, they've seized everything I own."

"Who did your uncle meet with?"

"I'll tell you everything I know."

Mathias was studying him.

"But I'm not like you . . ." finished the young man. He seemed apologetic. "Like my uncle, I mean. You know . . . I don't have . . . *friends* like you. Do you understand?"

Mathias smiled to himself. He understood that he needed to clear up this matter as quickly as possible.

CHAPTER 16

"I met him only once." Lorenzo was sitting in front of the fireplace. It must have been at least eight days ago . . ."

Mathias was warming up a decoction, a drink of brewed herbs that his mother used to make, and had set out some bread and sausages that Foscarini had sent to his house. The young man was clearly hungry.

"He was in the shop. My uncle had sent me out to buy some things, but I'd forgotten the money and had to go back. They were standing together, talking, near the bookshelves. All I heard was something like 'I'll call the others. We'll meet tonight.' I don't remember his exact words, but that was the meaning."

"That's all?" asked Mathias.

"As soon as they saw me, they changed the subject, and my uncle started rambling about a book he seemed to want to sell to the man."

"Do you remember what book it was?"

"I think it was a small collection of playful sonnets."

"Was it expensive?"

"Aside from a few copies of Cecco Angiolieri's sonnets, which in any case you can buy just about anywhere, the rest were all relatively cheap volumes. My uncle liked them simply because they appealed to his bizarre sense of humor."

"Can you remember any details?"

"When the man left, I asked my uncle who he was. He denied knowing him or anything about him, but I told him I'd heard what he'd said, and then he closed the door to the shop, took me by the arm, and led me into the printing room."

"What then?"

"He told me that the man had traveled here from far away in order to talk to him and some of his colleagues—printers, booksellers, people who were part of their world. But since they were discussing a very delicate subject, *we* wouldn't be a part of the discussion until much later."

"Did the meeting they'd talked about ever take place?"

"My uncle went out in the middle of the night, and stayed out until it was practically dawn. But he didn't say a thing about it when he finally returned."

"This stranger," said Mathias. "What did he look like?" An intuition.

"He was tall," said Lorenzo. "A robust man with long black hair."

Lorenzo would never be able to identify him, thought the monk, given the condition he's in right now. But the young man's description corresponded almost perfectly with the corpse Majid had shown him. The man who, according to the Arab, had taken his own life after he'd been horribly tortured. A man whose disappearance no one had reported. The fact that he'd been a foreigner might explain this aspect as well.

"That man is dead," said Mathias.

"How do you know that?"

"He was the other corpse they pulled out of the Canal Grande at the same time as your uncle's."

"What!" Lorenzo stood up.

"According to what you've said, this foreigner, perhaps a soldier, came to Venice to meet with some printers." Pulling his chair closer to the fireplace, Mathias kicked the logs to waken the fire. "When they met, they discussed something, then he and one of the booksellers—your uncle—were taken and massacred by the same monster who first killed another person the same way. We still haven't identified who that first victim is."

"Do you know *why* the demon killed my uncle?"

"Not yet, but I know that the demon is looking for something. Here's my theory: The foreigner was tortured and forced to reveal the hiding place of whatever the demon is looking for. Then the demon left him in order to go verify the information he'd revealed, and the foreigner took advantage of his absence by taking his own life." Mathias interrupted his narrative and turned to Lorenzo, his tone of voice changing, becoming softer. "I'm sorry to tell you this, but I believe your uncle was tortured for the same reason. Therefore, either he didn't know the answer, or he was willing to suffer pure agony in order to keep the answer hidden."

"He was killed because he refused to reveal a hiding place?"

Lorenzo was unwilling to believe him. He paced around nervously before flopping down on a bench. "What was he hiding?"

"Whatever it was, apparently a small group of printers were interested in it."

"Unfortunately, my uncle didn't have enough time to explain more to me."

"That's not true," said Mathias. Suddenly, the monk's eyes seemed to reflect a strange light. "In fact, he's given you key information. Think about it—what was your uncle planning to do?"

"He wanted to become a printer . . ." Lorenzo's face lit up. He understood what the monk was getting at. "He was planning to print something soon. That's why he went into such deep debt with that Jew."

"And after his death, someone came to rummage through his bookshop."

"Looking for something among his books."

"You said it seemed that your uncle already knew what he intended to print. Isn't that so?"

"Yes, that's right."

"So it's a book." Mathias struck his knee with one hand. "I knew it. Venice is the capital of publishing. This mystery couldn't be connected with anything else. A book. It's a book."

"*What* is a book?" asked Lorenzo.

"The object of the demon's search. He's after a book."

"And you think my uncle brought that foreigner to the demon?"

"I think that foreigner was carrying a book that a few minor artisans were supposed to print. I also think this book must have controversial contents, so much so that more important printers were unwilling to get involved. A network of small print shops, each working on its own, would have been an excellent way to avoid attracting attention."

"A group of small printers . . ."

"Something like that. Does that mean anything to you?"

"No," said Lorenzo, sipping the disgusting herb drink the monk had made. A thought was working its way through his mind. A group of booksellers and printers might share a special sign, a symbol by which they could recognize one another. Could that be the meaning of the rose engraved on Mariolino's ring? "Then what happened?" he asked the monk. He wasn't ready to share this new idea.

"I don't know. But apparently anyone who had anything to do with this book has met with a horrible destiny."

***

The carafe still held wine. A tired Giuntino was seated at a table at the Due Mori, near the fish market. Not even wine could chase away his fears. What had happened to Mariolino Scarpa? What had happened to the man who brought the book to Venice? Where were the others? They'd put the wrong ideas in his head. He should have taken his father's advice. The old man had always printed just a few things, carefully choosing to respond to the tastes of the most refined courtesans, concentrating on sonnets and comic operas. He should have done the same and avoided political things. He needed to get out of this situation and keep safe. The things he usually published would have been enough, if he'd led a life like his father's. But wine, women, and cards were terrible companions, and required a great deal of money to maintain.

The carafe was empty. He got up from the table and went outside, plunging into the cold night air and shaking off at least a little of his drunken stupor. Giuntino hugged his cloak tightly to his body and started walking home. He'd barely gone ten steps when he had to stop. He leaned up against a great door and emptied his stomach. The stench of vomit that clung to this corner of the city made it clear he wasn't the only one to have had this impulse.

Cold sweat. A heavy body. Weak legs. The ground rose and fell beneath his feet like a storm-tossed sea assailing a small boat. He leaned one hand against the wall and kept walking. His house wasn't far away. He'd lie down in bed and close his eyes. Everything else would disappear for a while.

He could feel his bladder swelling and complaining. He stopped again to urinate. He dried the sweat on his forehead with the edge of his cloak. And then he saw it. Empty eye sockets, a white face with a long hooked nose. A plague doctor's mask. It was flitting in and out of the shadows of a narrow calle. An enormous black cloak with a giant hood just barely revealed the grotesque caricature of the mask. Was it a ghoulish apparition? Was his wine-addled brain playing tricks on him?

The printer had finally made it to his front door when the strange figure emerged from the shadows again.

Darkness everywhere. His arms were in pain. Giuntino tried to move them, but a cord cut into his wrists.

Mariolino's body. He'd seen it. He'd run down to the banks of the Canal Grande as soon as the news began to spread. He'd seen the face of his friend transformed by a furious monster. It seemed that the same destiny lay in store for him. Terror exploded in his chest, constricting his breathing. He could barely make out soft lapping sounds. He was on the water.

An old black gondola. A funereal vessel. A windowless little felze upholstered with velvet. The boat slipped slowly across the waters of the lagoon.

CHAPTER 17

Caterina was still awake. From her bedroom window, she could see a light rain, the tiny drops breaking the reflection of the moonlight into miniscule fragments. She was crying. Ghosts of everything her life had never become moved around like characters in a theater set, but the rain helped her believe she wasn't crying alone.

Words reached out to her from far away, from across the years.

"Do you love me?" she had asked. "What would you do for me?"

"I would marry you, make you the happiest woman in the world."

They were in San Marco, walking together beneath the open gallery. Winter was at the doorstep, and neither one of them had any idea how long it would last. Lorenzo had brought her a marvelous white orchid, which Caterina held close to her chest. They'd been walking for hours. She had decided to tell her father that very day about this boy, this young man who wanted to make her the happiest woman in the world. Her father was an important merchant and knew how enormous the world really was.

After saying good-bye to Lorenzo, she dashed across the courtyard of the Marin family's palazzo. It was filled with tall flowers, but none as beautiful as her orchid. She ran up the marble stairs and straight toward the room where her father usually worked, filling his account ledgers for his various maritime trade ventures. She was going to explain to him what was happening in her life, and what decisions she'd made for her future. Her father would understand; he'd never denied her anything. He'd always told her that with the wealth her family was building, they would soon be able to buy anything they wanted, even happiness. But when she walked into the room, the look on her father's face gave her reason to pause. He looked tense, older somehow. He was hunched over at his table. She went over to him, frightened by what she saw.

"My child, your father has lost everything."

Alvise Marin had invested everything he owned in a commercial venture that was risky but had the potential to provide excellent dividends. He had taken over a small fleet of merchant galleys and sent them along a trade route he believed was safe. The difficulties seafarers faced along routes to the Orient had already convinced more timorous merchants to trade elsewhere. But it was a risk Alvise was certain would pay off, thanks to some private information he'd obtained.

Unfortunately, things hadn't worked out as planned. Pirates working for the Sultan had attacked the Venetian ships. One cool Tuesday morning in late October, Alvise Marin lost all his ducats, his properties, his reputation.

And his daughter's future.

"I have nothing left, Caterina. I've ruined you forever. I have no dowry left for you." He looked out at her with the eyes of a lost child.

"What are you saying, Father? What will happen next?"

"You'll have to go enter a convent."

Caterina's heart turned to stone.

"A convent? Father, you can't—"

"With no dowry, I cannot marry you off, my darling. But we still have a few friends in Rome who may help you obtain a position that is useful for the family."

The orchid fell to the floor. The flower ripped and fell apart on cold Istrian marble.

"We have nothing else left, my daughter. We need your help."

She would never forget those words. Thinking about them now, Caterina dried her tears. The moon reflected on the rippling rain-scattered lagoon reminded her of shattered porcelain. She went back to bed and tried to sleep, struggling once again to avoid dreams that would be difficult to awaken from at sunrise.

She tried and failed.

CHAPTER 18

"You didn't even know my uncle, did you?" Lorenzo placed the empty cup of Mathias's disgusting brew on the floor. The fire the monk had kicked to life was warming them both. "If you weren't his friend, not even his acquaintance, then why are you bothering to investigate his death?"

"Someone asked me to solve the mystery," said Mathias. "I cannot tell you more than that, at least not for now. But you need to try and help me. Have you spoken with anyone about these things, about that meeting?"

"I don't trust the night guards, and I'm not interested in airing my uncle's secrets in the public piazza. His memory is already disrespected as it is."

"What about those people who gathered outside San Giacometo the other night?"

"I don't know who they are."

"They wanted to burn your uncle's body."

"All I want is to get the printing press and shop back."

"Do you want to become a printer?"

"I have every right to. Mariolino recognized me as his nephew. The authorities should recognize my claim."

"The sooner we resolve this mystery, the sooner you can see to it that your ownership rights are respected. But if you know anything else, now is the time to share it with me."

"How am I supposed to trust you? I don't know anything about you."

"I'm a monk."

"One of the people stirring up the crowd outside San Giacometo was a monk too. You just said so yourself—everyone out there wanted to burn my uncle's body."

"He was a Dominican priest."

"That's wonderful for him. And what are you?"

"Augustinian."

"You all serve the same master."

"Everyone serves the Lord in the manner he or she believes is best. But in any case, he's not the one who got me involved in this affair."

"What are you, some sort of secret inquisitor, in the service of some lord who can pay for your loyalty?"

"You can think of things that way if you'd like, but don't share your thoughts with anyone else. The fewer people know what I'm doing here, the better chance we'll have of succeeding."

"You say *we* . . . So I can still be of use to you?"

"Perhaps, but after you've told me everything you know, you're welcome to go your own way."

"I don't have my 'own way' anymore."

That was true, and Mathias couldn't deny it. Involving Lorenzo any more deeply would be dangerous. He took a sip of his decoction. It was true the brew had a strong taste, but it helped calm the nerves and dissipate foul humors brought by cold weather.

"If you stay clear of this affair, you won't have any more problems, and I may be able to give you back ownership of your uncle's worldly goods," said Mathias, trying to reassure Lorenzo. "There's no reason for you to expose yourself."

"No reason?" The young man raised his voice. "They've massacred my uncle, and now they're stealing away everything I own. What would you have me do, sit around and scratch my belly until you've finished your job? And if you can't get it done on your own, what then? Don't you believe that's reason enough for me to help?"

"I'll get it done." Mathias began closing the window curtains.

"You don't even know what to do next," said Lorenzo.

"And what about you? Do you know what to do next? Hmm? Let's hear it."

Lorenzo took time to think that through. He trusted almost no one in Venice. And the few people who had remained close to him, like Niccolò, certainly couldn't help him solve the mystery of his uncle's horrible death. But if that mystery wasn't solved, he would never be able to disprove the popular theory that Mariolino Scarpa was executed by a demon because of his dissolute habits. He would never be able to go back to work. The echo of that horrible affair would follow him around forever, making him a target for all sorts of accusations. It would mean that any competitor, unsatisfied client, or common creditor like Luzzatto would be able to take advantage of Lorenzo.

He helped Mathias close the curtains around the room. Lorenzo didn't know why, but it seemed to him that this man was telling him the truth. This monk was the only one who could possibly help him.

"Maybe it would help for you to visit the room the stranger was staying in during his visit to Venice," Lorenzo offered.

"You know where it is?" Mathias walked up close to Lorenzo and stared at him with those clear blue eyes that seemed sculpted from ice in the northern lands.

"I saw him the day after the meeting, and I followed him."

"You should have told me sooner. At this point, he hasn't been back to the inn for several days, and the owner may have already called the night guards."

"You should have told me who you were sooner."

The monk slammed a window shut, displaying a grimace of anger. Then he took a deep breath. "All right," he said, turning to Lorenzo. "You can help me. But remember that this affair may earn you a lot of enemies. And some of them may be quite powerful."

"I just want to clear my uncle's name. Otherwise, it won't matter one whit whether I get the shop and printing press back. No one would hire the nephew of a sinner who drew a demon to the city." He looked Mathias in the eye. "We'll go tomorrow night."

"Why not sooner?"

"Because the innkeeper might be suspicious. Usually in the evening, he gets drunk and leaves his wife in charge of the rooms. Then all we'll need to do is tell her we want to pay the stranger's debt and she'll let us take anything we want."

"How do you know all this?"

"I know this city." Lorenzo had gone back to staring into the fireplace, busy with the thought that continued to work its way around his mind. The symbol on the small shiny ring his uncle wore. Was it connected to this mystery? If so, how? "And thanks to my uncle, I know things that very few other people know. He was accustomed to living a secret life and extremely talented at discovering the secrets of others." Secrets that Lorenzo would now have to reconstruct on his own. He turned once again to the monk. "As you can see, I can still be of use to you."

"As long as you realize what we're up against."

"You can explain it to me on the way. But first, I have a favor to ask . . ."

CHAPTER 19

Excruciating pain jolted Giuntino back to his senses. He was tied to a chair with leather cord. He looked around, struggling to make out anything clearly through the veil of blood obscuring his view. He was inside a warehouse. Was this, then, what Hell looked like?

A rag stuffed into his mouth prevented him from screaming. He looked at his hands. His fingers were deformed, and the nails were gone. They'd been ripped from his flesh with an iron pincer. The demon had gripped them in the mouth of that tool and torn them off, one by one, with a mighty jerk. Giuntino could feel blood running down his face. Suddenly, he remembered what had happened just before darkness had overtaken him. The demon had inserted a fish-scaling knife into the flesh above his cheekbones and started cutting his face away piece by piece.

He'd use the same rusty knife on Giuntino's eyeball.

All the while, nothing but a faint hissing emerged from that horrible mask beneath the black cloak.

He remembered the knife, resting beneath his eyeball. Pressure. Stronger and stronger. Then the pain. A blade digging around the socket. An eye ripped from his head. Blood on his face. The rag pulled from his mouth. The taste of his own blood filling his mouth instead.

"Where is the book?" whispered the voice, a serpentine sound. The noise of a snake waiting to strike, bite, poison and kill its prey.

"I don't know . . . I beg of you . . . There are others. They must know. I'll give you all their names. I'll tell you everything, but you must stop. I'm begging you . . ." The rag, reeking of vomit, was stuffed back into his mouth, and then Giuntino felt another explosion of pain as the demon continued carving up his body piece by piece.

He couldn't remain conscious any longer.

The idea of death seemed acceptable, even desirable.

He felt the knife enter his stomach. Searing pain moved in tandem with the opening of a great gash. Something dense pushed out into the world. He looked down and saw his own intestines burst from his belly.

The demon grabbed hold of them and squeezed. Slowly, hand over hand, he began to pull them out of Giuntino's body.

"You will suffer great torment until I stop," said the demon. "Tell me where the book is."

CHAPTER 20

The faithful were leaving San Giacometo after attending Sunday morning mass, walking down various calli toward their homes. It was pouring outside. Mathias and Lorenzo waited until the flow of people dwindled and then stopped before they went into the church.

The two men who had handled Mariolino's burial were busy cleaning the altar. When they saw the pair walk in, they spoke briefly to one another and the older of the two came over to them. Lorenzo recognized the wooden bench he'd spent the night seated on, keeping vigil over his uncle's body.

"Welcome to the house of the Lord," said the elderly man, presumably the church pastor.

"Greetings, Father," said Mathias. "We're here to pay the debts for the religious services you performed for Mariolino Scarpa, the man you buried the other morning, this boy's uncle."

The pastor's look grew severe.

"That was an unpleasant affair," he said. "Those people stayed outside the church all night, calling for bonfires. This young man disappeared in order to handle his own affairs."

Lorenzo was about to say something, but Mathias stopped him.

"You seem perplexed," said the monk.

"Absolutely not," replied the pastor. "Do you intend to pay your debts now, or would you prefer another mass?"

"In that case, you'd rather we settle later?"

"In that case, you would have to settle for the extra mass as well."

Lorenzo saw Mathias's eyes grow icy cold. He realized that if the conversation continued in this direction, soon he'd be the one forced to stop the situation from getting out of hand.

"I imagine you have a list of services, then." Mathias's voice was as sharp as a butcher's knife. "Would you please show it to us, the way an innkeeper does for his guests, so that we might choose a smorgasbord of God the way we'd like, along with the appropriate condiments . . . What do you think, hmm?"

"You are a heretic," said the pastor. "How dare you speak this way in the house of the Lord!"

"Leave him be, Pietro." The voice came from a shadowy area of the church, and they all turned toward it. "Pardon the impetuousness of this monk. He obeys the laws of Saint Augustine. At times he behaves like a bull ram from the mountains, but his dedication to the Lord is as sincere as a child's."

An old man walked into the light. He was wearing a Dominican friar's frock. Mathias's face lit up.

"Serafino!" he said.

"Magister Mathias," said the old man. "I know that's what I'm supposed to call you now."

The two men embraced.

"Go gently on me, my son, I don't want you to break my bones. The humidity in Venice has made me as fragile as their glass!" He took Mathias by his broad shoulders and stared into his face. "Let me see you, Mathias. For someone accustomed to looking into your ugly mug almost every day, I had to wait a long time for your return."

"I see you know one another well," said the pastor in a flat tone of voice. "If you've nothing else to tell me, you might as well leave your gift, if you feel it opportune to make a contribution to our efforts here. Otherwise, I have other commitments to attend to."

Then he turned on his heel and left.

"When did simony become so prevalent?" asked Mathias to his elderly friend.

"Pietro is a well-known figure here, you obstinate mountain goat, and if I hadn't been here he would have turned your day sour." Serafino turned to Lorenzo. "This boorish lout is only going to get you into trouble, you know."

"To be honest . . ." began the young man.

"Let's go. Come on, let's see what I can offer you to eat," said the older monk.

Serafino took both men by the arm and, leaning on them a bit, led them outside, toward San Zanipolo, where Serafino's monastery was located. During their walk, Lorenzo had a chance to listen to Mathias's strange story, as the monk explained how he'd been suspended from his job in Padua because of certain mentions of the teachings of an English theologian, who apparently wasn't a favorite of Serafino's either.

"Woe to the foolish prophets who follow their own spirit and have seen nothing!" said the Dominican.

"I see Ezekiel is still your favorite priest," said Mathias.

"So you still remember a few things from that strange book, the one that is supposed to be the only book you're interested in."

"This man was not merely my confessor," said Mathias to Lorenzo. "Over the years I spent in Venice, he became much more than that. But he has a terrible character, and that makes him decidedly unpleasant to be with."

"Ever the mountain goat," said the Dominican. "I didn't raise you up just to see you meet the same end as Jan Hus. How much longer are you going to insist on damning your own soul?"

"Who is Jan Hus?" asked Lorenzo.

"A Bohemian scholar," said Mathias.

"An excommunicated heretic," said Serafino.

"I imagine he met with an unpleasant end," said Lorenzo.

"You imagine correctly," said the Dominican. "So the next time you go into the church for worship, try to keep this silly mountain goat from prancing in behind you."

Mathias laughed.

"My friend, you're undoubtedly the least likable brother in the entire Dominican order," he said, giving Serafino a warm embrace.

Once they reached the monastery, the three headed for the refectory.

Someone came walking toward them. Lorenzo recognized him: the young Dominican who was stirring up the crowd outside San Giacometo, calling for Mariolino's body to be burned on a pyre. Mathias had to hold Lorenzo back again.

"Now's not the time, my son. Don't do anything stupid," he whispered in Lorenzo's ear.

Lorenzo was surprised. The monk seemed to know more about the affair than he'd realized.

"Brother Serafino," said the young Dominican. "I see that you've brought guests to share our worship."

"Once again, your sight serves you well, Brother Malachia," said Serafino.

The young Dominican's lips tightened to a thin line. It was clear he wanted to reply to the barb somehow but wasn't allowed to. "I won't steal any more of your prayer time then," he said.

"To tell the truth, we were just heading to have lunch," said Serafino.

"It's not yet time, Brother."

"Our guests are hungry. I don't believe it's necessary to wait for everyone else, at least not today."

"But Brother . . ."

"Thank you for everything, Malachia. We have no more need of you now."

The young Dominican stood as if frozen, but his face was livid. Serafino moved his two guests past the young brother. As they walked into the refectory, they could hear Malachia's quick steps walking away.

"Undoubtedly he'll run to the prior," said Serafino.

"That doesn't seem to worry you much," said Mathias as he sat down at a long wooden table with his old friend.

"You," said Serafino, "on the other hand, seem worried indeed."

"I've seen that young man before, the other night outside San Giacometo Church."

Lorenzo sat down next to Mathias. He was surprised to hear the monk say this. What did Mathias know? Lorenzo held himself very still, as if he didn't want to lose so much as a single word of what these two religious men were saying to one another.

"What was he doing?" asked Serafino.

"Yelling, mostly," said Mathias. "He was heading a group of fanatics who wanted to burn the body of a deceased man in order to drive the Devil from Venice."

"The bookseller, I imagine?"

"My uncle," said Lorenzo.

Mathias turned to look at him with fire in his eyes, and Lorenzo understood that he should have kept his mouth shut.

"Malachia is an idiot," said Serafino. "He's arrogant, presumptuous, and a coward. That's a mix of qualities that makes him someone to watch out for, my young friend. I'm sorry for you uncle, but you can rest easy. I don't believe the Devil has much to do with this affair."

"It sounds like you have a clear opinion on the matter," said Mathias.

"No opinions. I don't know the world of publishing that well, despite your fascination with it. But I know it's a world in which a great deal of money changes hands, and money often brings its own problems."

"There wasn't very much money changing hands in my uncle's shop," said Lorenzo.

"The young man would like to continue the business," explained Mathias.

"What about you? What have you come to Venice for?" asked Serafino. "Do you intend to dedicate your energies to the art of printing? Is that why you're walking around with this young aspiring businessman?"

"Nothing of the sort."

"I've already told you, young man," said Serafino to Lorenzo. "This monk will only bring you trouble. It's important you know that from the start."

"I'm headed back home," said Mathias, "toward my mountains."

That seemed to surprise Serafino. The old priest looked at him, betraying the shadow of a smile on his lips that Lorenzo could feel was born of deep feelings.

"So you're traveling again."

"The time has come."

"Then you've come here to settle your debts with the past?"

"I'm trying to understand what God has in store of me."

"God loves you. But he doesn't decide for you."

"They're building a new university, in Wittenberg."

"Where you and your companions will be able to come up with new ways to get suspended from teaching, I imagine."

"What happened in Padua has nothing to do with it."

"Nothing to do with it? Then what does? Your connections with Venice, perhaps? The ones you continue to run away from?"

Lorenzo listened to the two men go back and forth, but he didn't really understand what they were talking about. Mathias had described the older man as his "confessor." Apparently, Mathias had some unfinished business in his past to which the Dominican priest was privy.

"Do you think you'll resolve it in this manner?" continued Serafino. "Do you believe God appreciates a servant who, in order to continue to serve him, has to force himself to look the other way?"

"Should I stop serving him?"

"You and your companions have filled your heads with too many words. Faith is a simple matter. It's a calling, remember? Do away with everything else. Seek your calling."

"Mathias!" A voice came from the entrance that led from the refectory to the kitchen. Heavy steps. Then an enormous monk appeared at the transom. His happy expression was utterly without guile, betraying the child who remained inside.

"Hello," said Mathias, getting up to embrace the big man. "I see Serafino talked you into staying."

"I needed two strong arms," said Serafino. "And we discovered that *Brother* Berto has a hidden talent for cooking."

"Brother? So that tunic is no longer just something comfortable to throw over your shoulders," said Mathias.

"I'm like you now," said Berto.

"He's taken his vows, and now he's the head cook in our kitchen," explained Serafino. "And I have to admit that he already knows how to cook a great deal more than Brother Tobia, God rest his soul, ever learned during the many years he prepared our meals."

"As hungry as we brothers usually are, that can't be anything but good news," said Mathias.

Berto went back into the kitchen, a look of supreme satisfaction on his face.

"So you managed to convince the prior to keep him."

"There are so many orphans in the city," explained Serafino. "For most of them, once they become adults they find their path in life. But sometimes it's more complicated. And donations and contributions for these kinds of problems are nothing like what they used to be."

"Has the papal throne tightened the belt?"

"Don't blaspheme at my table, you boorish goat. The papal throne's got nothing to do with it. The Venetians are supposed to be the ones helping us deal with the fruits of their sins. They impregnate prostitutes as if they were sows, and then everyone turns the babies over to the convents."

"Apparently, this is not a great moment for the coffers of La Serenissima," said Mathias.

"It's got nothing to do with the moment." Serafino grew serious. "The greed and arrogance of some people has thrown a shadow even over charity. There are more ducats in two lines of the *Golden Book* than in the rest of La Serenissima combined."

"The *Golden Book*?" asked Lorenzo.

"The register of patrician families," said Mathias.

"The *nobil homini* of this sumptuous city," said Serafino. "I've said it before. There's too much money exchanging hands in certain circles. You know them. You know what I'm talking about."

Mathias's brow furrowed.

"Who am I supposed to know?"

"You have friends in high places," said Serafino. "In fact, your friends are so influential you can't convince this old monk that you've come back to Venice simply to make peace with your past."

Before Mathias could respond, Berto came back from the kitchen carrying a large pot of steaming cabbage soup.

"I trust that afterward you'll let me try a little of the excellent roast chicken you're making," said Mathias.

"How do you know about the roast chicken?" asked Berto.

"You've got a feather and a few spots of fresh blood there on your cassock, my friend. And clear signs of charcoal on your fingertips. Therefore, I imagine that when you went out, getting that fresh mud on your shoes"—Mathias pointed to the faint prints the monk had left on the flagstones behind him—"you went to set the chicken to roast."

"Why . . . that's exactly right!" said Berto, his face lighting up with enthusiasm.

Lorenzo was struck.

"Do you still want some of this soup?" asked the big cook.

"Of course. I'm sure it's exquisite," said Mathias. "And at least as good as the chicken, which I'm sure Brother Serafino won't want to eat all by himself before the other brothers arrive here for their meal."

"Oh, no," said Berto. "Brother Serafino always comes early when I'm making chicken, because he wants the drumsticks. He leaves the rest of the bird to the others."

"Thank you, Berto. That's quite enough," said Serafino.

"Yes, I'm sure you've said plenty more than you need," said Mathias. "I know Brother Serafino's tastes quite well, and I'll be more than happy with a bit of chicken breast."

"Our high inquisitor Mathias here would be more helpful hunting for the demon," said Serafino, "than he'd ever be chasing chickens."

Berto looked confused. He set bowls and the soup down on the table and returned to the kitchen.

All three enjoyed the meal immensely, especially the chicken, which arrived directly after the soup. When they had finished, they left the refectory, clearing the room before the other brothers came to eat.

Walking back down the corridor, they heard quick steps behind them. They turned around just in time to see a young monk in such a hurry that he'd pulled his tunic up over his knees.

"Brother Bernardo, why all the hurry?" asked Serafino. "Have you come to tell me Brother Malachia is busy babbling about my misbehavior to the prior?"

"No, Brother, nothing of the sort. Something's happened, and the prior sent me to find out what's going on. They heard yelling coming from the Canal Grande.

"Yelling?" asked Mathias.

"Yes," said Bernardo, "the demon has killed again."

CHAPTER 21

Another printer. That's what people were saying.

Mathias and Lorenzo had reached the canal. A crowd had gathered around a mooring, where a small boat had dragged something its owner has found in the rain-tossed waters.

A fourth body now lay stretched out on the ground. A woman broke forward from the crowd.

"Giuntino!" she cried, then collapsed in front of the mooring. A few people murmured that she was the man's wife.

The demon had taken his fourth victim.

The murdered printer's face was deformed, and partially devoid of flesh. His eye sockets were empty. As with the other victims, his arms were spread out and nailed into a large piece of wood. This time the demon seemed to have spared his victim the flames, leaving some resemblance of what he'd looked like in life.

Horror spread through those gathered: the man's stomach was split open, and entrails curled and spread out around him. A boy used an oar to pull the rest of the intestines up out of the water. The victim's wife fainted away.

They set the body against a wooden bench, attempting to put it back together somehow. One of the fishermen cut the intestines with a knife, letting them fall in the water, while another wrapped the printer's abdomen with a swathe of rough cloth.

"May God have pity on our sins," a voice said behind them. Brother Malachia. The monk knelt down, and one by one the other Dominican monks copied him, searching for guidance, for a way to gather their courage, in that simple gesture of humility.

Mathias felt as if he could see the shadow of the killer in front of him for a moment.

Your show is getting the welcome you hoped for, isn't it?

He looked around. Noble palazzi lining the canal, narrow passageways, a terrorized crowd . . . Everyone who had run down to the mooring was now on their knees, concentrating on the praying Dominican priest.

I think you're here somewhere, enjoying all this.

A gondola caught Mathias's attention. The prow of the lordly vessel was barely visible, sticking only slightly out of a rio that opened into the Canal Grande. He could swear it hadn't been there a few moments ago. Mathias moved closer, while the Dominican spoke of reconciling the Venetians with a Lord who was punishing them for their haughtiness and innumerable vices.

Once he reached the mouth of the rio, Mathias caught a glimpse of the boatman. His face was covered by a large hat that protected him from the pouring rain. The boatman opened the door to the felze and motioned to Mathias to get in.

The monk moved closer, trying to figure out who was waiting for him. It wasn't Foscarini's boat, nor the Doge's. All he could make out was a rich turquoise fabric with gold embroidery, clearly part of a feminine outfit.

He took a few steps back the way he'd come and waved to Lorenzo, who was still with the crowd, making it clear that the two would see one another later. Then Mathias returned to the gondola and got in. The boatman began maneuvering the small boat into the labyrinth of Venice's internal canals.

***

Lorenzo was making an effort to appear at least as devout as the others around him. He knelt down so as not to attract the Dominican's attention, who apparently still wasn't aware he was Mariolino Scarpa's nephew.

First, he tried to get as close as possible to the printer Giuntino's corpse. His heart beat rapidly as he thought about what he had just seen. Or hadn't he? He had to make sure, to remove any possible doubt about what felt more like sensation than a real, solid perception. He closed his eyes and lowered his head as a sign of penitence. With his hands folded in prayer in front of his face, he reopened his eyes and took a careful look at the printer's hand, still attached to the wood plank with rusty nails. The tips of his fingers had become grotesque in the absence of any fingernails. The blood had been washed away. And the thing Lorenzo was looking for was right there, right in front of his eyes.

The ring.

Rain and seawater had cleansed the ring, and the design on it was clearly visible. From where he was kneeling, Lorenzo could see a rose. What did it mean?

The image had been etched in his mind ever since Mathias had told him about a group of small printers who had entered into a pact. Was the rose the group's chosen symbol? Had Mariolino been a member of a secret society which, like the German monk postulated, had decided to publish a dangerous book? What book could possibly possess such power, be so important to motivate a demon to create all this horror?

Lorenzo felt it was time to go. He moved away from the group praying, still trying not to stand out. Malachia was imploring God to pardon the debauchery of Venetians. In particular, he asked God to forgive the printers. Men who had renounced their devotion of saints and the hard work of copying books by hand. Men who preferred diabolical machines that printed pages without help from a Christian hand to guide the words—like a plough that furrows the earth, leaving in its wake a testimony of faith.

"Two printers have been struck down by God's judgment," cried Brother Malachia, clutching in one hand the cross he wore around his neck. "This is a sign. The Demon sows his malevolent seed through their obscene books. Hellfire will rain down on our houses should we fail to put a stop to this madness!"

Lorenzo couldn't listen to the words anymore. He could think of nothing but the rose, which seemed to hide a solution, and a forbidden book that was capable of sowing horror and death. Turning a corner, he walked quickly in the direction of the Due Mori—he wanted to drink some wine—but when he rounded another corner, he was stopped short.

Someone dragged him through a large doorway—someone far weaker and more delicate than he but who took advantage of his shock to overwhelm him. The way this person took his arm, so familiarly, betrayed her. And the taste of her lips on his mouth reminded him forcefully of what it felt like to be in paradise.

"I was on my way to the market with the others, then I saw you coming," said Caterina as soon as their lips parted.

CHAPTER 22

Peals from the Marangona, the largest bell in the battered bell tower, called the Great Council of Venice together Sunday afternoon. Nobles from all over Venice came walking through the rain. They were wearing the *dogalina*, a formal black robe worn on official occasions, and arrived in Piazza San Marco in small groups. Some stopped to say hello to one another, or to make deals before they went inside to take their places. Others walked sedately as if they were on parade, echoing the *Procession in St. Mark's Square* that Bellini painted, below the forest of Byzantine arches of the building where San Marco's prosecutors resided. This slow movement of bodies converged on Palazzo Ducale—the center of Venetian government, the heart of La Serenissima, the symbol of the city's power.

About twenty years earlier, the building was destroyed by fire; it had cost one hundred thousand ducats to rebuild. With the war on the Turks under way, the Doge had decided to cut back on salaries for public offices, an act the patrician class was hardly enthusiastic about.

Once they'd passed the basilica, alongside Palazzo Ducale, Venice's nobility headed to the other side of the piazza, where a winged lion kept watch over La Serenissima from on high, set atop a giant column facing San Todaro.

Giacomo Foscarini was there, accompanied by his nephew Marcello. The Veniers were there as well, and before they all crossed through the entryway to the courtyard of Palazzo Ducale, Zaccaria Freschi had joined the group. He'd been waiting for the Foscarinis, to learn of the latest amendments to the proposal that the Council had called this meeting to discuss.

Foscarini had hammered out a peace proposal they could take to the Turks. He'd done this to save Loredan from having to expose himself personally before the Council, and had entrusted the proposal to Zaccaria. But unless the prevailing opinions of the Venetian noble class had changed, the proposal would be rejected, opening a path for the papists.

The Corner family walked past nearby. The family's elderly pater-familias took advantage of the moment to pay his respect to Giacomo, displaying a wicked smile that said he was already enjoying the show-down from which he would soon emerge victorious.

"They're going to eat us up and spit us out, Giacomo," said Zaccaria.

"We'll just have to do everything we can to prevent that from happening," responded Marcello.

"We will undoubtedly lose today," said Giacomo, trying to placate his nephew, who had only recently become a member of the Council of Ten. "But they don't yet possess the cards they need to deal us a deathblow, so we simply need to make sure the defeat is as painless as possible."

"But there's still a chance for us, uncle. There are dozens of unde-cided votes."

"And they'll remain undecided, Marcello. They'll abstain. There are certain mechanisms in play here, but you'll need more experience to understand them all."

"We're cutting it too close," said Zaccaria. "If the Doge doesn't intervene, and do so with a strong hand, they'll tear us to pieces. If not today, then next week."

"If the Doge exposes himself now, then they'll get the deathblow their thirsting for," said Giacomo, lowering his voice. "I'm sure you don't want to be the one to serve up that opportunity on a silver platter, do you?"

Zorzi passed nearby, walking to join the Corners. He was the one who would speak up to reject Zaccaria's proposal. Giacomo continued to look around. He still hadn't found his enemy, the supreme leader of the opposing party, but he knew he was here somewhere, weaving his web in order to catch and conquer Loredan.

**

"Please excuse my rather audacious methods, but I'm sure you'll understand that time is running out, and there is certainly no time left for fine manners." Alissa Strianese welcomed Mathias into the cabin on her gondola. She struck the roof of the felze. The gondola slid slowly away, maneuvering through a maze of canals.

Her hair was a bright, almost transparent blonde, the sign of long and expensive treatments, and she had a provocative figure that blossomed into a generous neckline. Her lips were scarlet red, and her eyelids were painted a deep, dark blue. In short: she was an anthem to sin. It was the look of a luxury courtesan, a woman that someone—and Mathias would soon find out who—was using in order to build relationships that were never meant to come to light. "You must be wondering to whom you owe this unexpected visit."

"I can't deny I'm curious," replied the monk.

"The information that concerns you comes from my lady, Caterina Corner."

She had once been the queen of Cyprus, but after continuous clashes with the Catalans, the Republic had asked her to abdicate and return to Venice, guaranteeing the lady previously unheard-of honors and privileges and conserving her title as queen in official acts.

"Why would the Lady of Asolo need a simple monk?" Mathias tried not to betray his surprise.

"The Doge sent to Padua for you and gave you a house in the Rialto, the theater for these terrible deaths. Your friend Foscarini had the bookshop of that poor Scarpa fellow seized and locked up. Someone has noticed you and has started to piece things together."

The secrecy Loredan was supposed to guarantee no longer appeared as impenetrable as it once had. But what surprised Mathias most was the speed with which this information had traveled through the most reserved circles of La Serenissima.

"You look perplexed," said Alissa. "Did you really think you could do all this in secret? Here in Venice?" She seemed entertained by his obvious embarrassment. "But don't worry. No one is interested in making your life difficult. At least we aren't. My lady simply wants to warn you about some potential dangers."

"The only danger is that what I am doing is on everyone's lips," said Mathias.

"Several people are asking questions about you."

"And who might these people be?"

"I know for certain that several men who work for a very powerful family are trying to figure out who you are and what you are up to."

"Did you come all the way here to talk to me about 'several men' and 'a very powerful family'? Or are you thinking of telling me a few names, given that you appear to know far more than I do about what I'm up to?"

"Don't get upset. We're on the same side."

"Then explain yourself."

"Surely you saw, just a little while ago, the people kneeling in prayer before the body they found in the canal. This mood is spreading across the city. Someone is taking advantage of the situation."

"You're not telling me anything I don't already know."

"Do you know Agostino Grimani?"

"I know who he is."

"His cousin is a cardinal and very close to the Borgias. If Venice were to ask for the Pope's help fighting the Turks, he would become the next Doge. And with him, the throne of Rome would reign over La Serenissima."

"What would he gain by becoming Doge if in return he were forced to sell the Republic?"

"Do you have any idea how many landed properties the clerics have in Venice?"

"You're talking to a monk."

"So you do know. And you also know that if jurisdiction over their possessions were taken from the Senate and passed along to the patriarch, and therefore to the Pope, the Borgias would find themselves in possession of wealth that would be more than enough to cover Grimani in gold. At that point, he'd be more than willing to surrender La Serenissima's autonomy."

"So it all boils down to money?"

"It always boils down to money. But if the city's autonomy were taken away at an economic and political level, it would inevitably lose its cultural freedom as well. Today La Serenissima is an island of safety for critics of the Church. If this were to end, the Pope would reign uncontested across all of Italy."

"Is that what's worrying your lady? Yet her family—the Corners—have not aligned with the Doge. In fact, if I'm not mistaken, they're quite happy rubbing shoulders with the Grimanis."

"You're not mistaken, but it's also a very big family."

"One that also boasts a cardinal among its members. Just like the Grimanis." Mathias was carefully studying the woman sitting in front of him.

"You're quite right," admitted Alissa.

"A cardinal who, if he were given the opportunity to intervene directly in Venice, could undoubtedly guarantee his cousin the chance to right a few wrongs she was forced to endure in the past."

"Clearly you're quite familiar with Venice," said Alissa, smiling like someone who wasn't entirely enjoying herself, as if she'd just lost a hand at the card table.

"Caterina Corner was compensated by La Serenissima for the loss of Cyprus," continued Mathias. "A substantial sum of money that made it possible for her to settle—in her own favor—a few controversial affairs dogging another Corner, if I'm not mistaken. A man who would be tickled pink to see his cousin return to Venice with the Borgias' blessing. Perhaps that's what you meant to say when you were telling me all about Venice's 'cultural freedom.'"

"My lady is afraid of falling victim to personal revenge. That much is true," admitted Alissa. "But what I said before is equally true."

"And no doubt such a wealth of beauty, and so brazenly displayed, was intended to convince me in as effective a manner as possible."

"You know full well that everything I've said is true."

"And you seem to forget that as a monk I might look quite favorably on the chance that the Church could increase its presence in your Republic." This wasn't at all what Mathias thought, but he was trying to coax the Lady of Asolo's emissary out into the open. What did the queen really want from him?

"So your Church is the same as the Borgias'?" asked Alissa.

"You're not the one to decide which Church is mine. If you've nothing else to say, please tell your lady I thank her for her advice."

"My lady is very busy preparing for a reception but would have the pleasure of meeting you," said Alissa, a strained smile on her lips.

Mathias had gotten more information out of her than she'd managed to get out of him. And clearly she wasn't accustomed to finding herself in this situation.

"Let me know when. I'll be happy to meet her."

The gondola came to a stop. Mathias took leave of Alissa, donning his velvet cap again to protect himself from rain that showed no signs of stopping. He took advantage of the long walk to his temporary home to reorganize his thoughts. Despite all the time he'd spent in Venice, he was still mountain-born, and needed to move his legs in order to think clearly.

Agostino Grimani was enlisting his men to spy on him. Mathias knew that the Grimani family was split into two factions, and that intervention by a cardinal might mend the rift—just as it would for the Corners. That's what lay behind the feud under way in the Republic: a battle between different noble family factions in a fight for power. Serving this side or the other was of no interest to Mathias. But the consequences of a Venice under the Pope's direct control weren't at all to his liking. His beloved books would be burned by ignorant, avid priests. Men like Malachia would win.

It was the same old struggle. The same fight Gheorg had chosen, the same fight that might take him to Wittenberg. But he wouldn't clear the way for Alexander VI. With what little strength he possessed, even though he was nothing more than a pawn on a chessboard that extended farther than he could see, Mathias would help those in power smash what had all the makings of a major plot, one designed to overturn the government in power in La Serenissima. And these thoughts allowed the monk to find the first answer to the many questions with which he still felt burdened.

He and the Borgias did *not* share the same Church.

***

Giacomo Foscarini sat down on the wooden bench. The enormous hall was slowly filling up ahead of the meeting.

Loredan was accompanied to his seat. His illness was growing worse, making him seem even weaker than before.

The first to speak was Zaccaria Freschi, who argued once again that a treaty with the Turks would save Venice from bankruptcy while preventing Rome from taming the lion. The strongest parts of his speech were underscored by the buzzing of the somewhat unconvinced.

Then Zorzi stood up to speak.

"Peace is a noble word, but what are we prepared to lose in order to obtain it?" The speaker looked around, gauging the effect his words were having. "In Venice they say that giving up the trade routes that would be lost, giving the Turks the territories my predecessor spoke of, would amount to an advantage for other trade routes and the merchants that use them."

Giacomo put a hand on his nephew's arm to hold Marcello back while Zaccaria stared at Giacomo, imploring the nobleman to say something. But Giacomo said nothing as he searched the faces alongside Zorzi, trying to locate his enemy.

"Our Doge would rather address these affairs within the Council of Ten," said Zorzi, "while we say that if a decision must be made on this affair, it would be better discussed here, in this hall. The honorable Trevisan has told me of a mountain of accusations deposited in the lions' mouths, denouncements of magical rites and demons. Fear is spreading throughout Venice, and we cannot remain indifferent. Make peace with the Turks and spurn the hand the Pope is extending to us? In a time of such darkness and despair? How long do we intend to wait before we take responsibility for our actions? For our lack of faith? Or would we perhaps prefer to relinquish every last ducat we possess in order to persist with this pride?"

"We must intervene!" whispered Marcello in desperation.

"Zorzi is simply stirring up the nobility," said Giacomo. "They don't have a majority. That means we haven't lost yet."

Giacomo was thinking about his next move when his eyes finally caught the gaze of the man he'd been looking for.

Agostino Grimani was seated on the opposite side of the immense hall. When he realized Foscarini was looking at him, he sent him a frigid smile, bringing one hand to his chin to caress his gray beard.

The fingers were covered with rings and precious stones, including an extraordinary ruby.

CHAPTER 23

They kissed for a long time. Then Lorenzo took Caterina by the arm and crossed through the open gallery of a courtyard until they reached a private warehouse. A strong shove on the rotting wooden door, and the two were inside. The small room was stuffed with all sorts of wares.

The couple lay down on a pile of straw, their bodies wet with rain. Weak light filtered in from the broken door. They ripped each other's clothes off hungrily, mad with desire, their breath blending with steam and vapor from the cold. Shivering skin brushed against shivering skin, generating a fierce heat. Caterina opened to Lorenzo, her back arching. Their bodies began to move together, first slowly, then more and more intensely.

For the two lovers, every horizon began and ended in that small space where they had been driven by an urgent need to leave the outside world behind and to exist, then and there, each for the other. They lay quietly for a long time, saying nothing. Their heavy breathing slowed and became calm. Still naked, stretched out beneath Lorenzo's cloak, Lorenzo gently moved a lock of blonde hair that had fallen across Caterina's face, caressing her from forehead to chin.

"You'll see. Soon I'll have the money we need. I've met a man who has important friends, and he'll be able to help us," he said. "You'll be my wife. We'll have a home, and a bed much nicer than this one."

"We promised, don't you remember? To never talk about the future, not even the next day."

"I can't keep that promise." Lorenzo pulled his body away from hers. "And I can't understand how you can live without thinking that someday we'll be together."

"Because I watched that certainty wither and die, my love. And now everything's much more complicated."

"But you can't—"

"Please, I'm begging you. Don't ruin everything. Not now, when it's all so beautiful." Her eyes filled with tears. She pulled him close. "I can't go back now," she said. "I can't leave the convent and run away with a man. I can't do that to my father. He needs me. He has friends that can help me give my family back the prestige they've lost."

"But I need you too. I love you, Caterina."

"Please, I beg of you . . ." She took his face in her hands and brought it in front of hers. "Don't ask anything of me."

She kissed him again. Lorenzo held her close.

He was ready to do anything, anything at all, to keep from losing her.

***

When he'd heard the shouts coming from the canal, like most people, Simone Luzzatto ran to find out what had happened. He saw Lorenzo Scarpa before he reached the wharf where they were dragging what looked like another corpse up out of the water. Simone's instinct had been to hide.

Scarpa was standing with a sturdily built monk with graying hair. It was the same man Simone had seen alongside Foscarini, that damnable nobleman who had taken what he knew Simone and his father had full right to possess. He watched while the young Scarpa knelt to the ground and prayed to his Christian god. Then Scarpa's new friend waved good-bye to him, disappearing around a corner, and Scarpa stood up and left. Simone followed him and watched him disappear through a large doorway.

Then he saw Scarpa and Caterina go inside the small warehouse. Simone stayed, hidden behind the little gallery, to spy on them. Envy, jealousy, rancor, and hatred coursed through his veins, corroding his spirit, as he listened to their urgent panting and their soft cries of pleasure. Every sigh ripped through his heart like a knife, yet he moved closer so that he could hear what they were saying to one another. He'd heard Caterina—beautiful Caterina—say that she could not give up her nun's habit. That it was her own father, Alvise Marin, who'd sent her to the convent.

Simone left the two lovers and walked away. His tears of rage mingled with the rain on his face. The hatred, the vitriol, it all had to stop. He had to free himself from this torment. And now he knew what to do.

***

Mathias was headed home. The seawater around Venice seemed to boil with raindrops. Walking along, hopping to avoid puddles, he was utterly lost in his own thoughts.

He laid out the pieces of the mosaic within his mind: A noble faction that wanted to overthrow the government of the Republic and open the door to the Pope. A forbidden book brought to Venice, from who knows where, so that it could be printed by a group of small printers. A ruthless assassin who left a trail of corpses in his wake as he searched for the book. A wave of terror that flooded the banks of the canals, convincing Venetians that everything happening was the scourge of God, and that the Pope's intervention was the only way they could hope to save their souls. Mathias was convinced that all these different pieces, like mosaic tiles, were somehow connected in a single design.

Reaching the door to his house, the monk almost ran right into two people who were standing there, waiting for him. He shook himself out of his thoughts, finding himself face-to-face with Majid and a gaunt, disheveled man who stank the way only someone accustomed to working with cadavers could possibly stand for long.

"This man came to find me this morning," said Majid. "He says he knows who the first corpse is."

CHAPTER 24

Simone returned home, slamming the door behind him. His father, Moses, saw him appear in the main room, soaking wet, his eyes red, his body tense with hatred.

"What has happened, my son?" he asked.

"I'm a Jew. That's what has happened."

"What . . . ? You're upset, my boy. Why would you say such a thing?"

"Why must we live in humiliation, Father? What right did that nobleman have to stick his nose in our affairs? Why did you stay silent in the face of such an offense? Scarpa's possessions were rightfully ours."

"Again with this Scarpa? Calm yourself and sit here with me." Moses pointed to a chair near the bench he was seated on, warming himself by the fire.

"I don't want to sit down," shouted Simone. "I don't want to sit by and let these people have fun walking all over us!" Simone walked over to the table and, with a sweep of one hand, knocked a mug off the tabletop. It shattered on the floor.

His father didn't move a muscle.

"Simone, calm down. You won't get what you want by smashing our house to pieces. Sit down next to your father, as you've always done."

Simone sat in the chair. His face was still twisted with rage, his eyes upset and full of tears. He was breathing heavily. Moses laid his hand on his son's leg.

"Life is not kind to our people, my son," he said. "You're an adult now, and you need to understand these things. The problems Venice is facing with commerce make us an easy target for merchants who are struggling. We must remain strong, but it won't always be this way."

"Things never go well for our people, Father. Unless we force our thinking on others, the way they do on us, no one will ever respect us."

"It's not that simple."

"Why shouldn't anything ever be simple?" Simone began to raise his voice again. "If the Venetians are allowed to do whatever they want, why can't we become Venetians too? Why do we have to remain the way we are? So . . . so . . ."

"So *Jewish*, Simone?"

"What is so irreplaceable about our identity, Father? Is it really so important to cling to the Law, to observe the Law, when we can't even guarantee our hold over our own credit?"

Moses lowered his gaze to the floor. He got up slowly and began to gather the shards of the broken mug. Taking a rag, he dried the water pooled on the tiles. Simone watched while his father worked.

"Don't I deserve an answer, Father?"

"You are beside yourself. You're neither ready nor willing to have a conversation."

Simone clenched his fists. He tried to summon the courage he needed to say something he'd decided on long ago. But his courage was lacking. His sense of weakness only made him angrier. Angry with his father. Angry with Scarpa, with Caterina, with Foscarini. Angry with the world.

"Do you have something else to say to me, Simone?"

If he said it, he would send an arrow through his father's heart. Simone stood up and shook his head. Once again. But this time, he needed to go do something. It was important.

He went to the room where his father kept their accounts. He took a piece of paper and a pen wet with ink and began to write. He was going to hurt the people he hated, but inside he didn't feel any real sense of satisfaction. He hated them all the more for having made him so small, so petty and mean, which was all he felt just then. But it wasn't enough to stop him. He kept writing, setting down everything on the paper. Then he folded the letter and slipped it into his pocket. His father had come into the room and was watching him.

"What are you doing?"

Simone got up and headed for the door, his face frozen in an angry grimace.

"It's getting dark outside Simone, where are you going?"

The young man pushed the older man aside. He opened the front door and went back out into the rain, dead set on seeing his plan through. His vendetta. Wrapping his heavy wool cloak across his shoulders, Simone looked around to see if anyone was watching. Then he headed for Caterina's convent.

Only once he was completely alone, far from his house, did Simone finally find the strength to say what he'd wanted to tell his father.

"I'm going to become a Christian, Father."

CHAPTER 25

"I don't know his real name, but I'm not sure even *he* could have remembered it anymore." The man standing alongside Majid was older than he first seemed. The dirt on his face seemed to be caked all the way into his skin, covering his wrinkles. His voice was raspy and guttural. They'd moved beneath the arch over the house's entryway in order to protect themselves from the rain. "But everyone called him Spider, because he was the kind of man who knew how to move around, if you get my meaning."

"Why did you search out my friend?" asked Mathias, pointing at Majid.

"I was looking for *my* friend. I was looking for Spider. He hadn't come back in for a few days, and when I heard about the bodies showing up in the canals, I immediately thought of him."

"Come back? Where?"

"We're a small community. We always sleep under the same portico, where we leave our belongings. Not much. Some clothing, a little wine to keep warm." The man stared into Mathias's eyes. "We're vagabonds. Haven't you figured that out yet?"

"Let's say I was beginning to suspect as much. But go ahead with your story." Mathias glanced at Majid. His investigation may have just reached a crossroads.

"I didn't know where the bodies were, so it took me a few days to find out. Rumors travel faster along the calli than they do in the palazzi. So I heard that some scholars had the bodies. And that's where I went."

"Why? Because you wanted to pay your respects to your friend, to say your last good-byes?"

"No, that's not really it . . . I mean sure, that too . . . I cared about him, you see." The old man seemed embarrassed. "I mean . . ."

"He was looking for money," interjected Majid.

"Spider had money?" asked Mathias.

"Yeah, that's it," said the old man, giving in at last. "He'd gotten some money from somebody. Somebody who'd promised him a lot more. An enormous amount of money. But Spider never told me what he was getting paid to do." The vagabond coughed, a deep rattling sound. "He often went off on his own. It seemed like he'd been given a really important task."

"What was his specialty? What kind of thing would a person pay him to do? What services could he provide?" Mathias was sure this detail would prove an important piece of information.

"He was a spy," said the vagabond. "Sometimes people would come to him to get information about what happened at night, in the calli. Jealous husbands, lovers, prostitutes. But this time it seemed like something really important."

"He doesn't know anything else," said Majid.

Mathias dug around in his pockets and pulled out a few coins to give the man.

"This is a first payment," he said. "I'll give you the rest when you bring me more information. Let me know if anyone else comes around asking about Spider. Make sure you tell me right away."

"Thank you, m'lord." The vagabond's face had lit up when he saw the ducats. The handful of coins was probably more treasure than he'd ever owned. "I'll do as you say, exactly as you say."

"If I should have need of you, how can I find you?" asked Mathias.

"Ask for the Worm. That's me."

"The Worm?"

"That's what they call me." Then the Worm smiled and leaned forward as if to share a secret. His breath was pestilent and foul. "Do you want to know why?"

"I'd rather not, thank you."

The Worm scampered off, clutching his newfound treasure in his hands.

"I don't know what you're getting yourself into," said Majid, "but I know I don't like it. Some things in Venice are pure poison." Majid's eyes looked like they could bore through a stone wall. "If someone has put you on a demon's tracks, you'd better make sure the demon doesn't find you first."

"What's that supposed to mean?"

"It means that behind every hand stained with blood there's another, and that one stays clean." Majid leaned in close, lowering his voice to a whisper. "What I'm saying is that behind a demon, there's always someone holding the creature on a leash."

"If you know something I don't, you'd do best to tell me now, Majid," said the monk. The pair moved inside. Majid warmed himself by the fire, sitting across from Mathias. The monk prepared two cups of his herbal decoction.

"This stuff tastes absolutely horrible," said the doctor.

"It helps keep you warm."

"A good wine would have the same effect."

"Do the sons of Allah drink wine now?"

"I was just speaking in general, Christian."

Outside the window, the rain had stopped pouring down on Venice. The sky was a dark leaden color, with a few faint wisps of red from the sinking sun.

After hesitating for a little while, Mathias spoke up, keeping his eyes on the spectral colors of a frigid Venice outside. "I can't explain what I'm doing right now, but if you have information that might help me understand why those men were killed, I'm begging you to tell me."

"Venice has changed." Majid took a long sip of the herbal drink and swallowed with a grimace. "It seems like someone is using wars and our economic crisis to spread distrust and rancor among the population. In times like these, those are dangerous feelings to spread around."

"You've already told me as much. I can't do anything about that. I'm a foreigner here too, and soon I'll be heading home."

"That's a good thing. If I had another home, I'd go back there too."

"Why did you mention a demon to me, Majid?"

As an answer, the doctor set something on the table alongside the bench where he was seated. Mathias heard the sound of a small object rolling around, and he got up and went over to see what it was.

A ring.

The monk picked it up and examined it carefully. It was a heraldic ring, boasting a family escutcheon, but there was no trace of sealing wax. It hadn't been used recently. The symbol engraved on the ring displayed a column surmounted by a crown.

"Okay, you've surprised me. Now you can explain what it means," said Mathias, watching the doctor.

"If you play with fire, you'll get burned."

"What are you talking about?"

"I found that ring," said Majid, "in the stomach of the cadaver you came to examine."

"Which cadaver?" Mathias tore his eyes from the little ring and sat down in front of his friend. "Which of the two, Majid?"

"Not the one with the rags. The other one, the soldier."

"In his stomach?"

"He must have swallowed it in secret. It's the emblem of an important Roman family."

The door opened. Lorenzo stood outside. He seemed upset. Mathias invited him to come in and take a seat, offering the young man a cup of his decoction.

"You do realize your drink tastes terrible, right?" said Lorenzo.

"A friend of yours?" asked Majid.

"More or less. I'd like you to meet Maestro Scarpa, a bookseller."

"And this is a friend of mine, a doctor," said Mathias to Lorenzo. "His name is Majid."

"So the Turks aren't all pirates who attack Venetian merchant ships."

Mathias was surprised. The boy had never spoken that way before.

"I have no idea what Turks do," said Majid. "I'm an Arab."

"You pray to the same God."

"I can't even remember the last time I talked to that God . . ." Majid seemed to be searching the hearth fire for the words he needed to continue. "It may seem strange to you, but I've lived in Venice for far longer than you have." The doctor turned back to Mathias. "Now maybe you can see why I've told you Venice has changed and that you'd do well to leave. Sooner or later, you Germans will be considered enemies of La Serenissima too."

"Please forgive him, my friend. And you," said Mathias, turning to Lorenzo, "do you want to tell me where you've been and what's going on with you?"

"What's happened is someone is stealing my life from me. And it's the fault of some pirate I'll never know and never meet."

"We'll get your bookshop back for you. I told you to trust me," said Mathias, putting a hand on the young man's shoulder.

"He's not talking about books," said Majid, smiling once again. "I hear the sounds of a broken heart in his words."

Lorenzo said nothing. Hesitantly he took the cup with the herbal drink that the monk was offering him.

"Are you going to explain yourself, or are you going to remain mute forever? Not that I'd mind," said the monk. I'd just like to know what to expect."

"I'll leave the two of you alone to talk. It seems like a delicate matter," said Majid, getting up from his seat. "Just try to be careful. That ring says a great deal."

"What ring are you talking about?" said Lorenzo.

Mathias looked hard at the young man. He had the impression Lorenzo was keeping something from him.

"A ring that tells us that one of the demon's victims came from Rome," said Majid.

"You're sure it's from Rome?" asked the monk.

"That's the emblem of the Colonna family," said Majid.

Mathias examined the ring again. Lorenzo stood nearby, staring hard at the object the monk held in his fingers.

"There's no trace of sealing wax because I pulled it out of his stomach, and for obvious reasons I cleaned it before I brought it here to you," continued Majid. "He must have swallowed it in order to hide the identity of his emissaries."

"Who are the Colonnas?" asked Lorenzo.

"Couldn't he simply have stolen it?" asked Mathias.

"That man had excellent teeth. He was healthy and fit, at least as far as I could tell. He wasn't a thief, and anyway, what reason would a thief have for swallowing his booty? That would only get him into deeper trouble. And then he couldn't try to exchange it for his freedom." Majid fingered his graying beard, a dark look on his face. "That man was an emissary sent by the Colonnas." Turning to Lorenzo, he added, "A noble Roman family that has clashed with the Pope in the past."

"Clashed? In what way?" asked Lorenzo, staring at the ring again.

"That's a story that is almost three centuries old," said Mathias.

"I'm interested. Let's hear it."

The monk sat down next to the fireplace.

"First of all, you have to remember that the Church is divided against itself. Within the Church, there are numerous different currents, each of which represents the powers of this or that noble house, and each, as happens in every other city, is focused on expanding its own powers." He looked for confirmation from Majid, who nodded. Then Mathias continued. "The Colonnas and the Caetani were sworn enemies, and when the Caetani managed to get one of their own cardinals elected pope, the two families went to war. Raids, scorched earth, and even the kidnapping of Pope Boniface the Eighth followed—although that was merely a backlash, since the war with the Pope led to the loss of many members of the Colonna family and the destruction of most of their possessions."

"And now they've sent someone here to Venice?" asked Lorenzo.

"Yes, and he was murdered," said Majid. "These crimes have not been committed by some fool, much less by a demon, unless you're inclined to actually believe that sort of stuff. This is an affair that has to do with noble houses and their eternal battle for power and influence. A war that has left a great deal of fallen victims in the field. It's very dangerous to play the role of pawn in this kind of game." Majid went to the door. "But I'm sure you've thought this through. Just try to make sure you don't wind up sending your own body to me for study."

"I will, Majid," said Mathias, handing the ring back to the doctor.

"You can keep that. No one knows I found it."

The doctor said good-bye to Lorenzo, and was just about to close the door behind himself when the young man stopped him.

"Please forgive me for what I said before, Majid. I had no right."

"I'll forgive you," said the Arab, "as long as you make me a promise."

"What promise?"

"That you'll keep an eye on this crazy fool here," he said, pointing to the monk.

"You have my word."

Mathias said good-bye to his friend, then Majid closed the door and was gone.

"So," said Lorenzo as soon as the door was shut, "the Colonna family may have been the ones who sent the forbidden book here to have it printed?"

"I think that's more or less how things happened," said Mathias. "Now we need to gather as much information as we can about this mysterious traveling emissary."

"Let's go visit the inn where he was staying. At this time of the evening, all it will take is a few coins and you'll get all the time you need."

Mathias forced Lorenzo to finish his decoction before the pair ventured back out into the cold. When the young man had finished the last sip—which he swallowed, wincing—he put on his cloak. The night enveloped them as they headed to the inn near Campo dei Frari, where the Franciscan basilica stood.

CHAPTER 26

Mathias and Lorenzo found themselves all but lost in a thick veil of frigid fog. Shadows snaked along the paving stones and loomed suddenly over the water of the small side canals. What little light spilled out various windows cast grotesque profiles on the fog. The two men crossed the island using narrow pathways. In some areas of the Rialto, the calli were less than a yard wide and wound their way between buildings with high walls, limiting their view to just a few steps ahead and behind.

When they reached the inn in Campo dei Frari, they found the owner sitting at a table with other people who seemed to share his grand passion for wine. From the way they were laughing and giggling, it was clear they'd already finished more than a few bottles.

Mathias went to talk with a woman sitting at the bar. She was the owner's wife and was watching her husband carry on with a look of utter disgust on her face.

"We're two friends of a guest of yours, a man who arrived from Rome," said the monk.

"Good for you," replied the woman.

"He asked us to please pay his bill and leave a generous tip as compensation for your hospitality."

"In that case, you're quite welcome at our inn."

"We need to pick up a few of his things, because he has to depart at once for Rome," said Mathias." In any case, he asked us to please leave behind the things that aren't strictly necessary, as a gift for charity, precisely because he needs to begin traveling immediately and doesn't want to be slowed down."

"Signor Marcelli was staying in the room on the top floor."

"Marcelli?" said Lorenzo.

Mathias glared at him. It should have been clear that since they'd presented themselves as the man's friends, they should at least know his name.

"Alfredo Marcelli," said the woman with a smile. "If anyone asks, *your friend* called himself Alfredo Marcelli."

"What the young man meant was—"

"No problem, m'lord. Doesn't matter one whit. I'm just happy someone has arrived to settle his affairs," said the woman, handing them the key to his room. "With everything you hear people saying nowadays, what with all those bodies showing up dead in the canal, I didn't want to get involved with the night guards over a missing client. Better to know he's left Venice on his own two feet, as you gentlemen have just explained."

"You're quite right," said Mathias. "That's exactly what's happened. It's been truly fortunate for everyone involved that this all worked out for the best, and there's no need to ever talk about this man again, is there?"

"I'm sure of it, m'lord."

Mathias gave the innkeeper's wife the money for the room, plus a handsome tip to buy the very silence she was so anxious to provide.

"You're very generous, m'lord," said the woman as she hid the money behind the bar, then cast a quick glance over to her husband to make sure he hadn't noticed what was going on.

"Your help has been of great value," replied Mathias, intuiting that the woman had something more to say.

"Unfortunately, I have to tell you that part of the room has been damaged."

"What do you mean?"

"I'll have to have it repaired. Fixed up."

"Then you'll need more money, I'm sure."

"I wouldn't want to take advantage of your generosity."

"It's my pleasure, ma'am. Truly." The monk added more coins. Taken together, he'd given the woman a sum totaling more than the inn would make in a month.

"You'll find that a board on the floor has come loose. Be careful you don't trip over it."

Having said this, the woman grabbed a carafe of wine and headed over to the table where her husband was still drinking and laughing loudly with his friends.

Mathias and Lorenzo headed to the room the woman had indicated.

"I'm sorry about before," whispered Lorenzo.

"It worked out well in the end," said Mathias. "The important thing is that our stranger isn't such a stranger anymore."

A variety of noises filtered through the doors to different rooms they passed. Most were moans of pleasure from those enjoying company, which the inn's management was apparently able to provide upon request.

"What did she mean about the loose floorboard?" asked Lorenzo.

"We'll find out in a moment."

When they reached the door, Mathias inserted the key into the old lock and opened it. The room had been turned upside down.

"Someone has already been here," said Lorenzo, following the monk into the room. Mathias motioned to Lorenzo to close the door behind them, then he walked around the room, studying what was left. There wasn't much to see, just an empty flask and a heavy travel cloak caked with dried mud, and there was nothing in its pockets. The sheets had been yanked off the bed.

Mathias knelt down to the floor.

"What are you doing?" asked Lorenzo.

The monk began tapping and knocking on the floorboards.

"They'll hear us downstairs," said the young man.

Mathias continued to move around, tapping here and there.

Then, suddenly, a short section of floor made a different sound. The monk knocked again and got the same result.

"The loose board!" said Lorenzo. "There's a hollow space here," said Mathias. "Evidently, among the various services this inn provides, there's also an option for a good hiding place."

"Do you think that whoever was here before us found it as well?"

"Let's find out."

The monk glanced around and found a plate left on the table, upon which sat an apple core turned rotten and a small knife. "Grab that."

Lorenzo handed him the knife. Mathias worked the blade underneath the floorboard, until he pried it up. There were two folded letters in the hiding space underneath. The monk took them both, then sat down on the bed to read them.

"I guess whoever was here before us didn't pay enough to get this information," said Lorenzo, sitting down beside the monk.

The first letter was a travel document, which showed that Alfredo Marcelli had passed through a number of different customs offices that separated the papal territories from La Serenissima.

"This confirms that our Signor Marcelli came from Rome," said Mathias. "At this point, we can only hope that the second letter reveals the reasons for his long voyage."

The second letter was just a few lines long.

> *The decision has been made. Maestro Valla's manuscript must be brought to Venice and entrusted to the Brotherhood of the Rose. May Truth abandon the Darkness and return to the Light.*
> *God watches over us all.*
> *Aurelio Cannizza Montebovi*

A starting point. Everything, the entire story they were struggling to reconstruct, began here. The letter opened other questions that raced around in Mathias's head the moment he took his eyes off it. Valla's manuscript. Could it be true? Was that the forbidden book that Marcelli had brought to Venice for the Colonna family? To hand it over to a sort of secret society made up of printers and booksellers?

"I know about the rose," said Lorenzo.

When he heard those words, Mathias turned to face Lorenzo. Then he set the letter on the bed and waited for Lorenzo to explain himself.

The young man told him the story of the small ring worn by his uncle and the printer whose body they'd found, Giuntino.

"Why didn't you tell me about it earlier?"

"Because I didn't know what it meant. I was afraid it would only further discredit my uncle's name. You know what I'm talking about."

Mathias waved Lorenzo off and got up, walking around the room again as he tried to put the new pieces of the mosaic together. He spoke out loud, letting the young man in on his thinking.

"The Colonna family gave their trusted emissary a forbidden manuscript, perhaps the most forbidden of all, so that he could take it to Venice and give it to a congregation, a secret society, or something of that sort, known as the Brotherhood of the Rose. Two men who were killed were members of this group. The emissary met with the same unpleasant end. If all this is true, then there can only be one conclusion."

"Someone betrayed the secret society my uncle was a member of."

Mathias turned to face Lorenzo again.

"Very good, Maestro Scarpa. And then?"

"And then sent the demon to look for the book."

"Very, very good." Mathias's lips tightened into a thin line. "And the demon is carrying out his task. But if he's still killing—and Giuntino's corpse proves that he is—then that means he hasn't yet found what he's looking for. He still hasn't located the manuscript."

"What *is* this manuscript the letter talks about?" asked Lorenzo.

"I'll explain it to you on the way. Right now we don't have time. We need to figure out which other booksellers and printers are members of the Brotherhood of the Rose, what they aim to do, and what they're about to face. Maybe we can put a stop to this river of blood."

"I know one," said Lorenzo.

"Then we need to go to him as fast as possible."

CHAPTER 27

They ran downstairs. Mathias took both of the letters with him, hiding them in the pocket inside his cape. In the main room of the inn, the hubbub from inebriated patrons had risen higher than ever. The innkeeper's wife was still at the bar.

"Satisfied?" asked the woman.

"Almost, signora. Almost," said Mathias.

"What else do you need?"

"You were right. The flooring is a disaster, and you'll undoubtedly need to do a great deal of work to fix it. That's going to cost a lot of money. As soon as I realized that, I thought it would be appropriate of me to offer you another contribution."

"That's very generous of you."

"Let me speak clearly."

"I'm listening."

"It appears that someone else went to see the room, before we did."

"Someone far less generous than m'lord, in fact. And I don't believe his visit was as satisfying as yours."

"I believe you, and I thank you. But what interests me most is knowing who came to make such a request."

"It is not my custom to reveal the secrets of other clients."

"Customs change," said Mathias, placing a fistful of ducats on the bar. The woman grabbed the money, holding the coins close to her chest and counting them quickly. Then she hid them, but not behind the bar with the others; this time she slipped the ducats into a pocket inside her bodice.

"A man came yesterday," said the woman. "He asked if he could look around the foreigner's room for a few minutes. That's when I figured out that there must be something hidden in there. I took his money, but I didn't tell him about the hiding place. After he left, I went upstairs myself to check, believing there might be money in there. The guest, Signor Marcelli, seemed quite well-off, at least judging from his clothing and the way he carried himself."

"And when you saw they were only letters, you left them where they were, hoping they might be worth something to someone else," said Mathias.

"It's a hard life, m'lord."

"Can you help us identify the man who came here before we did?"

"There are lots of rumors running around Venice, m'lord. Clearly, Lady Fortune didn't smile upon him."

"What do you mean?" asked Lorenzo.

"I knew him. He worked not far from here. A printer. His name was Giuntino. This morning I heard they dragged his body up from the Canal Grande, the same way they did with those other poor souls."

"And you said he didn't find anything," said Mathias.

"Well, I can't be sure, can I?" replied the woman. "If you don't know what you're looking for, you won't find anything, not even that table over there."

"And afterward? Did anyone else come here?"

"I haven't seen anyone." The woman winked at them.

They took leave of the innkeeper's wife and headed back out into the thick fog enveloping Venice. Once again the two men became shadows thrown onto stone by the weak lights glowing here and there.

"What does it all mean?" asked Lorenzo.

"I'd say Giuntino and your uncle had already met Marcelli. He brought them a book from Rome, a book controversial enough to strike fear into the Pope's heart." They walked quickly as Mathias spoke, using the vague outlines of buildings to orient themselves in the heavy fog. "Someone knew about the meeting—maybe a spy or, in any case, a traitor—and paid a vagabond to find out where the meeting would be held, and go and watch. Once he got the information he needed, he tortured the vagabond to death in order to make sure he couldn't tell another soul about what he'd seen." Mathias was walking so fast that Lorenzo practically had to jog to keep up, which was tricky on the damp, sometimes icy, paving stones. "Then he waited in order to find out where the foreigner was, and as soon as he found out, he set a trap for the man, in the shadows. He kidnapped the foreigner and tortured him in order to find out where the book was being kept."

"Didn't he have the book with him?"

"Evidently not, and apparently that was a good thing. It's possible the demon found a way to search the room without the innkeepers' knowledge. In that case, Giuntino would have found the room overturned as well. But the point is—the book is not there."

"Then Marcelli was the only person who knew where it was."

"And he took the secret to his grave. He gave the demon misinformation, and when the demon left him there alone, he found a way to take his own life. But our mysterious demon probably managed to obtain at least some information, all the same. Maybe the vagabond gave him the names of the other people who attended the meeting. Printers and booksellers who are associated with the rose symbol."

"My uncle," said Lorenzo. He came to a sudden stop.

"Keep walking, my boy," said Mathias.

"Why such a hurry?"

"Your uncle kept his silence. Either he didn't know where the book was, or he resisted the torture and didn't tell. Or he died sooner than his torturer expected. Only one thing is certain: he kept the secret to himself."

"He was a man who knew how to keep secrets," admitted Lorenzo.

"The demon has no choice now but to hunt down the other printers," said Mathias, picking up the pace again. "That's why he followed Giuntino to the inn at Campo dei Frari. When he saw him come out, he believed Giuntino had found something, so when the time was right, he grabbed him. Giuntino wanted to find the book, perhaps on behalf of the Brotherhood. He faced the danger of a demon assassin terrorizing Venice, and he lost."

"So the demon knew about the inn, and he grabbed Giuntino precisely because he saw him come out of there," said Lorenzo. "In other words, he grabbed him right after he did exactly what we've just done."

"Exactly."

Lorenzo started walking even faster.

They crossed a little stone footbridge.

A sound.

The pair stopped.

"What was that?" asked Lorenzo.

The fog, dense and thick, obscured everything around them.

A light in a window threw a shadow across the stone—the shadow of something just a few yards away.

CHAPTER 28

Mathias grabbed Lorenzo by the arm, and the pair ran back the way they'd come, turning at the little stone bridge. Behind them, the shadow moved and began chasing them. The sound of footsteps came closer and closer. Then, out of the thick fog, the silhouettes of two black-cloaked figures appeared, their hoods drawn down to cover their faces. Shimmers of light danced across the edge of a blade. A dagger.

Mathias became aware of his own body. He had become out of shape. He knew they would catch up.

So this is where it all ends . . .

He kept running, but his strength was draining fast. His heart in his throat, he could tell he wouldn't be able to last much longer. He decided he could make it a few more yards, but only so that he could give Lorenzo a chance to escape. He would turn and slam straight into the two men chasing them.

"Keep running!" he said to Lorenzo just before he stopped.

Mathias was about to turn around, ready to leap at his pursuers in the very last moment of his life, when he had an epiphany. Somewhere deep down inside, at the base of his very soul, he saw something that it was only possible to see when standing at the edge of the precipice.

Caught up in his own thoughts, he almost failed to realize that Lorenzo had stopped too, and that another pair of shadows had detached themselves from the fog in front of them, cutting off any possible escape.

They were trapped.

"What do we do now?" asked Lorenzo.

Mathias didn't answer, still stuck in his sudden realization.

"This is no time for thinking," said Lorenzo. "We need to make a quick decision!"

The monk came back to his senses. "Who are you?" he shouted. "Who sent you?"

Their faces were masked by black cloth, but their daggers were out and ready.

"Tell us what you found at the inn, and your lives will be spared," said one of the four.

"We didn't find a thing," said Mathias.

"Then we'll find it after you're dead. We'll dig through your lifeless bodies," said another, coming up behind them.

Mathias heard a lapping sound. Something was moving in the water. Out of the fog, a gondola appeared.

Heavy boots clattered up onto stone. Blades were drawn.

Lorenzo dragged Mathias to the side. Two men had leapt up out of the gondola with sharp swords. They were outnumbered, but their blades were longer than the daggers, and surprise was on their side. One of the cloaked men cried out, badly wounded.

"Mathias, quickly!"

The voice came from inside the gondola, and the monk recognized it. Mathias and Lorenzo moved as a single body, clutching one another, dashing amid the fighting figures and leaping into the boat. As soon as they were on board, the boatman shoved off and the two swordsmen abandoned the fight and leapt into the boat as well. The battle was over. The monk and the young man were safe.

"You needed far less time than I'd imagined to make yourself a host of new friends, magister."

Giacomo Foscarini was sitting in front of them.

"What were you doing here? Were you following me?" asked Mathias.

"That's not much in the way of a thank-you, you ungrateful fool!" Then he turned to other men aboard. "Cesare, did you see who they were?"

"I'm sorry, m'lord. They kept their faces covered," answered the captain of Foscarini's personal guard.

"You have my most heartfelt and unconditional thanks, Giacomo," said Mathias. "Now, would you please tell me what's going on?"

"What's going on is that I've developed a fondness for your life and the life of this young man you're dragging all over Venice, you worthless wretch." Then he turned to Lorenzo. "Do you have any idea what you two are up against?"

"Why don't you try and explain it to us," said the monk.

"Who do you think suggested your name to the Doge for this mission, magister?"

"I imagined as much, but I couldn't figure out why you didn't tell me so yourself."

"Because it would be better for everyone if you didn't know. Because if someday, in the none-too-distant future, you wound up being forced to explain the outcome of your investigation to an official magistrate of the Republic, my presence in this whole affair would discredit everything you've done."

"I can't see why."

"Because I have political aims and ambitions, while the Doge is worried only about the security of his city. Don't you see?"

"You live in a damnably twisted and convoluted world," replied Mathias.

"And you are trampling across it with all the delicacy of an elephant in a glass shop!"

"Who were those men?" asked Lorenzo.

"They weren't common thieves, my boy. That much you can be sure of," replied Giacomo. "They were sent by someone who has taken an interest in you two."

"They're looking for a book, Giacomo," said Mathias. "A book that the Church would like to see burned to ashes, once and for all."

"Why would the Church want that?"

"Because it might discredit the Pope's attempts to establish authority over the entire territory."

"Does a book with such power even exist?" asked Giacomo.

"It might, if it were printed and widely distributed."

"Explain yourself."

"Power plays are under way in Rome," said Mathias. "The Colonna family has a weapon to use against the Pope: this book. And they sent it to Venice, where a group of small printers have an important opportunity to change history. A secret society whose symbol appears to be the rose. But something didn't go as planned. They're the victims of a man Venetians are calling a demon, but who in reality is working on the Church's behalf. The dead men they've found in the Canal Grande are a printer, a bookseller, the Colonna family's emissary and a vagabond who was tasked with spying on them all. Those are the people who have been killed. Not divine punishment, but cold-blooded murder. Are you following me?"

"Continue," said Giacomo.

"Someone in Venice found out about the book and is working to find it and destroy it, because he knows if it were published it would put the Pope in grave difficulty, not to mention all of those connected with him. We're looking for that book too, because I'm convinced that the demon hasn't found it yet. Someone must have hidden it in order to keep it safe. Someone who might be party to this pact made between printers. Do you see what I'm getting at?"

"Lots of merchants join private groups. They exchange favors, clients, money, and work. It happens all the time. I don't see why printers shouldn't do the same."

"Yes, but these men had a plan that went well beyond exchanging a few clients. They wanted to print a book, the very existence of which the Church has denied. I imagine that this sort of secret agreement must have had the support of some noble family."

"What are you saying? Speak your mind."

"It might be someone very important, someone well-known, someone who decided to finance this publishing operation in order to gain an additional weapon against those who would like to sell Venice to the Pope."

"What would I know about that?"

"Someone like you, for example," said Mathias.

Giacomo snapped his head around and stared at him.

"Do you really want to know about my history of involvement in secret societies? As you wish," said Giacomo. "In my life I've been a member of the Society of the Sock. They called us the 'trouser sousers,' because we wore our pants low at parties and we were always drunk. Since then, I've never been a member of any other society."

"I had to ask."

"Do you really think I would have given your name to the Doge as an investigator if I'd been involved in this affair?"

"I had to ask, Giacomo."

"You're behaving a lot like an inquisitor."

"That's what you hired me to do."

"This whole affair has come at a difficult time, as I'm sure you've noticed. The war has devastated our markets, and the battle for control of Venice has reached a fever pitch. Every available weapon amounts to a resource that no one can afford to pass up. But if things have gone as you've said, the plan this secret society of printers cooked up has not only failed, but it's now actually helping our adversaries."

"They took advantage of these murders in order to double their efforts," agreed Mathias. He paused a moment in consideration and seemed to intuit Foscarini's thinking. "Or do you think that your adversary's hand may lie behind the demon himself?"

"If that were the case," said Giacomo, "then this whole affair would amount to a plot against the Republic."

Lorenzo piped up. "Is the same person behind the men who were following us?" He'd been sitting quietly, listening intently to every word.

"At this point, I'm inclined to think so," said Giacomo.

The gondola slid through the night, slicing apart the thick fog that hung over La Serenissima. Mathias thought it seemed like they were sailing on the river Styx. The three men sat inside the felze for a long time without speaking, each immersed in his own thoughts, following the shapes that rose up out of the marble-faced palazzi they could barely see alongside them, despite the pale moonlight.

"The Council of the Shadows," said Giacomo at last, interrupting the silence.

"What is that?" asked Mathias.

"A myth. A Venetian legend that people talk about only in whispers, looking over their shoulders for fear they might be discovered, for fear someone should hear that they know about such matters. It's an unofficial judiciary, similar to the Council of Ten, but hidden between the folds of official power. Their aim is to maintain control over the Republic."

"And you think they've chosen to achieve their goals through a secret agreement to overthrow Loredan?"

"For some time now, I've had the feeling that this is what lies behind our adversaries. These murders appear to confirm my worst fears. If I'm right, then La Serenissima's day is truly drawing to an end."

"What do you mean? Explain."

"Loredan will be beaten," said Giacomo. "It's just a matter of time now, and not much at that. The merchants are afraid. They can see that their profits are increasingly threatened. Soon Grimani and his cohorts will have the numbers they need to ask for the Pope's intervention against the Turks, and they'll give him Venice in return. If this is the plan the Shadow Council has put in action, once they've achieved their aims they'll have control over the entire Venetian state, both on land and at sea."

"Not if we find that book." Lorenzo's voice surprised the others. "If we find the book, we'll find who's behind this, and we can lay the plot bare for all to see."

"Slow down," said Mathias.

"What do we really know about this book?" asked Giacomo.

"It's a book written by Lorenzo Valla more or less sixty years ago," said Mathias. "Since then, it's been considered a forbidden book because of the danger it represents for the Church and the Pope."

"Exactly how does it threaten the Pope's power?" asked Giacomo.

"Are you familiar with the *Donation of Constantine*?" said Mathias. "It's the document upon which the Church has based its political legitimacy."

"And your dangerous manuscript deals with the *Donation*?" continued Giacomo.

"Precisely," said Mathias. "Valla's manuscript demonstrates that the *Donation of Constantine* is a complete fake."

CHAPTER 29

The fire was always kept burning in the Foscarini family home, in a fireplace so large that a man of average height might walk into it upright without stooping.

When the trio arrived in the middle of the night, the lord of the house called for the cook and had his servants reheat the rabbit stew *alla santoreggia* he'd requested for dinner but hadn't yet eaten. The meal was soon set out on the table, along with olive bread and a white wine that Foscarini produced on his land in Vicenza.

A servant worked the pulley that brought the chandelier down, and another lit the more than fifty candles it held. When they pulled it back up to the ceiling, the chandelier lit up the entire hall, setting its marvelous tapestries into relief.

Once the meal was over, they leaned back in their chairs, filling their glasses with a dense, rich red wine that Foscarini had purchased from a Portuguese merchant.

Before they'd arrived, Mathias showed Foscarini the letters he'd found at the inn in Campo dei Frari, and Lorenzo told them the name of Mariolino's friend who had a ring with the rose symbol. They agreed that Niccolò Zaugo had to be placed under protection as soon as possible, but without his knowledge. If he continued to move around undisturbed, he wouldn't arouse the suspicions of the demon or the people directing him. This would give Mathias a distinct advantage.

"Now that we're more relaxed," said Foscarini, pouring himself another glass of wine, "you can tell me more of what you know about this book."

"I should explain a few things first," said Mathias.

"Treat me as if I were one of your students," said Foscarini.

The *Donation*, said Mathias, "is the act with which the emperor Constantine supposedly gave the Pope the Western European Empire, including Gaul, as testimony of his Christian spirit after he'd been cured of leprosy." The monk was speaking in a quiet voice, as if the tale he was about to tell hid a few dangers that might rear their ugly heads if he spoke of them too proudly. "This was because the Roman Empire had been divided in two, and Constantine preferred the eastern half."

"A copy of that document is kept in Rome," said Foscarini.

"That's what they say," replied Mathias. "But according to Valla, the document that the Pope claimed was in his possession was written well past Constantine's time, after the year one thousand, in fact. At that time, the West was devoid of any true leader and grappling with what seemed like an eternal war, so it looked to the Pope as the only possible point of reference. And that document gave Rome the right to wield power over the entire empire."

"What power?" asked Lorenzo.

"Any power," said Foscarini. "The Pope is a monarch with his own realm, but unlike all the other monarchs, he has a say in everything, everywhere, even in lands he doesn't own."

"I don't understand."

"Lorenzo, the Holy Roman emperor is crowned by the Pope," said Mathias. "Even the king of the Germans has to travel to Rome in order to have the Pope place the imperial crown on his head."

"Each bishop has a say in every power structure that exists. Even the patriarchy we have here in Venice," said Foscarini. "And this Valla claims that the *Donation* document is a fake?"

"From the first to the last line," said Mathias. "And that it's rather poorly put together. Constantine even refers to the Apocalypse, which in reality back in his day, he couldn't even have heard of. Valla examined the document word for word and proved how the language and references it used are far more recent. The Church created a false document upon which to base its political claims. A perfect scam, ordered by the vicars of Christ."

"That's *your* Church, magister," said Foscarini. "Are you really convinced of what you're saying?"

"Valla's manuscript says a lot more," responded Mathias, choosing to ignore the question. "That's just the beginning. It goes on to question the very principles of the Church—principles like obedience, poverty, and chastity. It even casts doubt on the Pope's temporal powers."

"Was he a heretic?" asked Lorenzo.

"According to Valla, Christianity doesn't need forgeries, which only offend true faith and serve nothing if not the power of men," said Mathias. "In Leipzig we listened to people who claimed to have read the manuscript. True faith is threatened by a Church conceived of as the property of an emperor."

Lorenzo watched Mathias carefully. Even though he never considered his own father, who had abandoned him, a devout servant of the Lord, he found it hard to listen to such harsh words about the Church spoken by a monk.

"Why are you so interested in that book?" Lorenzo asked Mathias.

"Because it's an important volume."

"Because this man here," said Foscarini, "thinks he—and a few of his study companions—can reform the Church."

"I don't understand," said Lorenzo.

"Reformers like Wycliffe or Hus," said Mathias, "whose names you heard Brother Serafino mention, or even Valla, the author of this mysterious book, have never called into question the value of faith. They've attacked a spoiled, corrupt Church that has used its position as the sole path of true faith as a pretext upon which to base its power. But the Word of God is the same for every man, and it is intended for all ears. That's what my companions and I are talking about, what we're interested in, and we'll start putting our words into action as soon as we find a place where we're allowed to do so. For now, even the Venetians, who feel they're so superior to everyone else, have stopped me from talking about these issues in Padua."

"You were suspended in Padua because you're a hothead!" roared Foscarini. "We *Venetians* had nothing to do with it."

"Here in Venice, people are being tortured and murdered for the words written in a book," said Mathias. "Exactly what do you think makes you different from the inquisitors you despise so fiercely?"

"Open your eyes!" said Foscarini. "You talk to me of faith, of God, of manuscripts and prayers and study companions. The truth is that these printers decided to print a book, in Venice, that would amount to nothing less than an all-out attack on the Borgias' Church. We're not talking theology here, magister. We're talking about politics."

"We're talking about renewing the faith," said Mathias. "That book is more than just a tool to be used in a battle between noble houses. There's far more than just Venice at stake here."

"Of course. But if that book were to be printed here in Venice, there would be consequences, don't you think?"

"I think that the printers in the Brotherhood of the Rose were absolutely certain there would be," said Mathias.

"We're not talking about a few handwritten copies," continued Foscarini. "We're talking about print. Books produced very quickly and in enormous numbers. We're talking about the possibility of spreading this manuscript out among the people in an entirely new way. Imagine what would happen if this kind of book wound up at the bookstalls outside some shop, together with all the others. Out there, available to anyone, maybe even sold on the cheap. Imagine the effects something like that could have."

"It's strange, Giacomo. It almost sounds like you're scared," said Mathias.

And, indeed, Foscarini's face was contorted by fear. "We have to find that book," urged Foscarini.

"And what would you do with it?"

"That's a decision we'll make together. First, we have to make sure it's delivered to the Doge."

"The book doesn't belong to the Doge."

"That book doesn't belong to you and your friends either, Mathias. Don't forget that the Doge entrusted you with this investigation."

"You're the one who entrusted me, Giacomo. The Doge is merely one of the masks you wear, isn't that true?"

"Find that book Mathias." Foscarini's voice had become severe. "I guarantee you it won't be set aside. You have my word, and that has always carried weight with you."

"It still does."

Lorenzo watched in silence as the two men dueled with one another. Out of the many dark affairs swirling around him, he understood that their words extended well beyond Venice. He had the impression that far bigger matters were at play. And finally he understood who was behind the monk's mission, and where all that money he'd seen the German spend at the inn in Campo dei Frari came from. But he still didn't understand what lay between the monk and Giacomo Foscarini, nor how a simple monk could talk to one of the most important men in the Republic that way. Different thoughts crowded his head, taking on strange forms and traveling along new, untrodden paths. He reached out to pour himself some more of the red liquid, only to discover that the bottle was empty.

Little by little, Lorenzo felt himself drop down into a sweet, heavy sleep.

***

Niccolò Zaugo was walking quickly, under cover of fog and darkness. He felt out of breath. This was because he was carrying an enormous burden. It was not a burden that he had to balance in his arms or that anyone could see. Yet it was so heavy it weighed down every step he took.

Niccolò Zaugo had betrayed everyone.

Not for the ducats. Well, not only for the ducats. He needed to keep telling himself that as he raced through the maze of calli that would lead him to the meeting place. The money had been enough to tempt him into betrayal, but he didn't know about all the rest. If he had understood the suffering to which he was condemning Mariolino and the others, would he have done it all the same? In that moment, Niccolò Zaugo desperately needed to convince himself that he wouldn't have.

But those men with hidden faces had gotten to them. They'd discovered the Brotherhood's plans. So whether it was he or someone else who accepted all that money made no difference whatsoever. The game was up no matter what. But the murders, the torture . . . Niccolò hadn't been ready for all that horror. And now, as he ducked and dashed along like a criminal, shouldering such a difficult burden of guilt, on his way to the place where he'd been told to go, he felt deathly afraid.

He ran down the steep stairwell that led to the abandoned warehouse, carved out below the level of the canal. He entered a dark room and walked down corridors of wet stone. The only thing he could hear, apart from his own footsteps, was the noise of his pounding heart. He reached the door. Niccolò opened it slowly. The black-cloaked men were there, their faces covered with their hoods.

They were waiting for him.

The Council of the Shadows.

CHAPTER 30

"What news do you have for us, Zaugo?"

There were eight of them. A large candle was lit at the center of the room. The printer's was the only face that could be seen clearly. Zaugo couldn't tell which of them had spoken. He was breathing heavily.

His fear was palpable. They knew it. They could touch it, taste it.

They could do anything they wanted with him.

"I have no news, m'lords. I've told you everything I know." He could hear his voice trembling. He tried to look past the candlelight, but he couldn't see anything. "I don't know anything else."

"That's not enough. We want the book. You told us you could bring it to us. We paid you to do so, saved your life so that you would do so."

"I thought I could find it, but someone has hidden it. I don't know where it is."

"You need to find out."

So they weren't going to kill him. He could still be useful.

"How? If I start asking questions, the others will understand that I . . . that I'm the one who . . ."

"Betrayed them." Said with disdain.

"How can I . . . ?"

"You're the one who must tell us how you can keep your promise."

"I'll figure out a way." Zaugo didn't know how, but this was the only way he could stay alive: Convincing them that he might still find the book. Convincing them that he wasn't useless, and that keeping him alive still made sense.

"This is disappointing." The simple words cut through his heart like an icy blade.

"I'll find a way. Trust me." He could still escape. Leave everything behind, disappear with the money they'd given him. Go far, far away. Hide somewhere where they'd never look for him. In Spain, or Portugal. Set sail for the lands opening up on the other side of the ocean.

"Don't come back empty-handed."

If he did, he would never walk out on his own two feet again. He knew it in his heart.

Zaugo waited, but they didn't say anything else. He backed up without asking permission. They were letting him go. The candle stood motionless at the center of the eight hooded men, their faces shrouded in darkness. He reached the door and took the last step. He was safe.

Zaugo walked quickly back up the corridor. He tripped on something in the warehouse and fell, rolling on the floor. He was terrorized, struggling to understand what had happened, what he'd tripped over. He didn't know. It seemed like a large sack. He ran toward the door, the profile of which he could see outlined in weak moonlight. He burst outside, running up the stairs. Toward home.

"The printer is worthless to us now," another voice said.

"What do you intend to do with him?" This was the same voice that had spoken to Zaugo.

"What one does with all useless things."

"Your methods aren't bearing fruit," said a young, aggressive voice.

The silence that followed his words told him he'd gone too far. The voice he was addressing, the man they had all put their faith in to resolve this affair, was not a man you could speak to in such a manner.

Because that was the man who now governed the Council of the Shadows.

Because that was the man who held the demon on a leash.

"My methods have brought us to a point where the rest of you, left on your own, would never have arrived. Who are you to doubt me?" The young voice said nothing. "You have even failed in your pathetic attempt to capture the monk. Your men let him get away."

"They'll try again," said the voice in charge.

"Not now. I want the monk to continue. If *we* can't find the book, he'll find it for us."

"But that's exactly what we must prevent," said the young voice.

"Silence!" The other voice grew with power and anger. "In just a few days, I have discovered things that the rest of you haven't figured out in months. Our adversaries have had relationships with Rome for some time, well before they had the book sent to Venice, as this worthless printer has already explained. And you didn't know a thing about it. You could have intercepted the emissary who brought the book here before he managed to hide it, but you knew nothing. If the monk finds the book, we'll know. And we'll have it brought to us."

"How? How will you have it delivered into our hands?" said another voice, one that hadn't spoken before.

"There is always a way."

"If you know already, you should share it with us."

"Perhaps I should. And if I trusted each and every one of you, I would. But I don't."

"You don't trust us?"

"You have been given roles in events that are more important than your individual lives and all the goods you possess, and all of this has brought you here, to this place. Safeguard your interests, but don't ask for anything more."

"Our interests are the interests of Venice."

"Venice is a place like any other, merely an act in a much larger play."

The other voices were silent, saying nothing.

Outside, the first faint glimmers of dawn began dusting the sky red.

CHAPTER 31

That disgusting smell again. Only this time it seemed stronger than before. Lorenzo opened his eyes and found Mathias standing over him with a steaming mug in one hand.

"Portuguese wine is a good friend, but one you need to get to know slowly. It appears your friendship has taken a turn for the worse." To Lorenzo's ears, the monk's voice came from a distance, as if distorted. "Drink this. It will help you recover. I bought the herbs in the market."

Lorenzo took the mug. He felt nausea rising in his stomach.

"I also brought you something for breakfast," said Mathias, pointing to the things he'd set on the table alongside the bed where Lorenzo was lying. He'd woken up unable to remember how he'd gotten there. "Two nice red apples and a fresh loaf of olive bread. Last night you seemed to like it."

"Where are you going?" Lorenzo managed to groan, though merely saying a few words required all his strength. Before answering, Mathias opened the window shutters, and Lorenzo's pupils retracted to two tiny dots. "Must you do that?"

"You can stay here a little while longer, but don't stay too long. Giacomo Foscarini is a very generous person, but also an important public figure. The presence of a young man in his home who is having some trouble with the authorities is the last thing he needs right now."

"In trouble with the authorities?"

"You don't have a job. You don't have a house. All your possessions have been seized, and your uncle was brutally murdered. Is that enough for you?"

"You left out the fact that my uncle practiced a forbidden love."

"And that's exactly what the Venetians would think, seeing you leaving this house in the morning, even if they're unfamiliar with your late uncle's sexual inclinations. Therefore, make an effort to be inconspicuous and leave by a back door without drawing any attention to yourself."

"Where are you going?" Lorenzo tried to ignore the unpleasant thought of being considered unwelcome company.

"There is a wedding today," said Mathias.

"On a Monday?"

"Unusual, isn't it? It's a way like any other to remind people that the two people joining together are so important that it will turn even a Monday into a holiday for everyone. It's a rather delicate issue. You don't need to bother with it."

"Are you going to tell me what I should do?"

"Drink that decoction, have some breakfast, and then go back to my house. Light a fire in the fireplace and see if you can make something to eat. I don't know when I'll be back."

"Does this really seem like the time to be attending a wedding?"

"I was just invited, just now. The invitation came from someone I can't say no to. A good inquisitor can take advantage of any occasion to extract some useful information."

"Of course." Lorenzo managed to pull himself up and out of bed.

Mathias pushed the mug of steaming herbs back under his nose.

"Enough with your disgusting herbal decoctions," protested the young man. "I'll probably vomit if I try to swallow it."

"Summon your courage. In any case, it might not be a bad idea to liberate your stomach of that wine that's still tormenting you. If it happens, make sure you don't 'paint' any tapestries, do you hear?"

"I won't make a mess, and I won't let anyone see me. Is that all?"

"Drink the decoction."

Mathias turned away, about to leave. Lorenzo's voice stopped him just as he reached the door.

"I have an idea about the rose."

"What kind of idea?"

"I have to find my uncle's ring. I know he meant to leave it to me."

"Did he tell you that?"

"He never said things like that, but he made sure I understood."

"We'll have time to look for it. For the moment, we can't break the Doge's seals again. The risk would be too dangerous. You said that the books on display in the shop had been moved and put back in a different order, remember?"

"Yes, but that's not my point."

"The point is that they're looking for the manuscript. They've already been there searching for it. They know a lot more about you than you do about them. And don't forget that they're having us followed, so make sure you're not caught alone in some narrow calle."

"But it's my house."

"It belongs to the Doge for now, at least until he decides on the matter."

"You know the Doge. Can't you have him make his decision now?"

"I don't know the Doge. Not the way you're implying. And in any case, a different authority will have to decide the matter, and the Doge isn't a monarch. We're not important enough, right now, to be able to ask that he intervene on our behalf in a legal matter. Especially not one against a Jew."

"Why? Why not against a Jew?"

"It's a delicate issue."

"But they're taking my house from me."

"The loans the Jews provide are this city's lifeblood," said Mathias. "But right now, every Venetian is suffering the economic consequences of a foolish war; the moneylenders are viewed as demons." Lorenzo wasn't convinced by his words. "If the Doge were to intervene in a legal matter that concerns a Jew, he would effectively legitimize the hostility that already exists toward them. Venice isn't some country town with a local lord who can rule on any matter as best he sees fit. It's a far more complex place than that."

"You think everything's always more complex, more complicated. But the fact remains that I can't go back into my own home—simply because that idiot Jew has it out for me."

"Luzzatto's son?"

"Yes, that son of a flea-ridden bitch."

"Having enemies is never useful. You should have thought about that before making one."

"I certainly didn't decide to make an enemy for myself." Lorenzo got up off the bed, and only then did he realize how much his head was spinning. "I feel like a ship in the middle of a storm."

"What happened between the two of you?"

"Something stupid. But that idiot took it to heart, and he's sworn to get back at me." Lorenzo sat back down on the bed. "And he's never lost an opportunity to remind me, every time our paths have crossed."

"And naturally your behavior in this affair has been nothing but exemplary?"

"If someone swears revenge on me, I'm happy to return the favor."

"Is this why you were so upset the other evening, and you attacked my Arab friend? I should have guessed."

"You're not the only one with important issues to resolve, you know," said Lorenzo. He got up again, this time more slowly. He was starting to feel better.

"Of course. Just tell me one thing," said the monk. His ice-blue eyes bore into the young man with intensity. "What is *her* name?"

"Her? What her?" The young man tried to feign surprise. But he could tell from the expression on the monk's face that it was no use pretending otherwise. He'd only look ridiculous. "Her name is Caterina. But I don't know what concern it is of yours."

"I understand. When you feel like talking about it, I'll be honored to hear the tale. Right now, however, make sure you stay calm. Remember the encounters we had last night. Those people won't let a little daylight stop them. You understand what I mean, yes?"

"I'll be careful."

Mathias headed for the door once more.

"You didn't tell me who invited you," said Lorenzo, gathering his things.

"Her name is Caterina as well."

"Another of your friends in high places?"

"Caterina Corner."

"Then I'd say the answer is yes."

Mathias smiled and left the room.

Suddenly, Lorenzo remembered when his Caterina had first spoken of the queen of Cyprus. He remembered that her parents had decided to give her that name in honor of that famous woman. That memory, their first together, was never meant to be cloaked in sadness.

Mathias was headed to the appointment that Alissa Strianese had made with him just a few hours earlier. He'd met her in the Rialto, where he'd gone walking that morning. She had come up by his side, dressed quite austerely and covered in a heavy cloak, as if to guarantee that this time she wouldn't try to dazzle him with her sensual physique. She'd smiled at him, in a sense admitting that perhaps the two of them had gotten off on the wrong foot. The Lady of Asolo desired his company by her side on her balcony over the Canal Grande, to watch the nuptial parade, as was customary with noble families in La Serenissima. Mathias got ready for the encounter, trying to figure out why he'd been invited.

***

Unbeknownst to Mathias, Lorenzo was watching the monk from the window and hatching a plan. The man had proven he was a friend, but if Mariolino had wanted his nephew to find his ring, and along with the ring something else as well, who was Mathias to come between them? If Lorenzo had known that night in the shop everything he knew now, he would have understood why the books had been moved around. He probably would have known what to look for. If his uncle had been willing to put himself in such danger, he must have left something important behind. In any case, he would have tried to find a way—one of his own personal ways—to share his secret with Lorenzo without being obvious. Now that Lorenzo knew so much more, he simply *had* to go back to the shop. If he didn't find anything, Mathias would never even have to know about it. But if he did find something, then the strange monk would have to admit Lorenzo was right.

He wrapped his cloak around his shoulders and used a hidden exit that one of the kitchen servants showed him. Outside, the sky was gray and pale, swollen with snow that could start at any moment, draping Venice in an icy white mantle. As he made his way along the calli, Lorenzo's mind was racing as he thought about everything that was happening. And about the book. He had realized the night before, at least as far as his hangover allowed him to remember, that Giacomo Foscarini and Mathias had been busy debating the future of the forbidden manuscript. But if Mariolino had taken all those risks with Luzzatto just in order to buy a printing press, if Valla's manuscript was the book he had decided to print, if that was the project that was supposed to change their life—the aim of all their projects and planning together—then what right did others have to decide what would be done with it?

Lorenzo lost himself amid the crowd heading for the Rialto market. With his cloak wrapped close as protection from the cold, he was just another Venetian crossing the city.

The young man felt as if he'd woken up for a second time, shaking off an even deeper sleep. If somebody else found the book, what would happen to him and his little bookshop? Wouldn't Mariolino have left something behind, something that would help him? What if the forbidden book was that thing? The questions buzzing in his head all converged to a single point. One sole certainty that had remained hidden from him up to this point, but was now emerging clearly in his mind.

The forbidden book belonged to him.

CHAPTER 32

A festive crowd lined both sides of the Canal Grande. People were laughing, singing, and chattering excitedly among themselves. They made ready to toss flowers and rose petals as fidgety children gathered in groups on the wooden bridge that united the Rialto with San Marco. The wedding procession would be there soon. The nobles would drift past aboard their elegant boats, on display for the entire city to see. Their fine clothing and wellborn bearing would be a subject of conversation for weeks to come. The day would end with festivities for everyone, offered by the families of the two newlyweds.

Caterina Corner never participated in wedding processions. She never afforded anyone that privilege. She would watch from her balcony, paying tribute to the protagonists of the ceremony and their families while maintaining the detachment that befit her position. She still felt as if she were the queen of Cyprus, even though that crown had not sat on her head for over ten years now.

Yet the balcony was still empty. The Lady of Asolo would come out only near the end of the ceremony. Then everyone would turn toward her and the other illustrious Venetians she'd invited to join her—the most famous artists and the most beautiful women.

But while famous personages like Caterina Corner already had their assigned places for the ceremonies, everyone else—practically the entire population of La Serenissima—started running around at the first light of day in order to find a place from which to watch. They would wait there, in the lines that formed along the Canal Grande, making sure they didn't lose their spot. The last ones to arrive would have to make do with a place in the back of the crowd, where they wouldn't be able to see anything. All of Venice seemed to be elbowing for a prime spot. Only one person was walking quickly in the other direction.

Lorenzo realized that walking away from the hubbub could mean drawing the attention of anyone he passed. So he stopped to figure out which paths people were taking that would still lead him to his uncle's shop but give others the impression he was going to watch the parade. Once he figured things out, he set off again, this time using side calli. So it wound up being mere chance that he saw her.

Like everyone else, the novices were heading to the Canal Grande to watch the procession. But because of the crowd, they were not traveling all together, but spread out, separated into pairs and small clutches. Lorenzo recognized other girls who shared the same austere destiny as his beloved Caterina. Then he saw Caterina. She was alone, one among the multitude of faces in that continuous flow of people. Lorenzo moved to the mouth of a narrow calle. When Caterina passed close by, he grabbed her by one arm and dragged her close.

"You idiot! You scared me," she exclaimed as soon as she recognized who he was.

"Come away with me."

"I can't."

"In all this confusion? Nobody will know you're gone."

Caterina appeared to consider this for a moment, calculating the risk. She smiled.

"Let's go," she said.

The two went running down the passageway, dashing between the high walls of surrounding buildings.

***

Simone Luzzatto didn't go to watch the wedding procession. He was by himself, sitting in his house and taking one last long look at a place he would soon abandon forever. He thought, with contempt, of how the Jews were gathering along the banks of the Cannaregio while the rest of the population was gathering around the Rialto Bridge. Jews always had to stand out, to live separate from the rest of the world. Jews were different from everyone else, a source of torment for Simone. As a Jew, Christian boys would never truly be his peers. Just like Lorenzo Scarpa had done, everyone always got the better of him. He always had to give way to others.

Simone couldn't stand it. He hated his own people, his own family. Even his father. That's why he would become a Christian soon. He would leave home and go live in the Rialto. He'd pay for a nice, young, clean prostitute. He would play dice and get drunk. They'd treat him as an equal. They'd respect him, because he would no longer be forced to stay in Cannaregio like the rest of his kind. And with all his money, Simone would command fear and respect from people like Scarpa, a tribute no one had ever paid his father, who was the most Jewish of them all.

Moses Luzzatto always said to be patient during the hard times, that they would have to endure and make sacrifices while they waited for better times to come. He urged Simone and the other Jewish boys not to provoke the Venetians, saying they should remain separate and focus on their work. He said their traditions were crucial to their identity, just as they were for their fathers before them.

Simone hated words like these with all his heart. Because as long as they accepted them, the Jews would never be free to look arrogant Venetians like Lorenzo Scarpa in the eye.

But things were about to change for Scarpa, and not for the better. When the mother superior discovered what was going on, his little love affair would be over. Finished. That much was certain. The things he'd written in the letter left no room for doubt.

***

Lorenzo and Caterina ran, hand in hand, anxious to feel the tingle of skin brushing against skin, to burrow into the familiar scents of their lover's body. They slowed down only when they were sure they were alone, in a calle less than an arm's length wide, and their desire burst into open flame. Their bodies crushed together, their hands sliding everywhere. Lorenzo broke open the door to a storage space, and the pair fell together, laughing and breathless, into a large ball of hay. Caterina kicked the door shut, and half a breath later they were both naked, eager to possess one another.

Hiding discreetly in the shadows of a large building nearby, the mother superior of Caterina's convent had watched while the young couple hid. She'd received an anonymous tip about Alvise Marin's daughter.

So the accusations were true. A scandal would overwhelm them all. And she couldn't let that happen.

CHAPTER 33

A river of a thousand colors offered a wonderful contrast to the palazzi and warehouses and their backdrop of a gray, snow-swollen sky. The procession had arrived. In a few moments, the first boats would cut through the cascade of flowers and petals that were raining down from the bridge. Mathias and Alissa were sitting on the balcony with the Lady of Asolo. Alissa seemed to have been given the role of hostess during the ceremonies, entertaining the monk until such a time as Caterina Corner decided to speak to him directly. Alongside the former queen sat several of the most important personages in La Serenissima, including Aldo Manuzio, the most important printer in the world, and Pietro Bembo, the man who more than anyone else had helped Manuzio achieve this position. Bembo had overseen publication of Petrarch's *Canzoniere*, which Manuzio had printed the previous year in the new, small format and which Giacomo Foscarini had sent to Mathias as a gift. They were now working on a project that everyone was talking about, Dante Alighieri's *Divine Comedy*. But while everyone knew the Venetian Bembo's family and its history, no one could say the same of Manuzio.

"They say he comes from humble origins, out in the Roman countryside," whispered Alissa when she realized just how surprised Mathias was to find himself seated alongside the famous printer. "No one knows how he came into his fortune, and no one knows his real name. But everyone agrees it's not Manutius, which he uses to sign his publications. They say that his secret is hidden behind the symbol he's adopted to sign his books, a dolphin and an anchor. He claims he found it on an antique coin that his friend Bembo gave him. The truth is that his past, everything he accomplished before arriving in Venice, remains cloaked in mystery."

"It sounds like that makes you curious," said Mathias.

"I'm sure it makes you curious too."

"Am I such an open book?"

"That's not how I would describe you."

"And how would you describe me?"

"The most extraordinary missed opportunity I've ever encountered."

"Really?"

"This year." Alissa couldn't keep herself from laughing, so much so that Lady Corner turned around to bring her back to order with a severe look.

"Your lady seems perturbed," said Mathias.

"She just behaves that way when she's out in public. In reality she adores having fun just as much as I do."

"Not in the same manner, I hope."

That set Alissa laughing again. But she pulled herself together the moment Lady Corner gave her another look that was hard to attribute to someone who loves a good time. Then the lady's interest turned back to Manuzio.

Many people believed he was the author of *Hypnerotomachia Poliphili*, an obscure, blasphemous volume that he had published but whose authorship had never been clearly revealed. It was a masterpiece of typography. Foscarini had shown Mathias his copy not long before the monk left for Padua, pointing out a few of the secrets people claimed the book contained. An acrostic revealed the author's name, a certain Brother Francesco Colonna. But no one knew anything else about him. Mathias sometimes wondered if Colonna had anything to do with the affair they were currently investigating, but according to Foscarini, Colonna didn't exist—it was merely a fake name behind which hid someone else entirely.

The river of flowers parted as if it were a theater curtain for the newlyweds. They were seated on the first boat, the largest in the flotilla. They sat at the center of a large raised platform, around which an orchestra of flutes and violins played merry music. Wonder filled the faces of everyone assembled on the balcony, save Lady Corner, who appeared far closer to boredom than rapture. When the newlyweds' boat reached the center of the tableau and the other boats were moving in around it, accompanied by noisy applause from the entire city, Lady Corner motioned for Mathias to come closer.

"I'm pleased to see that you find Alissa's company enjoyable." Corner's voice was gravelly, and her eyes tiny fissures that were black as night.

"Alissa?" Mathias wasn't sure how to respond. He was surprised to find himself even more in awe of this lady than he'd been of the Doge. "Yes," he continued, "I have to admit that I find her company something few would have the strength to deny themselves."

"I wasn't trying to embarrass you. I know that you are a man of faith and immune to certain temptations. At least, so Alissa informed me after your first encounter."

"My lady, if you truly wish not to embarrass me, then you've certainly chosen the most difficult route."

Lady Corner turned her head, surprised. Her eyes bore into his, and the grave expression that seemed carved of stone fractured into an amused smile.

"As I'm sure you know," said the lady, "there are different moods and souls inside the family, and rarely do they get along with one another. Of course, these things don't concern you, but since you have influential friends, you should be aware that Venice is about to change masks."

"What does my lady mean?"

"You are attempting to investigate a matter that I hope is not larger than you are. Because you have very little time left. The adversaries of the Doge, which include my despised cousin, have already drafted a proposal which, if it is approved in the Senate, will officially ask the Pope to lead an alliance of Christians against our Turkish enemies."

"What?"

"Rodrigo Borgia cannot wait to get his dirty little hands on the Republic. Even my friends are worried about what may happen next," she said, pointing to Manuzio. "And, as you quite nobly pointed out to Alissa, this would amount to an entirely inauspicious occasion for myself. I tell you this in order to emphasize that if I share these things with you, I do so in part because of my own interests."

"How does m'lady know about this proposal?"

"My despised cousin is miserly enough that bribing his servants is as easy as paying a common prostitute."

"I understand."

"Does that offend you?"

"M'lady calls a spade a spade. That's not something that can offend a German."

"If this is how things stand, it means Grimani has won over a majority in the Senate. And the Senate of this thing we call 'the Republic' has the power to make such a decision. Therefore, whatever you and Giacomo Foscarini are cooking up, it would be better you finish the dish in a hurry." Lady Corner's voice grew deeper and more serious, and she appeared to speak even more in confidence. "Tell Giacomo. If you don't do something soon, they'll have won."

"When will they present this proposal to the Senate?"

"Perhaps as early as the next meeting."

There was very little time and a great deal left yet to do. If Mathias had believed in destiny, he might have accused it of having played a tremendous trick on him, the worst possible, by leaving him responsible for saving La Serenissima from indentured servitude to Rome. Gheorg would have loved this story. But then, only if Venice remained Venice would it be able to support the things he wanted to accomplish in Wittenberg. In fact, if he managed to locate Valla's manuscript, everything might even start here in Venice.

"We will do everything the good Lord allows us to, my lady."

"Then I'll pray to your God that he'll let you do enough."

Caterina Corner waved to the boats that were nearing the pier beneath the balcony. They had steered there to pay homage to the Lady of Asolo. The newlyweds knelt before her from the platform upon which they'd been dancing with their friends. Some of them appeared to be drunk already. The music was so close it was overpowering. Alissa appeared to be the only one really enjoying the clamor of hands pounding rhythmically on the wood platform. Then the newlywed boat continued down the canal. Other, smaller boats followed in its wake, each carrying an allotment of family members and their guests.

Mathias was staring at the waves left behind, trying to find some answers to the questions crowding his mind.

When he looked up again, he found Giacomo standing on a gondola before him with another man. Both saluted the Lady of Asolo, but Giacomo's gaze was fixed on Mathias as if he intuited quite clearly that his friend needed to tell him something. Giacomo certainly wasn't going to enjoy the news that Lady Corner was sending.

The boats would drift farther up the canal, beyond Cannaregio, then would turn around and bring their guests back to San Marco.

"Go ahead," said Lady Corner. "And make sure you put what I've told you to good use."

The monk bowed to her, fully appreciating the speed with which she'd released him from her company. What little time he had left was more valuable by the hour, and before he joined Giacomo in San Marco he'd promised himself he would take care of something else.

Leaving the balcony, he couldn't help but glance at Manuzio again. The printer appeared captivated by the showers of flowers tossed into the city's waters.

CHAPTER 34

They stayed folded in one another's arms, nestled in the hay inside that cold, damp little storage space, waiting for their breathing to return to normal. Lorenzo knew they were in a precarious position, poised on the brink of an increasingly uncertain future. Lorenzo knew that even though Caterina wanted to spend her life at his side, she would complete her novitiate and don a nun's habit. She was a much stronger person than he was, and could shoulder the burden of letting her own desires be trampled on and ultimately torn away. This scared him, because when that day arrived, he would no longer know what to do.

Music and the clamor of celebration in the distance interrupted their private silence.

"The procession must be passing nearby," said Lorenzo.

"Let's go see." Caterina shook off the strands of hay clinging to her body. She got up and began putting her habit back on. Lorenzo looked at her, naked. He reached out and ran a finger across her belly.

"Come on, get dressed. Let's go see," she said.

They ran out of their hiding place and down the calle, where they found a spiral staircase that led up to a raised warehouse set above a pig-sty. They climbed onto the wood roof, Venice spread out beneath them.

"Her name is Eleonora Donà, and he is Luciano Barbarigo." Caterina watched the wedding boat gliding through the colorful petals. "He's the nephew of our last doge—did you know that? He already wanted to marry her back then, but her family insisted that they wait."

"They wanted to wait for the Doge to die?"

"The family wanted an equal matrimony. That's the way it is with all noble marriages. If the nuptials had happened before, the Barbarigos would have had greater influence than the Donàs. But Eleonora and Luciano waited, patiently, and in the end they managed to get married. Do you know how they met?"

"Why? Do you?"

"Of course. Everybody's talking about it. At a party at the Barbarigo house a few years ago. They were all wearing masks, and Luciano mistook Eleonora for his sister, Stella. He whispered his secrets to her, confiding that he'd fallen in love with the Donàs' daughter but that he was afraid to admit how he felt because of the bad blood between the Donà family and his uncle, the Doge."

"That's a perfect excuse."

"What?"

"Oh, come on, Caterina. He only pretended he'd mistaken Eleonora for his sister. That way he had a perfect opportunity to give it a shot. It's obvious."

"I met Eleonora—did you know that?"

"You met her?"

"Yes, at a reception. My family was usually invited to such occasions, and my father always took me with him. I had beautiful dresses. There was always music at those parties. Thousands of rose petals. Everyone was so happy. They were always happy. At least that's how it seemed to me. Now it's strange. The girls who are with me in the convent all come from much more humble origins. All they talk about are the nobility, their clothing, the beautiful girls who marry handsome boys, love affairs. They talk about all that as if it's taking place in another world, which, in a sense, it is. Sometimes I get the impression that all this talk about other people's lives, dreaming of something different, helps them stand the simplicity of their own lives. One day one of them, Assuntina's her name, admitted to me that she'd once seen me dressed in a splendid turquoise dress embroidered with gold and silver thread. I don't even remember that dress.

"One day I'll be able to get you out of the convent. You'll see that—"

"The promise, Lorenzo. Remember the promise?"

"What promise?"

"We promised we would never talk about tomorrow. You always forget that."

"Without a tomorrow, the world wouldn't exist."

Caterina smiled then. Lorenzo was about to say more, but she put a finger on his lips. She leaned in close and kissed him tenderly.

They stayed there for a while, watching the procession travel along the canal, the city's well-to-do on display before the population of La Serenissima. The boats had already passed beneath the Corner balcony. Lorenzo knew that Mathias was sitting up there. That thought brought him back to what he had to do now, before the celebrations were over and people went back to their daily affairs along the calli and piazzas all over the city.

"Caterina, you have to help me do something."

"What?"

"My uncle's shop. I have to go in there and look for something."

"But you can't. You told me they seized the shop."

"It's extremely important. Right now there's nobody around. Everybody is over there," said Lorenzo, pointing to the Canal Grande.

"But it's dangerous. If they catch you, they'll arrest you."

"Nobody's going to catch me. Not if you help."

"I have to think about it."

"There's no time to think about it, Caterina. In a little while all those people will go back to work, and I won't be able to sneak in anymore."

"If you're in such a rush, then you should have told me about it earlier. We could have avoided wasting all this time."

"Why are you being mean to me?"

"Because I love you, and I'm afraid I can't go on without you."

Lorenzo was struck, and stood still as stone. He saw Caterina's eyes fill with tears. He took her and held her close.

"Okay, okay," said Caterina, pulling away from him and drying her eyes. "Never mind. I'm just being stupid."

"It didn't sound stupid to me."

"There's no use in thinking about it. Let's do the foolish, dangerous thing you were talking about before. Maybe we'll get lucky and they'll arrest us together."

The couple left the roof and went back down the spiral staircase. Lorenzo led Caterina through a narrow maze of calli until they reached the shop. They hid in the same warehouse he had gone to with Mathias the day the two of them first met. Lorenzo waited for a while, listening for the murmuring and scuffling of other people who might want to enter the shop.

There was no one there.

"Perfect," he said to Caterina. "I'm going in. You wait here. Warn me if somebody's coming, okay?"

"How am I supposed to warn you? They'll hear me."

"Knock on that window. Two knocks. They won't hear it, but I will," he said, pointing to the closed shutters. "And then run away, do you hear me? But don't worry, you'll see. Everything's going to be all right. Everyone else is at the Canal Grande."

Moving slowly, Lorenzo made his way to the door. He took a key he'd kept hidden and used it to open the lock.

Caterina watched as he disappeared inside the shop. She looked around. She couldn't see a soul.

CHAPTER 35

"That's a dangerous argument to put forth these days, my dear Foscarini." The gondola was sliding through the waters of the Canal Grande, enveloped in a pale, monotonous cold. The wedding procession was in full swing, passing beneath the Rialto Bridge, where hordes of children were waiting to shower everyone with perfumed petals. But Foscarini wasn't thinking about the wedding.

The man he'd invited to join him on the gondola during the ceremony was the first one who'd come to mind when Mathias told him about a secret group interested in printing such a dangerous book. And his intuition had proven correct. Francesco Falier didn't deny the information. Giacomo Foscarini's friendship was a privilege well worth protecting.

"The Brotherhood of the Rose is a dangerous subject," repeated Falier. "One that you risk being questioned about, now that everyone has seen you sitting here with me."

"How many people know you belong to this brotherhood? And who?"

"I can't answer that question anymore. In the beginning, it was a very small group of people. We set ourselves the aim of concentrating on anything and everything that might keep the Pope's hands off the Republic."

"Then the group grew larger?"

"In a certain sense."

"What do you mean? How many of you are there?"

"That's hard to answer. The members of the Brotherhood don't all know one another anymore. We recognize each other through symbols. It started to protect our safety. But it also made it harder to control."

"What happened?"

"Opposing the Pope attracted a lot of other people. Merchants, artists . . . You'd be amazed to hear the full list."

"Does such a list exist? A register?"

"I don't think so, and if had one, I wouldn't give it to you."

"I thought you trusted me."

"Not that far."

"Go on."

"The rose." Falier looked out over the crowd gathered along the edges of the Canal Grande as he spoke. "A rose as white as the wings of an angel. It started as a way to represent opposition to the Pope. Even for people outside Venice's city limits." He stopped and turned to Giacomo. "Opposing the Pope, Foscarini, means opposing the Empire. Enemies of the Hapsburgs are discovering their own sensitivity to issues like renewing the faith, if you catch my meaning. That's why some of them have begun financing a new university." Immediately, Foscarini's thoughts turned to Mathias, but Falier brought him back to the present just as quickly. "King Maximilian of Germany is still waiting for the Pope's hand to make him Holy Roman emperor, but their bond remains strong. And those who oppose him are springing up in the very belly of the Empire, but these adversaries need a new faith for their people. A faith that will free them once and for all from the Roman leash and the Pope."

"So," said Foscarini, "little by little, while the Rose attracted new followers, as well as new funding, I imagine, you all were quite careful to tell everyone it was just a group of noblemen intent simply on protecting their land and rights from any eventual redistribution by the Borgias, once they reached Venice."

"Moralism doesn't suit you, my friend. We may have had our own interests, but the core ideas behind the Rose extend far beyond all that."

"And you figured out religion is good business."

"A Church free of Rome." Falier's eyes looked off into the distance as if he were entranced by a vision. "Every parish represents the power of Rome. From the Venetian patriarch all the way down to the humblest country priest. But the Church is supposed to be an expression of its faithful, not of those who rule it."

"Theology doesn't suit *you*," said Foscarini.

"Simply whispering these ideas was enough," continued Falier, "to immediately unleash the forces of a hurricane. Then, one day I heard that someone had met with some people in Ferrara who claimed they had a copy of Valla's manuscript. And from here on out, I can only refer to things I've heard, because my role in this affair was already over."

"Did they offer the book to your brotherhood?"

"They offered it up on a silver platter. Thanks to that book, Venice would become the center of something so enormous you couldn't even imagine it."

"And you thought they would just let you do all this? You thought you could print a book designed to destroy the Pope's power and that nothing would come of it?"

"No one thought it would be that simple. But by affirming that the Pope is not the sole source for the Word of God, we would have started something that many, many people are waiting for."

"Not just in Venice . . ."

"There is no *Donation of Constantine*. The Pope doesn't possess any rights over Rome, let alone the rest of the West. Every man is free to pray to God in his own native language . . . Do you have any idea what all that would mean?"

"Every man free to rule his own land." Foscarini understood. "And that's what you're aiming for, isn't it?"

"Don't you think it's our right? Do you think the lands that feed Rodrigo Borgia's illegitimate children are imbued with the sacredness of Christ? Do you believe that the man who invented the *Donation* did so in order to render glory unto God?"

"Don't talk to me about God, Falier. I'm not a peasant you can dazzle. If someone in Venice were to print that book, the Pope would excommunicate the entire Republic. That's what you're aiming for."

"Raising up the level of conflict, Foscarini, could prove useful for your Doge. If someone did the dirty work, Borgia would react forcefully, and at that point it would be hard to pass him off as a friend of La Serenissima. It's called 'scorched earth.'"

"No, it's called 'war.' And right now, it would be the ruin of Venice."

"Borgia would be the ruin of Venice, Foscarini."

"Exactly how much is going on behind the Doge's back? Why didn't you tell me about this earlier?"

"Many people think you're already too compromised."

"*I'm* the one who's compromised?"

"If I found that book, the one you're looking for, what would you do with it?"

The book was worth a great deal. If it were printed, it would lead to an open conflict. A religious war. Foscarini was afraid it would give Borgia the excuse he needed to isolate heretical Venice and push it over to the Pope's side. A relatively simple task, now that Venice was struggling to extract itself from another war from which the Republic would surely emerge the worse for wear. Giacomo Foscarini couldn't deny that he would try to find a different use for the book. But what?

The gondola reached the canal's edge beneath Caterina Corner's balcony. Foscarini looked for Mathias among the people seated there.

He knew the monk had been invited there, since he'd told him so that morning. When he found Mathias, Giacomo stared at him meaningfully, hoping the monk would understand that they needed to talk, and soon.

The gondola continued its slow voyage behind the newlyweds' boat, which was now rocking back and forth to the sound of increasingly raucous music.

"Were you the ones who contacted the printers?" he asked Falier.

"They were already part of the Brotherhood. Mariolino Scarpa wanted at all costs to convince others to print the book too."

"Why not a major printer? Somebody like Manuzio, who's already got more than one bone to pick with the Church?"

"A network of small printers would have been able to work more quietly, and with fewer distractions. And if something were to happen to one of them, the others could continue."

"If someone were to accept a generous offer to turn over the book, you mean, the others could still continue."

"Apparently, things aren't moving much differently."

"You've condemned them to death, Falier. To a horrible death."

"The Brotherhood grew too large. Someone inside the Brotherhood revealed our plans. The rest I'd imagine you can figure out on your own."

"You know who's behind the murders. You know who your enemies are."

"They're your enemies too, Foscarini. They're all the noblemen in Venice who would only gain from the arrival of the Pope. Family factions that are fighting other family factions, merchants who want lands and ships, noblemen who want power and authority."

"Give me their names."

"Grimani, Corner, Zorzi, Morosini, Trevisan . . . Half the nobility in Venice. Don't you remember their names?"

"If we found that book, we could put a stop to this river of blood. Whose hand moved to kill the printers?"

"You know the answer to that question too. You can't possibly be so misinformed as to never have heard talk of the Council of the Shadows."

Giacomo tried to remain impassive. This subterranean war risked sinking the entire city.

"Apparently, an alliance has been struck around the papist faction," continued Falier. "Clandestine authorities keep an eye on guards and agents. Public officials who supposedly respond to the Republic are in reality working for others."

"But how is it possible that the Council of Ten doesn't know about this? Are you sure about what you're saying?"

"Yes, and I'm also quite certain that the Council of Ten isn't in the dark."

"What do you mean?"

"In the past, there have been certain rumors left in the lions' mouths."

"My nephew is a member of the judiciary, and he hasn't told me anything about this."

"Those accusations never made it to the judiciary. Someone is even going so far as to keep watch over which letters make it to the Council of Ten. Now do you see how far things have degenerated?"

"If you're right, the Republic is in their hands." Giacomo was struck by the power of what he'd just said.

"Now you get it. This is what that book is for."

"What is your brotherhood going to do now?"

"We're vulnerable. We're not ready for all this yet."

"What?"

"The Rose isn't organized enough. It can't accomplish anything against an adversary who, as you just said yourself, has the Republic in its hands. I know that one of our members is trying to figure out where the book is, but I don't know who he is, nor what he'll do if he actually finds it."

"Your brotherhood has gotten out of control."

"We needed more time."

"But without that book," said Foscarini, "the Rose has lost."

"Right now it's hard to claim you're wrong. But as I said before, it's only a matter of time. Even if it doesn't happen here, today, now . . . sooner or later, the Rose will blossom."

"So you feel it's worth waiting for."

"It won't be such a long wait," said Falier. "The seed has been planted, here and everywhere."

"But Venice may be destroyed in the meantime."

Falier did not answer. He stared out at the boat upon which the newlyweds were cavorting. "It seems like the city is busy having fun in the meantime."

CHAPTER 36

Lorenzo looked around the ground floor of the shop. After he'd gone in, he'd locked the door behind him. Books covered the shelves, but since he had no idea what he was looking for, it was impossible to figure out what had happened. They had searched the shop for a forbidden manuscript, but why did they think his uncle was the one who had hidden it?

Lorenzo blamed Mariolino for not having said anything to him about the hidden book or the brotherhood of printers, but he also knew full well that silence and secrecy was his uncle's way of protecting him. But without Mariolino, he didn't know what to do. And he didn't have much time, since once the wedding procession finished, everyone in the city would go back to their daily activities.

"The ring," whispered Lorenzo. He knew where his uncle had kept it. Mariolino had let him know how important that small object was to him, even though he'd never spoken of it directly. Lorenzo headed upstairs toward the bedroom, trying to make as little noise as possible. Mariolino always left the ring in the small drawer in his bedside table before he went to sleep. Maybe he'd deliberately let his nephew watch, as a way to safeguard that secret, dangerous inheritance.

He opened the bedroom door. There was the table, standing right in front of him. He remembered the hiding place where his uncle kept the key to the drawer. Kneeling on the floor, he searched behind the bed leg with one hand.

It was there.

He grabbed it.

Hiding outside, Caterina was afraid Lorenzo was doing something foolish. What would happen to him if he were discovered? What secrets was he trying to hide from her? He still refused to talk about Mariolino. Sometimes she was surprised that he hadn't given himself time to grieve his uncle's passing. But she knew that Lorenzo wouldn't waste so much as a second of the time they had to spend together, not even crying for his own uncle. She was thinking about precisely this when she suddenly realized that the procession was about to end and that a few people were starting to return to their businesses. Any moment, one of them might pass right by here . . .

The key turned. The tiny mechanism that held the drawer closed clicked and sprang open. When Lorenzo slid the drawer out, there was the ring, placed atop a folded piece of paper. He picked up the ring and walked over near the closed shutters, trying to examine it in a sliver of daylight. Lorenzo could make out the rose symbol, and he remembered that there was writing on the inside of the ring, words he wasn't able to read before. He had always wondered about those, but back then he hadn't wanted to betray his uncle's trust, sneaking around and rummaging in his drawer. Only now did he realize that Mariolino himself had set him on this trail. He scrutinized the words engraved inside.

Three words in Latin.

EX TENEBRIS LUX

Lorenzo was able to translate the expression using what little Latin his uncle had taught him with the books in his bookshop. It said something like "Out of the darkness comes light." He wasn't entirely certain what the phrase meant, or what those words might refer to. But before he could sit down and think about it, he went back to the drawer and pulled out the piece of paper that lay underneath the ring. It was a letter. The first few words struck the young man to his core.

È per te mio caro et amato nipote Lorenzo
To you, my dear and beloved nephew Lorenzo

He had been right: His uncle had led him here. He had kept Lorenzo in the dark about his affairs, revealing nothing more than a simple clue, providing his nephew with a trail to follow only if and when it became necessary. There wasn't enough light for Lorenzo to read the rest of the letter clearly. He moved the paper around near the shutter, but at that very moment he heard someone knocking on the window shutters downstairs.

Caterina!

Someone was coming.

Lorenzo put everything in his pocket. He closed the drawer, knelt down, and put the key back behind the bed leg. His heart felt like it was beating in his temples. Business was bad for everyone, and people caught thieving were shown little or no mercy. If he was lucky, he'd be dragged out into the piazza and they'd chop off one of his hands.

Was Caterina in danger, or had she escaped already? Who was coming? He was just about to leave the room when he realized that the key was now visible. If someone saw it, they would figure out that there had been something hidden in the drawer. He lay down on the floor and tried to hide it more carefully. That's when he heard the first voices drawing near. Another knock on the window. Caterina was still there. They would discover her if she kept waiting. After one last glance, he took the key to the main shop door out of his pocket and dashed down the stairs. Only he was moving too fast.

Lorenzo tripped on the last few steps and flew forward, sailing through the air, then crashing to the floor and rolling over a couple of times in the room downstairs.

"Lorenzo! People are coming! What are you doing in there?" It was Caterina's voice through the downstairs window.

"Go, go! Run away, right now. I'll come to you tonight and tell you all about it," said Lorenzo, his hand massaging his head. He looked around. He'd lost something, but he had no idea what. He was stunned from the fall.

"Hurry up or you'll get in trouble, you idiot."

"You need to go, now, Caterina. Trust me."

"What are you waiting for? Why aren't you coming out?"

Lorenzo realized what he'd dropped: the key to the front door.

"I can't find the key. I'll have to find another way out."

"What? Are you crazy?"

"Caterina, for heaven's sake, will you please *go*? I can handle myself."

The door was too heavy for him to force open, and in any case, that would make too much noise and take too much time. The voices were almost right outside now, and in a few moments they would see them.

"Okay, but be careful!" said Caterina, pulling away.

The key was gone, swallowed up in the darkness. He had to find another way out, and he had to do so before they discovered him.

CHAPTER 37

Giacomo would be busy for a little while. Mathias realized he had to take advantage of the short time he had to do something he couldn't put off any longer.

He thought back to everything that happened the night before: the hooded men, the chase, his tired heart and weak legs. The very moment in which Mathias realized it was over, when he'd decided to sacrifice his own life in order to save the young man by his side, the monk had found something fundamental inside himself. Deep in his soul, in that hidden place that can only be discovered when a person finds himself poised on the edge of the abyss, gasping what he thought was his last breath, he'd suddenly seen it. Only then did he realize what he held dearest in his heart. Because the last thing to cross his mind, what he'd thought about the moment he'd spun around, prepared to impale himself on the blade, had been a face. No thoughts of God or faith or of any other saint. A face. That's when everything became clear.

Angelica.

He walked quickly toward her inn.

It was no longer possible for him to remain in Venice. But he would take Angelica away with him. He entered the inn, walked up the stairs, and went straight to her.

Angelica was sitting at her desk. She was waiting for him. She would have waited for him no matter what—that was clear now. She took his hand and led him to her room in the back of the inn, locking the door.

Mathias hugged her close. His lips found hers. Her soft scent made his heart beat faster. He didn't need anything else. He let his monk's tunic fall to the ground. He caressed her hips and bathed himself in her. They made love.

CHAPTER 38

Lorenzo had just a few moments to come up with a plan. The key could be anywhere. It could have fallen behind a piece of furniture, behind a bookshelf, slid across the floor. He tiptoed back upstairs, careful in case anyone outside could hear his movement or steps.

He went back into his uncle's room. During nights when he couldn't sleep, sometimes he'd sneaked out the window and sat on the rooftop looking up at the stars. A cat used to come to him there, scampering across a formless mass of rooftops, terraces, and raised warehouses. He'd named it Rossino for its tawny fur. He would do what the cat did, moving away from the shop by skipping from rooftop to rooftop. They wouldn't see him. They wouldn't catch him. They wouldn't take what he'd found away from him. And they wouldn't chop off his hands like a common thief. He opened the window, trying not to make any noise as he opened the shutters. Down below he caught a glimpse of a nearby calle filled with people. He put one foot outside to test the ledge. The wood was rotten, the stones loose.

"Just this once, luck will turn my way," he said to himself, gathering his courage.

Lorenzo squeezed into the small space between rooftops and closed the window behind him. He hoped no one down below would be able to see that the shutters had been moved, that someone had forgotten to close them from the inside. He looked around, trying to find a route he could take to escape. The roof of a nearby warehouse looked close enough. But he would have to jump like a cat.

He made his decision and took the leap.

But Rossino was a lot more agile and lighter than Lorenzo. The wood crashed and snapped underneath him, breaking where he landed. To keep from falling into the warehouse and being trapped there, he rolled to one side, almost to the edge of the roof. He grabbed hold of a brick chimney to stop himself, but at that very moment, a small group of people were walking past below. They all looked up in unison, drawn by the noise.

"Thief!" shouted a man in the group. Other faces appeared. They all pointed toward the young man on the roof.

"Perfect," said Lorenzo to himself. Desperation fed his strength, and he managed to drag himself to his feet. He looked around, then started running along the roof. Now he was in trouble up to his neck.

***

Caterina couldn't stop thinking about Lorenzo. She'd left him in a bad situation, but she couldn't have done anything for him anyway. Night was still far off, farther still the hour in which he usually came to her window at the convent so that they could whisper to one another. Caterina wouldn't be able to relax until she saw him, until he came to tell her everything was okay. She tried to calm herself by walking quickly, threading her way among people who were walking back to their homes and businesses. Some of them had drunk a little too much, and now were singing bawdy songs at the tops of their voices. She walked down a narrow calle in which the smell of fusty wine was almost unbearable.

When she reached the convent, novitiates were arriving one after the other. They were all coming back from the wedding ceremony. She was too far away from them to hear what they were talking about, but she was certain they were talking about the bridegroom, Luciano Barbarigo, who was as handsome as a prince. Eleonora was the luckiest girl in the world—luckier than they were, that much was certain. Caterina walked through the doorway and into the convent, heading for her room. There she would wait for the evening to come, for Lorenzo to arrive and tell her it was okay.

"Caterina." The mother superior spoke behind her. Caterina turned to face her, trying to smile. The grave, troubled expression on the old woman's face made her feel afraid. Something had happened.

"What can I do for you, Mother?" asked Caterina.

"We have to talk."

"If you're angry about the choir rehearsal I missed, it was just that one time. But I can—."

"This is not about the rehearsal, Caterina. It's about that young man who was with you until just a little while ago."

The world fell out from underneath her.

It was over.

***

A flock of pigeons swept up and flew away as Lorenzo passed. He came to another open space between rooftops and leapt across it without looking. This time he managed to land on a more stable rooftop. From there, he ran toward a wood storage building. He doubled over and started crawling.

Down below he could hear people walking past. No one had heard him yet. If someone started yelling "Thief" again it would be over and the end for him. Somebody might still be looking for him back where they'd spotted him on the rooftop, but they couldn't have seen which way he went. He went over to an open window, slipped inside, and slid down between a large pile of uncut tree trunks. There he sat, hiding. He held himself motionless, surrounded by the strong smell of tree wood. He saw a few people walk past the entrance to the storage space, and he moved toward them. He took off one of his shoes, in such a way that everyone on the street could see him, pretending something had soiled it.

A woman came nearby.

"This time it wasn't mud," said Lorenzo, sniffing his shoe. "It'll be hard to clean off."

"Wash it in the canal, my child," said the woman.

"Maybe later, m'lady. I don't want to freeze my own foot off!"

He slipped the shoe back on and disappeared amid the moving crowd, surrounded by people still talking enthusiastically about the wedding procession. He was safe. Now he just had to find somewhere he could sit down and read the letter Mariolino had left for him. He was sure his uncle had shared his secrets with him, that he would find the answers he was looking for in those lines.

CHAPTER 39

"If you find that book, Giacomo, make sure you put it to good use," said Falier.

The procession had finished, and the boats were back in San Marco, where the nobility disembarked and returned to solid ground. Giacomo Foscarini, who was both tall and broad, stood out among the Venetian aristocracy. Falier, on the other hand, was small and unnoticed amid the elite crowd, and if it hadn't been for his limp would have remained unrecognizable. His family had once been important and had even enjoyed close contact with the Doge, but these days it kept itself apart from the fray surrounding the future of La Serenissima. Now Giacomo understood why his friend had made such an effort to remain discreet and almost invisible.

"I don't know if we'll agree what the best use for that book is," said Giacomo.

"I know that you only want what's best for Venice."

"Would your brothers agree?"

"As I told you before," said Falier, "it's hard to say. Maybe one day we can all get together and share our opinions with the rest of the world.

At least that way, you could finally see who these brothers of mine really are." Falier seemed to be enjoying himself.

He shook Giacomo's hand, and the two parted ways. Foscarini watched the small man as he walked away. Could the conspiracy still be broken up without declaring open war on Rome? Would their fragile equilibrium be broken apart for good? An underground movement in the belly of the Empire was clashing with an alliance the papists had formed with a dark coalition that extended and branched out farther than expected into republican institutions. It was a movement that fed off the fear and hatred it produced. This was about more than just La Serenissima; this was about the West itself. Could any one book really play such an important role in a power struggle of this size?

It was possible there was a single plan behind all of the disparate strands. And it might even call for black-cloaked agents, men tasked with attacking the monk who was investigating on the Doge's behalf. Unfortunately, Foscarini's men were unable to get a good look at their adversaries' faces. If they had, they could have identified them and figured out who sent them. Falier had spoken of the Shadow Council. If that organization truly existed and wasn't mere legend, then it undoubtedly boasted among its members the puppeteers behind the conspiracy, the very men who ordered the murders and who were spreading terror throughout the city's population.

Falier was already gone, disappearing amid the crowd the way he'd learned to do. Foscarini was left standing alone, shaking off his thoughts and looking around, standing still in Piazza San Marco. Not far off, he could see a large boat coming in to dock, with at least ten people who had joined in the procession standing near the prow. He recognized Zorzi, Corner, and the man who was directing them, Agostino Grimani, whose cousin worked alongside Alexander VI. Grimani represented the pale hand of Borgia, extending its reach to grasp at Venice. He stared back at Foscarini.

"How did it go, m'lord?" One of Giacomo's servants, Michelino, had come to fetch him, pointing back to where he'd moored his lord's personal gondola. "What with all this traffic, we had to tie up a little farther down, but if you'd prefer we can move and pick m'lord up here."

"It doesn't matter. What matters right now is the monk, my friend. Did you have him followed? Where is he now?"

"In Zanon's inn, in Rio San Silvestro."

Giacomo turned and took Michelino by the shoulders. His servant's eyes widened in surprise. "Now listen to me closely. You have to do something. It's extremely important." Giacomo could tell his servant was growing increasingly unsettled as he heard what his master wanted him to do. Foscarini's orders were usually much clearer, with aims that were far more comprehensible. When he'd finished and Michelino had left on his mission, Giacomo returned to his thoughts. He had very little time. As with card play, each match might be decided by a single point, won with the very last hand. The forbidden book was the only winning card in the entire deck. Somebody within the Brotherhood had hidden it, and if the man behind the demon was still busy killing off his enemies, that meant he hadn't found it yet either.

The boat carrying the Doge had moored at San Marco as well. Loredan disembarked with help from his servants. His illness was growing worse. He noticed Foscarini and waved to him. The Doge was surrounded by members of the Signoria, who followed him wherever he went. Perhaps some of them were members of the Shadow Council, thought Giacomo.

CHAPTER 40

Mathias was still naked, but he'd wrapped himself up in his cloak and walked over to the window to watch the city's denizens celebrating the unification of the Donà and Barbarigo families.

Behind him, Angelica was still in bed, snuggled in the sheets. Mourning her dead husband, the man she'd risked being executed for, she looked older, as she'd been forced to wear austere clothing and live a cloistered life. But her naked body revealed her youth.

When her husband, Sebastiano Zanon, was found hunched over his writing desk with a dagger planted between his shoulder blades, Angelica suffered a terrible loss. He had been generous with her and her father. But she was Zanon's only heir, and the inheritance raised suspicions. Envy and foul rumors had led to accusations of murder, and she'd been arrested and locked up in the *pozzi*. There she awaited trial while Venice's inquisitor attempted to establish proof that she worshipped the Devil. Only one person had believed in Angelica, willing to fight on her behalf. He knew she wasn't responsible for her husband's death, because that night he'd been lying by her side. Thanks to Mathias, the castle of infamies the authorities had built around her fell apart like sand in the tide. Then the real killer was captured: a homeless man who'd been hired by someone he didn't know by name and couldn't describe, because he'd never seen the man face-to-face. But his capture and confession were enough to drop the charges against Angelica and close the affair.

The authorities also dropped the charges because they saw that Mathias and Foscarini were prepared to go further, attempting to shed light on a murder for hire that was undoubtedly conceived somewhere in the world of merchants and commerce—the world of Venetian nobility. Mathias obtained Angelica's complete and total absolution in return for a guarantee that he would let sleeping dogs lie. The homeless man was executed, taking his secrets with him to the grave, while the inheritance Zanon had left Angelica disappeared almost immediately, swallowed up by debts her husband had kept hidden. Angelica still wanted to know who had killed him, and she went around asking questions, discovering a few things, but by then Mathias had already left Venice.

"They told me it was a Macedonian merchant," said Angelica as Mathias continued looking out the window.

"In the end you just had to find out, didn't you?" he said, turning to face her.

"I think that's a rather convenient truth."

"If it had been a Venetian, someone you saw every day, you would have felt obligated to take revenge, wouldn't you?" He sat down on the edge of the bed. The sheets outlined the form of Angelica's body.

"I don't know. But I know I felt relieved."

"It must have cost a great deal, money you don't possess."

"You'd already left."

"I've come back."

"For how long?"

"Not long." Mathias looked lost in his thoughts, his big clear eyes unfocused. "I'm finishing a job, and the less you know about it the better. It's a job that will make it impossible for me to stay in Venice any longer."

"What are you saying?"

"To tell you the truth, they sort of stuck me in the middle. And I don't think they did so because of my natural skills, either, despite what they told me. They did so because they believe I might uncover something that will create a mess when it becomes public knowledge, and they'll hold me responsible, at least in some way." Mathias's gaze returned to Angelica. "When I find what I'm looking for, it will deal a big blow to a number of very important people. People who, given the positions they currently fill, won't forgive my effrontery."

"Why did you accept the job?"

"It's funny. I don't even remember accepting it."

"Then why don't you walk away now, while you still can?"

"Because it's too late. And because there's something about this business that prevents me from doing so. I'm convinced that I didn't wind up in this situation by chance, that the people who put me here knew more than they've admitted. Now I have no choice. I have to push forward."

"Will there ever come a day when you put yourself first?"

"No, that day will never come."

"You're crazy, my old man."

"It will never come because I've finally realized that I want you by my side, now and forever. That I can no longer be just myself, standing alone. I need more."

Angelica's eyes filled with tears. She looked like she was fighting to hold them back.

"You really are crazy."

"Leave Venice. Come with me to Wittenberg."

"But you're still a monk! How can you possibly think that—?"

"We'll deal with that when the time comes. But we'll do it together. No more hiding."

"They'll call you a blasphemer. Do you want to be burned at the stake?"

"Something done with knowledge of God's love shouldn't be hidden from view. In Wittenberg I'm going to start teaching again, together with my friends, and we want to reform the Christian faith. There will be no more pyres, no more burning at the stake."

"Don't turn me into some sort of tool for your holy battle."

"This is all I have to offer you, and I'm begging you to accept."

Angelica grabbed his cloak and pulled him in close. She didn't say anything else. Their lips sought one another and met, devouring. She ran her fingers through his hair. It was her way of saying yes.

But just then, the couple was interrupted by someone banging on the door.

"My lady," said Mimosa, "there's a man downstairs. He says his name is Michelino, and that he was sent by Giacomo Foscarini."

Angelica looked at Mathias.

"I have to go now," he said. "For your own safety, it's better that we wait until this affair is over before we see one another again."

"Please be careful. After you've made me wait all this time, I swear if you get yourself killed, I'll tear myself in two!"

"I'll keep that in mind," he said, already pulling his clothes on.

"Can't your nobleman friend help you with this too?" Angelica was still sitting on the bed, holding the sheets up to cover her breasts.

Mathias turned around before heading out the door.

"He's the one who got me into this mess."

CHAPTER 41

"I didn't hear any divine calling. I didn't put this habit on by vocation either."

The mother superior's name was Benedetta. Caterina had followed her into a private room, and was sitting on a wooden bench facing her. The confidential, almost friendly tone with which the mother superior was addressing her had taken the young woman completely by surprise, helping her focus even more clearly on the older woman's words.

"To tell you the truth, out of all the girls you'll find here, I don't think you'll find a single one who is really, truly convinced that they've been 'called' to wear the habit. I don't think there's a single one who willingly, knowingly decided to accept a life of privation at such a young age. And among them, there are undoubtedly a few who will find lovers with enough money to marry them and take them away. They're all daughters of peasants, fishermen, sailors, or artisans, and none of them had much by way of a dowry. But things are different for you. You need to be aware of that, before you make your decision."

Caterina listened without saying a word. She already knew the things the mother superior was telling her, but she'd kept them hidden, even from herself.

"You are a nobleman's daughter, Caterina. The Marin family can make sure you achieve a certain standing in the Church. Even though the Church is governed by men, women can still play an important role—managing funds and donations, and earning the respect of our peers. Your father can help you achieve such a position. But if you decide to follow that young man, to abandon the novitiate in order to marry him, you will be dealing your own family a coup de grâce. The world of Venetian aristocracy can be pitiless, my daughter. They wouldn't forgive the Marins such a juicy scandal." Benedetta sat down next to Caterina and, running a hand through her hair, spoke in a softer tone of voice. "Every single one of us has been asked to give up the life we led, to sacrifice ourselves for a purpose that has nothing to do with God. Now it has come to you. It is your time to make this choice."

"I can't choose. I don't have the strength to choose." Caterina began crying, distraught. She'd barely found the strength to spit those words out. She wished she could lock herself up in her room and pretend nothing had ever happened. She'd abandoned Lorenzo in a terrible mess, and all she wanted was to be able to talk to him through their little window.

"I can't let you take this any further. I hope you understand."

"But until I've taken the vows, I—"

"Caterina, my dear." Benedetta sighed, as if her words represented a burden almost too heavy to bear. "It's no longer up to me. Someone wrote a letter revealing the details of your affair. If that person hadn't sent it directly to me, if he or she had simply put it in a lion's mouth, our convent would be in serious trouble. I would be relieved of my duties, you and that young man would wind up in prison, and you would both be punished in public. I don't dare imagine what kind of punishment you would receive. You're risking your lives—don't you see?"

"Yes." For Caterina it amounted to accepting her destiny. "I understand."

"I don't know who wrote that letter, but by sending it to me they protected you both from far more serious consequences. Nevertheless, it remains a threat to you both, one you can't afford to ignore. You have to leave Venice, Caterina. Finish your novitiate somewhere else, somewhere safe."

The words, uttered so gently and evenly, blew over Caterina's dreams, which toppled like a child's house of playing cards. She and Lorenzo would never see each other again. They would not stand by each other's side in the years to come. She would never have the chance to hear about his fondest wishes, to support his courageous, crazy way of tackling life. She would never again caress his hair, kiss his lips, look into his eyes, breathe in his scent.

A piece of Caterina Marin died that day.

"I'll do what you say, Mother. I'll leave Venice," she said. Caterina's voice had lost the musical quality it had always possessed. It was gray now, and flat. "Please choose a destination that you believe is best, and that's where I'll go."

CHAPTER 42

Lorenzo was sitting alongside a fountain that bubbled with fresh sweet-tasting water. He held Mariolino's letter in one hand.

He'd been waiting for a message from his uncle—some sort of explanation for what had happened—ever since the monstrous killings had begun. But the letter didn't contain what he was looking for.

He'd already read it over and over again as the rich red Venetian sunset washed across the marble fountain. Should he share this message with Mathias? Could he trust the monk? In a certain sense, the letter was testament to Lorenzo's right to keep the forbidden book. With just a few lines, Mariolino had confirmed that all his worldly goods and possessions—including the ring—belonged to his nephew, though he did so in a rather confused manner.

Ex tenebris lux.

Lorenzo took the ring out of his pocket again, searching those three engraved words for an explanation, a hint, something that would help him understand. Was there a hidden meaning? If so, what? Maybe it was the motto of his uncle's secret society . . . Maybe it was the password for brothers of the Rose . . . There were too many questions. And he didn't have any idea how to find the answers he needed.

He unfolded the letter and read it again.

To you, my dear and beloved nephew Lorenzo, I leave the few admonishments you sought, together with each and every object I have owned.

The few books we possess will reveal which paths destiny will open to knowledge, illuminating the shadows of ignorance.

There was something left unsaid in that message, something hidden between those apparently innocuous words. But it was clearly meant for him, and clearly written by his uncle's hand. Lorenzo had even found it in a hiding place that only the two of them knew about, even though Mariolino had always pretended he was unaware his nephew knew.

Lorenzo folded the letter back up and put it into the pocket of his cloak, together with the ring. He knew he should get up off the fountain. The evening was growing cold, and he could feel his fingers turning numb. He was about to head for the house Mathias was staying in so that the two of them could examine the letter together, but just then he saw Simone Luzzatto walk into the piazza.

He was taking a walk with his father. They stopped as soon as they saw him. Simone's eyes glimmered with anger. Moses tried to stop him, but his son was already racing across the piazza. The closer he came, the more Lorenzo could see something terrible hidden in Simone's eyes, and in his expression. His face was twisted with hatred, but there was also exaltation, a sense of victory.

"We meet again, Scarpa."

"We meet all too often, Jew. Leave me alone."

"Leave you alone? You're in trouble. I'm merely worried for you, and for my money. How can you pay your debts while you sit there doing nothing? How can a wastrel like you even think of offering guarantees for the kind of money your uncle took on loan? How do you intend to pay us back?"

"That's no affair of yours. I'll pay. That's all you need to know."

"No, that's *not* all I need to know. And you know it."

"What else do you want?"

"What makes you think you can talk to me the way you do? Calling me 'Jew' with all the scorn you can muster won't help you now. You'll see. You think you're better than me, don't you? Except now you've got nothing left. You're alone. More alone than you realize."

"I already told you to leave me alone."

Moses finally caught up with his son, grabbing him by the arm and pulling him away.

"Let's go, Simone. Leave him be. We're good people. You have to learn to—"

Simone tore his arm away and dashed over to Lorenzo again. The look of triumph on his face was clearer than ever.

"You thought you could keep her all to yourself, didn't you? You thought you were so much better than me that you could possess her, didn't you?"

Lorenzo felt his blood turn to ice. "What have you done to Caterina?" he said.

"I had her taken away. I just wanted to make sure you knew I'm the one who did it!"

Moses grabbed his son with both arms. Simone didn't put up any more resistance, letting his father drag him away, but he kept his eyes on Lorenzo, seeming to revel in his adversary's fear.

Lorenzo didn't understand. What had happened to Caterina? What had Simone done?

The two Luzzattos were still in the piazza. Moses was chastising Simone for his behavior. But Simone seemed deaf to his father's words, immune to his criticism. He kept staring at Lorenzo with that terrible expression on his face.

Lorenzo started toward the convent, leaving the father and son behind. Now that evening had fallen, he could talk to Caterina through the little window. He began to run.

CHAPTER 43

Michelino led Mathias to a pier. The last reddish hues of sunset stained the cold white marble palazzi. Night was almost upon them, and the sky was threatening snow. When they reached the canal's edge, Mathias saw Foscarini's private gondola tied up there. Michelino opened the door to the felze, and Mathias got in.

Giacomo was waiting for him. But he wasn't alone.

"M'lord," said the monk, speaking to Foscarini's guest.

"I'm pleased to see you're doing well, my friend," replied Doge Loredan.

"Things are coming to a head," said Giacomo.

"I know," said Mathias, "Your adversaries have a proposal they are ready to present to the Senate, perhaps as soon as the next meeting. They're going to ask the Pope to intervene on our behalf against the Turks."

"How do you know that?" asked Giacomo.

"Caterina Corner. She's on your side."

"If that's the way things really stand, our side won't exist for much longer," said Loredan.

"If they already have such a proposal ready," said Giacomo, "then they already have a majority in the Senate as well. We have to find that book."

Mathias had never seen Giacomo so tense. "What did you find out about the Rose?" asked the monk.

Giacomo told them everything he'd learned during his meeting with Falier. As soon as he heard about the Shadow Council, Mathias knew his enemy was more powerful than he had ever imagined. Loredan seemed inert, as if the threat were far too big for him to take on. This faceless, nameless specter. Or so it seemed.

"Zaugo," said Giacomo, "Scarpa's printer friend. This morning I told my men to keep an eye on him, just as you asked. They told me that this afternoon, taking advantage of the wedding procession on the Canal Grande, he met with several men on the edges of the crowd. They were wearing black cloaks, just like the men who attacked you."

"A black cloak is hardly an uncommon piece of clothing," said Mathias.

"Perhaps," said Giacomo. "But the man I met with just a little while ago is convinced that someone has betrayed the Brotherhood of the Rose. Someone who knew of Mariolino Scarpa's plan, the arrival of the forbidden book, and all the rest. Zaugo was close to the boy. Could he be the traitor?"

"We'll find out soon enough," said Mathias.

"We need to move, and move now," said Loredan, emerging from despondency. "We need to take the fight to them."

"I don't see how, m'lord."

"When you don't have the winning hand, my friend, you need to pretend you do. We need to convince the enemy that we're holding the trump card," said the Doge.

"I'm sorry," said the monk, "but I'm afraid I've never been good at cards." He was trying to figure out what Loredan was driving at.

"Nevertheless, you can help us score the points we need," responded the Doge.

"I don't—"

"The enemy still hasn't located the book, magister," said Giacomo.

Foscarini explained their plan. More than a plan, it was a bid for time, a way to keep their adversaries from trotting out their proposal requesting the Pope's intervention at the next Senate meeting.

Mathias listened carefully. He felt more and more like a tool in the other men's hands.

"You're entrusting me with your dirty work, aren't you Giacomo?" he asked finally. Giacomo didn't answer and avoided his eyes.

"Yes, it's pointless to pretend otherwise," said the Doge. "When you've finished, you will never be able to set foot in Venice again, no matter how things turn out. But I can promise you that the compensation for your role will be more than you need to go home and start a new life. Foscarini told me you intend to go to Wittenberg. I can promise you that I will do everything in my power to see that you're given anything you ask."

"What will happen to the boy?" asked Mathias. No one had said anything about Lorenzo. He wanted to stay in Venice, to become a printer and continue working in his uncle's shop, but he, too, had already passed the point of no return. If it would be impossible for Mathias to stay in Venice, then it would be equally impossible for Lorenzo. All the more so in light of the Foscarini and the Doge's plan.

"We have enough resources to provide for him as well," said Loredan. "I'll make sure the debt to Luzzatto, which Giacomo told me about, is taken care of quietly and efficiently. Then he'll be free to decide what he wants to do with his inheritance. If he should decide to leave the Republic, I'm sure he'll be given a very generous offer for his shop, in addition to the reward I myself will be honored to give him."

Mathias's thoughts turned to Angelica. They would leave together for Wittenberg, along with enough ducats to guarantee themselves an easy life.

"What a bizarre destiny for a monk," said Mathias. "I've become a weapon to use against the Pope."

Mathias got out of the gondola and headed home. He felt tired, oppressed by the weight that had been placed on his shoulders.

He should sleep—to gather his strength. The Doge's plan was risky, and he'd need to be as awake and aware as possible. And he needed the bookseller, Scarpa. But when he entered his house, the young man wasn't there. Where was Lorenzo?

CHAPTER 44

The route to the convent seemed longer than it ever had before. Lorenzo's mind was filled with Luzzatto's words, and his jaw muscles clenched in anger. He was breathing like an angry bull, the hot air coming out of his nostrils in twin jets of vapor. He couldn't feel the cold anymore. He didn't even realize it when the first snowflakes started falling.

The ground became slippery. He realized this at the same time he saw the convent wall appear between two palazzi. He took big steps to reach it more quickly, but the mud he was walking on had turned to ice. Lorenzo slipped and rolled on the ground, dirtying his cloak, but he didn't feel the pain in his frozen, bloody hands. He continued as fast as he could to the little window.

"Caterina!" His heart beat in his temples. "Caterina, are you there?"

No answer.

Lorenzo looked around. The few lights nearby were nothing more than pale brush marks in an opaque landscape painting. Snow was falling steadily now. He called her again, but there was still no response.

He couldn't go back home without knowing. Even if it meant knocking on the convent door and demanding to see the mother superior.

Lorenzo decided to wait a little while longer. He pulled his cloak up over his head. He had no idea how long he would stay. But he was willing to face any hardship in order to understand the meaning of the words Luzzatto had spewed at him with all the rancor he could muster.

"Go home." Caterina's voice.

Lorenzo spun around, slipping and falling again. He grabbed hold of the iron grate over the little window and pulled himself up.

"You have to go, Lorenzo. We can never see each other again."

"What are you talking about? Are you mad? What happened?"

"The mother superior received an anonymous letter. She knows everything."

Simone Luzzatto. Lorenzo felt his hatred grow overwhelming, clouding his reason.

"We can't risk another letter reaching the lion's mouth," said Caterina. "We'd wind up in the middle of the piazza, tied to the block. My family would be destroyed. You'd risk prison, the pozzi, your life. I'm going to leave Venice to finish my novitiate and don the habit somewhere else."

"You can't go. I don't want you to go!"

"We both knew this is how it had to end."

"But soon I'll have money. I can take you away from here. We can—"

"I've made my decision. I must serve my father, my family, before anyone and anything else. I am a Marin. I can do nothing less."

Caterina's voice seemed like it belonged to someone else. A gray, emotionless voice. Then Lorenzo sensed a change. For a moment, he again heard the voice of the woman he knew and loved.

"Lorenzo . . . Forgive me. I can't do it! Maybe someday I'll be able to come back and we can see each other again. Please don't make this harder than it already is!"

"You're breaking my heart. How can you think that? My life doesn't exist without you. Every corner of this city, every moment that we've—"

"You'll have those moments forever."

Those words went right to his core. Lorenzo felt his stomach churn. He felt lost. He felt alone, just as Luzzatto had said. He felt defeated. He fell away from the window. Tears filled his eyes and ran hot down his cold snow-dusted face. He would have those *moments* forever, but not her. He wouldn't have Caterina to share them with. They would be nothing more than memories, relics from a previous life.

"Where will you go?" he asked.

"I don't know yet. But I wouldn't tell you anyway. I don't want you to follow me." Caterina's voice had gone flat and lifeless again. Then, once again, he heard a last faint whisper of vitality, the last gasp of a girl who was no longer his. "I promise you that one day I will come and look for you, Lorenzo. I'll find you, no matter where you may be. But you have to make me a promise too."

"What?" Lorenzo was crying like a baby now. Caterina pressed her face to the window, and now he could see her. Her hair was covered by a veil. Her face was pale. She threaded her fingers through the iron bars of the grate, and Lorenzo grabbed at them, clutching them in his own. For a moment, Caterina's face seemed to come back alive. For a moment she looked as she had that day in the market, when Lorenzo saw her for the first time—her eyes clear and luminous, strands of hair curling down around her slim neck. A smile that seemed brighter than the sun.

"You have to promise me that you won't wait for me . . . For us."

Lorenzo kept weeping.

"You must, Lorenzo." Caterina was crying too. "I can't live with that remorse. You have to promise me that you'll live your life, that you'll try to be happy, that you'll become a famous printer. Promise me you won't spend your days pining for me. When we meet again, you'll have a mountain of things to show me. You'll have your books, your children. You'll have a marvelous life that . . ." She was overcome by tears. She couldn't go on.

Clutching each other's hands, they kissed for a final time, their lips meeting through the grate covering the little window. Then Caterina moved away, and Lorenzo saw her disappear into shadow. He collapsed on the ground. His desperation split open, and a face emerged.

I just wanted to make sure you knew I'm the one who did it!

The face filled out and took shape, its eyes bubbling with hatred.

Lorenzo couldn't live so much as another day, knowing that out there somewhere Simone Luzzatto was alive, and enjoying that triumph he'd seen in his face. His adversary had to die. He would wait for him in the shadows, entrusting the final chapter in his story to a dagger blade. His vendetta.

CHAPTER 45

The boy was in trouble. Lorenzo had done something stupid again, and now who knew where he'd wound up? The black cloaks were looking for him. They may have found him already. Mathias kept looking out the window, watching the snow fall. There is no such thing as destiny, he thought. The wind is the only thing that decides which flakes will fall to the ground, becoming ice on the paving stones, and which will fall into the water, melting into the lagoon. The wind had blown him to Leipzig, then Venice, then on to Padua and back to Venice. Now it would drive him on to Wittenberg.

Mathias felt the weight of his fifty years. He felt a sense of emptiness, as if all the books, all his studies, everything that seemed to have given meaning to his existence were becoming weightless, turning into something so light that it could be blown away by the wind. It was late at night. He didn't know how long he'd been standing at the window.

Then the front door opened.

Lorenzo staggered into the room. The acidic stench of cheap wine and vomit billowed around him. Mathias grabbed him and held him up with both arms.

"Where on earth have you been, you fool?" said Mathias, thanking God the young man had made it back. "Didn't you get enough of the black hoods the other night? Are you so determined to challenge destiny again?"

"He took her from me. That f-f-f-ilthy worm . . . has to die." Lorenzo slurred to the point where he was practically incomprehensible.

"Tomorrow you can tell me all about it. Right now you need to rest. We have a difficult task ahead of us," said Mathias, taking Lorenzo to his room and laying him on the bed.

Lorenzo was soaked through. The monk removed the young man's wet clothing, washed his face and neck, and covered him with warm blankets, trying to bring his body heat back to an acceptable level. He shouldn't have let himself get so involved with this young man, but he had to help.

Mathias watched over Lorenzo while the young man fell into a deep sleep. He stirred the fire in the fireplace and moved his chair closer to the bed so that he could stay close.

***

Alone in her room, Caterina sat on the bed, staring at the opposite wall. She couldn't even cry anymore. It was as if she had become consumed by nothingness, as if her soul had fled forever, seeking refuge in the places where she'd known the love of Lorenzo Scarpa.

She lay down and forced herself to close her eyes, hoping that sleep would come. But she knew it wouldn't. She would allow herself one last night of suffering. Tomorrow, a new life would begin. A different life, one she didn't want. To survive, she needed to forget everything else, tucking her memories away in a hidden corner of the soul that seemed to have abandoned her body. She would lock her emotions away and throw away the key, accepting her fate.

For his own good, she should have lied to Lorenzo. She should have made sure he wouldn't be tempted to follow her. That would only add to her torture. Not long before that one last desperate conversation at their window, the mother superior had come into her room. She sat down beside her and told her where she would be sent.

Far away. So far that it felt like there would be no return.

CHAPTER 46

At dawn, Venice was smothered in snow. Lorenzo sat still. He'd just woken up, wrapped himself in a blanket, and gone out on the balcony. He brushed a layer of snow off a chair, and there he sat, looking out over the surreal cityscape. The cold air was clearing his head and bringing him to his senses.

Caterina was the first thing he thought about. He'd made a promise to her. In order to keep his promise, he would have to convince himself that he'd lost her forever. Awareness of that loss tortured him. Caterina would never shame the Marin name by fleeing the convent in order to marry an artisan, but the fact that they'd come to this point was the fault of one person, and one person alone.

Simone Luzzatto.

A foul odor drew Lorenzo back to the present. He recognized the stench. Mathias had come out on the balcony, a blanket over his shoulders, carrying two steaming mugs of his herbal decoction.

"I think a mug would do me good as well," he said, passing the other to Lorenzo.

"Your decoction is the worst possible way to start a day."

"If you keep going out and getting drunk every night, not even this drink will be enough to fix your stomach. The wine they serve young people is nothing like Foscarini's Portuguese wine."

Lorenzo took a sip of the terrible decoction and felt his stomach churn. Then he felt a bulge break free in his abdomen and a sharp pang of pain. Acid rose in his throat until he finally released a booming sharp-smelling belch. He felt a little better.

"It's working," he said, bringing the mug to his lips for another sip.

"Last night you were babbling about a filthy worm that had to die," said the monk.

"Last night was not a great night."

"Why don't you come back inside and tell me about it. Sometimes it helps to unburden yourself with someone else."

Lorenzo took another sip, trying to gather his strength. Perhaps the time had come to share his story with someone. The strange monk that destiny had put in his path might well be the closest thing to a friend he had right now. Lorenzo also realized he was freezing, so he accepted Mathias's invitation to go inside and talk.

Sitting by a roaring fire, Lorenzo told him about Caterina and how the Marins wouldn't allow their daughter to leave the convent. The Venetian nobility would never forgive such an embarrassment. He asked the monk how it was possible to believe in a God capable of imposing such sacrifices on people. And he told Mathias about Simone Luzzatto and the letter.

"That Jew has to die," he concluded.

"I'm convinced that Caterina wouldn't want you to be locked up in the pozzi for the rest of your life," said Mathias.

"He has to pay. I won't forgive him this, if that's what you're asking me to do."

"I don't believe in the ethics of forgiveness."

Lorenzo was surprised to hear the monk say such a thing.

"I believe that each individual is responsible for his actions when done with deliberate intent," said Mathias. "And I believe that each and every one of us will be called upon to respond for what we've done in this life." Mathias took a long sip of his decoction, then spoke again. "But I also believe that you don't really want to become an assassin. Luzzatto's death would come by your hand, and the whole city would know it, given that everyone who is anyone knows about your situation and your debt with the Luzzattos. I'm quite sure you don't want to spend the rest of your life locked away in a stone hole, buried in darkness and cold with a chain locked around your neck and guards ready to beat you soundly for no better reason than a way to pass the time. And given that I believe all these things, I also believe that today you'll dedicate yourself entirely to me and to what I'm about to propose to you, putting off your other intentions until tomorrow, when cold hard reason will help you find a way to get the justice you desire without getting yourself killed in the process."

"I hope that you have better advice to offer me tomorrow, given that I've told you everything and you haven't offered me a single thing in return."

"Well, if nothing else, at least they haven't arrested you yet."

"All right, magister," said Lorenzo. "What are we supposed to do?"

"Stage a play."

"A play?"

"I hope you're ready, because you're going to have a starring role."

"Would you please explain yourself?"

"Rest up and gather your wits," said Mathias. "We're going to leave the house soon. There have been developments you don't know about. I'll have to bring you up to speed while we're walking. There are plenty of questions to which we still haven't found an answer."

This last affirmation reminded Lorenzo of the mysterious letter he'd found the previous day in his uncle's drawer. If he was going to share it with Mathias, trust the monk with everything he had, this was the time to do it.

Mathias was already getting ready to go out.

"What would you do with the book if we found it?" asked Lorenzo.

The monk stopped. He put the cloak he was holding back down on the chair slowly, then turned around to face Lorenzo. "And you? What would you do with it?"

"Do you realize you always answer my questions with another question?"

"Many different people are after that book," said the monk. Mathias shared everything he'd discovered about the Brotherhood of the Rose with Lorenzo, including what the secret society intended to do with the book they'd brought to Venice and how they planned to make Venice the epicenter of a cultural earthquake that would rock all of Christianity. Mathias explained why the Doge and Foscarini wanted to keep the Pope outside La Serenissima and what they were afraid would happen if Valla's book were published. How they feared an outright attack by Borgia as well as the threat of a religious war that would wipe out what was left of Venice, already struggling to deal with the effects of the war with the Turks. Last but not least, the monk spoke of what Foscarini had called the Shadow Council, a group of men intent on destroying the book or at least using it as a bargaining chip with the Pope to reinforce their position in the new Venetian order.

"You still haven't answered my question," said Lorenzo when Mathias had finished. "You still haven't told me what *you* would do with the book."

"I'll make you a deal," said Mathias. "For now, let's forget about that aspect. But if you and I are the ones who find it, then you and I will decide what to do with it together, okay?"

Lorenzo nodded. At heart, that was precisely what he wanted. He decided to trust the monk.

"My uncle gave his life for that book," said Lorenzo.

"I know," said Mathias. "And you've given up quite a bit yourself. You realize, of course, that when this whole affair is finished, it may no longer be safe for you to stay in Venice. We're making enemies with people who are powerful enough to sweep us both away with a brush of the hand."

"So much has happened in just a few short days," said Lorenzo, feeling lost again. Mariolino, the demon, the black cloaks, Caterina. "All we wanted to do was print books."

"We can talk about that when this is all over," said the monk, once again picking up his cloak. "Right now, however, it's time to get moving."

"I broke into my uncle's shop."

Mathias stopped short and stared at Lorenzo. Anger clouded his face. "That's a remarkably stupid thing to have done, given that we've got the black cloaks following our every move."

"I found this," said Lorenzo, handing him the letter.

Mathias put the cloak back down on the chair and read the letter. Then he read it again, and again. It seemed like he was having trouble understanding what was written there.

"It's my uncle's handwriting, but it doesn't seem like something he would say," said Lorenzo. "Do you think it's a hidden message?"

"It's possible we'll find a few answers amid these lines, but first we need to figure out how. I need to think things over. Can I keep it?"

Lorenzo nodded. Then he took the ring out of his pocket and showed it to Mathias.

"Ex tenebris lux," murmured Mathias.

"Do you have any idea what it means?"

"More a sensation than an idea."

"What?"

"I feel like we have all the pieces. Now we just need to figure out where they fit in, so that we can see the complete image they make."

He put the letter in his pocket, then put on his cloak as he walked to the front door.

"Where are we going?" asked Lorenzo.

"To set our play in motion."

CHAPTER 47

Niccolò Zaugo was in his shop. He had closed the door in order to make sure he wasn't disturbed. He sat at his table and looked through the papers he'd been given in return for his betrayal. They promised ducats to be collected through a Florentine bank. It was enough to get him out of Venice and invest in a business that could make him a wealthy man.

They insisted that he find the book, but he had no idea how to do so. He thought that perhaps he should talk to Lorenzo. Maybe his uncle had shared a few details with the boy that could prove useful. Lorenzo knew nothing, or almost nothing, about the Brotherhood, and wouldn't be able to interpret vague signals Mariolino had left behind. But Niccolò could. He was lost in precisely these thoughts when he saw Lorenzo's head appear in the window by the front door.

"Niccolò, where have you been?" asked Lorenzo.

"Lorenzo?" Zaugo dropped the letters of credit in a trunk he kept by his worktable. Destiny had just given him a perfect opportunity. He wasn't the one who'd sought out Lorenzo, and this meant he could be as curious as he liked without raising suspicion.

But behind Lorenzo, who had already walked into the shop, Zaugo saw someone else—a monk. And he knew that man was looking for the book. He'd heard that a monk had been seen visiting the inn where the messenger from Rome had been staying.

"I'd like you to meet Mathias Munster," said Lorenzo.

"Any friend of yours is a welcome here, my boy. Please, make yourselves comfortable." Niccolò realized he was having trouble hiding how unsettled he was by this unexpected visitor. The appearance of this German changed everything. What did the two of them want from him?

"How come you've closed up shop today?" asked Lorenzo.

"I needed to settle a few affairs. It seems like I never have enough time to attend to my business."

"Then business must be good," replied Lorenzo.

Did he know about the money? Had he already discovered everything? Should Niccolò throw himself at their feet and beg forgiveness, or should he continue to pretend in the hopes that those words had nothing to do with the sense of guilt overwhelming him? Niccolò kept his eyes on his visitors, trying to figure out how he should behave. The German was staring at him with an inquisitor's gaze. Lorenzo, on the other hand, seemed the same as ever. No sign of anger or rancor. Maybe they didn't know anything after all.

"Perhaps it would be better if you didn't sit around here on your own, Niccolò. It might be dangerous," said Lorenzo.

"Dangerous?"

"Don't make the same mistakes my uncle made," said the young man. "If he hadn't been so obsessed with keeping me in the dark, if he had shared things with me, maybe I could have done something to keep him from being killed."

"But what do I have to do with all that, my boy?"

"I know about the Rose, Niccolò. You should have told me about it."

Zaugo suddenly felt afraid. His hands jerked reflexively, moving to cover his ring. How much did they know?

"First my uncle," said Lorenzo. "Then Giuntino. All the men who took part in that meeting are popping up one by one in the Canal Grande. It seems like the demon has decided to drag them all down to Hell. I don't want you to run the same risk just because you're as stubborn about secrets as my uncle was."

"You're a dear boy, Lorenzo. But I don't know what meeting you're talking about."

"Then you're lucky. You didn't attend."

"A secret meeting, Lorenzo?" Niccolò felt the weight of the German's stare on him. Those ice-blue eyes were boring into him.

"My uncle knew a lot of things," continued Lorenzo. "But unfortunately, he took most of what he knew to the grave."

"I think that was for your own good, my son," said Zaugo.

"Most of what he knew. But not everything." Lorenzo spoke carefully, his tones measured. "You stayed with me all night when I was mourning my uncle, but you didn't say a word about what he was planning to do."

"I've already told you. I don't know anything about your uncle's secret meetings. Maybe it would have been better for us all if he hadn't had any."

"I don't understand," said Lorenzo.

"What's not to understand?"

"I don't understand why you kept me in the dark. He was like a brother to you."

The German kept his silence, but his presence, his behavior, was making Niccolò incredibly tense. "That's something you'd do best to forget about, Lorenzo."

"You're a member of the Brotherhood of the Rose, Niccolò. I've seen your ring," said Lorenzo.

Zaugo didn't move a muscle.

"Stopping now would be a mistake," said the German monk. He stepped forward, and a tenuous ray of light filtering through the window illuminated his handsome, weathered face.

Niccolò didn't know what to say—what to admit and what to deny. But he knew that he would have to tell the people who had paid for his soul about this encounter. He waited for the monk to continue.

"We want to publish the book, Zaugo," said the German.

"What book?" asked Niccolò.

"The one my uncle should have published," replied Lorenzo.

"Valla's manuscript on the *Donation of Constantine*." The German's voice had turned hard, powerful, and imposing.

Zaugo sat frozen as if made of stone.

"You know what I'm talking about, don't you?" continued Mathias, pressing him. "You knew what Scarpa was planning to do. It's not too late. You can still help us."

"How?" Zaugo was distraught. Had they found the book?

"My uncle wanted to use a network of printers," said Lorenzo. "But his plan was undone by a ferocious assassin and the men who sent him. We almost lost the book, but now that we've found it again we can finally press forward. That's why I'm here, Niccolò. You have to help us. You know the world of printers better than I do. I don't know who else is a member of the Brotherhood. You have to put me in touch with them, warn them that the book has been saved. That my uncle didn't die in vain."

"But where is the book now?"

"It's safe," said Lorenzo, reassuring him. His eyes were sparkling with an enthusiasm that left little doubt about what he meant to do with it. "It has returned to the light, Niccolò! From the shadows, the book has returned to the light!"

"To the light . . . of course . . ." Zaugo felt overwhelmed.

"That's right," added the German. *"Ex tenebris lux."*

CHAPTER 48

"I still can't believe he's the one who had my uncle killed." Lorenzo's words were rushed as he spoke to Mathias between hurried breaths. As soon as they'd left Zaugo's shop, the pair had begun walking as fast as they could through the calli, headed for Mariolino's workshop. "How did you figure it out?"

"Foscarini had his men follow Zaugo," said Mathias. "They were supposed to protect him, but instead they discovered he was meeting with strange people. Hooded, cloaked men just like the ones who tried to kill us. They tried to follow the men, but they vanished. That made me suspicious. Our little meeting a few minutes ago eliminated any remaining doubts. Zaugo was scared. You'll see—soon we'll have the proof we need."

"That lout sat next to me throughout the night. He sat right in front of my uncle's body."

"He'll answer for that as well. But right now we have work to do."

"There will come a time for everything, right? A time for Simone Luzzatto, a time for Niccolò Zaugo . . . But in the meantime, I have to sit still and let the people who chewed up my life and spit it out on the stones walk around undisturbed."

"Maybe you don't get it." Mathias stopped short in front of Lorenzo. "If Zaugo is what I think he is, we just offered ourselves up as bait for a band of assassins. And in case you're forgetting, we don't have any actual book to print. And while this little game may be useful to the Doge, may buy him time before his adversaries present the proposal they've prepared in the Senate, it certainly won't help us sleep at night."

"You might have thought of that before we visited him. What in God's name are we supposed to do now?"

"I'm thinking."

"Fantastic."

"In the meantime," said Mathias, "I've gotten you your shop back, and that's no small matter."

"It was the least the Doge could do for the mess he's gotten us mixed up in."

"I warned you. You knew the risks."

"I know. I'm just a little tense, that's all."

They kept walking as quickly as they could toward the bookshop.

"What do you think Niccolò will do?" asked Lorenzo.

"I think he'll tell them that we've found the book. And if the Shadow Council is truly behind all this, then those people will try to buy time and put the motion on hold before presenting it to the Senate."

"So if we have Foscarini's men follow Zaugo, we'll know who the protagonists are."

"They won't be the only ones to do so. Until we've decided what to do with the book, we'll need eyes and ears too."

"What are you talking about?"

"Forget it. Right now we need to concentrate on the task at hand."

"Finding the book."

"As long as that's still possible."

"Maybe it is," said Lorenzo.

Mathias stopped and stared at the younger man.

"What's that supposed to mean?"

Lorenzo motioned for them to keep walking. "Let's just say that while I was talking to Zaugo, I had an idea."

"And would you please be so kind as to share this idea with me?"

"Well, right now it's mostly just the inklings of an idea. But as soon as we get back to my uncle's shop, things may become clearer in a hurry."

"If you have something in mind, don't you think now's the time to spit it out? Maybe you haven't noticed, but we're risking our lives here."

"It's my uncle's letter," said Lorenzo.

"Have you figured out what he was referring to?"

"It's hiding another message. I'm sure of it."

"That makes two of us. Is that what your inklings of an idea are about?"

"Mariolino was a member of a secret society. I'll bet that the members of a secret society use secret codes to protect their most important messages."

"Codes," echoed Mathias. "Go on."

"My uncle and I used to play a game sometimes. It's so stupid . . . I can't believe I didn't think of it sooner. He would write numbers down on a scrap of paper, and I had to figure out what they referred to. They were simple codes. Sometimes they were the page of a book, other times certain lines on a page, sometimes the letters of words printed on a single page. It was a game we played to teach me how to count, read, and think. At least that's what he said. But everything Mariolino said had a double meaning. I think that letter has a double meaning too, one that we'll only be able to understand when we've figured out the code."

"But you don't know the code."

"You told me."

"What are you talking about?"

"While Zaugo was busy spouting lies, I realized that he would probably be able to decipher that message, since he was a member of the Brotherhood. But I also realized that if he is the person you think he is, he certainly wouldn't tell us what it says."

"Okay, that makes sense. But you still haven't told me about the code."

"That's what I was thinking about right when we were about to leave, when you said that thing to Zaugo. The phrase written inside the ring."

"I was thinking about *Ex tenebris lux* too, thinking out loud. That's an old habit of mine. The Brotherhood of the Rose was hiding an important secret, but it's as if that phrase communicated their very real intentions to bring something to light that would otherwise remain cloaked in shadow. I was trying to figure out if it comes from some volume, from some prophet. Writings that talk about truths denied, hidden, that are then given back to—"

"It's much simpler than that, magister."

"Have you figured out what it refers to?"

Lorenzo came to a stop. This time he was the one staring.

"Of course," said the young man. "It *is* the code."

CHAPTER 49

"You shouldn't have accepted."

Simone Luzzatto was livid. An unknown benefactor had paid all of Lorenzo Scarpa's debts, allowing his rival to inherit his uncle's possessions. Simone had no more power over Scarpa. Venice had shown once again just how generous it could be with that crooked Christian, more generous than it would ever be with even the most forthright Jew.

"What are you saying?" Moses was trying to calm his son down. "My son, where does all this rage come from?"

"*He* was supposed to come up with that money!" Simone was beside himself. "He was supposed to work his fingers to the bone in order to pay that debt. Why would some complete stranger do him such a favor?"

"Simone, business is difficult, and we needed to recover a little credit. What's more, I can't understand the hatred you feel for that young man. I don't know what happened between you two, but it's time for you to become a man and give up these infantile behaviors. Our people—"

"I *hate* our people!" shouted Simone. "We'll never be equal to the others. We'll never have the same opportunities, the same women, the same lives! What is our good name worth if any old bastard can play around with us? Who would have helped *me* pay *my* debts?"

"You're not yourself, my son. But I forbid you to speak of our people this way," said Moses.

"All our people know how to do is suffer. You may be able to suffer any wrongdoing, but I'm not like you." Simone's face was a mask of anger and violence. "I don't want to step aside for others. I want to be treated as an equal. I want to be able to look anyone in the eye and not feel inferior!"

"You are *not* inferior to anyone. Is that really what you think of us? Do you truly believe we're somehow inferior to the Venetians?"

"That's what they think. And we put up with the way they think, because it's good for business. Because we don't want trouble. Because we want to keep living in our own little community, maintaining our traditions. Our goddamned traditions! There are people out there who would see us locked up in prison, who would let us out only during the daytime, and they'd do it all for *their* safety. Are you going to put up with that when it happens?"

"You must calm yourself, Simone. Everyone will hear you if you keep yelling like this, and then what am I going to say?"

"Let them hear! What difference does it make?"

"You need to understand that many merchants have lost their possessions in the war, and people like us, people who give out loans and earn money on the interest we charge cannot help but become the focus of their discontent. But we're a part of this city, and things will get better here for us as well."

"If someone humiliates me in the street, do you know what happens?" Simone put his face close to his father's. His eyes were filled with angry tears. "People laugh! They enjoy it! They say, 'Oh, look at that silly Jew.' But if I say so much as a word in return, I can be arrested, or beaten. And then what happens? Nothing, that's what happens! Because guards would never arrest a Venetian for having beaten a Jew. Unless he's a drunk or a vagabond. Don't you see? I'm the son of a respectable family, yet I've got the same rights as a homeless bum! If we weren't Jews, people would *respect* us for our wealth. Someone I might even have been able to ask for a seat on the Great Council of Venice. But we're Jews. We'll always be Jews."

"I didn't know you were this ashamed of your own people." There was no criticism in Moses's voice, merely deep, far-reaching pain. "I haven't been a very good father, if I haven't been able to instill in you the pride you should feel as a son of Abraham."

"I want to become Christian."

Simone was surprised that those words managed to slip out. Instinctively, he felt a need to take them back, to gather them up and hide them away in the place reserved for unspeakable things.

Moses drew a deep breath as he looked at his son.

"If you believe that will make you a better person, then you must do so."

Simone was thunderstruck. There was no anger in his father's eyes. Ever since he had resolved to change his faith, Simone had been convinced that Moses would do anything in his power to change his mind. To stop him. He didn't understand his father's reaction.

"I have your permission?"

"Did you think I would stop you?"

"I know that it means a great deal to you."

"If you truly desire to become Christian, that means I've been a terrible father. That is not your fault, but mine. Therefore, I have no right to stop you."

Moses's gaze had turned severe. His voice was unwavering.

"You don't even want to try?" said his son. "You'll just accept my decision without a fight?"

"Must I fight my own son?" Moses ruffled Simone's hair with his fingers. "You will always be my son, Simone, no matter where you decide to go, no matter what decisions you make. And even though it may cause you shame, I will always be your father. All I ask is that you never let yourself be guided by rage. Hatred never brings anything good with it."

Simone felt powerless. Suffocated. He had always been convinced that his father would become enraged and try to force him to bend to his will. Instead, his father's subdued reaction was so completely surprising that Simone almost felt robbed of the anger he needed, that helped him feel strong. He pulled away from his father's gentle hand and grabbed his cloak.

A few minutes later, Simone was out on the street, running through the snow-covered calli of Venice. Scarpa had humiliated him once again. He, Simone Luzzatto, would take care of this injustice once and for all.

***

Niccolò Zaugo walked along, wrapped in his cloak, slipping and sliding through calli and past porticoes. He wouldn't be able to complete his mission. He wouldn't be able to recover the book, because others had already found it. But if he warned the others that the German and the boy had the forbidden manuscript in their hands, he would in a certain sense achieve the same end. In a certain sense, he kept telling himself in an attempt to drive away his fears, he really *had* found the book.

They'd given him a name, a person he could talk to in order to report developments. It was an important person, someone who could be generous with him. All Zaugo could think about was getting out of Venice with his money, putting this whole terrifying affair behind him. Forget everything. Forget Mariolino, his betrayal, that voice that emerged from beneath a shadowed hood and seemed to bubble up straight out of Hell.

Fear and anxiety were more than enough to make him walk quickly. That's why he didn't realize he was being followed.

***

The Worm seemed to have crawled up out of a gutter drain, just like the first time he'd met Mathias Munster, standing behind Majid. But he was skilled at hiding among the other vagabonds begging in and around the Rialto. The monk had been clear with him. The Worm was not to let that printer, Zaugo, out of his sight for so much as a second.

CHAPTER 50

"This is incredible. It wasn't just a motto, a promise, a prerogative of the secret society your uncle joined!" Mathias was still stunned by the boy's discovery. "It wasn't a citation, nor a prayer, nor even a popular saying. I'll be damned if it wasn't a code members of the Brotherhood used in order to exchange information!"

The monk was so excited by this idea that it took him a moment to realize Lorenzo was breaking down the door in order to get into his uncle's shop. Now that the Doge had intervened and paid his debts with the Luzzattos, the shop was entirely his. But he didn't have the keys, which he'd lost during the last visit, when he'd had to run away across the rooftops like a common thief.

"The members of the Brotherhood didn't know one another, yet they all shared the same code," said Lorenzo, finally opening the door and inviting Mathias in.

"They had the ring," said Mathias. "A friend would bring in new members, inviting each to obtain a ring of his own. Maybe there's a goldsmith somewhere in Venice who is a member of the Brotherhood, who made all those rings. That doesn't matter to us, though." He took out the letter Mariolino had left for Lorenzo, spreading it open on the worktable. "What we need is to extract the message your uncle meant to leave for you from this text. We have to use the code."

"Exactly."

"So . . ."

"So . . . ?"

"So now you should tell me the code."

Lorenzo smiled and shrugged.

"You said that *Ex tenebris lux* was a code your uncle used," said Mathias, anxious to hear the rest of it.

"I'm sure of it. It's just that usually the codes he used were numbers."

"Numbers," said Mathias, disappointed. "Numbers." He thought about this for a while, then he sat up suddenly. "Of course! Numbers! They couldn't write the code down on their rings, clear for all to see. They had to hide it somehow. They couldn't run the risk that an outsider, stumbling across one of their rings by chance, could use it to figure out the code. Their numeric code is hidden in the phrase."

"Every letter corresponds to a number," said Lorenzo, his face lighting up again.

"That's right. All we have to do is figure out which alphabet your uncle was using."

"I think that—"

"Not the Latin alphabet. Otherwise, he would have had to have written *L-V-X*, using a *V* instead of a *U*."

"Maybe you should—"

"Just a moment, just a moment . . . It could be the German alphabet, which Gutenberg used to print the first Bible, the first book printed using movable type."

Lorenzo grabbed Mathias's arm and pulled him into the printing room.

"What an idiot! We had the answer right here beneath our noses!" said Mathias, staring at a print hanging on the wall. He'd seen it already, during his first visit to Mariolino's shop. The print reproduced the letters of the alphabet used in Venice, but included symbols recently imported from other countries as well. There were twenty-six characters in all.

Mathias took the print down and laid it on the table alongside Mariolino's letter.

> *È per te mio caro et amato nipote Lorenzo che lascio i miei pochi avvertimenti che anelavi insieme a ogni mio avere e ogni oggetto che ho posseduto.*
>
> *I nostri pochi libri potranno rivelarti ancora quali vie apre il fato al sapere che illumina le tenebre dell'ignoranza.*

"Let's get started," said Mathias, picking up a quill and dipping the tip in an inkwell. "Our code is *EX TENEBRIS LUX*, which has to be translated into numbers through the position that each letter occupies on this print of the alphabet. Those numbers will tell us which letters of your uncle's writing we should use to find our hidden message. So we'll start with the *E* and take it from there." The monk pointed an index finger at the alphabet on the wall. The letter *E* was in the fifth position. Then he examined Mariolino's message, counting through the first letters. The fifth letter was the *t* in *te*. The monk wrote a letter *t* in the margin beside the text. If their guesses were correct, they'd just decoded the first of the thirteen letters that would make up their hidden message.

They moved on to the second letter in the code, the *X*. *X* occupied the twenty-fourth position on the print. Starting from the *t* they'd identified in Mariolino's text, Mathias counted twenty-four positions farther, finding the *r* in *Lorenzo*, the second letter in their hidden message. He wrote this letter down in the margin as well. Then they moved on to the *T* in *TENEBRIS*, which was twentieth on the print. Following the same procedure, Mathias counted from the preceding letter to the twentieth position, stopping at the *o* in *pochi*.

They did the same for the rest of the letters until they'd revealed the hidden message, written down the margin before their disbelieving eyes.

"He wrote that our books could show me 'which paths destiny will open to knowledge, illuminating the shadows of ignorance,'" said Lorenzo, staring at the words.

"That means we're close to the manuscript." Mathias turned and began to look over the bookshelves. "Closer than anyone else."

He put Mariolino's letter down on the table. Lorenzo took one last look at the message they'd deciphered. *EX TENEBRIS LUX* became *TROVA VIRGILIO.*

Find Virgil.

Whoever had broken in and searched the books before they did hadn't known what to look for. Now they knew. The answer to the mystery was right there, sitting in plain view.

"Virgil's works. Here it is," said Lorenzo, taking a dusty volume down from the shelf. "A handwritten copy my uncle bought from a monk who had abandoned his monastery. It's full of unfinished fragments, but by the time my uncle discovered that, the monk was long gone."

But when Lorenzo opened the book, the cover of which bore the Latin poet's name, they found there was no sign of the pages the monk had copied poorly from the original and used to cheat Mariolino. Instead, they found words written in elegant, flowing letters: *De falso credita et ementita Constantini donatione declamatio*, the title of Lorenzo Valla's manuscript. Mathias ran his fingers over the letters, as if to convince himself that they'd truly found the forbidden book.

"Young man," said Mathias, translating the Latin, "I give you the *Discourse on the Forgery of the Alleged Donation of Constantine.*"

"So we really found it," said Lorenzo.

"It appears so."

"We already told Zaugo as much, and he may have already warned others," continued Lorenzo.

"Yes. Our little stage production may well turn against us," said Mathias, "now that we really do have the manuscript."

Outside, the sun was setting and the sky growing dark.

"You know," said Lorenzo. "I don't think it's such a brilliant idea to hang around here much longer. And maybe you should ask Foscarini to send us a few bodyguards."

"We need to think this through carefully. We have the book. Out of all the people who are looking for it, each for his own reasons, we're the ones who found it. And now we have it. Our friends are convinced that the news Zaugo will share with others, the news that we've found the book, is false. But before we reveal the fact that we accidentally told the truth, I want to take a closer look at this text. I want you to talk things over carefully with me. We found it together. Now, together we need to decide what to do with it."

Mathias tucked the book beneath his cloak. They left the shop, and Lorenzo closed the door as best he could, locking it with an old trunk padlock. When he turned around, the monk was watching him.

"There's something you should know," said Mathias.

"What?"

"Your uncle had a brilliant mind."

"I know," said Lorenzo. His eyes filled with tears. Seeing his reaction, the monk gripped his shoulder and gave it a squeeze.

"It's the truth," continued the monk. "And I think he would have been extremely proud of you, proud of the way you solved this puzzle."

Lorenzo smiled and nodded thanks.

The pair made their way down the twisted calli crossing the Rialto and leading back to Mathias's house, where they could light a roaring fire and drive the cold from their bones.

They didn't notice someone was watching them. The man was hidden in the shadows, right next to the shop, waiting patiently for the right moment to act.

CHAPTER 51

"Forgive me, but I couldn't wait to share this news with you. I knew it was important to tell you about it immediately." Zaugo had crossed first the Rialto and then San Marco, going all the way to the house of the man they had told him to contact. He was the only person Zaugo knew by name—Graziano Morosini, nephew of the elderly member of the Council of Ten. Zaugo would have to speak through this young aristocrat, bartering the information he possessed in exchange for his life.

"This isn't the way to go about it, you idiot, hanging around and whispering through a window in my building while there are still people outside walking around. You should have left me a letter. You're a printer. I assume you know how to read and write."

"I was anxious to share the news with you, my lord. That made it hard for me to think clearly."

Zaugo was kneeling alongside a narrow building foundation that flanked a rio. He had knocked on a small window at the young Morosini's palazzo and asked to speak with the nobleman, believing that would guarantee him more secrecy than knocking on the front door. He knew that he should have written a letter, but the Shadow Council wouldn't read it until the following day, and wouldn't know how important it was until then. Then he'd undoubtedly be taken to task for not having communicated the news more quickly. He was making a mistake no matter what he did, but at least this way he was moving as fast as possible.

Darkness was descending on Venice. Zaugo was wrapped in his cloak, his face covered with his hood. He was still kneeling alongside that little window, through which Morosini was busy insulting him. But as soon as the nobleman finished and let him share what he'd learned, Zaugo began to feel better. He told Morosini that the German and Mariolino Scarpa's nephew had the manuscript everyone was looking for. More importantly, he explained that they planned to print it in Scarpa's shop.

Graziano Morosini realized he had some important decisions to make. As soon as he sent the printer away, he tried to figure out what he should do. It wasn't possible to gather up the Shadow Council then, at least not right away. He would send out letters in keeping with procedure, so that the men who received them could in turn send out others, until the message finally reached everyone. None of the recipients knew all of the other members, and this thick, impenetrable network of letters guaranteed protection and anonymity for each of them. But the book had to be safeguarded immediately.

Morosini decided to turn to the only man he knew for certain was a member of the Shadow Council, or at least played an important role. He called his servants for his cloak and had them ready his gondola. The best way to avoid suspicion during an unexpected outing was to be completely natural, with an open gondola and a few lanterns lit on top.

The Worm watched Zaugo walk away from the Morosini palazzo. This time he didn't tail him. Instead, he followed the instructions Mathias had given him and stayed put, waiting to see the effect of the printer's visit.

A gondola left the palazzo. Morosini was on it, wrapped up in a cloak of elegant fabric. The Worm smiled to himself: that damned monk had been right. He waited for the gondola to pass by, then watched to see which direction it went. He knew that at this hour of the evening there would be fewer and fewer people out on the streets, and it would be easy to keep hidden, slipping through the shadows.

CHAPTER 52

"Don't think for a minute that our task stops here." Mathias was speaking fast as he and Lorenzo walked toward the house. He almost couldn't believe that they had the book. A book shrouded in myth and legend that he'd heard talk of throughout his studies. A book that now had the power to change a great many things, thanks to a new invention that would make it possible to print and distribute multiple copies. Such a publication could support and strengthen ideas that he and his companions were preparing to divulge publicly at the university in Wittenberg.

"What do you think we should do?" asked Lorenzo.

"There's still a demon loose in Venice, my dear boy. And there's still a plot under way to overthrow the Doge, a plot we need to sabotage."

"Would that book save the Doge? Is that what you think?"

"No doubt it would."

"Mathias." Lorenzo took the monk's arm and stopped him. "What would Loredan and Foscarini do with that book?"

"They'd hold it hostage, use it to put a leash and muzzle on the Shadow Council."

"So the book's destiny is to stay hidden."

"That's what the Doge would do with it, Lorenzo. The longer and more effectively the book is kept hidden, the tighter that leash would be. They simply want to put a stop to the conspiracy, to earn the time they need to broker a peace with the Turks and lift Venice up out of these dark days in such a way that the city doesn't come out indebted up to its neck to Borgia. But the book has power for the Doge only as long as it remains a threat, something to blackmail people with."

"And that's what you think is best too, isn't it?"

"I know who Borgia is," replied Mathias. His tone was severe. "And I certainly don't want to see Venice wind up in his hands."

"But that means the book will never be printed."

"I never said I wanted that. But we need to take into account a series of priorities. I don't want to force my thinking on you. I'm just trying to make you see just how urgent the situation is. The Senate will meet tomorrow, and if it weren't for the trickery that got us into this mess, Loredan would be defeated—because yesterday I could never have imagined that we would actually find the book. The Senate would have formally requested the Pope's intervention in the war, and Venice would be finished. Do you know why the book was brought here?"

"Because *my uncle* brought it here," replied Lorenzo.

"Because no printer in Rome would have been able to print it," said Mathias. "Because the Church controls everything in its domain. And that can't possibly be what your uncle wanted for Venice."

"You're constantly contradicting yourself. If you have to choose between two paths, you can't take both, magister."

"Of course not. But once you've learned to think like a politician, then you'll see that there are two different ways of looking at the issue. There's the short view, then there's the long view."

"You keep saying things to confuse me. That's what you always do when you don't want to explain yourself clearly."

"I'll explain everything as soon as we're sitting in front of a warm fire."

They kept walking. The monk was thinking, going over every move in their elaborate game. The truth was that even he didn't know what they should do next. The only thing he was sure of was that they had put themselves in certain danger the moment they set hands on that manuscript.

The man who had seen them leave the shop continued to follow them, hidden in the darkness.

The enormous ruby on his hand shot reddish glints on Agostino Grimani's gray beard as he stroked his chin, thinking. Zaugo had told Morosini that the German and the young Scarpa were heading to the bookshop. As fate would have it, an unknown benefactor had paid off all Scarpa's debts with the Jew. It was rumored that this benefactor was the Doge himself, who was nursing literary ambitions. Grimani knew better, and had known better even before the young Morosini showed up at his palazzo to tell him the latest news.

The first thing to do, he'd thought, was to send someone to keep an eye on that cursed bookshop. He'd ordered his two most trusted men to do so. They wrapped themselves up in their black cloaks, covering their faces with large hoods, and headed out into the night. They knew the monk and the young Scarpa: they'd already had the pair surrounded a few nights earlier, until Foscarini's men had shown up to free them.

The second thing he'd had to do was initiate the procedure to organize a meeting of the Shadow Council. The third thing he'd had to do was put the proposal they'd prepared for the Senate meeting tomorrow on hold. They had a majority, and could keep it for a few days longer, but before they did anything else, they had to be sure that there was no chance of that book coming to light. The webs Grimani was weaving needed balance and equilibrium, and a book that might start a war would tear them apart. His cousin, the cardinal, had been clear on this point: protect their plans and move forward. Losing a little time wouldn't compromise their plans. It would allow them to see things more clearly.

The Worm was waiting again, this time outside Grimani's palazzo. A bone-chilling January cold had rolled in and was making the man suffer. But he was used to that. Among his companions, every year there were a few who didn't live to see the spring. But the Worm would. Those who made it through the winter considered themselves safe until the next winter came around. And the money the German had promised him would allow him to keep many men safe for a good number of winters to come.

He'd watched as the hooded men left the palazzo. Private assassins. Those men gave him another kind of chill. He'd seen noblemen whispering names in the calli between canals, and he knew their world well enough to understand what task they were paying for. The Worm's only skill was knowing Venice, just like it had been for his friend. Except Spider had been crushed under the heavy wheels of this affair—and indeed like a spider, hardly anyone had noticed.

That thought drove the Worm to be even more careful than usual, because those two black-hooded men were familiar with darkness. If they discovered him, he'd share Spider's fate.

***

And still another man waited in the shadows. After watching Lorenzo Scarpa and the German leave the shop, Simone Luzzatto followed them for a while. Scarpa seemed very satisfied. He would have to pay for his arrogance, for the way things always went well for people like him.

Simone kept an eye on them as they disappeared into the maze of calli running through the old quarter. When he was sure he was alone and would have the shop to himself, Simone turned around. He went to the door. It was padlocked. He took out a tool he'd bought earlier from an ironsmith. When somebody claimed they'd lost the keys to a warehouse and needed to break the lock, a good ironsmith should accompany the client to the warehouse, at least to check and make sure he's telling the truth. But it hadn't been hard to find an unscrupulous ironsmith. All he had to do was spend a little money. Now Simone had the tool he needed, and breaking into Scarpa's shop was easy.

When he was inside, he closed the door behind himself.

He looked around and found an oil lamp.

Now he just needed a flame.

CHAPTER 53

The Worm followed the hooded men as they slipped in and out of dark, snowy calli. He had a great deal of information to give the German. Maybe the monk would be even more generous than expected.

The hooded men moved between stone and wood buildings, shuttered stalls, and closed markets. They passed storage sheds and pigsties, and the Worm covered his nose against the acrid smells of feces and slaughtered beasts.

Then the Worm saw them stop. They'd seen something in the little piazza they were about to enter. One of them signaled to the other. There was someone there, around the corner, but the Worm couldn't see who it was. He decided to work his way down another calle and try to see from there, to figure out what was going on.

He dashed through the snow like a gust of wind. When he reappeared, near the entrance to the piazza, flanked by a few shop fronts, the Worm could see a faint light moving around inside what appeared to be a bookshop.

Dead men floating in the canal, black-hooded assassins slipping through shadow, and a bookshop owner who worked at night, he thought. What devilish story was this? What paths had that monk taken to fight the demon everyone was talking about? He watched the hooded men approach the shop.

Inside Mariolino Scarpa's shop, surrounded by books, Simone looked around. The shop was rather small. It wouldn't have made a very good warehouse. But that wasn't the point.

"You had no right to be saved, you bastard." Simone's eyes reflected the reddish-orange light of the flame in the lamp he was holding. Hatred gathered in him again, clouding his vision, but his plans for revenge became clearer and clearer. Destroy everything. Let the flames swallow that which had been taken from him and given to Scarpa. His father never should have accepted that payment. If his people continued to believe that humility would help them avoid problems, then others would only continue to take advantage of the Jews.

Yes, a nice blazing bonfire would set things right.

A sudden gust of air, a rustling, the sound of cloaks brushing across the floor. Simone turned toward the door. Two black-hooded men stood there looking at him.

"Stay calm, boy. We just want to know where it is."

"Who are you?"

"Don't make things difficult for yourself. Talk," said the other, pulling a long blade from beneath his cloak. "Give us the book, and this will all be over."

"I'm . . . I'm not . . . I was here to . . ."

"You're not? You're not what?"

"I'm not Scarpa, the bookseller."

The two men stopped. Their hooded heads turned slightly, and they appeared to look at one another.

"What do you think?" said one to the other.

"I'll admit I remembered him taller. But darkness and shadows can play tricks."

"Then who are you?" asked the other man, turning back to Simone.

"I'm a Jew."

"A Jew? What are you doing here, Jew?"

"This shop is mine." Simone felt better now. This is what he wanted, more than anything else. Even his fear seemed to evaporate. "Everything in here is mine."

"You must be crazy."

Simone looked around. They wouldn't stop him. He raised a hand up to his neck and touched the necklace his mother had given him. The little stone dolphin. No matter what else happened tonight, he thought, this shop would burn.

Simone leapt in a single motion, knocking over the lantern on the floor.

"What in God's name are you doing?" cried one of the hooded men, throwing himself on Simone.

The flames spread quickly, enveloping a pile of books set against one wall and licking rolls of dry parchments. The other hooded man jumped toward the flames, trying to put them out with his cloak, but the fabric caught fire and immediately burned up.

Simone struggled, trying to break free, and knocked another pile of stuff over in the process. Then an expression of complete surprise appeared on his face. It wasn't so much pain, at first, or even fear. He merely felt a very cold sensation in his abdomen. He understood what had happened only when he saw the blood-soaked blade one of the hooded men was holding in one hand.

"This whole place is about to burn," said the other man, shaking off what was left of his smoldering cloak. "We have to leave. Maybe we can grab a few books. It might be one of these."

Simone stared him in the face. Now that his hood was off, the man looked normal. He was balding, and had a long mustache. A man like any other.

Simone clutched at his stomach with one hand, then fell to the ground.

The flames were growing stronger by the moment. A wooden beam groaned and fell from the ceiling. It was impossible to reach any other books.

"Forget it. Let's get out of here," said the man with the bloodied blade, cleaning it off and slipping it back beneath his cloak. Then he hesitated. He remembered coming to check out this shop one night, upon the orders of his lord. He'd looked inside, but he hadn't stopped for long, because he'd wanted a little wine and the company of a woman. He glanced at the boy. Another beam came down, cutting him off from that crazy Jew.

"Come on, Righetto," said the man with the mustache. "We can't do anything else. That idiot has destroyed everything. Soon they'll be here to put out the fire. We need to disappear. *Now*."

They peered out the door to make sure no one was there, then they ran swiftly away, following their earlier path.

But Righetto knew he wasn't done for the night. There were other things to take care of. First, the printer, Niccolò Zaugo. He was a problem, and now it was time to get rid of him. Righetto motioned for the other man to leave, since the flames had consumed his cloak and he could no longer cover his face. They couldn't risk someone connecting them with their lord. Righetto would have to take care of the printer on his own. When he was done, he could give himself a little reward, warming himself between the hot thighs of a woman.

Right before the cloaked men had entered the shop, the Worm had moved to where he could see more clearly. He saw the shop go up in flames, and now he saw two men leave, one without his cloak.

***

Inside the burning shop, Simone felt the hatred that had consumed him melting away. It was completely unexpected. In a single moment that seemed to stretch out to infinity, he finally felt himself free of bitterness, free from anger. He held on to the necklace his mother had given him, before she'd died so many years ago. He'd never felt this close to her since. Then he thought of his father and realized how much he loved the man, the way he had since he was a child and played in his father's arms.

A day in winter. His father was crafting a little wooden rocking horse. His mother was making dinner. She was incredibly beautiful. Moses was carving the little horse's mane. He was a skilled woodworker. Simone stared at his father's strong, solid hands, thinking, "That's what I'll be like when I'm older."

There was a fire in the fireplace. The house was warm. Dinner smelled delicious.

CHAPTER 54

"Just once, I'd like to see the Pope be just Christ's vicar, and not also of the Emperor." Mathias had lit a candle in order to read the manuscript he finally held in his own hands.

His voice was dense with emotion as he read passages out loud that he'd only heard secondhand from those few people who claimed to have read them. Those words were now on the paper before him, written out by hand.

> *"I can hardly wait to see this, especially if it comes to pass thanks to my manuscript. We no longer want to hear the cry of fearful voices: factions for the Church, factions against the Church, the Church fighting the Perugians or the Bolognese. It is not the Church, but the Pope, that fights Christians; the Church battles the spirits of evil in high places. Then shall the Pope be called the Holy Father in fact as well as in name, the Father of all, Father of the Church; he will not provoke war between Christians but shall put an end to wars started by others, with all the majesty of the papacy."*

Lorenzo was sitting in front of him.

"They are villains," continued Mathias, jumping from one page to the next and back again. *"They do not understand that Pope Sylvester should have worn the clothes of Aaron, who was supreme pontiff, rather than those of a pagan emperor."*

In his *Declamatio*, Mathias explained to Lorenzo, Valla demonstrated that the language used in the *Donation* was that of a relatively uneducated clergyman, one who didn't know Latin very well. For example, the document claimed that Constantine wanted to build a *civitas* in Byzantium, when the right term would have been something else, given that what were actually built were called *urbes*.

Valla's manuscript was a careful investigation of the terms used, the circumstances, the historical context, and the aims and objectives that proved Constantine's document to be a fake. Valla hadn't been the first to draw such a conclusion, Mathias said, but it was the first time this conclusion was supported by such careful, leaving no room for alternate interpretations.

Valla wrote the *Declamatio* under the protection of King Alfonso V of Aragon, who clashed with the Pope of his day, Eugene IV, but it was still a dangerous undertaking. Not only did the manuscript dismantle the document, demonstrating that it was forged hundreds of years after Constantine's time to justify a universal role for the Church above any individual nation and their rulers, but it also struck a blow to the heart of the Church by saying that the customs of current popes no longer had anything to do with the original inspiration of Christianity. It was an attack on what the Church was turning into and presented powerful arguments, which, as Mathias knew quite well, reflected the growing hostility to practices such as the sale of indulgences.

The document was rendered even more dangerous by the fact that Valla himself was a man of the cloth. And that according to his reasoning, true faith was threatened by all of this distortion by the Church.

"True Christianity does not need to defend itself with falsifications," Mathias read. *"Its light and truth are defense enough, without these impostors' fables that offend God, Jesus, and the Holy Spirit."* Mathias felt the strength of those words as he translated them out loud for Lorenzo from Valla's Latin text. *"But our most recent Popes, rich and drunk with pleasures, seem to seek nothing more than to become as wicked and foolish as the ancient Popes were saintly and wise."*

The monk would have kept reading the text, words that promised to renew a corrupt Church, now distant from its original mission, but his attention was drawn to something happening in the streets of Venice. He went over to the window.

It was the middle of the night, yet the calle outside the house the Doge had provided for him was crawling with people. Not far off, the dark night sky, scattered with light snowflakes, was glowing a dull red. Squinting to focus his tired eyes, Mathias managed to make out faint traces of smoke billowing up into the night.

"Something's happening," he said.

"What?" asked Lorenzo, emerging from his own thoughts as if from a great distance.

"It seems like . . ." Mathias opened the window and walked out onto the balcony. The smell in the air removed any doubt. "There's a fire. We have to go see what's happening."

The pair left the house immediately. What was at first nothing more than a vague foreboding took more substantial form the closer they got to the fire. It looked like it might be at Mariolino's shop.

Anxiety gripped Lorenzo. Someone was trying to destroy the book. Or prevent him from printing it. If that was the case, there was no need for further investigations into who had betrayed the Rose. It was clear that Zaugo had warned his superiors that he and Mathias had the book.

When they reached the shop, flames were reaching up into the sky. The fire had destroyed the entire structure, including the nearby warehouse. Venetians were racing back and forth between the burning building and the closest rio. The power of flames versus the inadequacy of man.

Mathias saw desperation in Lorenzo's eyes. The young man cried out and started running toward what was left of his life. The flames were taking his home, his shop, the printing press . . . forever.

The books.

Lorenzo grabbed a bucket, while others were busy breaking the supports holding up a rainwater cistern that would fall onto the fire.

Mathias watched the flames as he clutched the manuscript hidden beneath his cape. At least it was safe. But Lorenzo Scarpa's patrimony was lost. What obscene will had driven such horrible destruction?

"Maestro." The voice came from behind him. But when Mathias turned around, he could only see Venetians running left and right, desperate to throw water on the fire before the flames consumed the entire Rialto. Then he noticed a thin, filthy figure emerging from the shadows. It was the Worm. He stepped in close.

"What news do you have for me?" asked Mathias.

"The man you sent me to follow went straight to young Morosini's palazzo."

"Morosini?"

"Graziano, m'lord. Apparently, he has chosen a very dangerous path in order to take his uncle's place."

"Apparently, you're well-informed about Venetian politics."

"More than you know." The Worm brandished a fetid smile. "I haven't always been a vagabond. In my day, I served people who taught me the importance of holding information. And amid these calli, there's a great deal of information for the taking."

"Go on."

"Morosini didn't wait for long. As soon as the printer left, I saw the young nobleman's gondola head for the home of someone even more illustrious."

"Who?"

"Agostino Grimani, my lord. It appears that you're swimming around in the affairs of some very big fish."

"Big fish that you'll forget about immediately."

"The moment I receive my reward."

"Tell me about this fire."

"Two men left Grimani's palazzo, but I couldn't see their faces."

"They wore long black capes, didn't they?"

"Precisely. With very large hoods drawn down to hide their faces."

"Did they light this fire?"

"I'm not sure."

"Explain yourself."

"When they came here, it was as if they'd noticed something. I moved to another part of the piazza in order to see better, and I saw a light inside the shop, moving around."

"There was someone already inside?" That may have been the one thing Mathias wasn't expecting. Who could have been inside the shop?

"Yes, my lord. I think there was someone in there. And I think that whatever's left of that someone is still in there, because I kept watch until the two hooded men left. The flames were already spreading up into the building, and one of the two had lost his cloak, but I still wasn't able to see their faces. They ran away, in the direction they'd come from. But no one else came out of that shop."

The answer to the only question left unresolved would arrive soon enough. They need merely wait until the flames died down.

The rest of the Worm's information was not so much news as confirmation. Grimani was behind the conspiracy. He was undoubtedly a member of the Shadow Council. He was the one who tried to have them stopped, and who tried to get his hands on the book before they could. He was also Foscarini's sworn enemy. It was entirely possible Foscarini knew more about Grimani than he'd shared. There were still a few details to clear up. But the mosaic that Mathias been patiently working on ever since he'd arrived in Venice was coming together.

"You're the last piece," said Mathias, talking out loud to the demon, still hiding somewhere.

"My lord?" said the Worm.

"Never mind. You've done well. Come begging outside my house in a few days, and I'll give you what I owe you."

"Your humble servant, m'lord," said the Worm, slipping back into the shadows.

"You won't stay hidden much longer," whispered the monk to himself.

Pieces of the mosaic: The bodies floating in the canal were chewed up as if spit out of Hell. The brutal murders were not the work of two hooded assassins like the men the Worm had followed. The torture was the product of one person's will. A sick, contorted mind bent on demonstrating something.

But demonstrating what? Another missing piece.

Where are you?

Who are you?

CHAPTER 55

The first rays of dawn cast reddish-pink hues on the white snow. The still-smoking charcoal remains of Lorenzo Scarpa's life were sprinkled with miniscule ice crystals. Lorenzo was searching through the ruins for something to salvage. But there was nothing left. Nothing of what had existed until just a few days ago remained intact. His uncle was gone. Their house. The shop, the books, the printing press they were planning such grand projects around—all gone. Those projects had cost Mariolino his life. Even the movable-type characters had been melted and deformed in the heat. They were useless now. Caterina was gone too, and all his tender encounters with her.

Mathias was watching the crowd that had gathered around the smoking ruins. The people in the piazza were abuzz about the chain of events. Seems they'd finally put out the fire just before dawn, and the cistern had made all the difference, dealing the monstrous fire a mortal blow when it overturned onto the shop. Otherwise, the flames might have engulfed the entire neighborhood. A boy was explaining what had happened to a curious onlooker, a man craning his neck to examine the ruins.

"We ran back and forth all night long. I found the body this morning. It was burned to charcoal," said the boy, making no attempt whatsoever to hide his pride.

"Does anyone know who it was?" asked the man.

"No, not yet," said the boy.

Righetto thanked the boy for the information. He was tired. He'd completed every task asked of him, but the fire had been an unexpected development and risked compromising his lord's plans. That's why he was here now, evaluating the situation and gathering fresh news. He recognized Mathias Munster. He watched the monk as a distraught young man went over to him. Righetto thought it must be Scarpa. He'd been right; Scarpa was taller and more robust than the Jew he'd killed a few hours ago.

The two were talking. Righetto moved closer, careful to look elsewhere, as if he were just another curious bystander.

He saw three men walk out of the ruined shop. Two were carrying a makeshift stretcher on which they'd placed the charred body, which a woman covered with a veil. The other man who'd come out appeared to be an Arab. He exchanged greetings with the monk. They knew each other. Righetto moved even closer.

"You're still alive," said the Arab.

"Does that surprise you?" asked the monk.

"I don't know what you've gotten yourself into, but it seems like one of those classic stories in which the protagonist winds up dead."

"Have any idea who that was?" asked the monk, pointing to the body they'd pulled out of the smoking ruins.

"None whatsoever," the Arab replied. "Whoever it was, he was wearing a stone pendant around his neck. One of the only things left.

We'll see. Usually, when someone disappears from home, sooner or later his family comes asking about him, asking if there are any unidentified deaths."

The Arab said good-bye and was about to walk away, but Scarpa stopped him.

"Zaugo is behind all this," he said. "There's no doubt, is there?"

The Arab stopped short.

"What did you say?" he asked Scarpa.

"The boy is tired. He needs to rest, my friend," said the monk.

"That name, Mathias. Did the boy say 'Zaugo'?"

"Yes," said Scarpa.

"The printer, right?" asked the Arab.

"That's right," said the monk.

"Did you know him as well?" asked the Arab.

"What are you trying to say?" asked the monk. "Would you please tell us what's going on?"

"The night guards found him this morning," said the Arab.

The other two men stood immobile. "He was hanging by a rope, right outside his shop. They told me they found him that way before dawn. The first person who saw him began yelling, believing he was the demon. He said the body seemed to simply emerge from the fog. Just another of the many strange and terrible events that keep happening here in La Serenissima."

"He's dead?" asked Scarpa. When the Arab nodded, he still couldn't find it in himself to feel sorry for the man.

"Did you get a chance to look at the body?" asked the monk.

"If you have a question to ask," said the Arab, "ask it."

"Did he take his own life?"

"I don't believe so."

Righetto wondered what he'd done wrong. After all, he'd set the printer's body up so that it would look like a suicide.

"There was a wound on the head," explained the Arab. "It was hidden beneath the hair, but clear enough with a close examination. Since it's hard to imagine he hit his head after tightening the noose around his neck, I'd say he was struck before he was hung."

"So they killed him," said Scarpa.

"I believe so, yes."

Righetto managed to control a desire to do the same thing to this damned Arab who was dismantling the hours of careful effort he'd spent hoisting that worthless body up into the air. He moved away discreetly, still staring at the burned-out ruin of the shop. He hoped the doctor's opinion wouldn't make a difference.

"If I were a guard, I'd have you questioned," said the Arab. "Either you bring bad luck, and therefore one would do well to stay away from you, or you know more about this trail of death than anyone else in Venice."

"Fortunately," replied the monk, "you're not a guard."

The Arab took leave of them and followed the two men carrying away the body of the unknown victim. Righetto moved away, to the edge of the small piazza.

"Oh, Lorenzo," said Mathias. He was obviously shaken but full of concern for his young friend. "I'm enormously sorry for all of this. I shouldn't have gotten you mixed up in this affair. This is all my fault. I hope I can find a way to pay you back once the Doge—"

"What are we going to do now?" asked Lorenzo. He was hardly listening to his friend. "If the Senate meets today and we no longer have a printing press, how will our 'play' end?"

"I wasn't thinking about that. I . . ."

"They've taken away everything I had. At this point, I'll do anything I can to make sure they don't win. You can count on it."

Lorenzo suddenly took Mathias's arm and began talking so loud that everyone in the piazza could hear.

"This is going to slow down our plans to print that book, my dear friend. Because now, out of the four printing presses we could rely on, only three are left intact." Their play, Lorenzo thought, needed an immediate plot twist.

A little group of people came over to them. They were all small printers who had known his uncle.

"This is a disgrace, Lorenzo," said one. "I'm terribly sorry for your loss."

"Thank you, my friend," replied the young man. "It's truly a shame that this terrible accident should happen now, just as I regained possession of my uncle's property. Especially now that we have such an important book to print. Fortunately, we haven't lost anything irreplaceable in the fire."

"You seem to be in good spirits," said another.

"When you have so much to do, it's always a good idea to stay optimistic. Don't you agree, my friends?"

It seemed like all of Venice was coming to the piazza to see what had happened during the night. The fire at the bookshop was all anyone was talking about, because the Doge himself had intervened to pay the former owner's debts. Righetto was preparing to leave when the arrival of someone else stopped him. The servants of aristocratic families all knew one another. Often they'd fought together as soldiers or mercenaries before winding up in the service of this or that nobleman. Righetto recognized Cesare at once. In fact, he'd fought the man just a few nights earlier, but his enemy hadn't known it was him, because Righetto had kept his face well hidden beneath his black hood when he and the other assassins attacked the German monk and his errand boy.

Cesare was the captain of Foscarini's personal guards, and he was accompanied by one of Foscarini's house servants, Michelino. They were both headed for Mathias. Righetto hid himself in the crowd and moved closer again, trying to figure out what was afoot. They spoke briefly, then the monk and young bookseller left, following Foscarini's men. Righetto thought he'd better find out what they were up to, before reporting back to his lord.

Foscarini was waiting in his gondola, moored in a nearby rio.

On their way to Foscarini's gondola, Lorenzo heard someone whisper his name. He turned around. A girl was standing just a few steps away. "I don't know if you remember me," she said. But Lorenzo remembered perfectly. She was a novitiate, a friend of Caterina's.

Finding Lorenzo no longer by his side, Mathias turned around to look for him. Their eyes met, and Lorenzo waved for him to go on, but Mathias wasn't sure if he should. Given the way things were developing, the monk was afraid for the young man. But it appeared that the young man had other issues to attend to for the moment, things Mathias couldn't help him with. He moved his lips, mouthing the words "Be careful." Lorenzo understood and nodded.

"I'm sorry, magister, but we have to hurry," said Michelino.

Righetto watched while the little group separated. The monk was leaving with Foscarini's men; Scarpa was with a girl who looked like a nun. But who was she?

CHAPTER 56

"Grimani is the hand behind the hooded men who attacked us the other night," said Mathias. He was seated facing Giacomo Foscarini, inside the felze of the nobleman's gondola. Cesare and Michelino were outside the cabin, keeping watch. "Graziano Morosini is involved, too. Zaugo went to visit Morosini right after we told him we had the book."

"Do you think Grimani is a member of the Shadow Council?" asked Giacomo.

"Let's just say he'd make a perfect candidate."

"So they want the lion's head . . . the end of the Republic. Grimani's cousin is the link to Borgia. If their proposal passes in the Senate tonight, everything will be over."

"It won't pass," said Mathias.

"What makes you so sure it won't?"

"I believe that the little play you and Loredan set in motion is beginning to bear fruit. If they're convinced that we have the manuscript, they'll think long and hard before presenting their proposal to the Senate for a vote. Grimani will want to bide his time."

"We'll know soon enough. The meeting starts in a few hours."

Realizing that Giacomo seemed to have other things to say, Mathias waited for his friend to continue.

"That book, Mathias," he said finally. "Where do you think it might be?"

"Why are you asking me?"

"Because we're bluffing. We don't have a thing. Even if they decide not to present the proposal today, sooner or later the truth will out. And then we won't have any more cards to play."

"What would you do with the book, Giacomo?"

"What kind of question is that? I'd save Venice! That book would be the best deterrent we could ever hope for in order to hold off the servants of Alexander the Sixth. With a threat like that hanging over the Pope's head, we could guarantee Venice's freedom."

"So you would hide it. Hide it and use it as a deterrent."

"What would *you* do with it? Would you really print the thing? Do you really think the Brotherhood of the Rose would have brought honor and glory to La Serenissima with its plan? After an offense like that, Borgia would knock on our door with an army larger than the one that conquered Jerusalem. Right now, while the war with the Turks has driven us to our knees. The end result would be the same. The Pope would have the lion on a leash."

"That book is about more than just Venice."

"But I'm a Venetian, Mathias. What would you have me do, sacrifice my Republic?"

"I'd have preferred to see you a little more conflicted about it."

"I've no more room for conflict. Not right now. What do you think would happen if Borgia got his hands on our city?"

"I think he would take away your lands and ducats, given how hostile you and Loredan are to him. Most people aren't familiar with what you're up to. They see the Doge and the patriarch getting along just fine. But the Pope knows about your intrigues. You and your friends would be finished the day Borgia reached Venice. It's not your city you want to save, Giacomo. You want to save your wealth and yourself."

"I'm sorry to hear you say that. You're like a brother to me." A shadow crossed Giacomo's face, as if Mathias's words had really hurt. "Once Venice has fallen, who will stop Borgia? Florence? Bologna? Genoa? Borgia's dominion will be unlimited. And if I know you at all, I know that's not something you want. Otherwise, you wouldn't be in such a rush to head for Wittenberg."

"What is Venice to you, Giacomo?"

"It is a grand idea of freedom, magister. It's a place where the world meets, because we're the door to the Orient or to the West, depending on which direction you're coming from. Depending on where you want to go. No matter which, you have to pass through Venice in order to get there."

"Spoken like a true politician," said Mathias.

"If I've earned your trust at all, magister, then tell me now where that book is." Giacomo stared hard at his friend.

"You can tell the Doge we've found it."

"What are you saying?" Foscarini looked upset. "I don't understand why . . . Have you really found the book?"

"We found it. The young Scarpa and I found it together. He deserves to be treated well for his efforts. Especially now, as I'm sure you've heard, that your little plan to stall the Senate has cost the boy his house, his shop, and every possession he owned."

"Everything we'd just returned to him, after paying off his debts."

"That's not especially *noble* of you, Giacomo."

"Don't be ridiculous. Of course the young man will have a generous reward, as I've already promised you. But the book . . . Where is it right now?"

"In a safe place."

"You don't trust me?"

"If I didn't trust you, I wouldn't have told you about it."

"Don't you think the time has come to hand it over to the Doge? Am I wrong or didn't we make a deal?"

"Everything in due time, Giacomo. Loredan will have the book. But there's still something else I want to find out."

"What?"

"The demon."

"If we stop the Shadow Council, we stop the demon too."

"I'm not so sure. The demon will keep hunting the book, no matter where it is. And sooner or later, he'll get his hands on it."

"You're crazy," said Giacomo. "Do you really believe the Devil is crawling around in the calli of Venice?"

"No, but I believe that you have the power to send a few of your men to protect me while I see my play through to its conclusion, the play that you and Loredan directed."

Giacomo sighed deeply. Mathias knew he'd get what he wanted.

"Tell me what you need, you crazy fool. And try not to get yourself killed."

Step by step, the monk explained his plans to Foscarini.

***

"We will not be presenting our proposal today." Grimani had called a meeting of the Shadow Council to inform the others about latest developments. The room was dark. As always, the room was dark, except for a single candle at the center. "We have to locate that manuscript and do away with it once and for all."

"That's something you should have done some time ago." That voice hung over the entire group. "But you've been too busy failing at it to realize that the monk was snatching the book right out from under your noses."

"You're being ungenerous." A young voice spoke up in Grimani's defense. "Nobody here has—"

"Do you think burning that shop was a good idea?" said the voice they all feared more than any other.

"It was an accident," said Grimani. "Someone else was already in the shop.

"Someone else was there, and you don't know who it was. You know that the monk found the book, but you don't know where the monk is. Is there anything you actually *do* know?" The voice breathed a heavy sigh. "I'll no longer put up with your half measures."

Those last words sounded like a threat to them all. Each of them knew what it meant. The demon would crawl back up out of whatever hellhole that voice had kept it hiding in.

***

Lorenzo was running so hard he thought his lungs would burst. He bumped into other people, tripped, fell, and got up again. His throat was on fire. But he couldn't stop running.

The girl he'd met, the novitiate, had told him Caterina was about to leave. He didn't even stop to ask the girl whether Caterina had sent her just to tell him, or to say good-bye one last time. He didn't ask a single question. He simply started running toward the piers in San Marco, from which he knew Caterina would depart. He crossed the Rialto Bridge, running past kids playing at throwing stones into the water. He ran between stone palazzi and down narrow calli. He ran in front of the basilica, past the Doge's palazzo, beneath the lion. He ran all the way to the piers, but he could see the boat preparing to pull away from its mooring.

"Caterina!" he cried with what little breath he had left. There was no one else around. No family members had come to see her off. It was a sudden, almost clandestine departure. When he drew closer to the boat, Lorenzo saw that she was wearing a veil to cover her hair. There were two oarsmen with her, and the mother superior. When she saw

Lorenzo, she gave the oarsmen orders to bring the boat back to shore. If she hadn't, Lorenzo would have thrown himself into the icy waters of the lagoon. Caterina stepped to the side of the boat closest to the pier, taking Lorenzo's hands in her own. She wiped tears off her face with the sleeve of her dress.

"Let me go, I'm begging you," she said.

"How can I?"

"I'll always be with you, Lorenzo. Just close your eyes and you'll find me. But you promised me you would live your life."

"And you promised me that you would find me again."

They embraced, caught in a dangerous balance, Lorenzo on land and Caterina still in the boat. Then the mother superior motioned to the oarsmen, and the boat pulled away again.

Lorenzo didn't move. He watched each single oar stroke, each movement that took Caterina farther away. The faces were getting smaller, but he kept his eyes on Caterina as long as he could, until the boat was nothing more than a tiny black stain on the horizon, headed far beyond the Venetian lagoon.

Lorenzo sat down on the pier. With the warm afternoon sun on his face, he wept in desperation. He could still hear Caterina's voice in his head.

You'll have those moments forever.

That's the way it would be.

Forever.

CHAPTER 57

Angelica was seated at the table in her inn, holding a letter that Mathias had sent.

In just a few lines, he explained that he had wanted to tell her this in person, but it would be too dangerous for her if they were to meet. The affair he was caught up in would be over soon, and then they could leave Venice together.

Angelica folded the letter back up and held it close. She got up from the table and gave a few last instructions to her staff. Then she retired to her room. Outside the window, the evening was growing dark. The weak January sun was quick to abandon the heavens above La Serenissima. Angelica watched the snow falling. It was a white mantle draped over the ground now, but it would turn to mud up and down the calli.

She didn't see the dark, tormented figure standing motionless beneath an overhang.

A large hood drooped down over his well-hidden face, also covered with a white mask. An unnatural grimace. A grotesque, misshapen nose. Dark holes where eyes should be.

***

Mathias stopped at a fountain and sat down on the stone rim. Weak moonlight filtered through the thick blanket of fog and snow covering the city, barely illuminating the spot where he'd stopped at the center of the little piazza. The monk looked like a statue erected alongside the fountain. He took Valla's manuscript out from beneath his cloak, careful to keep the snowflakes off. He kept looking around, trying to hear every sound around him, though he pretended to be concentrating fully on what he was holding. He began reading a few passages.

Even exposed as he was, even as he waited to meet the truth face-to-face, Mathias couldn't help but grow excited by the pages he held in his hands.

Valla's words had the potential to rupture centuries of tradition far beyond Venice, indeed, throughout Europe.

Soon he would have to satisfy Giacomo's requests. He would have to tell Lorenzo about the meeting. But where was the boy now? Didn't he understand that wandering around Venice was dangerous? It was even more dangerous than sitting here, motionless in the middle of the night, waiting for a bloodthirsty beast to find him. It was the biggest risk he could take, but he didn't see any other way. He needed to see the last face the Shadow Council would produce—the darkest, most terrible visage of all—in order to find the mosaic piece that had eluded him.

He couldn't hear a thing moving around him. Not even the slow slip-sliding across snow of two men who had come within a few yards of where he sat.

They looked at the monk, immobile in that small pool of moonlight. In the midst of that oppressive silence, they could even hear him breathing.

Hiding in the shadows near Mathias, they stood absolutely still, sharp daggers in their hands, waiting to leap.

The monk kept reading.

***

The monk is in grave danger, my lady.

Angelica had left the inn, frightened by the words in the anonymous message.

Around the corner, there was the swift movement of a predator. A black cloak. A face as white as death. Horrible. The enormous nose. The empty eyes. Fear constricted her chest so that she couldn't make a sound, much less breathe.

The demon had taken her.

CHAPTER 58

Clear peals from the Marangona echoed across Venice. Lorenzo could hear the bell all the way out on the pier, where Lorenzo was still sitting. He'd been there for hours and was now covered with a thin layer of snow.

He'd been watching the tiny snowflakes fall in the lagoon water as if they were his memories of his brief time together with Caterina, melting away one by one. He'd done nothing else since the boat carrying Caterina away from him had disappeared over the horizon.

The pealing bell shattered his reverie. Turning around, he caught a weak ray of sunlight as it struck a lion, painting the symbol of Venice a deep red. For days the leaden, snow-swollen sky hadn't allowed so much as a single ray of sun through. This ray faded, and he knew it was time to return to the nothingness for which he was destined. All around him, the oppression of that white monotony, turning dirty and gray wherever people walked, seemed to mirror his fate.

Darkness came quickly, almost as if it were bent on attacking him, shutting him down. Lorenzo ran his hands through his hair, wet with snow and crusted with tiny ice crystals. His legs hurt, and his back felt like it was made of twisted metal. It was as if he'd spent all that time somewhere else, far away, leaving nothing more than his own body, an empty shell devoid of a soul, sitting on the pier in San Marco.

Mathias. His mind turned to the monk, pushing aside everything else. They'd talked about a plan that afternoon, just before they split up. They'd talked for just a few minutes. They'd decided what to do. It was dangerous, but Mathias was his friend, and his friend needed him. He had to force himself to move. Their play wasn't over yet.

Lorenzo tried to remember the details of what he was supposed to do. It occurred to him that he'd disappeared for half a day without telling anybody where he was or what he was up to. He would have to face the narrow calli alone in order to get where he needed to go. The same narrow calli the assassins used.

He felt life coursing through his frozen veins again, now that he felt danger. He turned toward the piazza. He would have to run. The Marangona rang for a third time, peals filling the air. He still had an important role to play in this story, before it was all over.

Lorenzo ran across the piazza, passing through what seemed like a ghost of the Venice he knew. Weak, sickly light reflected in the fog on the pale marble of its palazzi. The water of the lagoon, black and impenetrable.

There was no point in blaming himself for the hours he'd spent wandering through a world that no longer existed. Mathias would carry out his crazy plan with or without him. But he would try to get there in time. He simply had to run until he reached his friend—the only one he had left.

Suddenly, Lorenzo's instincts told him to stop. He wasn't far from his destination now. Everything seemed frozen in snow and ice. But there was a sound, almost imperceptible, of something slipping along the water.

Lorenzo was near a small wooden bridge. If the sound was a boat, then it was coming from the Rialto. If he kept running alongside the waterway, whoever was on the boat would see him. If it was the night guards, they'd stop him. He couldn't leave Mathias alone as bait for the demon.

So he hid, flattening himself on top of the bridge, in the hopes that whoever was producing those soft lapping sounds would take another route. All he could do was remain still.

A boat was coming down the rio, headed straight for him. He would have to wait until it arrived, then slide down the bridge as the boat passed underneath, so that he would be on the other side once it passed. If it was the night guards, then the smallest mistake could be enough to get him into serious trouble.

And if it wasn't the night guards, a mistake could cost him his life.

He stuck his head out just far enough to see how far away the boat was. It was a gondola, entirely black. The wood squeaked in the water. It seemed quite old, with a large cabin, the windows of which were entirely covered with black cloth. It looked like a funereal gondola, only a run-down and decrepit one. A phantasm floating through icy nothingness.

Lorenzo pulled his head back, but the vision was so fantastical that he couldn't help but look at it again. An enormous figure was busy working the oar. He was gigantic, covered with a long black cloak that ran all the way down to his feet. Something white and deformed was sticking out from beneath his hood.

If Death were a person, this is what he would look like, he thought. Terror clutched the young man's chest and overpowered his senses.

The demon.

So it was true. Hell had freed one of its most terrifying creatures here, among the calli of Venice. And that was his ferryboat.

The image of his uncle's body torn apart loomed large in Lorenzo's mind as the black gondola drew closer, announcing its proximity with squeaking sounds and the musty smell of rotting wood. He saw the first ripples on the water and waited a few more moments. The prow of the gondola appeared on the other side of the bridge. If he reached out his hand, he could touch it, just to see if it was real, or merely a specter in his mind.

Lorenzo slid along the stone, staying hidden. He caught a glimpse of the stern on the other side of the bridge. And the languid black cloak of the thing guiding it, though only for a moment. Lorenzo closed his eyes, praying with all his strength for God to save him, even as he realized he couldn't expect a God he had largely ignored to intercede on his behalf. He even tried to stop his own heart from beating in order to be invisible. The demon was passing beneath the bridge. At that moment, Lorenzo smelled a strong scent of spices. The water slowly returned to motionlessness. He looked out and saw the black gondola continuing down the rio.

Lorenzo waited until it disappeared completely from view, then he started running again.

He had to find Mathias and tell him everything.

But what if he was too late.

CHAPTER 59

Pieces of the mosaic: A shadowy silhouette standing in the foreground, a shadow Mathias could not make out. Conflict between great powers in the background. The Empire, the Church. The swollen belly of the Church grew fatter as the Empire's belly boiled with controversy. Men who possessed the power of the Word might well tip the balance.

These men could manage that knowledge, control it. They could disseminate it, render it immune to the power of others. Free it.

They could do it by printing. No more hands crippled by cold, tracing lines of ink, sewing letters and words together into books destined only for the few. With printing, the Word would reach the people. Multiplied. Liberated.

Wycliffe. Hus. Valla.

A book. Pages testifying to the solid faith of a believer who harbored contempt for powers who abuse that faith, who control it. Heresy. Reform. That book was capable of anything.

A passage from Psalm 80 ran through Mathias's head:

Restore us, God Almighty; make your face shine on us, that we
may be saved. You transplanted a vine from Egypt; you drove

out the nations and planted it. You cleared the ground for it, and it took root and filled the land. The mountains were covered with its shade, the mighty cedars with its branches. Its branches reached as far as the Sea, its shoots as far as the River. Why have you broken down its walls so that all who pass by pick its grapes? Boars from the forest ravage it, and insects from the fields feed on it. Return to us, God Almighty!

The boars were ravaging the vines of the Lord. A rose was blooming in the belly of the Empire. War was in the air. Printing the book in Venice would mean advancing the front to La Serenissima. Venice, with the book a casus belli, a reason to go to war.

Rome. The Colonna family wanted to make things difficult for the Borgias. The book was sent to Venice. There were agreements made in secret. A secret group of printers united around a rose. They would have printed it. The book would have sown chaos, but the Shadow Council, puppeteers of Venice, had learned of the plan.

Mathias was peering into shadow. He could see faces there. Agostino Grimani, surrounded by his men. Another face, still cloaked in darkness. The demon.

Majid's voice.

If you want to catch him, try to understand his mind, the way he thinks.

The hunt for the book. Deaths. The Spider. The Colonnas' messenger. Scarpa. Giuntino. Zaugo. The bookshop in flames and an unnamed victim. Fear. The people of Venice, terrorized by those deaths, ready to deliver themselves into the hands of those who promise to save them. Papists riding the wave of terror. Feeding it. Spreading it. A conspiracy to overthrow Loredan. A game of lands and titles. And money. Lots of money. That game had the power to shake the marble palazzi.

Giacomo's voice.

Do you really think the Brotherhood of the Rose would have brought honor and glory to La Serenissima with its plan? After an offense like that, Borgia would knock on our door with an army larger than the one that conquered Jerusalem.

The book had to be stopped. The balance had to be protected. The book could become a weapon for blackmail, for Foscarini or for Grimani. But it shouldn't be opened.

The rose blooming in the belly of the Empire wanted to turn Venice into the theater for this battle.

The last face in the conspiracy that remained shrouded in darkness.

Where are you? Who is hiding you?

Pieces of the mosaic: A ferocious beast. One that causes pain. A harbinger of death.

Grimani. The papists. The Shadows. Rome.

Who is involved?

My Lord, show your servant where to look.

CHAPTER 60

Lorenzo came dashing into the little piazza where he knew Mathias would stop. They'd talked the plan through in just a few minutes, while they were still standing outside the smoldering remains of his bookshop. But there was an aspect of the situation that he couldn't have known.

Men were waiting in ambush. Near the monk.

He felt a hand on his shoulder.

Lorenzo slipped and slammed into a wall. He saw someone in front of him, an armed man. Then he felt a sharp pain in his head and fell to the ground. Out of the corner of his eye, he saw a man in the center of the piazza, walking over to him.

He heard voices, but they seemed very far away.

He recognized Mathias's voice.

"Stop. It's the boy."

"What boy?" asked the man who'd struck Lorenzo.

"Scarpa," replied Mathias.

The monk's voice. Lorenzo fainted.

***

Angelica opened her eyes, but she was surrounded by darkness. She could feel herself rocking, hear the lapping of water. Her hands were bound and tied. A rag was stuffed in her mouth. She remembered hearing a noise. A giant shadow with the white face of death fell on her. Then, nothing.

She tried to free herself, but the ropes tied all around her body only became tighter.

She was a prisoner.

Rumors about those brutal murders had reached her inn. Rumors of disfigured corpses floating in the Canal Grande. She breathed in through her nose. There was the smell of rotten wood mixed with another, more penetrating smell. Oriental spices . . . Pepper, perhaps. This, then, was what Hell smelled like.

Anyone watching could have seen the black gondola easing its way through the maze of small internal canals. But no one was watching. The imposing demon moved the oar ever so slightly. Beneath the formless hood, a pale, frozen face. Dark, lifeless cavities where the eyes should be. An obscene, horrible vision.

The door was not far.

The black gondola came to a stop before a small wooden door, beneath a bridge, that opened directly onto the water. A hidden entrance, shielded from anyone who didn't already know it was there. The demon took out a key and opened a heavy padlock. He had to struggle with it, because the door reached below the waterline, and he had to move a great deal of water to get it open.

There was a large pulley system set up just inside the entrance. The demon grabbed the pulley and began turning it. A mechanism opened the rest of the wooden door. The demon gripped the oar again and guided the gondola inside an underground gallery. Once inside, he turned the pulley to close the door. It was pitch-black inside, but the gondola kept sliding slowly, through the darkness.

He reached a wider, open space. A mooring. The strong odor of spice was everywhere. The demon tied up the gondola, got out, and lit a candle. Weak light. An enormous room, the walls of which were barely visible.

He returned to the gondola to fetch his prey.

In the feeble light of a votive candle, Angelica saw large knives hanging on the wall, as if in a butcher's shop. And a large wooden chair. It had heavy leather straps attached to the arms and legs. She screamed instinctively, but the rag in her mouth muffled her voice. The room smelled of rot and death.

She was lying on the ground. On cold, slippery mud. The thin candle flame projected an obscene interplay of shadows across the demon's deformed face. The rag made it hard enough to breath; now spasms of terror made it feel like she was suffocating. She tried to figure out where she was. Judging from the time she'd spent in the gondola, it couldn't be that far from her inn. Then she heard the voice, almost a raspy whine.

"You're beautiful . . . So beautiful . . ."

***

Marigo was Loredan's most trusted servant, the one the Doge had relied on to fetch Mathias from Padua. He'd brought a second man along, Antonio, who was also in service to Loredan. Evidently, word of the favor Mathias had asked Giacomo to perform had reached the Doge, who had sent two men to protect the monk. When Lorenzo managed to open his eyes again, he saw their faces looming over him.

"How do you feel?" asked Mathias.

"I was better before."

"Where have you been?"

Lorenzo didn't answer. He didn't know what to say. The two men helped him pull himself to his feet.

"I think I struck you quite a blow," said Marigo.

"I think so too," said Lorenzo.

Mathias inspected his head. The young man was bleeding.

"We have to go home. Your skull is as hard as a rock, but we still need to wash this wound with boiled water."

"We have to stay here," said Lorenzo. "We have to wait for the demon . . . I . . ." Suddenly, the black gondola he'd seen rushed to the forefront of his mind. But as soon as he remembered it, he felt another sharp pain in his head, which kept him from speaking sensibly about the eerie scene he had witnessed.

Marigo and Antonio carried the young man to Mathias's temporary Venetian home. They took him upstairs, the monk leading the way. At the bedroom door, a dagger was stuck in the wood, holding up a letter.

CHAPTER 61

No one could remember another time when the Senate had gathered after sunset. But Venice was in great difficulty, and every family faction had its own reasons to participate in a meeting that might resolve a number of different problems for a great many senators. The majority seemed ready to vote in favor of the proposal that the Corner family would read out loud before the assembly, even though each senator was already fully familiar with it. It committed La Serenissima to sending ambassadors to Rome to request the Pope's intervention in the war with the Turks. A Christian alliance to combat the Muslim enemy, just as had happened in the conquest of Jerusalem. The Pope would carry the cross, and Venice would recover the cities it had lost to the Sultan.

This was enough for the merchants, who were reeling from the war's effects on their commerce. The way Alvise Marin had fallen from wealth and grace was all anyone was talking about. But the circle of noblemen in Antonio Grimani's faction wanted even more.

The content of the pact the Pope would grant the Doge, who was its de facto applicant, was so completely binding for the lord of La Serenissima that it would turn Loredan into an empty figurehead. It would allow Borgia to maneuver the mechanisms of power necessary to make Grimani a shadow Doge, who could rule Venice as a feudal territory of Rome. The arrival of an Inquisition tribunal would remove any difficult adversaries and establish a new order. Accusations of heresy were easy to come by, and required no additional proof. Once the war with the Turks was over, any new enemies could be sent directly to their deaths.

Everything had seemed perfect to Grimani. But the surfacing of Valla's manuscript had forced him to put his plans on hold. He'd requested to postpone the assembly in order to inform his allies and decide their next move. Corner had another proposal ready to present, a less important issue that had to do with creating a ruling authority to oversee management of the lagoon waters. This was the perfect justification for the requested assembly, even though everyone knew full well it was a stopgap solution, used because something had interfered with the papists' plans.

The youngest members were the first to reach Palazzo Ducale. They were all talking about the fire at the bookshop. Those who had seen the remains of the burned-out structure were astounded that the flames hadn't consumed the entire neighborhood. They argued for public services that could protect the heart of La Serenissima in the event of another fire. Some of them were quite excited about what everyone was calling the "nocturnal assembly" and by the extraordinary events unfolding around them. Even Caterina Corner had asked to attend, though she had no vote to cast.

Whispers ran along the benches, and the younger members behaved more rambunctiously than usual. People were convinced that something big was afoot, because there was still no sign of the most powerful aristocrats in the Republic.

***

Lorenzo opened his eyes again and saw Mathias. The monk was sitting in front of the fire, holding what looked like a letter in one hand. His gaze was lost, unfocused, extending far beyond the flames he was staring at. The boy looked around. There was no sign of the two men who had attacked him. He touched his head and felt bandages.

"Is it serious?" he asked the monk.

"You'll heal quickly. The bandages are just a precaution," said Mathias. His voice was flat, devoid of emotion. Something had happened.

"Mathias . . ."

"They've kidnapped someone who is very important to me. They want the book in exchange for her and her safety." He turned and handed Lorenzo the letter. There were only a few words written on it, but their meaning was clear.

> *A sinner hangs poised upon the brink of Hell*
> *But the demon may take pity on her soul*
> *If you show you're willing to repent*
> *In the church at San Marco before the twelfth bell.*

"A *sinner*." Mathias seemed ready to give up. "I've involved too many people in this affair. Too many people who didn't ask to get involved and should have stayed clear of it. Including you."

"It's a little late to back out now. Who is this person?"

"A woman."

"A woman? Don't you think maybe you should tell me a little more about her?"

"The woman I love," said Mathias. "The woman I was planning to take with me when I leave Venice."

"You should have mentioned her."

"It's not that simple. But everything is much clearer now." Mathias's eyes had returned to the fireplace.

"Clearer?" asked Lorenzo.

"By taking Angelica, the demon has revealed his identity."

"You know who he is?"

"Now I do, but it doesn't matter anymore. I can't let him hurt Angelica. I'll bring him the manuscript, and I'll leave this cursed city for good."

"You're going to give up? What about me? That book is mine too, remember?"

"We have promised it to too many people, Lorenzo. Please, I beg of you, you have to understand. That woman is more important to me than anything else."

"When you talked about Valla's work, it seemed like that was important to you too. You said it had the power to change things. To change the Church."

"What do you care about changing the Church?"

"I've lost the woman I love to your Church . . . I have a right to have a say in this too, don't you think?"

Mathias turned to Lorenzo.

"If what you said about the book is true," said Lorenzo, "then we can't afford to lose it. Remember? We had a plan."

"Yes. But I can't condemn her to death. Don't you see?" Mathias seemed to be struggling, as if in great pain.

"Where are the other two?" asked Lorenzo, referring to the Doge's guards.

"They're in the other room, resting."

"Mathias, I saw the demon."

The monk stared at him.

"What did you see?"

"I was running to the piazza where we were supposed to meet," said Lorenzo. "It was very late. That girl who came to me today was a friend of Caterina's, and she told me that Caterina was about to leave Venice. I went to the pier, and I must have lost track of time. Then I started running. When I came to a bridge, I saw an old black gondola heading away from the Rialto. I hid, but I managed to get a look at the person navigating it."

"How do you know it was the demon?"

"I don't, not for sure. But the oarsman was huge and covered by an enormous black cloak, and he had something on its face. I couldn't see clearly. It wasn't one of the men in black hoods who attacked us. There was something different about him. And now you tell me a woman was kidnapped. She might have been on that gondola."

"Where on the gondola?" asked Mathias, growing anxious.

"The gondola was like the ones they use for funerals, only much older. It had a long covered cabin, like the ones they put dead bodies in. That would be pretty useful for carrying someone away, don't you think?"

"Do you know where it was going?"

"I don't, but I could retrace my steps to where I saw it. It happened just a little while ago. We could search in that area."

"Let's go. Now!" Mathias went to wake up Marigo and Antonio. But when they were ready, Lorenzo stopped the monk.

"I'll take care of it," he said. "This time you have to trust me."

"Why?"

"Because you have an appointment to keep before dawn, and we don't have any guarantees we'll find what we're looking for. If anything happens, you wouldn't be able to ransom her."

Mathias started to protest, but Lorenzo cut him short.

"There's no other way, magister."

"You shouldn't be the one risking your life this way."

"Sometimes things go the way they should. Other times they don't."

The monk told Marigo and Antonio to follow Lorenzo and do what he ordered. He warned them to prepare to meet the demon. The two men tucked their swords beneath their belts, and Antonio wore a strange double-curved crossbow over his shoulder. Mathias explained more about what they'd be facing, because he believed he'd found the last piece of the mosaic.

Once they'd left, Mathias picked up Valla's manuscript off the table and hid it in the inside pocket of his cloak. He looked at the fireplace again.

"So you were the one holding the puppet strings of this monstrosity." The monk addressed the flames, where he envisioned the form of his enemy.

CHAPTER 62

Lorenzo, Marigo, and Antonio began running as soon as they left the house, retracing the route they'd taken from the little piazza where the monk had waited as bait for the demon. When they reached the piazza, Lorenzo noticed a few light traces of blood on the snow and touched his bandaged head.

"Does it still hurt?" asked Marigo.

"I'll get over it."

Lorenzo located the narrow calle he'd taken to get there, and he headed that way. The maze of calli crisscrossing the Rialto was a confusing labyrinth, and it wasn't easy for him to orient himself. The snow had already covered his tracks, but he knew his encounter with the black gondola had taken place on San Marco.

When they emerged from the maze of narrow calli, they paused to catch their breath, staring at the strange world around them. The falling snow seemed to plunge the city into impenetrable silence, and the accompanying fog seemed to suspend the surrounding palazzi as if in a dream.

Yet they had no time for reflection; they began running again. Lorenzo couldn't remember the name of the calle he'd been in when he saw the black gondola. He'd been so confused, so anxious to get to Mathias that he hadn't paid attention to anything around him. Even so, he managed to find the little bridge the black gondola had gone beneath.

"That's where I was," he said to the others. "The gondola came from that direction, and it was headed that way." In other words, it was heading west.

"Try to remember any little details. Anything," said Marigo. "From here, it could have gone anywhere."

"Let's try walking along the rio," said Antonio.

"There are too many here to just follow one by chance," said Marigo. He was staring out at the narrow waterway. "Isn't there anything that can help us?"

"I smelled an extremely strong odor," said Lorenzo.

"What do you mean?" asked Antonio.

"When the gondola passed close by, I smelled an extremely strong, spicy odor. It might have been pepper. But there were other smells too."

"Spices?" said Marigo.

"It's just a detail. I thought maybe—"

"A warehouse," said Antonio.

"Maybe, maybe. Is there one nearby?" asked Marigo.

"I know of one in Rio Fuseri," said Antonio. "Near the Rio dei Barcaroli."

"How do you get there from here?"

"Rio Fuseri is close-by, but I don't know where the entrance to the warehouse is."

"Wouldn't the entrance be visible?" interrupted Lorenzo.

"There are secret warehouses spread out around the city," explained Marigo. "Merchants use them to store part of the merchandise they import. That way they only have to pay fees on the remainder, and they can sell the hidden merchandise to other merchants, who sell the wares somewhere else. It's a way to dodge some taxes, and the Doge casts a blind eye on the practice because it keeps the price of spices under control."

"The odors you smelled . . ." said Antonio. "I'll bet that old gondola was being used to transport contraband. It's probably kept in one of the secret warehouses where they store spices. It may even have had spices on board. Sometimes they're ground up so fine that they become little more than a powder. It's impossible to get off your clothing."

"Trust him," said Marigo, smiling. "Antonio was a smuggler for years, before he entered the Doge's service."

"Then what are we waiting for?" said Lorenzo. "Let's go!"

The three headed toward Rio Fuseri. The entryways to clandestine warehouses may have been well hidden, but at least now they knew what they were looking for.

***

Angelica was horrified by the demon's face. A white mask. An enormous, obscene nose. Dark, empty cavities where the eyes should be. A mouth twisted into an eager smile from which emerged a noxious stench.

The demon put his hands near his prisoner's mouth. Angelica could see his fingers out of the corner of her eye. They were horrible, but human. She felt the rag in her mouth loosen, then a current of air on her lips. She tried moving her mouth. She could talk.

"Who are you?" she asked.

She earned nothing more than the wheeze of rapid breath in return, like that of a beast waiting for the chance to leap at its prey.

"What do you want from me? What have I ever done to you?" Angelica could feel terror taking over again. She tried to hold back her tears, to keep from appearing vulnerable. But the feel of that hellish creature's fingers brushing along her face was more than she could bear.

They felt like claws, talons. She realized that this dark soul was feeding on her terror.

"So beautiful," he said.

***

"Pulling back now doesn't make any sense," said a young senator named Dolfin. "And for what reason? How is it possible that nobody knows why?" Dolfin was excited by the nocturnal assembly. He felt like he was taking part in something extremely important. He puffed his chest out and behaved like an authoritative member of the Senate, forgetting for a moment that he was merely supposed to just do as he was told. He was talking with a few friends, boys his age who weren't part of the assembly, but whom he'd insisted he bring along. Now he was showing off outside the entrance to Palazzo Ducale, where bright torches glimmered against stone. Beyond this, his friends were not allowed to set foot.

"The fact that nobody is telling you why doesn't mean there's not a good reason."

Dolfin turned around and found Graziano Morosini standing behind him. Morosini was just a few years older than he was, but far higher up the power structure. Dolfin had to pay his respects, his stomach churning for the loss of face in front of his friends. Morosini was Grimani's friend, so Dolfin couldn't possibly respond to his disparaging comments the way he would have liked.

Graziano Morosini passed them by and headed down the corridor that led to the assembly hall. When he arrived, he was surprised to see how few people were there.

Doge Loredan was nowhere to be seen, and the Lady of Asolo, Caterina Corner, wasn't there either, even though she'd requested and obtained permission to attend. Also absent were Grimani, Corner, Venier, and Trevisan. And there was no sign of Foscarini.

There was nothing to do but wait.

Mathias was sitting on a wood chest in the piazza beneath the open. Hidden behind a column, looking out at San Marco Basilica before him. Inside that church, someone was waiting for him.

He saw a small group of people walking across the piazza, headed for the Palazzo. Members of the Senate, the executive authority of the Republic, which had once been known as the Pregadi, since its members were *pregati*, or "requested," to give the Doge advice.

Everyone would remember this assembly. It was convened as usual by messengers sent to all the members' houses, but given the affairs under way, it was an unprecedented event. The assembly had been put off and delayed all day long, and it was clear to Mathias who was behind these maneuvers. The final piece of the mosaic now had a face.

CHAPTER 63

"Look for a door on the water." Antonio, the former smuggler, knew how people who wanted to hide things operated. "A well-hidden warehouse needs to have direct access to the water," he explained to his companions. "So the entrance will have to open directly onto the rio."

Lorenzo was following Antonio's instructions when instinct drove him toward a bridge he'd never paid attention to before. It still wasn't entirely clear to him how you could hide an entrance. But when he reached the bridge and walked down the little stairs leading to the rio, he saw a padlock. It was open, and a chain was hanging from the door. He motioned the others over.

Two gondolas were tied up to a little wood pier outside a nearby palazzo. Marigo climbed up and untied one, then went aboard and pushed off the pier, gliding silently toward Lorenzo. When he reached the bridge, Lorenzo and Antonio had already opened the hidden door. There was a pulley contraption just inside. Lorenzo boarded the gondola, with Antonio right behind him.

The little boat floated quietly into the underground gallery.

***

"How much longer are we supposed to wait, Agostino? Before long it will be midnight. We need to make a decision." The elder Trevisan was the oldest member of the Council of Ten. As a senator, he was anxious to see what would happen. And he couldn't stand the mysterious methods Grimani was using with them, his most trusted friends. "Maybe we were mistaken to put our faith in him."

Grimani turned around and stopped stroking his gray beard, his usual habit while he was thinking. "I'll be sorry to tell him how little faith you had in him, once all this is over and Venice is in our hands," he replied with malice in his voice.

"Don't be angry, Agostino." Trevisan spoke softly. He didn't want the others to hear. "You shouldered this burden, and we're all grateful for it. But your cousin couldn't give you the leadership of the Shadow Council on his own. So stop putting on airs and tell us how things really stand."

Grimani looked long and hard at Trevisan. He couldn't stand the old man's silent presence within their clandestine assembly. He saw Trevisan as someone entrenched in his ideas and clinging to his seat, devoid of ideas and courage, and capable only of waiting for others to suggest what to do before expressing his own opinions. But this wasn't the time to create additional tension. He simply stared at Trevisan.

After having recovered his composure, Grimani turned to the others who had gathered in his house before heading for Palazzo Ducale. They hadn't heard what Trevisan had said, but it wasn't hard to intuit his meaning. Rumors of the existence of the Shadow Council had begun to circulate among the papists, and the principal exponents of the theory had gathered around Grimani that night.

When Agostino Grimani heard talk of the man holding the Shadow Council on a leash, it made him more than a little uncomfortable. He was convinced that *he* deserved such a position. But the voice everyone on that clandestine council feared was the same voice that had promised them he would have his hands on the forbidden book by the twelfth stroke of the Marangona. And Grimani knew that once he did, nothing else would stand in their way. Then Corner would read their proposal before the Senate, requesting the Pope's help in their war against the Sultan.

"Let's leave for the Palazzo," he said to the others, displaying a calm he didn't feel. "But I must ask you to be patient just a little while longer. I can't guarantee that we'll be able to present the proposal tonight. But if we can, the sun will rise on a new Venice tomorrow morning. *Our* Venice."

"What's going on, Agostino? Why all the mystery? Don't you trust your old friends?" asked the elder Morosini, a member of the Council of Ten. His nephew Graziano was anxious to take his place, and Grimani had immediately found a way to use the younger man's ambition, not caring one whit about hiding it from the elderly uncle.

"My dear friends, I'm truly anxious to tell you everything you want to know," said Grimani. "And I'll do so as soon as we're all gathered together back here, in my house, to drink wine from my cellars and celebrate our victory." Then his voice took on a darker tone. "But until that moment, I must ask you to trust me. The destiny of La Serenissima may well pass into our hands tonight."

***

Marigo was directing the gondola as it slid along the subterranean canal. The lapping sounds the boat's passage made as its wake knocked against the stone walls echoed along the underground tunnel, covering up any other sounds.

Lorenzo's eyes had become accustomed to the dark when suddenly he could see a faint light coming from what appeared to be a sort of cove to their right.

Antonio raised the strange double-curved crossbow he'd slung over one shoulder. He motioned for Marigo to slow the boat down a little, then he reached inside his leather boot and took out two bolts. He positioned them on the crossbow, used the lever to draw the first and second cords taut, and motioned for Marigo to move up.

Lorenzo felt that Mathias should have been there with them. That it would have been better, more appropriate somehow, if the monk who had chased the demon all over Venice were at their side. But if anything went wrong and he hadn't been able to reach the church by the twelfth bell toll, then the person Mathias cared about most deeply would be condemned to death. So it was up to Lorenzo, with the help of the Doge's most trusted guards, to stop this demon, this monster who had killed his uncle and four others within the span of a few days. And seeing the expert movements with which Antonio loaded his weapon, Lorenzo felt utterly certain the demon was there, hidden nearby in some small subterranean hellhole.

As they drew slowly forward, Marigo kept the gondola close to the wall until they were just a few yards from that open cove on the right. Ahead, the tunnel continued on into darkness. Antonio lay flat in the prow. The first thing to appear around the corner would be the sharp tips of his crossbow bolts. As soon as he saw light reflected on those, he would tighten his finger on the trigger: at the slightest pressure, those bolts would fly.

***

Mathias saw Agostino Grimani, followed by other noblemen loyal to him, cross the piazza in silence. The monk stayed hidden beneath the open gallery as the group disappeared inside the Palazzo. The torches burning at the entrance reflected on the blanket of white snow covering the ground and illuminated the flakes still falling from the thick clouds overhead.

Suddenly, he heard quick-paced steps. Someone was running. Mathias hid behind a few crates and held himself motionless. He heard the footsteps draw closer. When the runner appeared around a corner, Mathias recognized him at once.

The monk stepped out of his hiding place and went over to meet him.

"What's happened?" he asked.

***

Grimani and his men stopped outside the entrance to the Senate assembly hall. A senator came forward, saluting Grimani and informing him that the Doge hadn't arrived yet. Everyone turned to Grimani, trying to read even the smallest sign that his impenetrable face might betray.

"What are we waiting for, Agostino? Do we go in or not?" asked the elderly Morosini.

"Didn't you hear? The Doge hasn't arrived." Never before had Grimani felt so tantalizingly close to realizing his objectives.

Then everyone heard the sound of many footsteps crowding down the corridor. A large group was coming in.

***

He was kneeling before the altar in San Marco Basilica. Votive candles were flickering. Deep within himself, he felt the full weight of the sacred task he had accepted as his own. He felt absolutely no hesitation.

Mathias would find him here. He wouldn't understand. But that didn't matter anymore. Only the book mattered now. He stood up and pulled the hood to his shoulders so that the candlelight illuminated his face. Then he walked to the door, behind which he would wait for the monk.

***

Grimani immediately recognized the pomp and splendor of the nobles processing down the corridor to the entrance of the Senate assembly hall. The magnificence of the Lady of Asolo's retinue was impossible to confuse with any other. He heard Corner clearing his throat next to him, preparing to salute his hated cousin.

Caterina Corner appeared, surrounded by members of her private court. At her side walked Alissa Strianese, attracting stares from all the senators present. The Lady of Asolo had been given a place of honor within the Senate from which to watch the proceedings. Although she didn't have the right to vote, her presence was taken as a sign of support for the Doge. Everyone knew her feelings on the matter, just as everyone knew her cousin's. Caterina turned to look at him now.

"I see you are healthy," she said, "and that brings me joy."

"Not nearly as much as I feel for you," responded Corner. He held two documents beneath his cloak: the papists' proposal and another creating a new authority to oversee the lagoon waters. Grimani gave him a look, and Corner pulled his cloak a little tighter.

"In the name of the entire Senate, I welcome you here," said Grimani, making no effort to hide his hypocrisy. "With all your commitments, it is truly commendable that you should find the time to dedicate your attention to our boring little political issues."

"Only men can make political issues boring," replied the lady, "because they often make the mistake of believing themselves more intelligent than they really are. Thereby becoming not merely boring, but even pathetic."

"Perhaps. But it would be an error to underestimate certain men." Grimani's lips drew into a sharp, thin smile.

"An aunt of mine often repeated an interesting thing about men," said Alissa, intervening in the verbal clash with a perfectly calibrated display of ingenuousness, "that rarely can one underestimate them enough." Then she burst into a peal of innocent, girlish laughter, forcing the others to smile at her joke, lest they appear rude.

Caterina Corner saluted her enemies and proceeded into the assembly hall, collecting homages from all present.

The Doge's chair was still empty.

***

The demon was circling her. Angelica could feel his fetid breath blowing hot against her neck. His excited panting was heavy, sickening.

"What are you waiting for? What do you want?"

"You must be patient . . ." That hiss, the voice of a serpent. "We have to wait."

"Can you tell me what we are waiting for?"

The demon grabbed her face with one hand, staring at her from those empty cavities. He put the rag back in her mouth.

"Death," said the demon. He hesitated like an actor drawing out his lines for dramatic effect. "Death need not hurry."

Angelica felt herself gripped by a new, even more powerful wave of terror. Death. *Her* death.

Wait. Something was out there. On the water.

The movement in her eyes seemed to arouse the demon's senses. He turned in a heartbeat, grabbing a dirty and well-worn knife that hung on the wall behind him.

A gondola with three people aboard came around the corner.

"Stop right there," shouted Antonio. "Put that knife down! It's over!" He was still lying in the prow, the crossbow pointing at the demon. Marigo was driving the oar, but his free hand was already on the hilt of his sword so that he could leap ashore and stop that enormous black monster.

Antonio stayed still, cool and concentrated. He could see the tension in the demon's hand holding a large knife.

Antonio tightened his finger on the crossbow trigger.

The demon turned to Angelica. A malevolent cry had barely escaped his lips when he felt a sudden sharp pain in the arm holding the knife. A crossbow bolt was sticking out of his cloak; it was covered with blood—his blood. He looked, stupefied, at the knife he had dropped. A man, the one who was working the oar, jumped to the ground. There was a younger man there with them too.

"Don't move!" shouted the man with the crossbow.

"*Requiescat,*" whispered the demon, stooping with difficulty to grab the big knife with his left hand. He had less strength in that arm, but more than enough to prove he hadn't given up. Just as he'd promised God, who now seemed to have forsaken him. The demon threw himself at the man standing before him. But before he could reach him, he heard a cursed whistling noise and then felt an even greater spasm of pain.

He couldn't breathe. It was as if he'd swallowed something too big for his throat, as if an unnaturally large fishbone were stuck there. His hand went to the strange arrow in his neck. He tried to pull it out, but the pain was too great. The demon tried to scream, but he could only groan in pain. Yet his enemy was near. The knife could still reach him . . .

Lorenzo found himself face-to-face with the demon. He was petrified. Here was the beast that killed his uncle. The thing that tortured and destroyed human beings, that sent lacerated corpses floating in the canal. And he'd done it with the very knife he was brandishing now. Lorenzo realized the creature was leaping at him, but he was too terrified to move. He would have died, but at that very second, Marigo drove his dagger into the creature's side.

The demon fell down on the ground, defeated. A few final gasps shook the enormous body, then it was still.

Marigo ran to Angelica's side. He untied the leather straps and removed the gag.

Lorenzo knelt by the body stretched out, lifeless, on the ground. Beneath that cloak, beneath that white mask, lay the face of Hell. Mathias had already told him whose face he would find beneath the mask. But Lorenzo needed to make sure. He knelt close and grabbed the mask with one hand. He could felt his heart beating in his temples.

It was him.

"We have to warn the monk," said Marigo, pulling Lorenzo out of his reverie. Lorenzo came to his senses, finding the white mask still in one hand.

"You go. And take him this," he said, handing Marigo the mask. "Antonio and I will come as soon as we take care of Angelica."

Marigo jumped into the old black funereal gondola and worked the oar to send it toward the exit.

Lorenzo went over to Angelica and stroked the frightened woman's head gently. "My name is Lorenzo Scarpa," he said. "Mathias Munster sent us to find you. Stay calm. It's all over now."

Hearing the name Mathias, Angelica finally felt the terror leave her heart. She clung to the boy, sobbing uncontrollably.

***

Antonio took a long look around, making sure the gondola they'd used to come in was ready to go. Only then did he see the enormous bags set against the wall. The strong spice smell was coming from them.

"Some merchant must have let that insane monster use this place," he said.

"There are powerful people behind this affair," said Lorenzo. "People beyond suspicion."

As he left the watery tunnel, Marigo worked the oar to speed the boat up. The twelve bells hadn't rung yet, but he knew he needed to hurry. He went as far as he could over water before getting out on land and running the rest of the way to the piazza. He didn't stop until he saw a small group of people walking toward San Marco. Marigo hid behind a doorway and soon recognized Grimani and his cohorts. He waited until they'd passed, then followed them.

The group of noblemen crossed the piazza, heading for the Palazzo, where the Senate was assembling. Marigo waited until they were far enough away, then dashed beneath the open gallery, where the monk would be waiting for him.

When Mathias stepped out from behind a column, Marigo stopped short.

"What's happened?" asked Mathias.

Marigo took the white mask out from beneath his cloak and handed it to the monk.

"Everything was as you expected," he said, still catching his breath.

"The woman?" asked Mathias.

"She is safe and unharmed," said Marigo. "Now let's put an end to this affair."

CHAPTER 64

"Take your seats," said Grimani. "There's no point in all of us standing out here. We're just drawing attention to ourselves." He was more nervous than he should be. He still hadn't received any news.

"Is something wrong?" asked Corner.

"We have victory in our grasp. Don't look nervous," said Grimani. "We might scare someone into changing his mind."

"There are still a lot of people missing," said Trevisan. "And there's still no sign of that bastard Foscarini."

Grimani cast an icy glare at his little group.

"We'll go in then," said the elderly Morosini. Turning toward the room, he caught a glimpse of Graziano, and waved to him with one hand. "I see my sneaky little son-of-a-bitch nephew is already there."

"Go in," said Grimani. "I want to wait for Loredan."

***

The monk, wrapped in his cloak, was walking across the snowy piazza, headed for the basilica. Marigo entered from a small side door. He walked along a corridor, went up a short set of stairs, and went through a door hidden behind a painting.

The Doge was waiting for him. Marigo smiled.

Mathias let his eyes feast on the basilica. San Marco was an enormous church. East and West met and interwove in its Byzantine mosaics, a blend of gold and stone. The church was the symbol of La Serenissima, under the Doge's jurisdiction, not the Pope's. It was administered by the procurators of San Marco, an important authority within the Republic. To Rome, it was the symbol of Venetian pride and arrogance. A church that was not run by religious figures was a daily affront to the patriarchy and the Pope.

With San Marco looming over him, lofty and proud, Mathias thought how small every man is before God. He took it all in: Light from the votive candles glimmering on the frescoed dome. Marvelous paintings in blue and red on sparkling gold. Pillars holding up the vault. Rows of columns extending along the naves.

The monk heard nothing but the sound of his own footsteps echoing inside that miracle of human construction. Then suddenly, he sensed movement amid the glimmering lights. A candle flame flickered, perhaps blown by a draft. He turned toward the flame and saw a door start to close. It remained open barely the width of a palm. Mathias went to the door. He could hear a man breathing on the other side.

"It must have been difficult to get San Marco all to ourselves," said the monk.

"I know how much you love this church. I had hoped it would reawaken your ardor, magister." That voice confirmed everything Mathias suspected. The mosaic was complete, laid out clearly before his eyes. Rebuilt down to the tiniest detail, to the final face.

"You've never been more wrong," he said.

"We'll have time to talk about it. Right now you have something you need to give me."

The man on the other side of the door was asking for Valla's manuscript. He didn't know that Lorenzo, Marigo, and Antonio had freed Angelica and killed his attempt to terrorize him. For a moment, Mathias felt compassion for the man. Then he remembered the dead. He took out the white mask and passed it through the door.

The man took it. Silence.

"Turn yourself in and confess your sins," said Mathias.

"You . . . Your arrogance knows no limits," said the voice on the other side of the door. It seemed different now. Creepy, evil. A voice Mathias didn't recognize. "You will pay for this!"

"Open the door. It's over," said Mathias. "You have to own up to everything that you've done."

"God already knows what I've done."

The door slammed shut. Mathias found himself standing alone inside the basilica. He knocked on the door, pounded on it. He remembered where that passage led. He tested the door, feeling for its strength. It wasn't very thick. Mathias picked up a heavy candelabra and ran at the door, slamming the bottom of the candelabra into it like a battering ram. The weak lock gave way, and the wood split open. He put the candelabra down and headed for the stairs. Stairs that led to the terrace where the *Quadriga*, the statue of the four horsemen, stood.

***

"What do you think of all this?" Alissa was sitting alongside Caterina Corner. They couldn't figure out why the most powerful people in the Republic were behaving so strangely. The senators were palpably nervous.

"I believe that most of Venice's destiny is on the table tonight," said the Lady of Asolo. "But it's not being decided here."

They'd taken their places in a small balcony that had been set up specifically for Caterina and her small court. The lady was passing the time by watching the senators. But she knew that the protagonists of the subterranean conflict that was tearing apart the Republic, doing perhaps even more damage than the war against the Turks, had yet to enter the room.

Outside the assembly hall, Grimani saw a small effeminate man approaching him. It was Giulietto Mascari, one of the Doge's servants.

"My lord, the Doge would like to speak with you before the assembly," said Mascari, inviting Grimani to follow him. Grimani was surprised. Maybe Loredan knew that he'd lost the book, and now wanted to bargain for his capitulation.

**

Mathias ran down the narrow stone staircase. He still had questions that needed answering. There were still things that needed explaining. He could feel his heart pounding in his ears, pulsing in his head. When he came to a small door, he opened it so forcefully that it bounced back and almost shut on him.

He was there. Standing, looking out at the lion of San Marco. The four imposing gilded bronze horses alongside him. The Venetians had brought them here centuries ago from the hippodrome in Constantinople, after the city was taken in the name of the cross.

"It's over," said Mathias, struggling to catch his breath.

"Do you believe that?" answered his adversary. "Do you really believe it's so?"

**

As Grimani followed the Doge's messenger, he knew victory was at hand. The web he had been so carefully weaving all this time was about to trap his prey. The Republic was within his grasp. He need only demonstrate he was capable of ruling it with a firm hand and, at the same time, achieve stability by being generous with his defeated adversaries. Perhaps he could rely on his Roman friends in order to secure his position. But someday he might free himself of his friendships, dusting off his native Venetian spirit in order to become Doge, the undisputed leader of La Serenissima.

His own enthusiasm was driving him beyond the plans laid out by the Shadow Council, the conspiracy he'd set up with the other noblemen, who would soon clamor for their share of the spoils. Grimani hated their avidity, because it limited his own.

In time, he would be able to get rid of the Shadow Council as well, and with it the man who had led it up until today, demanding obedience not only from the others, but from him, Agostino Grimani.

The Doge's servant led him into a small room used for private meetings prior to assemblies. Often the most important decisions were made in places like this, well before the official proceedings started.

He opened the door and invited Grimani to go inside.

"Hello, Agostino, please make yourself comfortable," said the Doge. Loredan was sitting in the seat his servants used to carry him around, now that his illness was wreaking greater destruction than ever on his body. "We have a few things to discuss before we meet with all the others."

Grimani walked over to the seat Loredan pointed to, but he could tell something wasn't right. The expression on the Doge's face . . . He didn't look defeated. In fact, quite the opposite. But why?

"If you'll agree, I believe we can set political prudence aside for a moment and speak to one another frankly."

That wasn't Loredan's voice. Grimani craned his neck around. Behind him stood Giacomo Foscarini. Grimani could see his own defeat in the triumph of Foscarini's expression.

CHAPTER 65

"How can you think this is over? You haven't understood a thing. Venice is descending into chaos!"

Mathias stared at him. He recognized the features and the voice. But the man he was facing wasn't the man Mathias once knew. He wasn't the man who had supported him, who had sustained him during his spiritual education, who helped him deal with his difficult relationship with the faith. This wasn't the man who had taken his confessions, guiding him back to God each time, pardoning his sins of arrogance and rationality. It wasn't the man who had been his friend, even when the German monk confessed his love for a woman.

And yet the moment Angelica had been kidnapped, Mathias finally understood. Because only Giacomo Foscarini and one other man knew Mathias's secret. Only Giacomo and Brother Serafino, who was now standing before him, knew the truth about his relationship with Angelica.

Mathias knew what the priest had done. Yet he was surprised to discover within himself one last, residual glimmer of compassion for the old man he was facing. For the way Serafino had damned his own soul, for the abyss into which the old priest had plummeted.

Serafino had armed the hand of a man with a child's mind. He had used Berto's unconditional love to transform him into a demon who had terrorized Venice. He'd manipulated a guileless man in order to disseminate pain and death.

"In whose name have you transformed Berto into a monster?" Mathias asked his former guide. "When I saw him the other day, that wasn't just chicken blood splattered all over his clothing, all over the cassock you yourself put on his shoulders. Is that why you kept him with you? In the name of merciful God, Serafino, whose service are you in?"

"God's service, Mathias. I have only ever been in God's service." Serafino turned to the monk. Their eyes met. "You still don't understand?"

"No, I don't understand."

"Your arrogance prevents you from seeing the game you've let yourself play. A pawn in the hands of skillful deceivers."

"Deceit, Serafino?" said Mathias, pointing to the white mask the priest was still holding in one hand.

"Your false doctrines will be the tool of powerful people, and they'll use it to attack the house of the Lord," said Serafino. "We are small men, Magister Mathias, tools in the hands of others. The Empire, the Church, princes."

"You're confusing faith with politics. That's your mistake."

"You stubborn man. You're the one who refuses to see that they are one and the same! If you let yourself be maneuvered by those who will question faith, then you'll only become a weapon for those who want nothing more than to escape the Church's leadership. Is that what you want? To let yourself be used to humiliate the very people you should be serving?"

"Everything I have done," said Mathias, "I have done by my own choice."

"Your choice? Was it your choice to return to Venice and prevent God's will from being done?"

"You're confused again. You're talking about Borgia's will, not God's."

"So much pride, Mathias. Those books you worship like pagan idols have planted the seeds of the Devil in your heart. You've forgotten who you are."

"Pride? *My* pride? Was it my pride that slayed all those people?"

"Do you remember the words of Saint Paul? *'I know that after I leave, savage wolves will come in among you and will not spare the flock. Even from your own number, men will arise and distort the truth in order to draw disciples after them. So be on your guard.'*

"You haven't been 'on your guard.' You've had people kidnapped, tortured, and murdered in order to get your hands on a book. You've turned Berto—an innocent man who looked up to you as a father—into a monster. All this just to keep a book from being printed. A book, Serafino, a book!"

"A book that would have offended all those who represent God here on earth." Serafino grimaced. "It would have started a war. That's what they want. They want to force the leader of Christianity to withdraw the hand he's offered this 'Sodom on the water,' which he's done only to save it from its sins and the infidels who are knocking on its door. Whoever doesn't want this desires the destruction of Venice. And you should know."

"What should I know?"

"There are maneuvers that begin far away, places that you, a German, know full well. Do you think that it's mere chance that the diabolical invention that prints books comes from your lands?"

"So, after the Jews, now you want to point your finger at the Germans?" said Mathias. "These are simply the ravings of a madman."

"They want to use that infernal contraption you admire so much to turn Venice into a wall of flame, one the Church cannot see beyond. One it cannot rule over, where God cannot reach. That's the plan your printer friends choose to serve."

"I can't believe I have to remind you. The first book that 'infernal contraption' printed was the Holy Bible."

"You cursed mountain goat! Without a fear of God, they'll be able to print and spread any blasphemy they choose!" Serafino's mouth twisted into a livid rictus. "God gave man the gift of handwriting. He did so in such a way that tracing the Word in ink would be like plowing the field with a plow. Only the Church can guide a copyist's hand. Only prayer and sacrifice can inspire it. Not the money flowing through the shops of printers, men who see and sell smut and prayer in books with identical forms. Or do you believe that the Word of God can be sold at the marketplace like a piece of meat?" Serafino's eyes were lit with an almost mystical exaltation that Mathias had never seen before. "Only the Word of God is worthy of being written and venerated. Everything else is lies! Thirst for power. Vanity. Don't you see? You who *were* a man of God!"

"I *am* a man of God."

"No, you're not. A man of God would never have salvaged a book that questions the power of faith. A man of God would have helped me. We would have found the book together and destroyed it."

"You're getting confused again. The book doesn't cast doubt on the power of faith. It questions the power of the Pope."

"The two cannot be divided!"

"I believe they can."

"Heresy! You'll burn in Hell, Mathias. You and all those cursed friends with whom you offend the Word of God, speaking it in your filthy German language. Did you think I didn't know?"

"So that's what you fear." Mathias's voice grew harsh. "Faith, printing presses, jealously guarding your manuscripts, Valla, the Empire. You've wasted so much time staring at the finger of the wise, never once understanding what it was pointing to. What the Church truly fears is losing the power it has over the Word. Because the Word is what governs men. And if every man had free access to it, your pulpits would have no more meaning."

"You want to destroy the Church." Serafino's eyes were almost in awe, alive with wonder. "You are the Antichrist. *Your* words will be rife with blood, Satan. They will open the doors to an era that will devastate this world like an apocalypse. You don't realize it, but you're staining yourself with crimes far worse than mine."

"I'll let the Republic's magistrates be the judge of that," said Mathias.

"Still you fail to understand." Serafino began backing up. "God is my only judge."

Mathias wasn't quick enough. Serafino climbed up on a wood crate, and from there up onto the stone balustrade. Mathias leapt toward him, but he caught nothing. His eyes witnessed a scene that he would never forget, as long as he lived.

Serafino opened his arms, as if to welcome his own destiny, and threw himself off the balcony.

The absolute silence of the snowbound city was broken only by a dull thump as the priest's body hit the ground. Mathias stood there, staring down at his old mentor stretched out in that unnatural position, while a bloody stain seeped slowly out, coloring the snow red. The white mask, which Serafino had let slip during his leap, floated down and came to rest along the priest's side.

"May God have pity on your soul."

CHAPTER 66

Rain had returned to the lagoon, turning the snow into a swampy mess. The Senate assembly ended quickly, and most of the senators couldn't figure out why Corner's proposal to institute a new lagoon water authority had been considered so urgent that it required such an unusual meeting, or why the meeting had been postponed repeatedly. Grimani took part but seemed quite distracted. He'd spent the entire evening fixated on the image of his castle crumbling around him.

It was time for Grimani to figure out what was left standing, and how he might use it to his advantage in the future. The Shadow Council was now free of the cumbersome presence of that Dominican priest Rome had imposed on them. And even with tonight's defeat, he knew that leadership of that secret brotherhood was in his hands. This helped render his adversaries' victory a little more palatable, and make the future a touch brighter.

Mathias spent the following morning closed up in the Palazzo, a guest of the Doge and Foscarini, with whom he recounted the entire affair, down to the last detail. They intended to respect in full the promises they'd made, as long as the monk gave them the manuscript. At the end of their long discussion, he did.

"I know what you're thinking," said Giacomo, seated alongside Loredan. "We have no right to do this. But maybe that won't always be the case. Maybe a day will come when your manuscript can be printed."

"If that day ever arrives, it certainly won't be here in Venice," replied Mathias.

"Why do you say that?" asked the Doge.

"It's just my impression, m'lord. But I believe the Republic will always need a bargaining chip in order to keep from being overwhelmed. The new century before us is going to be full of changes."

"Important changes," said Giacomo. "Now that you're a rich man, perhaps you can think of a few new ways to invest your money."

"I was thinking of other changes," said Mathias.

"Your heart is already in Wittenberg, isn't it?" asked Giacomo.

The monk said nothing, simply smiling and giving a vague nod of his head.

"In addition to what we agreed upon, I've added a considerable sum for the possessions you intend to leave behind," said the Doge. He was referring to what was left of Lorenzo's and Angelica's properties.

"I'm sure Lorenzo Scarpa will appreciate your generosity," said Mathias. "Especially because his involvement in this affair, like mine, will make it impossible him to remain here in Venice without spending the rest of his life looking over his shoulder to make sure someone doesn't plant a dagger in his back."

"No one asked him to get involved," said Giacomo.

"I know, Giacomo. You asked only me. A teacher suspended from his duties because he was considered dangerous and subversive. You'd already decided not to create conflict with the Church. My only mistake was to believe you entertained higher ambitions. Instead, I was merely the right person to use and thereby rid yourself of forever. The best man to burn for the cause. That's why you had Marigo come all the way to Padua to summon me here."

"Don't hold on to your grudges, magister," said Giacomo. "That baggage is too heavy to lug into your new life. Let's part as friends, just as we met."

Mathias nodded. He didn't want to take leave of Giacomo with harsh words either. He'd been used, and he knew it. But he'd gotten what he wanted, since he had already decided to return to his homeland when Marigo arrived at the University of Padua.

After having said good-bye to the Doge, Giacomo accompanied the monk out of the Palazzo. "As soon as you've settled down, let me know where you are so that I can send you Manuzio's new volumes. I'd like to maintain our old traditions," said Giacomo, warmly.

"I'd like that too," said the monk.

"Do we still have enough time for that beer I promised you? The best in Venice, remember?"

"There's always time for a beer."

They both knew they would never see one another again. But they didn't speak of it. They drank their beers together at a favorite tavern of Foscarini's, talking of times past as if they wanted to etch them in their memories, each taking his favorite experiences away with him. It really was the best beer in Venice, and to Mathias it tasted like a homecoming. Giacomo paid for drinks for everyone in the tavern, inviting the crowd to raise their mugs in honor of his friend. And Venice.

***

Lorenzo wanted to take one last look at the ashes of his uncle's shop. A tear threaded its way down his cheek as he gazed upon it everything that was left of his life. Remembering his uncle and everything the man had done for him, everything they'd done together, was like remembering what Venice had first meant to him the day he'd arrived here from a place he could never return. The city had welcomed him, given him a job, projects to develop, plans and aspirations. It had also given him a woman to love, and the heat from that fire still burned inside him. Then the city had taken it all away again.

Angelica went with him to the shop. Together they took refuge beneath an overhang, waiting for Mathias to join them. Angelica took Lorenzo's hand and encouraged him to be strong. Then Lorenzo realized that someone's eyes were upon them.

He turned around. Moses Luzzatto was standing just a few yards away, soaking wet in the rain. There was something in the old man's eyes that drove Lorenzo to go over to him.

"My son was not the person you believe he was," said Moses.

Lorenzo said nothing. Simone had set in motion the wheels that drove Caterina away from him. He didn't know where Simone was now, but he'd had to fight back a powerful desire to murder the young Jew.

"I don't know what happened between you two," said Moses, "but it wasn't you he hated. He hated what he felt you represented. Simone was born in Venice. He wanted with all his heart to be Venetian. But his hatred ruined him."

"I don't know what you mean," said Lorenzo.

"The body they pulled out of the ashes"—Moses pointed at what was left of the bookshop—"it was his."

Lorenzo stood still, completely shocked.

"He was a good son," said Moses. "I know he was. Don't let hatred poison your life too. I ask for your forgiveness on his behalf. Please forgive him." Moses held out a small object in the palm of his hand. It was a little stone dolphin. "This is all that is left of my son. All except the memories I have of holding him in my arms. I want you to have it. Perhaps it will help you see how hatred always ends in defeat."

"I can't accept this . . . I didn't know . . . I'm sorry," Lorenzo managed to say.

"Please. It will help me believe that all of this had meaning somehow," said Moses, pushing the pendant into his hand. Then the older man left, walking away slowly in the rain.

Lorenzo was surprised to discover he felt compassion. A knot that had been tied tight around his heart loosened and fell away, leaving him an unexpected feeling of profound relief. Mathias had told Lorenzo he didn't believe in the ethics of forgiveness. Maybe that was true, or maybe he was simply saying that because he knew that right then, that was what Lorenzo needed to hear. He stared at the small stone in his hand. He would make a necklace out of it and wear it always, a reminder of rivalry and forgiveness.

CHAPTER 67

The boat was ready, moored at San Marco. Lorenzo and Angelica were waiting for Mathias there. The rain was thinning now, fading into a light drizzle. The piazza's golden lion reigned supreme as the monk walked toward them. Then he stopped and looked around as if he were expecting someone.

A small figure, walking with a slight limp, came out from beneath the open gallery. Mathias had met the man before. The day of the wedding procession on the Canal Grande, while he was seated alongside the Lady of Asolo, he'd recognized the man in the gondola with Foscarini. When Giacomo had told him that he'd met a member of the Brotherhood of the Rose, Mathias understood that it was the same man, Francesco Falier.

Keeping his plans secret from everyone, Mathias had sought out and spoken with Falier.

The pair had agreed on one thing right from the start: they had to make a copy of Valla's manuscript. They both knew that the book would never be printed in Venice, not now, not ever. They also knew that the papal authorities would do anything they could, directly or indirectly, to keep it from being printed anywhere.

So Falier brought together a dozen members of the Brotherhood of the Rose. He divided the manuscript between them and gave each an equal section. They worked day and night to copy it. They were under strict orders not to print it, in order to keep from raising any suspicions. When Falier gave him back the original to take to the Doge, they made a deal. Mathias would receive the Brotherhood's copy of the manuscript only when he was about to leave La Serenissima. Until then, it would be kept hidden and safe.

He couldn't be sure that Falier wouldn't make a second copy. But even if he did, it wasn't a problem. In fact, in a certain sense it would be further guarantee that Valla's work would not be lost. Respecting their pact, Falier arrived in San Marco the very day the monk was set to leave.

"A pleasure to see you, Falier," said Mathias.

"At this point, we consider you an honorary member of the Brotherhood of the Rose. I hope you can take this burden and carry it into the lands where you're headed," said the Venetian, handing the monk a leather-bound folder.

"Have you double-checked the work?"

"Of course," said Falier. "Word for word. It is a perfect copy of Valla's manuscript. And now we're trusting you with it."

"The Rose has accomplished its mission."

"The Rose merely handled part of the mission. We've done everything we could here. The rest must be done elsewhere. And I'm sure you'll play an important role in what's to come."

Mathias took the leather folder and headed straight to the boat, where Lorenzo and Angelica were waiting for him.

The boatman directed the vessel away from the pier. The three passengers huddled in the slight rain, covered by their heavy cloaks.

Falier watched the three figures until the boat disappeared from view. Then he went back the way he'd come, stopping only once, to look at the lion. No one could doubt its pride, its courage. Then, accompanied by nothing more than the sound of his own footsteps, he disappeared amid the sodden, snowy calli of Venice.

EPILOGUE

Wittenberg

Early April 1507

Five years. But she hadn't forgotten, because it was as if her life had stopped, frozen forever in the instant she'd accepted her destiny. In those five years, Caterina had accomplished everything for her family that she needed to.

Her father had received a hefty note of credit from a cardinal, and after the Republic made peace with the Turks, thanks to a pact Zaccaria Freschi established on the Doge's behalf with the Sultan's emissaries, his trade routes were open and working again. Like the other merchants, Alvise Marin never paid back his debt. Now the Church was preparing an unprecedented offensive against the impudent city. But this was no longer Caterina's affair.

Caterina had returned home to the lagoon. She'd gone to visit Lorenzo, just as she'd promised, only to discover that he'd abandoned Venice a few days after she had. He'd left La Serenissima in the company of a monk, a shadowy character that no one knew much about, except that he enjoyed friendly relationships with some very important men, including Giacomo Foscarini.

When Caterina arranged a meeting with Foscarini, now one of the most influential noblemen in the city, she found him tired, resigned. A new alliance between Rome, France, and Aragon was extending over the lion. A devastating war was coming. Foscarini was more involved than ever, weaving a thick web of relationships that was supposed to stop armies led by papal soldiers from entering the city. For this reason, he'd been interested to hear what the nun had to say.

He'd been told Caterina Marin had influence in Rome yet avoided talking about politics. She only wanted information about Lorenzo Scarpa, the young bookseller who'd left the city with Mathias Munster.

Foscarini knew where the monk was, because he was still sending his friend books via Manuzio. The great publisher had promised him a first edition of his upcoming collaboration with a very important scholar who was about to arrive in Venice, Desiderius Erasmus. Mathias couldn't wait to get his hands on his book.

The monk had given up his vows and taken Angelica Zanon as his wife. Over time, he'd sent a few books back to Foscarini, and Foscarini showed these to Caterina now. They'd been printed in Wittenberg by a young printer who used a little dolphin as his trademark. At first, Caterina didn't understand, but Foscarini explained that this printer was the Venetian who had moved to Wittenberg with Mathias Munster: Lorenzo Scarpa.

So Caterina set out for the north. It was a long voyage, but she had enough money to guarantee an easy journey. When she reached Wittenberg, she didn't immediately ask around about the publisher with the dolphin trademark. She didn't know how to behave, nor what she really wanted. She'd asked Lorenzo not to wait for her, to go out and live his own life.

But Caterina had never loved anyone else.

With time, she'd learned to appreciate the company of her fellow nuns. Her spirit had been soothed by the peace and tranquility of the places she'd gone to fulfill her role. Her education and intelligence had allowed her to manage donations, lands, and money received by the Church, supporting the careers of other religious authorities, all men, who were indebted to her. She'd grown to become the respected sister she was today.

Still, she'd wanted to honor a promise she'd made to a young man long ago. The moments she'd spent in his company had been her constant companions over the past five years of her life. The time had come to put them to rest.

When she summoned her courage after a few days in Wittenberg and asked about Lorenzo, she was directed to a tiny print shop, and she walked there straightaway, threading her way among the crowd that filled the city streets. She was almost there when she saw a man wearing an ink-spattered apron step out of the shop into the street, as if needing a breath of fresh air. It was Lorenzo. She stopped and watched from a distance.

A woman with long blonde hair and a baby girl in her arms walked over to him. She kissed him, and he smiled, looking down at the little girl.

Lorenzo had his life—the life that had been denied to Caterina.

She stayed where she was for a while, watching the simple tableau of daily life. He had changed, and the changes surprised her. He'd become a man. He had put on weight. Most importantly, he'd become precisely what he'd wanted to become: a printer. Venice was a distant land to him now, in both space and time.

Finally, Caterina understood what she'd come looking for in this foreign land. She wanted to be sure that Lorenzo had done what she'd asked—gone on and lived his life. With that certainty, she turned around, staying out of sight, and went back the way she'd come.

She decided that it was all for the best. That things had gone as well as they possibly could, and she didn't want to upset Lorenzo and his wife with her presence. She felt she had kept her end of the bargain, and that thought made her smile. She was surprised to feel happy. She would pray for Lorenzo, every night, now that she'd seen his daughter and understood that seeing her was the best thing the trip to the north could possibly have given her. The Marin name had required her to pledge her life for its cause, but she would have never sacrificed Lorenzo's life.

As Caterina walked, her mind was full of the moments she and Lorenzo had stolen away amid abandoned warehouses and the rooftops of Venice. For the first time in years, those memories made her feel serene. She would keep them with her, like polished jewels, forever.

Not far away, the Castle Church rose up, powerful and imposing, at the center of the city. It was a majestic monument, presiding over the hubbub and cry of students attending the young university founded by Frederick the Wise. Some students were seated just outside the church, intent on listening to their teacher, Magister Mathias. He'd arrived from Venice full of ideas that seemed to foreshadow enormous changes.

Behind them stood the massive wood door to the church.

AUTHOR'S NOTE

Lorenzo Valla's Discourse on the Forgery of the Alleged Donation of Constantine was formally published in 1517.

That same year, Martin Luther is said to have nailed his Ninety-Five Theses to the wood door of the Castle Church, calling into question some practices of the Roman Catholic Church.

That day, October 31, is widely considered the beginning of the Protestant Reformation.

The symbol chosen to represent Lutheranism is a white rose.

ABOUT THE AUTHOR

Riccardo Bruni is an Italian journalist, writing for newspapers, magazines, webzines, and blogs. He's authored the novels *La lunga notte dell'Iguana*, *Nessun dolore*, and *Zona d'ombra*. For more information, please visit www.riccardobruni.com.

ABOUT THE TRANSLATOR

Photo Credit © 2012 Davide Carlesso

Aaron Maines is a freelance writer and literary translator based in Milan, Italy. He has written for a number of publications on both sides of the Atlantic, including the *Wall Street Journal*, the *Washington Post*, and the *New York Times* in the United States, and *L'Europeo* in Europe.

He has translated numerous books and essays, including works by Umberto Eco, Oriana Fallaci, Elisabetta Dami (Geronimo Stilton), Tullio Kezich, and Andrea De Carlo. In 2007, he was chosen to translate filmmaker Federico Fellini's private diary, *The Book of Dreams*.